**"Maybe you'd like to come with me and show
how well you can ride."**

Had Noah meant to say those exact words in that exact order? The mental picture of him atop a horse, thigh muscles straining as he guided the animal around, was enough for Avery to want to decline. Then she pictured them together, him behind her in the saddle with strong arms wrapped tightly around her. She almost came undone in her chair with thoughts of his thighs cradling hers. Her imagination really was overactive.

"I'm sure I can ride just as well as you can."

He lifted a brow and his mouth quirked just as he brought the iced tea bottle to his lips. "Is that a challenge?" he asked after taking a long sip. "Because I'm sure I can outride you."

Avery cocked an eyebrow and shook her head. "We'll just have to see…"

Also by Erin Kern

Here Comes Trouble

LOOKING FOR TROUBLE

ERIN KERN

FOREVER

NEW YORK   BOSTON

Copyright © 2010 by Erin Kern
Excerpt from *Here Comes Trouble* copyright © 2011 by Erin Kern
All rights reserved. In accordance with the U.S. Copyright Act of 1976, the scanning, uploading, and electronic sharing of any part of this book without the permission of the publisher is unlawful piracy and theft of the author's intellectual property. If you would like to use material from the book (other than for review purposes), prior written permission must be obtained by contacting the publisher at permissions@hbgusa.com. Thank you for your support of the author's rights.

Forever
Hachette Book Group
237 Park Avenue
New York, NY 10017

www.HachetteBookGroup.com

Printed in the United States of America

First Edition: July 2013
10 9 8 7 6 5 4 3 2 1

OPM

Forever is an imprint of Grand Central Publishing.
The Forever name and logo are trademarks of Hachette Book Group, Inc.

The Hachette Speakers Bureau provides a wide range of authors for speaking events. To find out more, go to www.hachettespeakersbureau.com or call (866) 376-6591.

The publisher is not responsible for websites (or their content) that are not owned by the publisher.

To my husband, for bringing Avery and Noah together. Without you this book would still be sitting on my hard drive. Thank you for never letting me quit. I love you.

ACKNOWLEDGMENTS

I would like to thank my husband and his genius mind for working on so many more dimensions than mine does. And also for scooting the kids out of my hair, so I could get more than ten uninterrupted minutes to myself. To my editor, Lauren Plude, and editorial director, Amy Pierpont, whose enthusiasm for the Trouble series was far greater than I could ever expect. You came to me at a time when my confidence was cracked. And Jessica Somberg, you are a marketing genius.

Also to my tireless, hardworking superagent, Kristyn Keene, whose late-night e-mail changed the course of my career. It seems impossible to put into a few words everything you've done for me. Thank you for giving me the chance that no one else would.

FROM THE DESK OF
ERIN KERN

Dear Readers,

I'm a small-town girl at heart who loves living in a small town, visiting small towns, reading about small towns, and writing about small towns. Wyoming is full of picturesque "dots-on-the-map" that are nestled among foothills and aspens. The town of Trouble, although fictitious, has a place in my heart as the quintessential Middle American small town.

The people of these towns are your average, hard-working American families with real stories to tell. People who battle the same everyday dynamics and family-centered idiosyncrasies we all face. The McDermotts are a blended family with the same quirky but lovable relatives we all deal with in our own families. The four brothers, along with their outlandish younger sister, all had their own happy endings waiting for them.

These are their stories, and the stories of the women who bring four devilish, very tough men to their knees.

Happy Reading,
Erin Kern

LOOKING
FOR
TROUBLE

ONE

THE MAN WITH A DARK-BROWN Stetson pulled low over his eyes appeared in Avery Price's rearview mirror a split second before her back bumper knocked him down. Her Christian Lacroix wedge sandal slammed on the brake pedal before her tires could roll over him and snap his bones like fragile twigs. Her cell phone, which had been pressed to her ear for ten minutes while her brother peppered her with questions, slipped out of her hand and clattered to the wood-grained middle console. Moisture seeped out of the corners of her tightly closed eyes, and she wrapped her hands around the fine Italian leather–stitched steering wheel.

A few seconds stretched into an eternity while she inhaled deep breaths and kept her eyes closed. When she opened them, the dented metal door of her motel room came into view along with the early-morning sunshine.

Okay, you barely nudged him. Chances are he's just sore and pissed off. Now would be a good time to get out and check on him.

Her internal lecture was pathetic at best and warranted no action from her hands other than to pick up her discarded cell phone. Her trembling fingers grasped the device and brought it up to her ear.

"Avery, what the hell is going on?" Her brother's unusually demanding voice vibrated through the phone and added to her already jittery nerves. As good as his intentions were, she couldn't deal with his you-need-to-start-making-some-decisions speech.

"Avery, if you don't start talking in two seconds, I'm going to send the Wyoming State Patrol after you."

The man who'd been forced to the ground by her car had yet to pull himself to a vertical position. "I gotta go. I just hit somebody."

"What? See, this is what I'm talking—"

Her thumb hit the end button on her phone, effectively cutting off another one of her brother's annoying but painfully predictable rants.

Her brain fired away commands for her legs to move, to do *anything*, with no success. After several seconds, a thump came from the back end of the car as though the man on the ground was taking his retribution for being plowed over. The sound prompted a squeak from her, and she fumbled for the door handle.

As far as mornings went, this one ranked down in the shitty category. First, she'd slept through the alarm clock's weak *beep-beep*ing, and then the fleabag motel couldn't provide her with a decent cup of coffee. Far be it from her to wish for a double-shot latte with no whip. All the shoebox-size lobby offered was the bottom scrapings of hours-old brew and stale English muffins. Not exactly an appealing spread.

Now, in her haste to find something edible and caffeine to rev up her system, she'd bowled over a man who had the bad sense to walk behind a car that had its reverse lights on.

She threw the car in park and exited on shaky legs. The

early-morning sun was still weak enough that the temperature hovered in the tolerable range.

As she rounded the back of the car, trying to swallow her irritation at her own carelessness, the man on the ground pushed himself not-so-gracefully to his feet. He swayed, as some drunk people did when they couldn't walk a straight line, and placed a hand on her car. The fierce protectiveness she had for her German-engineered vehicle almost had her demand he remove his hand from her sunflower-yellow custom paint. The fact that she'd hit this poor man, and would probably have to grovel to keep him from suing the pants off her, stopped the words from flying out of her mouth.

A deep, gravelly groan flowed out of the man, now minus his cowboy hat. Burnt sienna–colored hair, mixed with sun-kissed shades of caramel, was smashed down in untidy disarray to the man's skull. The cowboy hat, which now lay about six feet from where he'd hit the ground, had flattened the edges of his hair to a greasy, slicked-down look. Avery considered herself an expert on personal hygiene and keeping one's appearance as perfect as possible. She'd be willing to bet all the money in her trust fund that this man hadn't seen a shower in at least twenty-four hours or his wrinkled, untucked chambray shirt and faded jeans a washer and dryer. For all she knew, he could be some bum who skulked around motels, looking for a place to rest his head.

Nevertheless, that didn't change the fact that her car had come in contact with a human being, and she needed to make sure he was okay.

With his mile-wide back to her, he bent over and placed both his hands on his knees, dropping his head as though he couldn't catch his breath.

Geez, had she hit him harder than she thought? She certainly hadn't meant to.

"Are...are you okay?" she stammered while taking a tentative step toward him.

He straightened much faster than she expected considering he'd been swaying like a drunk a second ago. When he turned, a gaze grayer than blue—and definitely not pleased—hit her. Thick brown brows slammed down over his eyes, which flashed with anger.

"You hit me, lady. What do you think?" The accusing words came out of a full mouth surrounded by dark growth of beard stubble. It wasn't a full beard; it looked more as if he hadn't made the time to shave, as though he didn't care that his unkempt, wrinkled appearance was less than appealing. Or, maybe, he simply didn't own a razor because he was homeless.

"I know that fancy, expensive car of yours has mirrors, so why the hell weren't you paying attention?"

It's not as if she hadn't looked. She *had*. Her one quick glance had shown a man just standing there, as though he had all the time in the world. She'd lifted her foot off the brake and had already been backing out of the parking space. She'd scarcely rolled two inches before she tagged him and set him on his ass.

Her fingernails bit into the inside of her palm. "I had my reverse lights on because I was backing out of my space. Didn't you see them?"

He snatched his cowboy hat from the uneven gravel and placed it back on his head. "I was walking and not paying any attention to you. You're supposed to look before you back out."

"I did, and it looked as if you were just standing right behind me. I couldn't stop in time. I'm sorry, but I really didn't mean to hit you."

"Your fault, not mine." His words were short and

clipped, evidence that anger, not pain, was his dominant emotion.

Okay, so he had her on that one. Technically it was her fault, regardless of what he'd been doing. She was adult enough to admit when she'd made a boo-boo. As a consolation for hitting—no, *nudging*—him, she tried to be nice even though she felt like a complete imbecile for not paying proper attention. Despite her put-on cheery attitude, she sensed some serious hostility. Maybe she'd messed up his one and only wrinkled shirt.

She stared back at him and tried to dodge the daggers his stony eyes threw her way. "You don't look seriously injured. Again, I'm really sorry." She bounced from one three-inch platform to the next before pivoting and reaching for the car door handle.

"Now wait a minute."

She paused with her hand on the door and tossed him a look over her shoulder. The cowboy hat shielded his hostile gaze and lent only a view of a straight nose and wide mouth.

"You can't just flee the scene of an accident. How do you know I'm not injured?" The words had lost their heat and rolled off the man's tongue with a deliberate slowness.

Other than his disreputable clothing and stubble-covered jaw, there was nothing to suggest he was anything other than normal. No blood sprayed from an open head wound, no bruises or scrapes decorated his masculine face. He had swayed and stumbled at first, giving her the impression of maybe a mild head injury. Since replacing his hat, he'd only leaned one hip against the bumper of her car and regarded her beneath his hooded gaze.

She wrapped her arms around her midsection. "You're not going to call the cops, are you? I already said I was sorry."

Then a terrifying thought hit her. *He could easily file a report against you.*

He slid one hand under his hat, lifting it crookedly to one side. "I don't know. My head's a bit tingly, and I feel a little light-headed. You might need to take me to a hospital for some medical attention. Or better yet," he continued while rubbing a hand along his rough jawline, "I know the sheriff pretty well. We can get him down here to straighten this whole thing out. I'd call him myself but"—he dug his hand in his back pocket and produced a small black device—"you crushed my cell phone."

Okay, the cell phone was a good indicator that he probably wasn't homeless. Although his attire suggested someone who'd just crawled out of a cardboard box, he was evidently one of those people who just didn't give a damn what he looked like. His nice little speech was also his way of threatening to have her ass thrown in jail if she didn't do . . . whatever it was he wanted her to do. This was *so* not how she wanted to start her new life.

He nudged his hat lower on his head. "I think the sheriff is on duty today and wouldn't mind coming down here—"

"All right," she said through gritted teeth. "Just tell me what I can do."

He held his hands up in front of him. "I don't want to put you out. I can tell you're in a hurry."

She forced a smile. "It's no put out at all. Is there somewhere I can take you?"

The grin that crept up his face resembled the one the big, bad wolf used to lure the three little piggies. Unfortunately she was at his mercy until he decided to let the whole fake-injury thing drop. "I'm so glad you offered. I need a ride to my car."

She tightened her hands around her keys. "That's it? Just a ride?"

"Oh, I want a lot more than that."

She crossed her arms, then let them drop. Maybe she should have stayed in bed and watched the rabbit-ear-adorned television at the motel. "All you're going to get out of me is a ride to your car."

A lone passing car filled the silence between them. "Okay."

Without giving him a chance to make more threats, she jerked open the car door with all the force her arm would allow and plopped herself in the driver's seat. She had the car started and was rolling backward by the time he yanked the door open and sat himself next to her.

"Are you trying to run me over again?" he asked after folding himself in the seat until his knees bumped against the glove compartment. Her little roadster was not designed to hold men the size of the Jolly Green Giant. His hat remained firmly on his head.

"I can't help it if you don't move fast enough." She jerked the wheel and maneuvered her car around a pothole.

His narrow hips shifted until he'd slid lower, as though he were settling down for a nice Sunday drive. "I think you were trying to ditch me." The leather beneath his backside squeaked when he moved again.

"Can you sit still? You're going to scratch the leather."

"Can you not shout? My head feels as if it's going to crack in two."

Avery eased the car to a red light. "You haven't heard loud yet. Get one scratch on my car and you'll know the meaning of loud."

One corner of his mouth turned up and created shallow

lines in his stubble-covered cheek. "Poor princess. Daddy might have to buy you a new one."

She tucked a strand of hair behind her ear and decided to let the "daddy" comment roll off her back.

The light turned green, and she tapped her manicured index finger against the gearshift. "Would you like to tell me where your car is, or should I drop you off wherever I please?" *Like here?*

"Go straight and make a left turn at the fourth light down," he replied without so much as moving a muscle.

She wound her hand tighter around the steering wheel and cursed herself for being so stupid and careless. Avery was the sort of person who treated everyone with respect, regardless of how that person treated her. She'd been caught off guard and lost in her own thoughts about what she was going to do with her life. With practiced patience, she eased off the brake pedal and set off down the street. The inarticulate man next to her didn't so much as utter a grunt. Instead, he remained slouched low in the seat with his hat pulled down so it covered half his face. Only his deep, even breathing indicated he was still alive.

Over the years, she'd worked to develop an ironclad backbone, so she rarely let situations or people intimidate her. The man who sucked all the breathing space out of the car, with his massive shoulders and long legs, sent her nerves tingling in a way they hadn't in a long time. Was it intimidation, or fear that she'd injured another human being? Avery didn't know, nor was she comfortable with the feeling. She couldn't say it was his looks, because so far all she'd seen was half his face and hair that hadn't been combed in days. Perhaps it was just the sheer size of the man. Even though he sat perfectly still, there was an edge to him but also an air of confidence, as though he knew how he looked and damn the world if they didn't like it.

The characteristics defied everything she knew about men. A heavy breath left her lungs.

"You sigh a lot."

Another light turned red, allowing a man hunched over like a question mark to cross the street. "I'm just mad at myself. I'm usually much more observant."

He was silent for a moment. "Don't feel so bad. I'm not that hurt."

The look she threw him went unacknowledged. "But I do feel bad, even if you don't seem that hurt."

"I thought I saw you checking me out." The grin in his voice was unmistakable, although Avery didn't see the humor. Nor did she appreciate it. Whatever. Let him make his wisecracks. In a few blessed minutes, she'd be free of him.

After the old man shuffled his way across the street, the light turned green, and she made her way toward where she was supposed to turn.

Her phone vibrated in the middle console, where she'd dropped it in her haste. She kept her hands on the steering wheel, having no desire to listen to her brother call her incompetent while the stranger who'd kissed the back end of her car listened to her humiliation.

She made the left turn as instructed, then looked to him for the next set of directions. "Go down about half a mile then turn right on Beach Street." The deep timbre of his voice had her mind wandering to unsuitable thoughts as she passed a hay-and-feed store.

"What were you doing at Dick's Motel if your car is way down here?" She'd already come to the conclusion that he wasn't homeless; homeless people didn't have cell phones and wear brand-new Timberland boots. He was just a man who didn't iron his clothes and woke up two miles from his car.

For a moment he sat as still as he'd been since entering the car and didn't answer. Then he said, "What people usually do at motels."

O-kay. That could be anything from doing drugs to cheating on a significant other. For whatever reason, the former didn't seem likely. As for the latter, well, what did she know? Maybe the woman he was with had kicked him out and refused to take him anywhere, leaving him stranded without transportation. Then Avery had gone and knocked him down, destroying his cell phone in the process. For all she knew, he could have a wife at home who was pacing herself sick at this very moment. And Avery could be an accomplice to his sordid love triangle. Now she felt even worse than she did before.

Her desire to attempt a conversation with a man who'd strong-armed her into driving him across town was minimal. She kept her gaze on the street in front of her and both hands on the wheel. Under normal circumstances, Avery was a pretty chatty person. She didn't like uncomfortable silences that stretched into eons of nothingness. The silence made her fidgety, and it felt as if worms crawled underneath her skin. Oh, but the cowboy loved it. His answers were clipped and to the point as though he couldn't be bothered with trivial things like speaking to another person.

"It's on the left-hand side of the street at the very end," he muttered after she'd made a right turn onto Beach Street.

A metal sign that read DAVE'S WATERING HOLE sat crooked on top of a masonry building as though someone had just tossed it up there and hadn't bothered to make it sit straight. There were no windows, no landscaping, or anything that was minimally appealing about the place. The building sat away from the street in the middle of a cracked, weed-adorned parking lot. This definitely wasn't an establishment that screamed fine family dining, though Avery was pretty sure anything with the word "hole" in it wasn't suitable for little children. Given the behavior and the dozen words she'd exchanged with the man next to her, she hadn't expected something with gold-plated front doors.

She cringed as the front bumper of her car scraped the pebbly ground when she drove into the parking lot. A handful of early-model trucks and a later SUV sat in the parking lot without any sort of rhyme or reason. Apparently the owners didn't feel designated parking spaces were necessary.

"Just stop right here." The man straightened in the seat and reached for the door handle.

When the car purred to a stop, he opened the door and unfolded his long limbs from the low-slung vehicle.

She grabbed his arm before he had a chance to exit. "Wait a minute. Are you sure you're okay? Can I take you to a doctor?"

His stunning gray eyes lit on hers. "Nothing more than a bruised ego, princess."

She let the "princess" comment slide and withdrew her hand from his arm. "I really am sorry."

"I know."

The car door slammed shut before she had a chance to grovel for more of his forgiveness. What was wrong with her? She didn't just go around hitting innocent people with her car. She was a better person than that.

Executing an abrupt U-turn, she left him in the dust of her Mercedes and hauled ass away from Dave's Watering Hole as fast as she could.

What a way to start your life over, Avery.

Well, son of a bitch. Noah McDermott withdrew car keys from his pocket and hit the unlock button.

The Mercedes princess was all spitfire and sass.

The curved backend of her car sprayed all sorts of dirt and gravel in the wake of her swift retreat. Maybe Her Highness was late for her manicure.

Or maybe she just wanted to get away from your grumpy ass.

It certainly wouldn't be the first time. Mary Ellen hadn't wasted any time kicking him out of the motel room this morning after she'd had her way with him. Not that he'd been heartbroken. He hadn't been expecting to find a hot meal in his lap and a ball game on the television. Instead, Mary Ellen had emerged from the shower and told him he needed to be on his way. She didn't have to tell him twice. He'd quickly thrown on last night's wrinkled, stale-cigarette-smoke-shrouded clothes and let himself out the door. Just before exiting he thought he'd heard Mary Ellen asking him to call her. Yeah, that wouldn't be happening. She was the type of woman who sat around in bars, as she had last night, and waited for a man to pay her any sort of attention.

The argument he'd gotten into with his father had propelled Noah into the dingy and disreputable interior of Dave's. Once there, he'd immediately spotted Mary Ellen, with her too-tight jeans and dark, overly processed hair. Initially he hadn't been looking for a woman, only the comfort of a pool table and a longneck bottle of beer.

By his third game, Mary Ellen had wormed her way into his game and bought him another beer. She'd spent the remainder of the time slipping her hands in his back pockets and rubbing her double Ds against his arm. He'd been just drunk and pissed off enough to allow her to drive the two of them to Dick's Motel and promptly handcuff him to the wooden headboard.

Hours later he'd woken up with a bitch of a headache and blurry memories of new sexual positions he'd been introduced to.

The interior of his car was cool, having not yet been affected by the heat of midday. He tossed his hat on the passenger seat and slid in with deliberate slowness so he didn't make the pounding in his head worse. After dropping his eyelids closed and inhaling several deep breaths, he started the car. A morning meeting with one of his subcontractors prevented him from returning home longer than to take a shower. With the condition his head was in, he'd love nothing more than to wash off the previous night and dump himself into bed.

As he exited the parking lot and headed toward the outside of town where he lived, Noah's thoughts returned to the Mercedes princess.

Someone like her didn't enter the town of Trouble very often. Her sleek dark hair and perfectly pressed clothes screamed wealth. Of course her car was also a dead giveaway. He didn't need to see the little roadster to know she'd grown up with privileges most people in this town only dreamed about.

Having a hundred-thousand-dollar car knock him on the ground had upgraded the pounding in his head to freight-train status. He hadn't noticed anyone sitting in the car when he'd stepped out of the motel room. His mood was already dangerously close to black, and allowing a woman, who hadn't been paying attention, to catch him off guard had pissed him off big-time. Never mind the fact that she was a delectable little thing who smelled like vanilla and peaches.

She had guts and looks that would send most men drooling at her feet. Not him. His mind had been too foggy and his limbs too achy for him to notice anything beyond the fact that she was a knockout with bags of money.

A small smile turned up the corners of his mouth. Sparring with her over who'd been at fault had been enough to erase the previous evening from his mind. For that much he was willing to forgive her affront of hitting him.

Okay, so she'd been genuinely sorry and only his ego had been hurt. The only other thing he'd suffered from was lack of sleep and a broken cell phone. Just to lay it on extra thick, he'd antagonized her into giving him a ride. He'd never had any plans to call law enforcement into the picture. But there hadn't been any harm in making her think he would. The steam coming out of her feminine little ears had been satisfaction enough. And being in the car with her had given him the chance to poke at her some more. So far the morning had been more entertaining than he'd anticipated.

Fifteen minutes later he pulled into his driveway, and as he stepped out of the car he realized his pocket was empty.

His wallet had fallen out in the princess's car.

TWO

AFTER HUNTING DOWN AN ESPRESSO as though it were the Holy Grail, Avery chugged the barely drinkable sludge down in three rapid gulps. The coffee was bitter and entirely too strong. The town's one and only coffee shop was closed due to renovations, leaving her no other choice but to go to the self-serve machine at a gas station. Luckily for her they offered other flavors besides straight black coffee. She opted for an espresso, thinking it would vaguely resemble something other than tar. After taking one sip, she realized she'd set her hopes too high.

On her way out of the gas station, she picked up *The Trouble Citizen*, the town's newspaper. She tossed the paper on the passenger seat and set off to find a place where she could sit and drink her sludgy espresso and browse the classified section in hopes of finding a job.

Grinning, rosy-faced children held hands with their *Leave It to Beaver* parents as they skipped across the crosswalk. Bouncing curly pigtails and golden retrievers on leashes screamed of a Norman Rockwellian society, and Avery had grown fond of it during the past week. *Who knew?*

After half the population of Wyoming crossed the street, the light turned green, and Avery eased her foot off the brake pedal. Jittery nerves dancing across her body from the accident had her driving slower than normal. She stayed a good two car lengths behind the wood-paneled station wagon in front of her. Lord knew one ticked-off person with her car's imprint on his backside was one too many for her. Guilt still tore at her. How had she managed to be so careless? It shouldn't have mattered what the man had been doing. No one deserved to get hit by a car. Had she apologized enough? Had he really not been hurt or had he just been saying that? She now chastised herself for not making completely sure he was okay. If he ended up with a concussion and crashed his car, she'd never forgive herself.

Just as she was about to start her search for a place to stop, her cell phone chirped from the cup holder it rested in. Gritting her teeth against having an unwanted conversation, Avery left one hand on the steering wheel and picked up her phone with the other.

"Please have a good explanation for what I just heard," her brother demanded after she pushed the answer button on the touch screen of her phone.

"Don't worry; everything's fine," she reassured him halfheartedly.

"So, you didn't just hit somebody?" The hope in Landon's voice almost made her say, "Yep, false alarm," and hang up on his overprotective ass.

Alas, Avery could never lie to her brother. He meant too much to her. "No, I did. But don't worry; I was practically crawling, so the guy walked away unscathed." Unless you counted his personality.

Don't think things like that, Avery. You're not a mean person.

A colorful array of expletives flew from Landon's mouth. "Whether or not the guy was hurt doesn't matter. It'll get back to Dad, and then you'll be screwed like a Cinemax B-movie actress."

"Nice, Landon." She steered her newly scratched Mercedes into the uneven, cracked parking lot of the Greasy Spoon, a place that dared anyone to eat their one-pound hamburger. "Don't worry your handsome little head, because I didn't give him my insurance card."

"How in the world did you manage that? Don't tell me you fled the scene of an accident."

"Do you really think I'm that irresponsible?" *Well, you did just hit someone.* Her car purred its way into the only free space behind the hole-in-the-wall hamburger joint. "On second thought, don't answer that. I just used my beauty and charm on him."

Static-filled silence stretched across the cell phones. "No, seriously."

"You're impossible to talk to, you know that?" She left the car running and adjusted the vents to blow refreshing air on her heated face. "The guy was kind of in a hurry, and all he asked for was a ride to his car."

"Say what?"

She ran her fingernail over the stitching of the steering wheel. "I didn't want to risk pissing him off even more. The last thing I need is him filing a report against me. Plus, I felt really bad for what I did. I didn't think it was too much for him to ask." *Please don't let the noble thing backfire in my face.*

"Just how long do you plan on staying in that place, anyway? You've already been there for a week. Don't you want to move on to someplace else?"

Avery pulled in an air-conditioning-filled breath. "I

don't know. I was thinking about giving this place a try. I kind of like it here."

More silence flowed from the other end of the line. "You actually want to stay in a place that doesn't have decent shopping? Where will you buy your Chanel handbags?"

She could never accuse her brother of being clueless. "Not funny. Plenty of people survive on knockoffs. I'm sure I'll get by just fine. I have more than enough Chanel and Balenciaga to keep me happy for the rest of my life. Besides," she continued when Landon started to interject, "I don't exactly have the money to buy couture right now."

"Uh, yes you do. If you weren't so damn stubborn and used your bank account, you'd be just fine."

Avery mentally counted to ten and managed not to roll her eyes. "I *am* just fine. And I already told you, I don't want to use that money unless I absolutely have to."

"Because it keeps you tied to Mom and Dad, I know." A deep-throated groan flowed out of her brother. "Your stubbornness is going to get you into trouble, Avery."

She let her head drop back to the cushioned headrest. "I'm not in trouble, Landon. I use it for necessities like gas, food, and the motel where I'm staying. But other than that, I refuse to touch it."

"Avery..."

Her head jerked back up. "How can I demand independence from them and use their money for stuff I don't need? Hypocrisy isn't something I want to add to my list of assets."

"Okay, okay, you make a valid point. Look, if you need it, I can float you some cash until you get things figured out."

"That's sweet of you, but I can do this on my own." As

she'd boldly stated in the note she'd left her parents minutes before walking out of their house. She *had* to stick to
her guns.

A man and woman exited the restaurant and climbed
into their faded sky-blue Cadillac. One of the taillights
had clear tape over where the glass shield used to be.

"Maybe you should get a job," Landon suggested after
he'd been silent for a second.

Hmm, you think? "The thought has crossed my mind a
time or two." What in the world could she do here? Milk
cows? As appealing as the small-town atmosphere was,
Avery still wasn't sure what sort of job market Trouble
offered its citizens.

"I know a couple of developers in Cheyenne. I could
give them a call for you."

"Landon—"

"You want to do it on your own. I got it."

Landon, bless his big, soft heart, got her better than
anyone else she knew. Yes, he pushed and tried to get her
to do what he thought was best. At the end of the day, he
always stepped back and let her take her own footsteps in
her own time, even if she fumbled over her footing; a trait
Avery cherished above all else.

"I'm running short on time, so I need to get to the reason for my call. You need to get in touch with Mom."

At Landon's announcement, her forehead landed with
a *thud* on the hard steering wheel. As noble as his intentions were at keeping her relationship with dear old Mom
and Dad from unraveling completely, Avery simply
wasn't at that point yet. The rusty blade that had pierced
her heart during her last conversation with them was still
embedded too deep.

"Do I have to?" Her voice had a mousy sound she

hadn't intended it to have. Damn it, she would *not* go weak at the mention of them.

"Mom was less than pleased with your runaway note." The smile in her brother's voice was unmistakable.

The sand-colored concrete building stared back at her when she lifted her head from the wheel. "First of all, it wasn't a runaway note. Second of all, I didn't write it with the intention of pleasing her. I've stopped trying to do that."

"Well, anyway, she's relentless in her pursuit of you. She must have called me a dozen times demanding I tell her where you are. 'Your father and I are just worried about her,'" her brother repeated in a below-par imitation of their mother's breathy voice.

Despite the frustration of the day, the corners of Avery's mouth turned up in a mood-lightening smile. "She did not say that."

Landon's deep, chesty laugh made Avery's grin turn brighter. "No, she really did, though I'm inclined to doubt the sincerity of it."

"It certainly wouldn't be the first time her sincerity's been doubted. What have you been telling her?"

"I tried to tell her as little as possible without actually lying to her."

A burdening weight had her shoulders slumping forward. The even, neutral tone in Landon's voice hinted at someone who thought lying to one's parents was a big deal. Landon was no Boy Scout, and he'd told his fair share of white lies to their parents over the years. Keeping something of this caliber from the people who'd raised them had to be like a cloud hovering over his head. On the one hand, he'd do what he felt he needed to do to protect his little sister, and she blessed him for that. On the other hand, guilt jabbed a sharp pain in her chest at the thought of one of her closest confidantes carrying this around with him. Considering what a tenacious lion their father was, it couldn't have been easy for Landon to fend them off this past week.

Huffing out a weary breath, Avery squared her shoulders and leaned back in the car seat. "I'm sorry, Landon. You've already done so much for me. I don't want you to have to lie to them."

"I haven't lied to them yet. But you need to pull it together and give one of them a call." He paused and some background noise pierced Avery's ear. "Just tell them how you feel. Explain it to Mom in a way she'll understand."

A snort popped out of her. "How? And I already tried explaining it to them. They didn't want to hear it. I tried telling them I can't marry a man who'd cheat on me, but they don't care. All they care about is how my actions reflect on them."

"True, they tend to have tunnel vision. But, sis, you can't hide from them forever. Enough time has gone by that you should be able to have a rational conversation with them."

"I'm not hiding; I'm starting over. I just don't think they'll understand that."

He was silent then said, "Avery, I don't blame you for leaving. They were suffocating you to the point of insanity. But you're not going to solve anything by ignoring them. Be strong. Drop them a line and let them know where you are, at least."

"I left them a note." The conviction in her voice was weak at best.

Don't try to get in touch with me. I'll call you when I can.

Her emotions had gotten the better of her when she'd grabbed a pen and scribbled irrational words on paper before absentmindedly tossing it onto the marble table in the foyer.

"That you did. But I have to be honest; the note you left wasn't very informative. All it said was that you were leaving because you needed independence. There wasn't anything in there about where you were going."

Her fingers gripped the steering wheel with a ferocity she rarely expressed. "That's because I didn't *know* where I was going."

"And now that you're there, you should be the strong, independent woman I know you are."

His words created a pocket of warmth around her heart and eased the pain that had been residing there. The feeling had her smiling. "I can always count on you to lift my spirits."

"At the end of the day, it's your decision. What I think you should do and what you're going to do is probably not the same thing. You need to do whatever you're most comfortable with. But listen, I gotta run. Think about what I said."

She ran her index finger over the Mercedes emblem on the steering wheel. "You're the best, Landon. I love you."

"Right back at you, kiddo."

They said their good-byes and disconnected the call.

She dropped the phone in her lap and let her head fall back on the headrest. The provocative purr of her car hummed beneath her as she ran Landon's words through her head again. While she did admit he had some legitimate points, she wasn't quite at that comfortable place with herself where she could drop a line to her mother. Their parting hadn't been your typical kiss-kiss, hug-hug good-bye that mothers and daughters generally shared.

Not that Avery had expected anything more than the stony silence that had filled her father's study when they'd finished lecturing her. In fact, the word "good-bye" hadn't even been exchanged between them. They'd probably been blindsided by her departure. Just as her brother said, Priscilla and Darren Price tended to see things through tunnel vision. This wasn't anything new to Avery. She knew full well how her parents' minds functioned. The note she'd left had simply been a way to be responsible. She held no illusions it would improve matters between her parents or make them understand.

The deep rumbling of her tummy reminded her she hadn't eaten anything since early that morning. Avery pulled the key out of the ignition, grabbed her Kate Spade shoulder bag, and exited the car. The warm summer breeze brought with it the greasy aroma of deep-fried potatoes and fat-riddled hamburgers. Normally she wouldn't be caught dead eating anything other than a spinach salad with grilled chicken. But what the hell? Lately she'd been doing things she normally didn't do. For example, telling her fiancé to shove his marriage proposal up his pretentious backside after she'd caught him red-handed screwing his bottle-blond assistant.

If she could do that, then she could indulge herself by putting something into her system that hadn't been organically grown. Since arriving in Trouble, Wyoming, a week ago, she'd told herself she was the new Avery. And by God, she'd see it through.

Noah McDermott had eyes like quicksilver and a mouth meant to kiss shivers over a woman's skin.

Avery pulled in a sip of her thick triple-berry-with-a-shot-of-ginseng smoothie while gazing at the picture on the motel man's driver's license. Normally she didn't go around fantasizing about men who had holes in their jeans and growled instead of talked. There hadn't been anything particularly fantasy-worthy about him—except the thickness of his shoulders and maybe the melodious sound of his voice. But any number of men possessed those qualities, so what made Noah McDermott, owner of McDermott Construction, so different?

It wasn't a single defining quality she could put her finger on. Half a dozen things contributed to the fact that her insides trembled like cottage cheese when she got a look at his license photo. The square, slightly stubborn shape of his jaw. His nose, which sported a faint, crooked bump, as though he'd been punched and the bones hadn't healed properly. Thick, conservatively cut sun-streaked hair that looked like it'd been tamed with fingers rather than an actual comb. And his eyes. His gray eyes pierced through the grainy photograph as though looking directly at *her*.

She tried to make a connection with the man she'd met that morning and the man in the picture. Except the shape of the jaw and the color of his hair, there wasn't anything remotely similar about the two. The man in the picture prompted goose bumps to rise up in waves over her skin. The man she'd met that morning had set her nerve endings on fire with his smart-ass short statements.

After gazing at his photograph a moment longer, she flipped the brown trifold wallet closed and set it down on the tabletop. It hadn't been until after she'd perused the classifieds, with no results of a promising job, and gotten out of her car at a smoothie shop that she'd noticed his wallet tucked in the crack of the passenger seat. Curiosity led her to grab the wallet and bring it inside so she could gather a name and address while she enjoyed her drink.

After she'd gotten the necessary information, she'd given the rest of the contents a cursory glance and pulled out a white business card.

Not only was Noah not homeless, but he was also a business owner—a fact that was pretty good evidence that a slight responsible streak ran though him. She'd begrudgingly granted him the benefit of the doubt even though he'd been less than pleasant. His lack of fault for being hit made it easier for her to admit she'd wrongfully judged him.

So, okay. Yeah. She clearly hadn't been paying attention. She'd succumbed to the cell phone distraction millions of other people fell victim to every day.

Running Noah down could have been a debilitating problem for her. Luckily for her, and she supposed him too, he'd walked away unscathed.

And left her with his wallet.

Now *that* could be a debilitating problem for *him*.

By now, several hours after their introduction, Noah had probably realized he was minus some very important documents.

Her initial reaction, after spotting the wallet, had been to toss it to the backseat and shove the matter to the bottom of her long list of priorities. Then, right about the time she'd realized there weren't any promising jobs in the town, she'd thought to herself, *What would I want someone to do for me?*

The answer had been as plain as the cracked plastic tablecloth in front of her.

The uneven chair wobbled beneath her when she stood. Unfortunately for her, doing the right thing meant seeing Noah again. *Not* something she'd planned for her day. She was supposed to get up, have her morning coffee, find a job, and everything would be right with the universe again.

Yeah right, in a perfect world.

The mild afternoon heat surrounded her like a warm blanket when she left the smoothie shop. After hitting him, the least she could do was return his wallet and make sure once and for all that he really was all right. "Do unto others" had been a mantra she'd tried to live by, no thanks to her parents. They did unto others as they saw fit. As a result, Avery had always vowed not to be like the vain, self-serving type of people her mother and father were.

Because of her promise to be a better person than her predecessors, she had no other moral choice than to show her face at McDermott Construction and attempt a civil encounter with its owner.

How could she do this with as little pain as possible? Hand him the wallet, say, "Have a nice day, Mr. McDermott," and leave him to his own devices.

Yes, that sounded like a very smart plan.

THREE

"YOU'RE FIRING ME?"

Noah leaned back in his black leather desk chair and tried not to roll his eyes at the woman he'd hired less than a week ago. His patience had been hovering in the nonexistent category for the last couple of weeks. The tears that rolled down Belinda Johnson's cheeks were not the best way to nudge his patience back into the tolerant area.

Another sniffle made Belinda look like a child who'd been scolded. She was only forty-three but easily passed for fifty, with her gray-streaked brown hair and eyes that housed bigger bags than the grocery store. Noah didn't know the full extent of her past. He'd gotten a sob story about how she needed a job to get back her kids, who were currently living with her "dirtbag" ex-husband. His softer side had gotten the better of him, so he'd given her a job for no other reason than he'd felt sorry for her. That was what he got for trying to be nice: a woman who was never on time, took bathroom breaks every fifteen minutes, and couldn't pick up the phone without stuttering the greeting. He wasn't *trying* to be an asshole. This business was his livelihood. He needed someone on board who could be presentable to clients and didn't make him look like a pushover because he couldn't get a handle on his employees.

Belinda pressed her thin, age-lined lips together and dashed away more tears with her hand. "I need this job, Noah. Give me another chance." The last word turned into a tear-filled whine. Big, fat tears crept out of her blue eyes and rolled down to her pointy chin.

How many chances did this woman want? He'd given her another chance after she came in thirty minutes late on her first day. He'd given her yet another one when she'd accidentally deleted an e-mail from his biggest client before he had a chance to read it. The woman was a walking disaster and needed to be in a position where she wasn't in control of important tasks.

He leaned forward in his chair and held up his index finger. "This is the fourth time since I hired you that you've walked in more than fifteen minutes late." His middle finger popped up. "You sent a contract to the wrong client, essentially giving out private financial information, and you made a very detrimental typo in an e-mail that turned into a curse word." With each tick of his fingers, her silent tears turned into full-blown sobs. If this were anywhere but his place of business, he would have patted her on the back and told her everything was okay. Unfortunately for her, that wasn't the case.

She yanked a tissue out of the box on his desk and blew her nose. Thick black mascara lines streaked her cheeks, which she failed to blot away. Her chin trembled as she tried to control her meltdown. "I promise I'll do better. It's just I've never really done anything like this before." The tissue she'd been twisting around in her hands had all but dwindled down to dust. "I just need some more time to get used to all this."

That was her problem, not his. He didn't have time to let an employee get "used to" the way he ran things. The handful of women he'd fired in the last two months had told him he was overbearing and difficult to work for. He ran a tight ship at McDermott Construction. Call him crazy, but impressing clients was sort of important to him. This was what paid for his house and put food on the table. No way would he jeopardize his hard work because the current woman standing in front of him begged that he give her another chance. He had no choice but to let her go.

He pulled in a breath and tried to rein in his patience. "I'm sorry, Belinda. It's just not going to work out. This is too much for you to handle." He stood from the chair. He wound a comforting arm around her shoulders and walked her to the door. "If you want, I'll have Rebecca type a letter of recommendation." Man, he felt like a complete dog for having to do this. Belinda was a nice woman, but she wasn't office manager material.

Her brown hair fell in her face when she hung her head in defeat. When they stopped in the outer office, she turned to face him. "I don't need a stupid letter; I need a job."

And he wished to hell he could give her one. He didn't know what else to say besides, "I'm sorry. I really am, Belinda."

Deep wrinkles cut into her forehead when she narrowed her eyes at him. "I was told you were a bastard to work for, but I didn't believe it until now." With an indignant lift of her chin, she pushed through the double glass doors and disappeared down the street.

"That went well," Rebecca said from behind him.

The twenty-year-old college student came in only three days a week, when she wasn't in class. With the nagging of his stepsister, Courtney, who rarely took no for an answer, he'd given Rebecca a job to come in and do filing and answer phones on her days off from school. She was the only employee he'd hired who was intelligent enough to stay with him long-term. Much to his chagrin, she planned on leaving for medical school at the end of summer. Wasn't that just his luck? He'd finally found someone he could depend on, and she couldn't even stay permanently.

"There was no way I could keep her on staff." A knot twisted in his gut. "I feel terrible. She was a nice woman, but clients were starting to complain. I have to put their needs first."

Rebecca shoved a strand of fiery-red hair off her forehead. "I know. This morning she came in and filed a client correspondence in the miscellaneous file. In the wrong job section." The young girl shook her head, shifting her corkscrew curls around her shoulders.

Noah turned around. "I'll be in my office if you need me." *Debating what the hell I'm going to do now.*

After clicking his door closed, he resumed his seat behind his desk. He'd gone through four office managers in the past two months. They were either incompetent on the computer, couldn't work enough hours, or simply couldn't handle him. Rebecca seemed to be the only one willing to put up with his shit, and she planned on leaving. And his wallet was now the property of Miss Ice Princess.

Never in his life had he been that careless with his belongings, nor had he figured out a way to get his wallet back. The fact that she had been at Dick's this morning was a pretty good indicator she'd stayed there. Perhaps he could go back and...what? Sit there and hope she'd come back? For all he knew, she could have robbed him blind and tossed his wallet. Or she could have just been passing through and was now halfway to Canada. Someone who knocked down innocent bystanders with their I'm-so-rich vehicle certainly didn't seem honest enough to do the Good Samaritan thing. Luckily, he'd already taken the necessary precautions by canceling his ATM and credit cards. Unluckily for him, he'd had sixty bucks cash in his wallet.

As far as luck went, his day had quickly plummeted into the dumps.

Noah pulled his computer out of sleep mode and tried to point his brain in the right direction. He had a meeting later in the morning with the mayor about possibly building an apartment complex. A job of that size had the potential of nudging his company from small potatoes to large cojones.

Rebecca finished updating one of his older proposals to fit the needs of the job. The manager he'd hired before Belinda had done a fairly decent job starting the project. However, she'd saved it on her computer and accidentally e-mailed the partially finished document to one of his subcontractors. He'd fired her that day. Rebecca said he'd been too harsh with that one. She told him Patricia displayed real potential to be a competent office manager. Noah had laughed. He didn't have time to hold his employees' hands and kiss their boo-boos when they made a mistake. He needed someone with thick skin and a take-charge attitude.

"You're going to fire every woman in this town, and then what'll you do?" Rebecca scolded him after Patricia had cleaned out her desk.

"I'll go to the next town" was his only reply as he slammed the office door behind him. Rebecca's laugh had penetrated the thick wood, as though she hadn't taken his sour mood seriously, as she often didn't. If there was a way to talk Rebecca into ditching medical school and running his office for him, he'd have done it a long time ago. As it stood now, she worked only about four hours a day and he had approximately three months left before she abandoned him. Which left him with what? Probably some jerk-off moron who wouldn't know her ass from her elbow. He'd hire his stepsister, who was the most take-charge person he knew, but she was off at Colorado State, learning how to be a graphic designer.

After getting halfway through the proposal, which was mind-numbing to say the least, his eyes started to cross. He leaned back in his chair and dug the heels of his hands into his blurry eyes.

All jokes aside, he had a serious problem. Every day his workload grew. The countertop space in the outer office ran short due to neglected piles of filing. The laughably archaic filing system simply didn't do his office justice. The computer system was unorganized and half the time there wasn't anyone to answer the phones when he was out on a job site. He needed someone he could depend on, fast.

He jabbed the intercom button on his phone. "Rebecca, send the help wanted ad back to the newspaper and tell them to run it ASAP."

"You got it."

Rebecca would get it done. She could type a contract with her eyes closed.

For the next thirty minutes, Noah scanned the proposal to make sure the document was one hundred percent ready for the mayor to read. He'd just hit the print button on his computer when Rebecca opened his door and poked her head in.

"Uh, Noah, there's a woman here to see you."

He waited for her to elaborate, to give him a name or something.

Her full, glossy lips twitched. "She says she's the Mercedes lady. Whatever the heck that means."

This he had not expected. Seven hours after their interesting encounter, the woman who'd hit him wanted to go another round? Were the Fates finally smiling at him for a change? Noah had learned long ago not to hold his breath. The woman possessed something he desperately needed. She was also a woman with an attitude the size of Alaska.

"Give me three minutes, and then send her in."

His part-time secretary narrowed her bright-green eyes at him. "Okay."

He rubbed his calloused hands over his eyes one more time and then assessed the disaster zone that was his office. How would a person who'd never been here before see this space? Um, yeah. Totally and completely unprofessional.

Jumping out of his chair, he grabbed the stacks of papers off the two seats that faced the desk. Rebecca had come in one day, barely containing them in her arms, and asked where to put them. With an absent wave of his hand, he'd told her to set them on the chairs. That had been weeks ago, and he'd been too busy to find a home for them. Now he stood with his arms full of documents and no place to put them. The only filing cabinet in his office, housing information on closed jobs, was packed ridiculously full.

"Screw it," he muttered as he set them down on top of the filing cabinet. It really wasn't a better alternative than the chairs, but at least the Mercedes woman would have a place to sit.

He surveyed his office again. Rolled-up plans were scattered haphazardly on the floor, just waiting to trip anyone walking by. That was a surefire lawsuit waiting to happen. Geez, had his office always been this much of a catastrophe? He came in every day, yet failed to notice the plans on the floor, and how pitiful the plant in the corner of the room wilted from lack of water. This was why he needed someone trustworthy and responsible.

He scooped up the dozen or so plans and tried to find any sort of available space to put them. There wasn't any.

"Oh, hell." They landed with a plop and scattered when he dropped them behind his desk. *Let's hope Little Miss Million Dollars doesn't notice them.*

He turned in a circle. Clean walking space and a place to sit. That's about as good as it would get.

No sooner had he lowered himself in the chair than his visitor opened the door. Oh, this woman undoubtedly came from money. The subtle scent of what he was sure had to be expensive, designer perfume immediately filled his office. A floral print skirt made out of some sort of girly, filmy material swirled around her knees when she moved. Yellow shoes with heels so high they could have been lethal weapons encased her petite feet. In all his adult life, Noah had never understood how women walked on shoes the size of stilts. Her sleeveless white blouse left her toned shoulders bare.

"Have a seat, Miss . . . ?" He lifted his brows and waited for her to answer.

She lowered herself in the chair across from him and didn't respond for a moment. "Price," she said and left it at that.

Had her voice been this soft and airy this morning? He'd been too hungover and pissed off to notice anything other than the fact that she'd *hit* him.

Her hair had even more color and depth to it than it had seemed to this morning. All different shades of brown were layered in her shoulder-length locks. The strands were so shiny they reflected the commercial lighting coming from the ceiling. He'd never seen any woman's hair pick up specks of light the way hers did. Her almond-shaped eyes tilted up slightly at the corners and were the deepest shade of brown he'd ever seen. Pink shiny gloss accented her full, wide mouth. A mouth that most men would picture doing certain things. Not that he *ever* pictured anything like that.

"I have something you need," she said without as much as a lead-in.

He folded his hands across his stomach and tried not to sound too eager. "I believe you do."

The princess actually smirked. "How badly do you want it back?"

Some of his relief turned to apprehension. "I beg your pardon?" Had he jumped the gun when he thought she'd come to do the right thing? No way was she even thinking about blackmailing him. He leaned forward in his chair. "All right, how much did you take?"

Her perfectly shaped brows pulled together in confusion. "I'm sorry?"

"How much money did you take out of my wallet?"

"You think I'd take money from your wallet and then try to return it?"

When she put it that way, it did sound like a stupid thing to do. What other thing could she possibly want besides money? Granted it was ludicrous considering she probably had more money than she knew what to do with.

"Then how much do you want for it?"

Her eyebrows pulled even lower. "What do you—?"

"Well, you didn't come here to return it for nothing." People didn't do nice things like that anymore.

Her delicate chin lifted and her brow smoothed out. "Actually, no."

Just as he suspected. The princess had an ulterior motive. Equal amounts of disappointment and annoyance had him gritting his teeth together. "So, what do you want?"

She hesitated for about two seconds. "A job."

Okay, seriously, was someone playing a joke on him? Too much clutter and other shit crowded his office to tell whether or not someone had placed a hidden camera at his expense. Maybe Courtney had found this girl and paid her to mess with him. Or maybe this beauty-pageant woman had just enough of a sadistic streak in her to play with him like this. Either way, the games ended here.

He couldn't help the laugh that popped out of him. "No way."

Both her shoulders lifted. "Okay," she said, then stood from the chair and headed for the door.

"Wait a minute," he said before she could make a fast getaway with his stuff.

She tossed a cool, expressionless glance over her shoulder. "Yes?"

"You're not really going to walk out of here without giving me my wallet back, are you?"

"That depends on whether or not you're willing to hire me."

He crossed his arms over his chest. "What makes you think I'm looking for help?"

Her deep-brown eyes scanned the disorganized surroundings. "Something tells me you could use some help."

He needed someone so badly he was willing to pay ungodly rates to hire a professional organizer. But her? A person who couldn't see out her rearview mirror worth a damn and wouldn't hand over personal belongings without blackmail? Okay, a very small part of him said, *Screw what sort of person she is. You are in dire straits. Plus, she's hot.*

The sensible part of him said, *Who cares what she looks like; you don't even know her.*

She must have taken his silence to mean a big fat no. Miss I-Look-Down-My-Nose-at-You turned again and almost made it out the door before he grabbed her elbow.

"For hell's sake, woman. You're forgetting I memorized your license plate and could easily file a report against you." Actually, he hadn't memorized anything. Sometimes threats served a purpose.

Her full, painted pink lips flattened together in frustration. Her chocolate eyes darkened even more.

"Let me see the wallet before I consider giving you a job," he demanded before she could reply to his threat.

Without a word, she dug her free arm in her duffel-bag-size purse and produced his brown trifold.

With a small smile, he snatched the wallet out of her hand. "Thanks," he said and released her arm.

"What do you think you're doing?" she asked when he turned away from her and walked to his desk.

"I hate to leave you hanging, but I have a meeting I'm running late for." Too bad, so sad, princess.

She jammed her hands on her thin hips. "You said if I gave your wallet back, you'd give me a job."

One corner of his mouth kicked up in triumph when he grabbed the proposal from the printer and jammed it in his bag. "I said I'd *consider* it." He glanced at her.

"Unfortunately for you, I don't have time to consider anything right now. But I sure appreciate getting this back." He held the wallet up before stuffing it in his back pocket.

The muscles in Miss Price's jaw tensed as her eyes narrowed to slits. *Yeah, I outsmarted you, didn't I? Not bad for an ornery, hungover jerk, huh?*

He touched two fingers to his forehead in a mock solute. "Have a good afternoon, Miss Price."

Avery Price stood, dumbfounded, as the finest man she'd ever laid eyes on walked out into the glorious Wyoming sunshine. What the heck had just happened? One minute she'd been executing a poor attempt at blackmail and the next he'd gotten the better of her. Man, he was a quick thinker, much quicker than she was.

The girl with the brand-new-copper-penny-colored hair moved around in the outer office. Avery walked back into the reception area. Rebecca, as Noah had called her, hummed some peppy tune to herself while practically floating around and gathering papers. Honestly, this place was a nightmare. Avery had been in dozens of offices, and none of them had been this cluttered, this uninviting. Didn't Noah have some sort of staff to at least water the poor dracaena drooping like a forgotten child in the corner?

A water cooler sat against one of the walls. Avery filled up a little Styrofoam cup and gave the plant the drink it desperately needed. She dropped two more cupfuls in the soil.

"Oh, hey, thanks. The poor plants around here get neglected, because I'm too busy being this business's backbone." Rebecca came to a stop next to Avery, barely holding on to a stack of papers at least a foot and a half

high. The girl didn't look like she was any older than
maybe nineteen or twenty. Her pearlescent skin was dotted with a smattering of light-brown freckles across the
bridge of her nose. A few corkscrew tendrils had come
loose from the bun on the back of her head and hung
down like red streamers. Her eyes sparkled when she
smiled and were the color of emeralds. Avery instantly
liked Rebecca.

"The plants never get watered?" Avery gestured to the
one behind her.

"When I remember. But I'm here only three days a
week, and when I am here, I'm so busy with the workload
that watering the plants is the last thing on my mind." She
graced Avery with an openmouthed smile. "I don't know
why Noah bothers to keep them around. I think it would
look better to just take them out."

"You're the only employee here?" Avery found that
hard to believe. How did one run a business with just two
people? See, he did need help.

Rebecca hefted the papers higher in her arms. "He
fired our office manager this morning for incompetence,
not that I blame him. Although the woman was really
nice, she wasn't a great employee. Yesterday I asked her
to shred some legal documents, and she faxed them to a
client instead. Noah had to get on the phone with the guy
and explain the mistake."

Her father would have hit the roof if one of his employees had done anything that stupid. And he certainly
wouldn't have kept them around another day.

"So now it's just me."

Avery was just about to offer to take some of the papers
from the obviously overworked girl when the phone rang.

Rebecca lifted her green eyes to the ceiling. "Great."

She scampered across the room. "Will you grab that for me? Just say, 'McDermott Construction' and write down whatever they say. There're some sticky notes and pens next to the phone," she called out from down a hallway.

Avery had been in stranger situations than this. Surely she could handle answering a phone and taking a message.

On the third ring, Avery snatched it up and repeated the greeting Rebecca had given her.

"Yeah, I need to talk to Noah."

She paused. *Now would be a good time to say something, Avery.*

"I'm sorry, Noah's not here." Whew.

"Okay, I need to leave a message for him. This is Ray from DDM Project Management. Just tell him there's been a delay in the permits because the wheelchair ramps on the plans for the Pelican Club need to be modified by three inches. I gotta go into a meeting. He's got my cell. Thanks, sugar."

The dial tone rang in her ear a second later. What the heck? The guy had rambled off his message and hung up before she could unstick a sticky note.

"Oh, good." She breathed in relief when she saw a stack of Post-its right in front of her face. She pulled key words from the conversation out of her brain and tried to re-create the message. Something about wheelchair ramps and three inches. And his name was Ray. That was about the extent of her knowledge of that one-sided conversation.

Rebecca stepped back into the room, paper-free. Avery spun around and held up the note. "A message for Noah."

The redhead scooped up another monstrous pile. "Oh, you can just stick it in his office. He'll see it when he gets back." She left the room as quickly as she had come in.

Avery let herself back into Noah's office and stopped short

in front of his desk. "Okay, where?" she asked herself when not even the surface of the desk could be seen for all the crap he had scattered on top. Noah McDermott needed some organization coaching. If only he had accepted her help. On a sigh, she stuck the note to the screen of his computer.

When she walked to the reception area again, Rebecca was back, going through more papers. "Wow, it's kind of nice having a second set of hands." She stuck her hands on her slim hips and regarded Avery. The corner of her wide, red-painted lips kicked up. "Would you by any chance be looking for a job?"

"You *hired* her?"

Noah's perky secretary held up her hands in defense. "Okay, first of all, calm down. Second of all, I didn't *hire* her." She made quotation marks in the air with her hands. "Technically, that's your job. All I did was ask her to help me out with a few things. She was more than happy to give me a hand. She even said she'd be willing to come back tomorrow."

"I don't want her coming back tomorrow, Rebecca." *You know you do, so stop denying it.*

"Noah, look at this place." She lifted her arms out, encompassing his small office. "We're drowning here. I'm only one person, and you fired the only other office person we had."

He scrubbed a weary hand down his prickly face. "I know, and I'm sorry I put you in this position. But I couldn't keep her here."

The younger woman lifted her eyes to the ceiling like a teenager. "I know. My point is I had a perfectly able and willing body here today. And she's willing to help out some more. Why not take what's being offered?"

Of course she was willing. She'd tried to blackmail him into giving her a job. But hell, he didn't want the woman who'd hit him and also made him think of lazy afternoon sex sashaying around his office like a tempting piece of fruit. He did *want* her; there was no denying that. Just, not here.

"Look." Rebecca continued her case for Avery's employment. "We got all the paperwork for the Dennison property filed today and made new files for the Pelican Club. That's like a week's worth of work for me."

Clearly, the woman knew her way around an office; he'd give her that. But work here?

"Just give her tomorrow. If you don't think she's really helping or you can't stand to look at her, which I would find very hard to believe considering she's beautiful, then tell her not to come back."

Well, when she put it that way...

FOUR

THE PEELING CAULKING IN THE bathtub stared back at her as though it had a thousand slimy little eyeballs beckoning her to come sit in its filth. A shudder wracked her tired, dirty body after she saw the blackened corners of the tub that had failed to be cleaned, probably since the day it'd been built. The showerhead was nothing more than a pipe sticking out at a ninety-degree angle from dingy, cracked white tiles. The walls of public bathrooms were probably cleaner than the orange-and-brown-streaked transparent shower curtain. Some of the plastic rings were broken, leaving the curtain to droop pathetically in some places. Someone needed to enter this place in the book of Guinness World Records for the world's dirtiest bathroom.

Her skin felt sticky and dry from going nonstop for more than twenty-four hours. She'd grabbed her papaya-scented bubble bath, hoping it would diffuse some of the nastiness that was the bathtub. But after eyeing stains that looked dangerously like human fluids, a big fat *Hell, no* flew through her mind. No amount of papaya bubble bath could get her in that grime. She couldn't stomach taking another shower in this place.

"Blech," she said as another quake coursed through her body. She padded across the slimy tile floor and the shag green carpet in her bright-pink fuzzy socks. Since there wasn't any sort of air-conditioning in this negative-five-star establishment, the temperature in the room hovered at a humid ninety degrees. Despite the heat, she'd refused to put her bare feet on flooring that had Lord only knew what embedded in the fibers. She returned her bubble bath to her plastic bathroom kit and tossed the contents in her suitcase. The piece of paper on which Rebecca had scrawled her address was still folded in her pants pocket. Avery dug it out and debated whether or not she should really go.

Rebecca was a virtual stranger but was nicer than any human being Avery had ever encountered. She *talked* to Avery, which was something people rarely did, except for Teeny, her best friend, and Landon. *And* she'd given Avery a job. Granted, the girl probably didn't have that sort of authorization, but so what. Maybe if Avery showed up enough Noah would give up and let her stay. Tomorrow she'd walk in and say, "Take that, Noah McDermott. Who got the better of whom this time?"

"Living in the spare bedroom of a stranger's apartment has to be better than this place," she muttered to herself.

Seriously, the little black alarm clock was bolted down to the particleboard nightstand. "For Pete's sake." She sighed while shaking her head. That did it. She could not spend another $57.99 to sleep on a cardboard mattress and look at the peeling furry wallpaper. What in the world sort of people put fur on their walls? They had to have lost a bet on that one. The metal grating sound of the zipper on her suitcase echoed in the silent shoe-box-size room. She tore the fuzzy socks off, stuffed them into the top pocket of her suitcase, and slipped her feet into her ballet flats. Bidding the hotel *bon adieu*, Avery pulled the heavy metal door open and blinked at the man standing on the other side.

The man she'd knocked down in front of this very door leaned casually against one of the brick columns. His body radiated a relaxed I'm-just-waiting-for-the-bus air. He'd slipped a soft-looking brown leather jacket over his light-gray polo. He wasn't even standing near her, and his powerful presence crowded her. The light in his gray eyes ate up her face before roaming over her linen button-down top and dropping to her denim capris. Worn blue jeans covered his long, solid legs—legs that had probably gotten that way from squatting school buses.

"Good evening, Miss Price. Or can I call you Avery?" His deep, gravelly voice washed over her skin like intimate little fingers.

A sharp breath filled her lungs when he said her name. "How—"

"Rebecca told me," he answered.

A cool gust of wind whipped down the open hallway and ruffled his light-brown-and-dirty-blond-streaked hair. Why hadn't she noticed his hair before? Sun-kissed strands of blond were threaded all through his otherwise oak-colored hair. The look she'd spent appalling amounts of money to achieve in her coif, he probably got naturally from being in the sun. He *did* own a construction company, which meant he most likely spent a lot of time outdoors. That would also explain why his hands were big and had thick veins running just below the surface of his tanned skin.

That doesn't explain anything. All men have hands like that.

No, Noah's were different. They were hands meant for running over a woman's sensitive skin or threading through her hair.

"Rebecca told me you helped her in the office today." His words brought her thoughts back to the situation at hand.

Avery crossed her arms under her breasts to ward off the chill from a sudden burst of wind. "No offense, but your office needs some serious help. And Rebecca was fun to talk to. She made me laugh."

Little smile lines bracketed his sensual mouth. "Yeah, the place is pretty quiet when she's not there." His brown work boots scraped the ground when he shifted his feet. "I actually wanted to talk to you about what you did today."

"I know, and I'm sorry. It was wrong of me to hold your wallet hostage. But I'm kind of desperate for a job." She sure was doing a lot of apologizing today.

He scratched part of his five o'clock shadow with his thumb. "That's the reason I came over here. I have a little proposition for you."

Given her history with her parents and ex-fiancé, Peter, Avery didn't really do well with propositions. They usually benefited only the person doing the propositioning.

Another quick gust of wind stirred her hair around her face. "Oh?"

"I will pay you to organize my office."

Didn't sound like much of a proposition.

"The job is temporary until I can find a full-time manager. And I won't report you for our little incident this morning."

She straightened from the door. "You already said you wouldn't do that."

"No, I never actually said that. I think you assumed it."

O-kay. Yeah, she probably had. While she certainly could use the distraction of doing something she enjoyed, it also meant seeing Noah. Every day. Talking to him, being in close proximity to him. Hearing his hypnotic voice, drooling over how the tight muscles of his thighs moved underneath his slacks. Sitting on the other side of his massive wooden desk earlier in the morning turned out to be more torture than finding a designer dress that wasn't in her size. She didn't think she'd endured that much torture since she'd waited to eat the homemade pies her nanny used to make. Noah was a man she could lose herself—and possibly her heart—to. Avery wasn't sure if the fragile little organ could really stand much more grief. But then again...he had offered to pay her. And one of the first things she needed to do when she found a place worth staying was find a job. Spending the money in her trust fund was like drinking poison, a very delicious poison, but poison nonetheless. She needed to stop ASAP, so her mom and dad didn't have any more strings to pull.

Noah must have taken her narrowed eyes as resignation. He held his hands up in front of him. "You're the one who said you needed a job." Then he pulled his wallet out of his back pocket. "I already got what I needed." His smile cut shallow lines in his cheeks, one of them resembling a dimple. The sight of his devilish mouth grinning turned the pit of her stomach into cottage cheese. She'd never felt anything like that before, especially not with Peter. The only thing she felt with Peter was...well, nothing. The somersaults her stomach did by simply looking at Noah were leaps and bounds more than she'd had for any other guy she'd dated. Avery had never known her stomach could actually do a somersault.

"So what do you say?" The smile on his face grew to

resemble the Cheshire cat's, as though he knew exactly the effect it had on her.

Maybe her suddenly uneven breaths or the perspiration coating her forehead were strong indicators. She'd always been a bad actress.

Against her better judgment, she nodded, and her mouth turned up in an involuntary grin. "Okay. Wait," she called out just as he turned to leave. "I just wanted to say sorry again." Swallowing pride was not easy, or fun. The way she'd acted today had been completely out of character for her and unacceptable. For some reason she needed him to know she wasn't that sort of person. "For hitting you and..."

"Blackmailing me for my wallet?" he finished, when words failed her.

"Yeah," she said on a weary sigh. "I should have just given it back to you."

His mouth pulled up in a devastating smile. "Luckily for you, I'm a forgiving guy."

The thick, deep-piled carpet in Rebecca's spacious apartment was like walking on feathers compared to the Fleabag Motel. An hour ago, Rebecca had opened her front door with a welcoming smile and an enthusiastic "Come on in!" The colonial-style apartment building, accented with mature trees and a duck pond, was quiet and secluded on the outside of town.

"The second bedroom is down the hall. Just help yourself to anything in the kitchen," Rebecca had said as she grabbed her school supplies and stuffed them in a bag. "My anatomy class starts in thirty minutes, so I have to go." With a cheerful wave of her fingers, she let herself out the door and left Avery alone.

Now she paced across the living room floor, trying to get in touch with her friend. "Come on, Teeny, pick up," Avery whispered into her cell phone as the other end rang and rang. Trying to predict when her best friend would be home was like trying to pick a winning lottery ticket.

The phone stopped ringing as someone picked up. There was a muffled curse, and Avery waited through the background shuffling until Teeny finally came on. "Hello," her childhood friend said in a breathless voice.

"Tee—" Avery broke off as there was more background noise and what could only have been Teeny muttering to herself. "Teeny? Are you okay?"

"Sorry," she said finally. "I . . . had to run for the phone. Then I dropped it." Her friend laughed, but it sounded strange, high-pitched, and nervous. "Clumsy me. So how was your day?"

Teeny didn't sound like herself at the moment, but Avery ignored that and told her about the accident and the man she'd hit and how he turned out to be the most delicious man she'd ever seen.

"So let me get this straight. You hit a guy because you weren't paying attention, and now you're helping him organize his office." Teeny chuckled. "Tell me you're joking?"

"Hey, don't judge me. I'm desperate here. I could use the money. I refuse to use the money out of my trust fund."

"Why? It's got like millions of dollars in there. I bet your parents wouldn't even notice."

Avery plopped herself down on the worn leather couch and let her head drop back. "Teeny," she groaned, closing her eyes. "*I'd* notice. What sort of hypocrite would I be if I go around begging for independence then use money they gave me?"

"I'll never understand you, Avery."

Biggest lie of the decade. Teeny was the only one who really understood her.

"So how hot is this guy?"

Avery thought back to that morning and the sheer size of the man and how he filled the entire room with his massive shoulders and impossibly long, muscular legs. Her bones practically melted when he opened his mouth and his deep, smooth, rumbling voice poured out. He had a bedroom voice. That's what Teeny had said about some of the men she'd dated. A voice built for seducing a woman. Murmuring to her in low, melodious tones, as though she were the only woman in the world who turned him on.

Avery sighed. "Words cannot describe how good-looking he is. He has stunning gray eyes that are like looking into his soul, or something. And his hair—" She placed a hand over her chest and felt her heart beating a rapid rhythm against her rib cage. "You know how I have a thing for hair," she reminded her friend. "He has the most beautiful, sun-streaked, touchable hair I have ever seen."

Teeny let out a hoot of laughter. Avery winced and held the phone away from her ear. "Girl, you are busted."

Avery's smile faded as she stared at the fireplace mantel with pictures of Rebecca's family. "What do you mean?"

"You are totally in lust with this guy." Teeny's voice continued to boom at unnatural decibels over the phone.

Avery lifted her eyes to the smooth ceiling. "Please. How could I be lusting after him? I barely know him."

"You don't have to know a person to lust after him. It's all about how your body chemically reacts to him."

She ran her short, painted nail along the edge of the couch. "It's not lust." Who was she trying to convince?

Teeny was silent for so long, Avery thought she'd lost the connection. A cricket sang on the other side of the sliding glass door, and she heard more muffled sounds from Teeny's end followed by more muttering. "What are you doing?"

"Huh? I'm not doing anything." Teeny's raised voice turned soft and breathy.

Her friend answered too quickly. "You sound like you're running a marathon or something."

Teeny laughed again, a nervous chuckle that had Avery thinking her friend was doing something she didn't want Avery to know about. "I'm just doing some laundry and trying to carry the basket with one hand, so I keep dropping clothes. Sorry if I seem distracted."

"You're doing laundry at"—Avery glanced at her silver wristwatch—"nine o'clock?"

Teeny sighed. "Yeah, I had a really busy day and didn't have time earlier. Plus I'm out of clean underwear. I'm wearing a pair of swimsuit bottoms right now, and they're not comfortable because they have these beads that keep digging into my hips."

A little tug of guilt pulled at Avery's insides for doubting her friend. Especially after all Teeny had done to help her leave her parents. "I'm sorry. You can call me back tomorrow if you want."

"No, it's fine. I'm not done drilling you about this guy."

Whether or not she lusted after Noah wasn't something she wanted to discuss. It was bad enough she had to see him again, with her lustful thoughts about his hands caressing her body.

"I can tell by your silence the subject has exhausted itself," Teeny said, as though she'd read Avery's thoughts. "Your mother hasn't called you yet?"

Priscilla Price was an entity Avery would never fully understand—or relate to. Earlier that afternoon, she'd pictured her mother reading the note, then neatly folding it back into the envelope and asking her cook about that night's dinner menu. There had to be some small part of her mother that worried about Avery's whereabouts. That was most likely wishful thinking on her part. Worry would cause stress and tiny lines to crop up in her unnaturally smooth face. Priscilla didn't indulge herself in things like that.

"Not a word from either of them."

"I still can't believe they wanted you to reconcile with Peter after you told them you found him in bed with his assistant. I would have castrated him."

Satisfaction pulled at the corners of Avery's lips. Teeny didn't put up with shit from anyone. A spineless weasel like Peter Hanover wouldn't survive a confrontation with the fearless Teeny Newberry.

More background noise and scuffling came from Teeny's end of the line. How strange for a woman who was home by herself to be making so much noise by just doing laundry.

Avery looked outside the sliding glass door; she saw nothing but open cattle fields and horse ranches with an occasional house spotted here and there.

The city of Denver had been so riddled with different noises—police cars, traffic, and people yelling at one other—that Avery found the silence of southern Wyoming almost deafening. Nothing could be heard right now, not a moo from a cow, and even the lone cricket had quieted. She thought an environment like this, so different from what she was accustomed to, would take her ages to get used to. Instead, Avery found the serenity and slow pace of Trouble made it a place where she could happily spend a lot of time.

"Do you think I'd be crazy if I stayed here?" she asked her friend after a long silence.

"In Wyoming? Heck no. You said you wanted nowhere and it sounds to me as if you're there."

Avery gripped her cell phone tighter. "Would you have left town?"

"Are you kidding? Leave the big city for cow country? Never. But you're stronger than I am, babe. You'll do fine. You just have to get back on your feet."

Avery sighed and dropped her head back against the couch. The ceiling fan overhead turned in slow, hypnotic circles. "I don't know. Sometimes I think..." Avery paused. What sounded like a man whispering filtered through the phone line. Teeny hadn't mentioned having someone with her. The words he said weren't discernible, but clearly someone was there and trying to have a conversation with her. "I'm sorry; I didn't realize you had company. Was I interrupting?"

"What?" Teeny sounded dazed. "Hold on a sec, Avery."

Avery waited while thumps and grunts came through her cell phone. She had no idea what her friend was doing or who was at her house, but clearly something other than washing her clothes had her distracted. "Sorry, babe. It was my television. I just turned the volume down."

If there had been whispers on her friend's television, Avery wouldn't have been able to hear them so clearly through the line. But if Teeny said it was her TV, then it was her TV. She'd never known her friend to be a liar.

"That's all right. But I think I'm going to turn in for the night. I'm beat. Thanks for listening, Teeny. I'll call you in a few days and let you know how everything's going."

Teeny giggled, and a few more seconds went by before she responded. "Good luck. I want all the details on this Noah guy. Ciao, babe."

Avery disconnected and barely had time to reflect on her friend's strange behavior when her cell phone chirped a tune from *Saturday Night Fever*. The caller ID read "Peter."

The urge to answer and tell him where he could shove his marriage proposal almost beat out her pride. This was the first attempt he'd made to contact her since she'd left Denver. She hadn't really expected to hear from him, knowing there was no love lost between them. She supposed he'd called with some BS explanation about how her catching him in bed with his assistant wasn't what it looked like. Or go so far as to tell her the woman meant nothing. She didn't need to hear from him to know he'd probably been carrying on an affair with this woman for quite some time.

Her phone stopped ringing and a message scrolled across saying she had a new voice mail. A rambling boo-hoo apology wasn't something she was interested in hearing right then. She'd heard enough excuses from her parents when she told them the man they picked out had cheated on her.

"I don't think I've ever been so disappointed in you, Avery." Little snippets of her last conversation with her parents invaded her fatigued brain. Her father had stood in his study, like the force to be reckoned with that he was, and droned out yet another lecture.

"Your mother and I give you everything in life you could ever want, and all we ask is that you do something for us in return. Your mother and I don't think it's too much to ask that you reconcile with Peter and accept his

proposal. Do you know what sort of political connections his family has? My candidacy for governor would be in the bag if we had a family like the Hanovers on our side. And yet, just to spite us, you're going to turn down an offer for a solid, comfortable future?"

The convulsive swallowing she'd done since her father started talking had been barely enough to hold back tears. Like the good little girl she'd always been taught to be, she sat in a chair across from her mother and listened to her father continue his speech.

"I've never seen such selfish behavior. We introduced you to him to secure yours and our future. You will marry him or you're on your own, Avery Price. Do you understand me? I don't want to hear any more on the matter. The next time I see you, you'd better have his ring on your finger."

She'd exited her father's study, barely containing her tears, and had felt as if someone had carved her heart out with a dull, rusty knife. A deep, sharp ache settled in her chest and had accompanied her all through the night as she wrote her note with shaky hands and packed her bags. Teeny listened with comforting silence as Avery cried her heart and soul out. Fifteen minutes later, her best friend had shown up with fury in her eyes and a compassionate touch. Teeny had always been a good ally to have on one's side. Luckily for them, her parents had gone out for the night, leaving them the perfect opportunity to slip out the gold-plated front doors.

The ache in her chest had subsided to a manageable level throughout the day. But as she thought of the last encounter with her parents, once again, the pain returned. She dropped her cell phone on the leather couch and rubbed a hand in small circles over her chest. Why did it have to hurt so much? Why couldn't she be emotionally detached the way they were? Why was she the only one affected? A softball-size lump traveled up her throat and refused to be swallowed. After several failed attempts to push it down, the lump went all the way to the top of her throat. One stray, unwanted tear crept out of the corner of her eye, rolled over the edge of her eyelid, and slid down her cheek. She dashed it away with her hand before it reached her jaw. Before long, another tear, then another, forced itself out. In a matter of a few short seconds, she'd gone from trying to push the ache out of her chest to allowing the tears to fall freely. She didn't bother wiping them away. They fell like raindrops on her Pink sweatpants, soaking through to the skin. Like the night of the confrontation with her parents, she cried until she had nothing left. She cried until her insides hallowed out and dried up. She cried until she lowered herself down to the couch and drifted to an exhausted, dreamless sleep.

FIVE

NOAH LET HIMSELF IN THE front door and tossed his keys on the table. He undid the top two buttons on his shirt as he made his way to the kitchen to check messages. He'd just popped the top to the beer bottle he'd grabbed from the fridge when the mechanical voice said there were six new messages. The first three were hangups. The fourth message was from RJ, asking why he hadn't been at the staff meeting today.

Noah sighed and shook his head. His father owned two restaurants in town, a rowdy sports pub and a steak house. He wasn't willing to delve into the reasons his father pushed himself at a young age to become a successful entrepreneur when most people in town made their living from cattle and beef. His father's mind was too complex and mysterious to try to make sense of it. Nevertheless, he'd opened the restaurants years ago and expected his children to follow in his footsteps, earning their keep by working in the family business.

His stepbrother, RJ, tended bar at the Golden Glove, the sports pub located in the heart of town, where his youngest brother, Brody, was the general manager. Chase, his other brother, was the GM of McDermott's, an upscale steak house outside town. That life suited his three brothers; however, Noah had never had a desire to put up with temperamental chefs and high school students who wanted nothing more than to wait tables for the summer. His father had taken it as a personal offense that his eldest son had no interest in being part of the family business.

Noah just didn't have any passion for the restaurant industry and had given up trying to explain himself to his father. Instead, to appease Martin McDermott, a proud man, Noah bought into the business as a silent partner. But that wasn't good enough. Martin wanted his oldest son to be an integral part and follow in his footsteps. Noah refused, saying he had his own passions in life. He eventually came to the realization that he and his father would never see eye to eye.

Their relationship had been strained ever since.

The fifth message was from Brody, also wondering where he'd been. Noah closed his gritty eyes as he sat down on the sofa. The sixth message was from Mary Ellen.

Her feminine, shrill voice filled the room and grated on his last remaining nerve. She went on and on, saying how they'd had a good time, how she missed him and he could call her any time he wanted. Yeah right. While she'd been dynamite in bed, she annoyed him with her high-pitched giggle and incessant desire to drag him all over town so people could see them together.

Why did women always equate sex with a commitment? Every time he slept with a woman, she'd call nonstop, wondering when he was going to take her out again. Sometimes he wanted to be left the hell alone.

Mary Ellen ended her message, but not before rattling off her phone number, just in case he'd lost it. Like that was the only reason he hadn't called her. The machine beeped, indicating there were no more messages. Noah took another long sip of his beer and savored the cool liquid gliding down his throat. Silence and peace at last. He didn't want to think about his father and the monumental disappointments he'd caused the man. And he definitely didn't want to think about the sexy-as-hell, knock-you-on-your-ass woman he'd recently gotten involved with.

Someone must have smashed him over the head with a two-by-four in his sleep. Only a person who wasn't right in his mind would offer a job to a woman who stirred things in him he hadn't even realized were there. Avery Price was a force to be reckoned with. She stood out in Trouble, Wyoming, while women he'd dated in this town blended in. He wasn't sure yet if that was a good or bad thing, but it would be interesting to find out. He had no idea what brought her to their small cattle town, other than the song and dance of just passing through, but he intended to find out.

Her sassy speak-her-mind attitude intrigued him. She was like a Christmas present with numerous layers to unwrap. Maybe that's what made her all the more appealing. The need to chase her, tackle her to the ground, and force her to explain more about herself was one small contributing factor for hiring her.

Noah pulled his pack of cigarettes out of his back pocket and stepped outside to the front porch. Man, it would be fun to draw out the same fire she'd shown yesterday.

Noah ran her name through his mind over and over as he sat in a wooden rocking chair. Avery Price. The name suited her perfectly—a high-society name.

He lit the cigarette and stacked his booted feet on the wooden porch railing.

In order to "purify" his body, as his stepmother put it, he'd been trying to cut back on the smoking. His stepmother, Carol, made him feel guilty by constantly reminding him his body was a temple. Noah laughed out loud in the quiet, cool night. He already knew too much smoking, alcohol, and sex had ruined any chance of keeping his body pure.

A deep, growling rumble drew near his house and finally quieted in his driveway. Noah immediately recognized the sound of Chase's Harley. Not ten seconds later his brother came up the walkway, unzipped his leather jacket, and tossed it over the railing next to Noah's feet. The wooden rocking chair creaked under Chase's weight as he sat down and stretched his long legs in front of him.

"You missed the staff meeting today," his brother informed him.

Noah inhaled from the cigarette before passing it to Chase. "So I heard."

"I take it someone already got to you before I did?"

Noah took the cigarette back. "I got messages from RJ and Brody. I stopped going to staff meetings years ago. Everyone knows that."

"Yeah, but you're a silent partner."

Noah inhaled once more before crushing the cigarette out in the ashtray next to his feet. "I didn't realize being a silent partner meant I had to attend every single meeting Dad calls."

Chase held up his hands in defense. "Dad's words, not mine. I'm just relaying the message."

"So what was the meeting about anyway?" Noah asked, trying not to picture his father waiting in anticipation, then being disappointed when Noah didn't show.

His brother shrugged. "Dad spent a half an hour explaining why we were there. Then he went on about how the chefs are inefficient getting the food out and the waiters take too long with the checks and aren't pushing enough customers through. Afterward, the management staff debated about putting pool tables in the Golden Glove. Brody and RJ think they'll bring more paying customers, but Dad thinks they'll draw the wrong kind of clientele."

"A pool table will definitely draw more of a crowd."

"I agree. I suggested Dad put one in as a test to see how it works out. If he doesn't like it, he can always remove it. But then he bit my head off because I don't work at the Golden Glove and I don't get to weigh in on that discussion."

Noah turned his head. His brother leaned back in the Adirondack-style chair. "Yeah, but you still have a share in the Golden Glove, so technically you do have a say."

Chase shrugged his shoulders again. "Try telling Dad that," he said quietly. "Anyway, he was pissed off to begin with, because Brody showed up twenty minutes late."

"But Brody's never late."

Chase nodded. "I know. Don't tell him I told you this, but I think he and Kelly are having problems. It's the second time Brody's been late this month."

"What makes you think he and Kelly are fighting?"

Chase took a deep breath and folded his hands across his stomach. "When I called him one day last week, Tyler answered and said his mom and dad were in their bedroom, arguing. And that's not the first time Tyler's told me something like that."

"That kid was always too observant for his own good," Noah muttered. "Has Brody told you anything about this?"

"Nah," Chase said, shaking his head. "You know how

he is. He doesn't like to talk about his problems, but their marriage has been rocky from day one."

Brody had met Kelly in college, and a month later, she'd turned up pregnant. They'd married out of obligation and had managed to stay that way for the past seven years. They moved back to Trouble after graduation, and Brody went to work for his father. Noah had always suspected his brother's wife wasn't too fond of Trouble and harbored some resentment toward her husband. The fact that Kelly and his brother were fighting made him worry about his nephew's well-being.

"I'm sure whatever it is, they'll work it out," Noah said.

Chase rubbed a hand along his chin. "I'm not so sure. Haven't you noticed how different Brody has been lately?"

To be honest, Noah hadn't. He didn't really spend a whole lot of time in his father's restaurants. He had noticed that recently, Tyler's attitude had taken a subtle shift from bouncy and outgoing to quiet and watchful. No matter what went on between Brody and Kelly, hopefully they would try to keep their son from being affected by it as much as possible.

"Anyway, Dad wanted me to come over here and rip you a new one," Chase said, looking at him. They shared quiet chuckles.

They sat in silence for a few moments, then his brother's cell phone vibrated. He reached to dig it out of his back pocket. He glanced at the screen for a second before shoving it back in his pocket.

"Damn woman won't leave me alone," Chase muttered.

A grin turned up the corners of Noah's mouth. Half the women in town followed his brother around like lost puppies. Chase never minded, as he bounced from one female to the next like people go through pairs of socks. It seemed, at twenty-eight, he was not finished sowing his wild oats.

"Who is it this time?" Noah asked.

"Jessica Reilly," Chase murmured.

Noah's head whipped around toward his brother. "The mayor's niece?"

Chase laughed. "Yeah. I don't know how she found out where I live, but I came home late from work and she was sitting at my front door. The woman practically shoved me into bed. She gives new meaning to the word 'stamina.' "

"What the hell were you thinking getting tangled up with her? She's got the biggest mouth in the entire town."

"She's got a big mouth all right," Chase said with a mischievous grin.

Noah lifted his eyes to the bead-boarded ceiling.

Chase continued, "It was just a one-time thing, but now she won't stop calling me, as if we're supposed to get married or something."

"Women don't usually like to be blown off."

Chase snorted. "You're one to talk. Besides, she's the one who came on to me. I didn't promise her anything. I don't do relationships."

That much was obvious from the long string of one-night stands on his brother's record. But Noah wasn't going to analyze his brother or lecture him on not sleeping around. Chase was young and single. If he wanted to be with a woman without offering her a commitment, then that was his business.

Besides, his brother was right. Noah was no authority on how to treat the opposite sex. Especially since he'd hired a woman who'd hit him and then tried to hijack his wallet. He decided then and there that would be a non-issue. He would treat her like every other employee and pretend she didn't turn him on like no other woman ever had.

Someone was following her. Avery was as sure as she knew her own name. The prickly, hair-raising sensation had been with her for the last twenty-four hours. It had started that morning when she left for work. Even now, watering the poor, neglected plants in Noah's office, she felt as though someone waited outside for her. She hadn't actually seen anything out of the ordinary, but the feeling of someone's eyes following her every move went from uncomfortable to downright creepy.

No one she knew was low enough to have someone tail her. Well, except maybe Peter. However, Peter had never seemed the type to stoop to private investigators. It was so desperate.

He never seemed the type to cheat on you either, and look how wrong you were about that.

The dull pain that slid next to her heart last night was still very much present today. Every few minutes, she had to pull in deep breaths and massage her chest with her hand.

A phone call to her mother would have to be made later, however much she didn't want to talk to her. Despite the fact that she and her parents would never see eye to eye, it wasn't fair to remain silent this long.

"Noah needs these files for his meeting this afternoon. But he doesn't need the whole thing, just copies of the memos. After you make copies, paper-clip them together and set them on his desk." Rebecca placed four thick files in Avery's arms. Immediately after arriving, the two of them began filing to clear some of the clutter off the desk-

tops. Noah had only one pitifully organized filing cabinet, which was way too full and not clearly labeled. It was
almost as though someone had tossed all the papers in
blindfolded and scrawled sloppy labels on the files. There
was absolutely no attempt at any sort of proper organization. Avery suggested they organize the cabinet first, and
then put away the papers.

Rebecca shook her head and sent red curls flying out
of her bun. "We sometimes have clients come in here and
we need to make this space as presentable as possible.
Organizing the cabinet will take way too long." The girl
pushed the long sleeves of her knit sweater her forearms. "So far, I've just been transferring the piles into the
conference room. Noah got mad and said he uses the conference room when clients come in." Her green eyes lit
up with amusement. "Now I don't know what to do with
them. Every time I make headway with the files I have to
stop and modify a contract, pay the bills, or answer the
phone. And for every pile of papers I clear out, we accu-
mulate three more. It's never-ending."

"Sounds like you're a one-woman show now."

Rebecca turned to pick up more papers. "Don't I know
it? Noah doesn't pay me enough for what I do." The files
landed with a heavy *thud* when she dropped them in the
hall. "But as important as this is, we need to put it on hold.
I have to go over some things with you because you have
to go with Noah to a meeting today and take notes."

Accompanying Noah in public was not in her job
description. Her senses had a hard time handling his
spicy, freshly showered, manly scent. When he'd walked
in that morning, a come-and-inhale-my-knee-weakening
aroma trailed behind him all the way to his office. Avery
had tried to ignore the lingering scent and had failed

miserably. Her thighs turned to Jell-O, and an unfamiliar heat burned in the pit of her belly and spread up to her breasts. All the paper-gathering in the world couldn't quiet the salsa dancing her heart had been doing.

Rebecca grinned at her with a row of straight white teeth. She must have noticed the widening of Avery's eyes. "All you have to do is write down what people say. I normally go, but I have a twenty-page contract for a potential client I've been working on. I won't be here tomorrow, so I have to work on it today. Trust me; you're getting the easier of the two jobs."

Easy was not something she cared about right now. She'd rather fumble her way through foreign contract language than be within touching and smelling distance of Noah.

"Go ahead and make copies of the memos from the files I gave you and give them to Noah. When you're done, we'll go back to the filing." The old desk chair squeaked when Rebecca sat down. The long skirt she wore floated and settled gracefully around her. "I'm going to work on this contract while you do that. Just give a shout-out if you have any questions."

As soon as Avery turned and faced the copy machine, every hair on the back of her neck lifted. The boogeyman was out there. He'd grab her at the first opportunity and drag her back to Denver.

You're stronger than this, Avery. No one can make you do anything. That's why you're here, remember? Your parents couldn't make you marry Peter, and no one can make you leave here if you don't want to.

The motivational speech didn't erase the goose bumps that had surfaced on her flesh, nor did the hairs on her neck return to normal.

Her breasts pushed against her Yves Saint Laurent

rose-printed blouse when she inhaled a deep breath. She let her eyes drift shut and tried to wash away the unpleasant feeling with thoughts of something pleasant. Like, say, Noah? Noah's calloused, strong hands. Noah's thick, muscle-corded shoulders. Noah's masculine legs covered in fine dark hair. Noah, Noah, Noah.

Yeah, it worked. Her heart still tattooed against her rib cage, but for a reason that was much more welcome than the feeling the boogeyman caused her. An involuntary smile curved her lips. She clamped her mouth shut so Rebecca wouldn't notice her grinning like a psycho at the copy machine. Copying wasn't *that* exciting.

The last of the memos slid out of the machine. She gathered them up, stacked them neatly, and made sure they were in chronological order.

Avery rapped her knuckles lightly on Noah's closed door to announce her arrival before stepping inside.

His chair was turned away from her, and his long legs, covered in a pair of gray slacks, stretched out in front of him. An incredibly immature and sick urge to sit on his lap just to get a feel of his thighs flexing had her sucking in a sharp breath.

He didn't hear her enter as he talked on the phone, his low voice rumbling in conversation with whoever was on the other end. She stepped toward his desk and placed the papers down as quietly as possible so as not to disturb him. But the man must have had hearing like an eagle's, because almost as soon as the papers left her hand, he turned.

"We'll have to postpone the walkthrough until next week, then," he said, his gray eyes burning into hers. A sexual jolt coursing through her body reminded her she wasn't unaffected by him. The corner of his mouth kicked up, and Avery averted her gaze to the window behind him. The view was nowhere near as exciting or attractive, but the rolling green hills didn't threaten to make her spontaneously combust.

"Send me a fax when you have those numbers worked out."

Avery turned to leave, but not before Noah lifted a finger, asking her to wait.

"Thanks, Joan," he said and hung up. He glanced at Avery, quickly raking his gaze down to her toes, and then picked the memos up and thumbed through them. "Did Rebecca mention you're coming with me today?" he asked, his attention focused on the papers.

His hair, which looked soft and touchable, yet masculine, distracted her from answering.

Be professional, Avery.

"Yes, but to be honest, the filing in your office should be your first priority. You can hardly walk in there."

Noah took his attention off the papers, leaned back in his chair, and tapped the stack against his thigh. "Do you always say the first thing that comes to your mind?"

"When it's important, yeah."

He ran his gaze over her again, pausing briefly on her shoes, as if he wanted to say something about her wearing gold pumps to a job site. More ripples of goose bumps surfaced on her bare legs in the wake of his penetrating gaze. Ever so slowly, his eyes lifted back to hers and remained locked there for several heartbeats. Her heart thumped harder against her insides with each passing moment their gazes remained fixed.

The chair squeaked under Noah's weight as he swiveled back and forth. He tossed the memos back on the desk and linked his hands across his flat stomach. "I understand this isn't exactly what I'm paying you to do, but at the moment you're needed more with me out there than in here."

She opened her mouth to tell him she doubted that, but he lifted a hand to stop her. "The papers aren't going anywhere. And, trust me, no one knows more than me the state of emergency my office is in. The meeting will last only an hour, and then you can come back and organize your little heart out."

Okay, he made some sense. But she refused to let the subject of his office drop. She jerked a thumb over her shoulder. "Do you have only that one filing cabinet?"

His low, throaty laughter was like hot, seductive breath over her skin. "Geez, you have a one-track mind."

She stabbed her fists on her hips. "It's overflowing. There's no way it'll fit all the rest of those papers."

"A fact that I'm well aware of."

Her brows shot up. "And?"

His massive shoulders lifted in an I-don't-give-a-damn shrug. "And what?"

"How do you plan to fix that? Rebecca can't just keep stacking papers in the hall. We can barely walk down there as it is. It's a fire hazard, for one thing."

He ran a hand down his square jaw. "I suppose I should get another cabinet. You think one will be enough?" The words were spoken around a sneaky little grin that had the one dimple appearing in his cheek.

Her toes curled in her uncomfortable, pointy shoes. "You're making fun of me."

Mischief lit up his smoky eyes. "Never."

Her teeth clamped together. The insufferable man was laughing at her. "Forget it," she bit out through gritted teeth, then spun on her heel and exited his office.

Avery dropped herself at the temporary desk Rebecca had set up for her and huffed out an aggravated breath. Of all the nerve, he had to make fun of her when she was *trying* to help him. It was a wonder anyone was able to locate anything around here. The man probably couldn't find his driver's license if he needed it. She dug her fingernails into the thin folding chair until her temper subsided. Noah McDermott was a hardheaded man who would never take anyone's advice, especially from little ol' her. She could live with that. If the man wanted to run a disorganized business, it was no skin off her back. Until then, the papers wouldn't pick themselves up. As she stood, the front doors opened and a man came through, one of the most breathtakingly gorgeous men she'd ever laid eyes on.

He was exceptionally tall, probably well over six feet, and had the type of golden good looks that reminded her of a Greek god. In fact, all he needed was a loincloth and a pair of leather sandals, and he could pass for Hercules. He pulled his dark sunglasses off, revealing a pair of stunning green eyes, and hooked them in the front pocket of a pair of well-worn, faded jeans. Jeans that sat low on his lean hips and hugged his manhood like an intimate touch. A clean white T-shirt stretched tightly across a rather large chest, so tightly, in fact, that the shirt strained to hold itself together. She had no doubt she would be extremely attracted to him if Noah McDermott hadn't already caught her attention. But as a woman, she couldn't help but appreciate a stunning example of the male gender when she saw one.

"Good morning, ladies." He greeted them with a dazzling white smile that could have had any woman melting in a puddle at his feet. He leaned his impressive forearms, covered with a light dusting of golden hair, on the counter in front of Rebecca's desk. "Is my workaholic brother ready for me?"

Avery pointed a finger toward Noah's door. "I think he's just finishing up."

"That's all right. I rather like the view from up here," he said with a wink at Avery before shifting his attention to something on the floor behind her. Brown-and-white swirly printed material flashed in the corner of Avery's eye. She swiveled around in her chair and saw Rebecca crawling on her hands and knees, gathering little dots of paper that were supposed to go in the garbage can from the hole punch, but had flittered to the ground instead like cheerful confetti. The young redhead muttered to herself. Was the always-sunny Rebecca cursing?

"Is he gone yet?" she asked in a whisper. Avery wasn't sure if the words were meant to be heard. "Did he see me?" This time Rebecca looked up. A faint blush, the color of a pink carnation, stained the girl's high cheekbones.

"Um..." Noah's brother's green gaze was still fixed on Rebecca's backside, with unwavering interest. "I think he sees you." Avery stuffed down a giggle while Rebecca recovered the last dot and her composure and stood.

The golden god's eyes followed the young woman until she sat down at her desk. While she, on the other hand, ignored his presence. An unaffected grin poked dimples into his smooth cheeks.

He directed his attention toward Avery, who'd been trying to hold in her smile at Rebecca's flustered state. "I suppose I'll introduce myself since Rebecca has forgotten her manners."

The other woman whipped her head around. "Oh, right," she said with a shake of her head. "Yeah, Avery this is...um—"

RJ shook his head and walked around Rebecca's desk. "I'm RJ. Noah's brother."

Avery shook the man's hand and offered her own smile. "Avery Price."

"Clearly that was too hard for Curly Sue over there," he added with a nod of his head toward Rebecca.

Avery could have sworn she heard Rebecca mutter the words "shut up."

Noah's brother grinned, as though getting shits and giggles over making Rebecca suffer. "You know, you ought to be more careful when driving through cross-walks. You could really hurt somebody," the man said, leaning precariously close to Rebecca's chair.

"Maybe you should learn to read crosswalk signs before you start crossing the street," Rebecca responded with an unsteady whisper. The attention Rebecca kept on her otherwise monotonous contract was obviously forced. Her ramrod-straight spine reminded Avery of her own posture when listening to one of her father's lectures. The sexual tension between Rebecca and Noah's brother was as thick as chocolate pudding, and Avery vowed to ask Rebecca about their relationship later.

"Touché" was all he said as the smile on his face became even more alluring and charming, but Rebecca wasn't having any part of it.

Just as Avery thought the encounter between the two would get even more interesting, Noah's door opened and he stepped out. "Stop harassing my secretary, RJ."

The two men didn't look anything alike except that they both exuded sexuality the same way cheesecake exuded calories. These two were really brothers?

"We'll be back in a little while," Noah said. His eyes touched her the same way RJ's ran over Rebecca, with possessiveness, before the two walked out the front doors. Rebecca's shoulders relaxed and she dropped her head on the desk, groaning aloud. "I hate that man."

SIX

USUALLY NOAH DIDN'T LOOK FORWARD to weekly meetings. He'd rather be out meeting potential clients or breaking ground on a new project.

But this week's meeting might be more interesting than recent ones, thanks to the woman seated next to him in his SUV. She'd hardly said more than two words since leaving the office a few minutes ago. It probably ticked her off that he wouldn't drop work, run out, and buy another filing cabinet.

The woman was pure spit and fire. He'd never known anyone who had such passion for filing as she did. For crying out loud, filing was about as exciting as watching grass grow. She acted as though she were hunting for buried treasure. Yes, his office needed help. Labeling folders and putting correspondence in chronological order wasn't something that lit his fire. That's why he had employees. Poor, overworked Rebecca did the best she could. He had no earthly idea what he would do with himself after she left. That was a bridge to be crossed when he came to it. So far, Rebecca had taken the shorthandedness in stride.

Noah cleared his throat and glanced at Avery. "As I

said before, you don't have to write down everything we say. Only the key points. The meeting shouldn't take more than an hour."

"I'm sure I can handle it." The sarcasm that dripped from her voice like pure, thick molasses wasn't lost on him.

Call him crazy, but it actually turned him *on* and had the material of his pants growing tight around his swelling erection.

The best way to keep his thoughts away from getting into Avery's designer pants was to keep talking. "Are you finding your way around the town okay?"

"It's a pretty easy town to get around. It's not that big."

He strummed his fingers on the leather steering wheel. "Has Rebecca offered to show you around?"

"She's busy with school and I don't want to take up more of her time. She's being nice enough to let me stay with her. Why? Are you offering?"

Hell, if she wanted him to, he'd be more than happy to show her around. And not only the town, but his house as well.

She's your employee, McDermott. Knock it off.

The craving for nicotine reared its ugly head and had his fingers trembling. Not only did he not want to be rude and smoke with her in the car, but he was allowing himself only two cigarettes a day. In the meantime, he dug in the middle console for gum. The minty stick wouldn't compare to a cigarette, but it was better than nothing.

"I'd be happy to show you around. If you want," he added, tossing the gum wrapper into a cup holder.

"Only if you promise to buy some new filing cabinets." Her brown eyes challenged his.

The fire he'd become used to since meeting her made

his mouth turn up in a grin. "You're a tenacious little thing, aren't you?"

Her feminine chin lifted. "You say that as if it's a bad thing."

The light finally turned green, and he made a left turn to the construction site. "Tenacity can be entertaining in the right hands."

Her pale-pink mouth pouted into a frown, which should have been a sin. "You're laughing at me again."

He wasn't actually laughing, but he did find her stubbornness to be a breath of fresh air. "No one's laughing. Did you see me laugh?"

Her accusatory gaze dropped down to his mouth. "You don't have to. You had a mocking tone."

"What's got your back so stiff, anyway?" Tension radiated off her sexy, curvy body.

A tune from *Saturday Night Fever* filled the car. She leaned forward, exposing a slice of creamy back, and dug her phone out of the purse at her feet. She put the device back after studying the number. More tension drew her shoulders stiff.

Just what was it about her anyway? What had happened to her?

"Have you been to any of the restaurants in town?"

"Just a few. I've tried not to spend more money than I have to."

This coming from a person who drove a car worth enough to put money down on a small house? Yes, there was undoubtedly more to Avery Price than she wanted people to see.

"Well, you haven't had a steak if you haven't eaten at McDermott's."

"McDermott's," she repeated. "Do you own that also?"

"My father owns it. Their steak is from locally raised

cattle and is probably some of the best I've ever had. Before you say anything," he added, because she opened her mouth to speak, "I'm biased because it's my dad's. And I can eat there for free because I'm family."

Silence was his answer. He lifted his eyes to the roof of the car. "I'll buy a new damn filing cabinet, if it makes you happy."

A triumphant grin lit up her classically beautiful features. "I knew I'd break you."

One brown strand of hair came loose, and she tucked it behind her ear. She ought to let her hair down altogether, so he could run his hands through it and mess it up.

She looked at him through long, thick black lashes. He met her gaze as her brown eyes dropped down to his mouth and briefly touched lower to his lap. Her tongue darted out and touched her bottom lip. *Yeah, you're not so bad to look at yourself, honey.*

The construction site came into view ahead. Noah maneuvered his SUV into the dirt parking lot and pulled to a stop in front of the trailer he used as his on-site office.

"Trust me; the only way us working together will be a problem," he said, taking the keys out of the ignition, "is if you keep giving me looks like that."

Avery paced the small expanse of Rebecca's living room, holding her cell phone to her ear, with one part trepidation and three parts fear. In the time it took her to dial the phone number to her parents' penthouse in Denver, she'd almost talked herself out of making the call. She'd gone in determined to remain calm and in control of her emotions, especially when trying to convey her decision to her mother. But with each ring on the other end of the line, her hands trembled, her palms sweat, and her heart thumped higher up in her throat. It wasn't all that unusual to feel that way when dealing with her parents.

She turned and paced toward the kitchen, taking a deep breath and closing her eyes. Maybe no one was home, and she'd be off the hook for at least another twenty-four hours. Of course, that meant carrying around this anxiety all day tomorrow, and it had already hindered her happiness enough.

Lord only knew why she was so worried. They were only her parents. How upset could they really be? Then again, Darren and Priscilla Price weren't your average, all-American mom and dad. They didn't take their kids camping or let them have ice cream before bedtime or have pillow fights. In their eyes, children were to be seen and not heard. It was ridiculous. Like they'd stepped out of Victorian England and raised their children as British nobility.

The phone rang one more time, and just as she was about to hang up, she heard the traditional Price household greeting, "Good evening, Price residence."

Regret pushed away all feelings of fear when her old nanny's voice sounded in Avery's ear. Gina was the one person who never judged Avery and let her behave as a kid when her parents weren't looking. She used to let Avery sneak cookies in bed and talk on the phone late at night with her friends. Gina had been her one source of affection, besides her brother, throughout the years.

"Hi, Gina."

Gina gasped. "Avery? Good Lord, where have you disappeared to? Your parents have been very quiet about what happened before you left. And your brother's been so mysterious."

"I'm sorry, Gina. I shouldn't have let you worry this long, but . . . I just needed to get away and think about some things." She didn't want to divulge the whole story to her nanny without talking to her mother first. But she had to reassure the woman she was okay. "Is Mom around?"

"She and your father are about to leave for dinner with the governor. Would you like me to catch them before they go?"

If she didn't talk to one of them now, she'd never work up the nerve again. "If you would be able to catch them before they leave, I'd appreciate it. Oh, and Gina?"

"Yes?"

Avery hesitated and chewed her painted nail. "I'm sorry for making you worry. I should have called you sooner."

"Don't think about it, honey." The smile in the other woman's voice was unmistakable. "I'm just glad you're okay."

A small amount of relief had her sinking to the couch. "Thanks." The line went silent as Gina placed the phone down. Her mother's loud, demanding voice gradually grew louder.

Here goes...

"Avery Josephine Price, where in the world have you run off to? I've called you a half-dozen times over the past few days, and you haven't returned any of my calls. And I know you don't think that ridiculous note you left me was any sort of explanation. I want a real answer."

"You don't have to worry anymore, Mother. I'm at home."

There was a beat of silence. "You're here, at the penthouse? I didn't see you. Where are you exactly? Downstairs?"

Her mother was so obtuse. "I'm not in Denver."

"Oh, did you go to Beaver Creek, then?" Her voice held

a tone of relief and Avery almost clicked the end button, allowing Priscilla to think Avery was at their ski resort estate. But that would only be putting off the inevitable; her parents would soon figure out she wasn't there.

"No, I didn't go to Beaver Creek either, I—"

"Well, don't tell me you drove all the way to Newport Beach?" her mother said, with her annoying, fake laugh. Avery bit back a sigh and reminded herself whom she was dealing with—a woman who saw only what she wanted to.

"Mom, stop. I'm not in Colorado, and I'm not in California. And before you ask," she continued after her mother started to speak, "no, I didn't drive to the beach house in the Hamptons either."

"I'm sorry, honey, I must be confused." Now she was being condescending, which made Avery's guilt subside. Just a little. "The only other home we have is the villa in Italy, and I know you're not there. Now, I really don't have time for this. Your father and I have a dinner engagement with the governor, so please just tell me where you are."

Avery took a deep breath. "I'm in Wyoming. I live here now."

Her mother was silent for so long that Avery thought her phone had dropped the call. Then the laugh that came across the other line sounded similar to Cruella de Vil's. "That's a very funny joke, Avery, but be serious. No one lives in Wyoming."

A typical response from a woman who didn't think a world existed outside her own snooty social circle. Trying to explain it to her, or argue about the population of Wyoming, would be like trying to nail Jell-O to a tree. Instead, Avery took another deep breath and tried to ignore the previous comments. "I didn't call to argue with you, and I don't want to talk about what happened. I simply called to tell you I'm safe, which I am, thanks for asking. And this is my home now, and if you and Dad ever need me for anything, you'll have to call my cell phone. Good-bye, Mother."

Just as she was about to push the end button, her mom spoke. "Avery, wait. If this is about what happened with Peter, then we can talk about it. I understand you're upset about what happened and how your father and I reacted, but... you've never been a liar, and if you say Peter was unfaithful, then we believe you."

Yeah right. You're just telling me what I want to hear, so I'll come home.

Her mother continued, "All your father was saying is to give your relationship with Peter another chance. He's financially secure and could be a good husband."

"Then *you* marry him, if you think he's so great," Avery snapped. But she had promised herself she would not let her parents see how deeply their betrayal cut. "Look, I don't want to be married to Peter. I told you that before and nothing has changed now. I don't love him. Hell, I don't even *like* him, and I don't want to marry a man who can't keep his dick in his pants."

A soft gasp penetrated Avery's ear. "Don't you swear at me, young lady. I raised you better than that."

" 'Dick' is not a swear word," she argued. She gripped the edge of the couch with white knuckles. *Stay calm and controlled.* "It doesn't matter. I'm sorry I spoke to you like that. But the fact of the matter remains, I'm not marrying Peter. I don't know why a marriage to him is so important to you guys in the first place."

"Because your dad and I know what's best for you. I, for the life of me, can't figure out how you turned out so selfish and ungrateful."

Avery bolted up off the couch and stomped barefoot across the floor. "*I'm* selfish? This isn't the Dark Ages, Mother. You can't just pick out a husband and expect me to agree. Why can't you let me make my own decisions and be supportive?"

Her mother sighed, and Avery wasn't sure why she was surprised. The conversation had gone exactly as she'd expected.

"I don't have time to do this with you right now. Your dad and I are running late. We'll be in Stockholm next week for business, and after that, we'll discuss this further. I trust by then you'll have come to your senses and returned home where you belong."

The line disconnecting was like a loud crack in Avery's eardrum. Once again the woman issued demands and Avery was expected to obey, like a good little daughter: a classic Priscilla Price characteristic.

The cell phone slipped out of her fingers and clattered on the coffee table. Her intention had been to be assertive and tell her mother how things were going to be without sounding as if she was asking for permission. But as always, her mother had the last word without hearing what her daughter had said.

How foolish she'd been to think anything had changed in the last week. Not even something as drastic as her leaving home could get them to see what they were doing to their daughter. Their tunnel vision wouldn't let them see beyond the person they thought she should be.

An ache twisted inside her heart, carving out a hole unconditional parental love should have filled. She'd always harbored the silly fantasy that her mother would give her a big hug and tell her she was proud of the woman Avery had become. Instead she felt like a big, fat disappointment because she refused to marry the man they wanted her to and pop out six sons to carry on her father's publishing empire.

She supposed it had been only wishful thinking to assume she would grab their attention with all she'd accomplished with her charity work. Last year, she'd single-handedly brought in half the yearly earnings for the Make-A-Wish Foundation. They'd even held a ceremony and presented her with a plaque to show their gratitude for all her dedication. It had been one of the most humbling, yet heartwarming, moments of her life. Landon had been there, along with Teeny and Gina, snapping pictures then accompanying her out to dinner. Her father had been in Paris that week but swore he'd read about it in the paper. Her mother... well, she still wasn't sure what her mother's excuse had been. She'd told Avery she'd looked positively glamorous in her beaded Stella McCartney gown.

Maybe Avery had made a bigger deal out of the event than it really was. The whole thing surrounded her heart with a warm sensation, as though she'd found her calling in life, the reason God had put her on this earth. Without her parents' support, she'd felt empty and lost.

She supposed it was an inner fault to always want to please her mother and father, and without their attention, she'd given up her charity work. Ever since, she'd been meandering around not sure what to do with her life. Shortly after, they'd introduced her to Peter... and the rest was history.

She placed a quick call to Landon, but he wasn't home. He hadn't been answering his cell phone either. Her brother had been MIA a lot lately, and his absence had only made her feel even lonelier.

She stood, shaking herself together, determined not to let the overwhelming sense of disappointment ruin her Friday night. After all, tonight was her dinner with Noah.

This did not qualify as a date. That's what she had been telling herself since Wednesday afternoon, when Noah had first asked her. She wanted to reiterate that by insisting she meet him at the restaurant instead of his picking her up. He'd agreed only after she'd conceded defeat when he'd badgered her about paying for dinner. It was merely steaks with a friend, so she could become more acquainted with the town. The fact that she wanted to jump his bones every time he was within a five-mile radius had nothing to do with it...

Yeah, just keep telling yourself that, Avery. You want his body.

This was a mistake. She should call and cancel. Nothing good could come of going out to dinner with one's boss. How could she keep her cool when the man sent her hormones into overdrive every time he looked at her? But then again, what else would she be doing? The people she worked with were the only people she knew in town. Friday was Rebecca's late night at school, so she wouldn't be back until ten o'clock. If she didn't go to dinner, she'd most likely be sitting watching television anyway.

Oh, the joys of living on one's own.

Avery checked the mantel clock. Thirty minutes before dinnertime. Trouble happened to be an exceedingly small town, so it would take her only about ten minutes to get to the restaurant, which left her twenty minutes to... stew in her own thoughts. That was never a good thing. It was during times like this that her mind got the better of her. Teeny said Avery became the worst version of herself when left alone to think for too long.

Avery paced the living room once again and forced her mind to safer things, such as whether or not she chose the right outfit for tonight. Shorts were not plentiful in her wardrobe, since Avery spent most of her money on pants, skirts, and dresses. She did, however, own a few pairs of capris, which she'd decided was a far better choice than a pair of slacks. A skirt would no doubt be much too dressy.

She stopped pacing and walked to Rebecca's room, where a full-length mirror hung on the back of the door. Avery stood in front of it, turning this way and that, assessing her appearance, wondering if she looked appropriate. What *was* appropriate for a steak dinner with her boss? One would think with all the many evenings out she'd spent, she'd know how to dress for one simple dinner. *Oh, what the hell?* Her heather-gray capris and maroon sleeveless turtleneck would be as fitting as anything else she might put on.

Instead of her traditional French braid, the way her mother used to do her hair as a child, she'd taken it down and gone daring, letting the strands fall to where they ended just past her shoulders. Her hair was one of her best assets. Why not show it off? In order to give her brown tresses a wild, windblown look, she ran her fingers through them and shook her head. A different person stood before her in the mirror. A person she hardly recognized, wearing her one and only pair of sandals and with her hair falling down around her face.

With a final look-over, she gave herself a smile of approval and grabbed her purse. A crystal-studded clutch seemed too fancy for this kind of thing, so she put it away and went for a less formal leather shoulder bag.

Avery took a deep breath, hoping she wasn't making more out of this than there was, which would be typical of her, and walked out the door.

SEVEN

MCDERMOTT'S, SITUATED AT THE END of town, with a backdrop of cattle fields and farms, boasted a classy atmosphere. Its stucco siding and shiny copper roof stuck out like a sore thumb among turn-of-the-century masonry buildings.

This would be the first meal since Avery left home that didn't come out of a greasy paper sack or a cardboard box with microwave instructions.

Noah had told her to look for him in the waiting area. Avery's heart danced as she neared the entrance, and her hands shook a little too much for something that wasn't supposed to be a date. Heck, she couldn't remember the last time she'd been out with a man. Peter didn't count, since he never took her to places that weren't filled with her father's associates. But this was something different, more…personal. When Noah had asked her to dinner, his concern for her happiness had rolled off him in waves.

She pushed through the heavy wooden doors and was greeted by a dim interior with low-hung chandeliers and candle-lit tables. She'd expected peanuts on the floor and a jukebox. Instead, McDermott's had a romantic, personal atmosphere, with deep-red carpet and walls paneled with dark wood.

She spotted her host in the waiting area, just as he'd said he'd be. He took her breath away like no man ever had. She hadn't expected such a jolt of lust, but it was there just the same. The feeling confused her and made her wonder if this was a mistake. She pressed her fingernails into her leather shoulder bag to ease their trembling.

Rooted in place, Avery watched him. He leaned up against the wall, next to the hostess's podium, deep in conversation with the young girl. He said something to her, a smile upon his handsome face, and the blond, high school–age girl burst out laughing. Unexpected but powerful, jealousy surged through her veins, sending her blood to a boil.

Something as useless as jealousy would never do her any good, so she shoved the feeling down and smoothed a hand over her hair. But the jealousy returned when she realized how positively delicious he looked in a pair of khakis that hugged his legs like a second skin and a white polo shirt that clung to his shoulders. The clothes were casual but they had the same effect on her as if he were buck naked. Although she had no problem visualizing him as such, with the way his shirt stretched tightly across his chest, outlining his muscles and leaving nothing to the imagination. He ran a hand through his hair, and a strand fell over his forehead as he laughed at something the hostess said.

My, aren't we good buddies?

How childish of her. Noah was certainly entitled to speak to any woman he chose. She had no claim on him. They were merely boss and employee having dinner. Nothing more.

Avery repeated that last line over in her head as she took a step forward. In that instant, Noah moved and his gaze connected with hers; his gray eyes brightened. Her steps faltered, and something inside her shifted at his sensual scrutiny. She managed a smile, and he grinned in return, which had a more devastating effect than his looks alone. He was so freakin' sexy; she wanted to rip his shirt off and just...lick him all over.

Lord, Avery, control yourself.

She came to a stop in front of him, and by that time, she'd managed to get her breathing under control. He did another one of his slow assessments, dragging his gaze from her face down to her black strappy sandals, leaving behind a trail of scorching heat on her cool skin.

"Were my directions easy to follow?" he asked, pushing away from the wall.

"Your directions were great. I had no problems."

The blond hostess looked from Noah to Avery. "Are you ready to be seated?"

"Yes," Noah answered, placing his hand on Avery's lower back as they followed the young girl through the restaurant. He waved to several people, most of them women. Okay, whatever. So he had female friends.

The hostess led them to their table in a secluded area in the back, handed them menus, then left. Now they were alone, surrounded by the intimacy the restaurant was aiming to achieve by its wall sconces and dim lighting.

Noah smiled at her again, picking up his menu and opening it. "You need to relax, Avery. This isn't a big deal."

Avery narrowed her eyes, annoyed at herself for being so readable. "I'm perfectly relaxed."

"Are you kidding?" he asked, lowering his menu. "I could practically feel your tension when you walked in the door."

Remember how Teeny used to tell you that you're a horrible actress? Now would be a good time to remember that.

She shook her head and smiled. "It's not that I'm tense. It's just... I haven't been on many dates before. At least not like this."

"Well, you can relax, then, because this isn't a date."

"I didn't think it was," she responded with a smile.

He folded his menu and set it in front of him. "Right. We're just two friends having dinner."

"It's not often my big brother brings a beautiful woman into my restaurant, but when he does I have to make it a point to say hello." The deep, smooth voice came from behind her a split second before a man wearing black slacks and a blue button-down stopped next to their table.

Oh, they were unmistakably related. The same wide, heavy shoulders filled out the man's blue shirt and similar light brown mixed with blond hair curled just over his ears and brushed his collar. Noah had a penetrating gray gaze, and this man's eyes were the color of a clear blue sky. The women of Trouble probably lined up to eat here, just to get a look at this guy.

Noah rolled his eyes. "Avery, this is my brother Chase. He's the general manager. Avery's helping Rebecca out for a little while," he remarked to his brother.

Chase gave her a megawatt smile, showing a row of perfectly white teeth; he lifted her hand, pressing a kiss to it. Heat crept up her cheeks and continued to her hairline. Did all the McDermott men emanate such smooth charisma?

"I'll have to make it a point to visit my brother's office more often. You're certainly nicer to look at than this ugly guy over here," he said with a playful punch to Noah's shoulder.

"Get lost, Chase. Don't you have some books you need

to go over, or a chef to deal with?" Noah asked, with a smile that belied the irritation in his voice.

"Did it already," he responded, still smiling at Avery. Then he focused his attention on his brother. "You just missed Dad. He mentioned he needed to talk to you about something."

Noah shrugged. "Guess I'll have to catch him later."

The note of sarcasm in his voice was unmistakable. Why wouldn't he want to see his father? Would it be inappropriate for her to ask? She shifted in her seat as the two brothers stared at each other, sensing some sort of family issue. Obviously there were others in the world that came from less than perfect households.

Chase lifted his wide shoulders. "Anyway, it was nice meeting you, Avery. Feel free to come back anytime, and I'll give you a family discount. Any woman who could get my brother to eat here must mean something to him." He swaggered away, leaving Avery gaping at his comment. The skin between her breasts itched under Noah's unblinking gaze.

"I apologize for him. My brother has made a career out of being a womanizer."

And what are you?

"I like him," she said with a small grin. "How many brothers do you have?"

Noah waited while a young waiter appeared and set two glasses of water in front of them. "Three," he answered, taking a sip from his glass. "I'm the oldest. Then there's Chase and Brody. RJ is my stepbrother, and my stepsister, Courtney, is his younger sister."

"You have a pretty big family. I have only one brother."

"RJ and Courtney's mother married my dad six years ago. But I love them like a real brother and sister."

Avery ran a finger around the rim of her glass. "And your mother has remarried also?"

Noah stared at her for a moment, as if he didn't want to answer, and she shifted in her seat to ease the tingling running down her spine. "My mother died of breast cancer when I was nine."

Wasn't she just the most insensitive person on the planet? Here she'd been complaining about her mother, and Noah had grown up without one. Yet he'd made the statement as though it hadn't been a life-changing event for him. "I'm sorry," she said with a shake of her head. "I shouldn't have asked you that. It's none of my business."

"Don't be so hard on yourself, Avery," he said in a reassuring tone. "You can ask me anything you'd like. Yeah, I miss her, but it was a long time ago, and I don't remember that much about her. Don't get me wrong; I love my stepmother...but sometimes it's like..."

"You miss the nurturing bond of a real mother," Avery finished for him.

Something flashed in his eyes, darkening them for a split second. It happened so fast that Avery almost missed the change of color. It seemed as though they had more in common than she'd originally thought. "Exactly," he replied in a soft voice. His bottomless eyes bore into hers for a moment longer. Maybe she'd touched a nerve. Then he spoke, his voice lighter than before. "What about your family? Why are you so eager to get to nowhere?"

Ah, there it was: the million-dollar question. She had a vague answer all made up and rehearsed, but she didn't think it would make her this wary. "There's not much to tell. My family isn't very exciting. As I said before, I have one brother, and my parents raised us in Colorado." Avery lifted her shoulders, not wanting to say much else.

"I had a pretty normal childhood." Except for the fact that she was homeschooled by private tutors and her parents owned four vacation homes, plus a yacht they used to sail the Mediterranean. Yeah, your average American kid had that kind of upbringing. "As far as the 'nowhere' thing... I just needed to be away, on my own." Hey, it was close to the truth. That was about as much as he'd get out of her right now.

Noah looked as if he found her explanation less than convincing. Luckily their server came and took their order, but after he left, Noah opened his mouth as though he wanted to say something. She jumped in before he had a chance. "I don't want to bore you with tales of my childhood. Have you lived in Trouble your entire life?"

"Mostly," he answered before taking a sip of his water. "I was born in Casper, and my parents moved here when I was three, just after Chase was born. I've never lived anywhere else since. My brother Brody lived in Minnesota while he went to college but"—he shrugged—"I've never had any desire to leave Trouble." He narrowed his eyes at her while tapping his finger on the tabletop. "I'm still curious as to what caused you to leave Colorado and end up here."

Being under his scrutiny was worse than listening to one of her father's repetitive lectures. People she'd met so far seemed to be immensely interested in why she'd left her life in Denver. What, people weren't allowed to move to a new city? Was she expected to live her entire life in her parents' household? Why was it so hard to believe that she'd wanted to start a life of her own? Irritation made her cheeks heat again, and her back straighten.

"I just wanted a change of pace. I got tired of living in the city, and this seems like a nice town."

He nodded. "And you like it here so far?"

"So far," she said, smiling.

Noah returned her smile, and a moment of...under-standing passed between them. For now he accepted her answer and respected her privacy. He didn't ask a million questions as her father would have, demanding an answer that pleased him.

The table between them wasn't very big, and Avery, being five ten, couldn't stretch her long legs out without brushing against Noah. Every time she did, his eyes touched hers, and another one of those sexually charged moments passed between them. She lifted her left leg to cross it over her right. When she did, her foot nicked his knee, and he shifted. The movement, however, didn't improve matters. When he did so, one of his legs some-how maneuvered between hers, creating an intimate posi-tion Avery wasn't entirely comfortable with. Noah cleared his throat and tried to move his leg out of the way, and Avery scooted farther up the seat to give him room. A nervous, awkward laugh slipped out as the heel of her sandal got caught in his shoelace, preventing his leg from going anywhere. He wiggled his foot, and her leg wiggled along with his, her knee bumping against his hard thigh.

"I hate being tall sometimes," she muttered.

"Hold still a minute," he said and reached under the table to fiddle with their feet. Avery held as still as she could while his fingers worked with his shoelace, trying to unhook it from her shoe. In the process, his fingers brushed along her foot, sending a fiery jolt up her legs and settling in her stomach. The encounter lasted only a sec-ond, but his fingers were warm and soft and she imagined what they would feel like on the rest of her leg. A long sigh flowed out of her.

Please hurry.

"You okay?" he asked, lifting his head from under the table. Their gazes connected and Avery nodded. His eyes lingered on her for a moment longer, a lazy smile creeping along his mouth and causing a laugh to burst out of her. "I've almost got it, so sit still for a second longer."

A second, my left butt cheek.

Fortunately for her sanity, he got them untangled, and Avery quickly moved her leg away from his and into safe territory. And not a moment too soon.

Noah must have sensed how she felt, because he broke out in a big grin as he settled back in the booth. "Now, that could have proved to be very interesting. Maybe I should have left it and then you would have been attached to me all night."

The way he said "all night" in that sexy, suggestive manner of his made her toes curl and her mind conjure up all sorts of interesting ways they could've been glued together. She feigned nonchalance. Badly. "I don't think that would be very good for business if you had to cart me around with you everywhere. What would your clients think?"

"I think my clients would like the view. It might make our meetings more enjoyable."

Flattery will get you everywhere.

The words "take me now so we can get this out of the way" were on the tip of her tongue. Avery didn't normally go around sleeping with men she hardly knew, especially men she worked for. In fact, it had been ages since she'd had sex and even longer since she'd had mind-blowing sex. Noah looked like the type of man who could blow her mind in bed.

He was so big, his broad shoulders consumed all the

space around him. And his long legs kept hitting the bottom of the table when they weren't sliding along hers. The sensation was enough to make her eyes roll back in her head and send her comatose. She'd never known a man like Noah before. He ignited feelings inside her she didn't even know she had. The only men she'd felt sexually attracted to like this to were Johnny Depp and Matthew McConaughey. And those feelings didn't make her squirm like this. She had as much of a chance of hooking up with a Hollywood hottie as she did getting struck by lightning.

This man was real and in the flesh, not strolling across a screen, reciting memorized lines. This time the man who caused said feelings looked back at her with the same fire and interest. Not only was it new, but it excited her and made her want to do things she'd only seen in the movies.

"Have I told you tonight how great you look? I'm not used to seeing you dressed so casually. It looks good."

"Thank you." *I was thinking of you when I got dressed. And when I showered. And when I climbed in bed...*

"I'm just going to say this and get it out of the way so we both can relax. I want you, and I'm pretty sure you want me too. So what do you suppose we do about it?" He stretched an arm along the back of the booth and looked at her as though he'd just asked how her day was.

You expect me to relax now?

If she lied to him and said she was offended by his basically propositioning her, would he drop the subject? Or if she was honest with him and told him she reciprocated his feelings, would they have a hot, dirty, torrid affair?

Decisions, decisions.

She chewed her lower lip and met Noah's gaze. How would he react if she said what was going through her mind right now? Only one way to find out...

"I think maybe we should indulge ourselves until we get it out of our systems. That way we can go on working together without this hanging around us. Sound okay to you?"

Who was this person making these suggestions? Certainly not the woman her parents had raised. But she rather liked this alter ego. She was fun, scandalous, and fearless.

Teeny would be so proud of her.

Noah blinked at the woman seated across from him. He almost asked the server to pinch him as their food was delivered, thinking he'd conjured the words himself. Had she really just propositioned him? Maybe she meant something else?

He shifted in his seat, while the steak on the table beckoned to be eaten. "Are you talking about us having an affair?"

Avery lifted her delicate shoulders, not quite meeting his gaze, and picked up her knife and fork. "If you think it's a bad idea, I understand. You are my boss, at least temporarily, and it would be unprofessional for us to sleep together, wouldn't it?"

No answer came to him. He wasn't sure what would be a correct one anyway. Yes, it would be very unprofessional. But then again, no one would have to know except the two of them. So, who could it hurt?

"Don't you think?" Avery asked after he'd been silent for a moment.

He shifted his attention from his food to her face as she put a piece of steak in her mouth. She closed her plump lips over the fork and pulled it back out slowly, as if it were some sort of phallic toy. Noah nearly exploded in his pants, and he had to shove some food in his mouth to keep from sputtering. Women had propositioned him before, but for some reason the suggestion sounded different coming from Avery. As if it were more than just sex for her, and it had an entirely different effect on him. He felt as though he'd been sucker-punched.

And why the hell was he thinking about saying no to a woman who was offering him uncommitted sex? Had the waiter put something in his water? Her offer was every man's fantasy. Casual, no-strings-attached sex whenever he wanted. It was all he'd ever looked for in a relationship. So why was this time different? Noah knew it was something more than just her being his employee. He was sure that a simple affair would lead to more with Avery. She didn't strike him as the type to go around having meaningless sex. No, she was the commitment type, someone who'd expect a ring after so many months of being intimate.

On the other hand...if she wanted more, why would she offer only this?

"Uh..." He cleared his throat and cut another piece of steak. "What happens when the affair is over?"

"Well. I suppose we'll just go on, but we won't have to pretend this thing isn't between us because it won't be there anymore. Right?"

"I guess."

She narrowed her eyes at his unsure tone.

The way her nose wrinkled when she laughed and the way her lips slightly parted when she scrutinized him, as she did now...she was so damn cute. He loved what she'd done with her hair. Normally, she had it pulled back tightly from her face, as if she were giving herself a face-lift. But tonight the strands flowed free from their restraints, falling around her face and brushing over her collarbones. Her skin looked soft and creamy, like glaze melted over a cinnamon roll, and all he wanted to do was reach over and run his finger down her cheek. And then maybe graze it across her lips, which were full and free of color; he was used to seeing them painted red. That's how they'd look after hard, rough kisses or the morning after all-night lovemaking.

"Let me see if I understand what you're saying," he said after she'd been staring at him. "You think we should sleep together, which we probably shouldn't do in the first place, until we—and I'm quoting you here—get it out of our systems? And then just go on working together?"

"As you said before, we want each other, and we're only working together temporarily. You asked what I thought we should do."

She said it so matter-of-factly, as she put another piece of steak in her mouth, that he couldn't help but laugh out loud. Shaking his head, he stabbed his fork into his own steak. "You really are something, Avery Price. Most women want a relationship to go along with sex."

"I'm not most women. So are you up for it, or not?"

Hell yeah, he was up for it. The question was: What would happen when it ended? Everything always came to an end.

"You mean casual sex anytime I want, with no strings or expectations afterward? Hmm," he contemplated, rubbing his chin. "I don't know. It might make me feel a little cheap and used. Can I think about it?"

Avery laughed; it was a soft and airy sound that traveled over his skin like feminine hands. "I thought this was every man's fantasy, a woman who won't be needy and expect a call every day. You don't even have to take me out."

"So, you just want sex?"

She nodded.

He leaned forward, resting his elbow on the table. One side of his mouth turned up. "If I didn't know any better, I'd say you were propositioning me. There's something about you, Avery, and I'm going to figure out what it is."

EIGHT

Noah must be out of his damn mind. Too many tequila shots in his early twenties and hits to the head in high school football had damaged the part of his brain that provided rational thought. Or maybe it was the bewitching scent of the woman who'd so unabashedly propositioned him into an affair, a completely terrible idea.

But hell, he was only a man.

He'd made up his mind. Instead of an affair, this would be just a one-time thing, then he'd graciously back out, citing a conflict of interest.

After dinner, he'd managed to let her talk him into taking her own vehicle. He'd wanted to drive her, saying he'd bring her back to the restaurant in the morning to get her car, but she hastily shook her head no. Probably so she could cut out on him in the middle of the night. The thought should have relieved him. Hell, it would make this less complicated, less intimate. But the thought of waking up next to her, seeing the early-morning sunlight catch the blond highlights in her hair, made him want to break his rules of dating.

This is dangerous ground you're treading on, McDermott.

He glanced in his rearview mirror to make sure she still followed and saw the fluorescent glow of the Mercedes's headlights.

Noah shook his head.

When he'd asked about her life back in Colorado, he'd seen something flash in her eyes. Wariness. Reluctance. It was the look of someone not entirely comfortable with people digging into her childhood. The rehearsed speech she gave him about coming from a normal household and a boring childhood was interesting, indeed. But it was a lie.

A young woman who came from a normal family, with no work experience, didn't drive a hundred-thousand-dollar car and wear designer shoes. She was hiding something. For some reason, she didn't want him to know about her life before Trouble. Who was Avery Price? What made her tick?

What had made her pack up her belongings, leave her home, and head to a small cattle town that couldn't possibly have anything to offer her? But he'd accepted her answer, not wanting to pry and make her uncomfortable by asking questions she didn't want to answer. If she'd wanted him to know her life history, she'd have told him.

Nevertheless, here he was on his way to his home, about to start an affair with her.

He shook his head, lit a cigarette, and rolled down the window. She certainly wasn't like any woman he'd ever known, that was for sure. But one thing she had said tonight surprised him. She'd pegged him about his mother with her comment on motherly love. He had the feeling it was the one moment he'd caught her with her guard down. Her tone of voice indicated she had experience in that particular area. And the soft, vulnerable look in her eyes, just before averting her gaze, told him it was a touchy subject. Noah was similarly sensitive to the topic of his own mother, and knew when to leave well enough alone. If there was a story behind her brief comment, and he guessed there was, he knew that was the one area where she'd appreciate the privacy. He knew how it felt to be peppered with questions about growing up without a mother.

He wasn't sure why Avery was different or why he felt the need to bring her to his home. But he'd seen the question in her eyes and then remembered she shared an apartment with Rebecca. He didn't want to be a source of a sticky, uncomfortable situation between the two women, and he knew Avery wanted to keep their agreement under wraps. Frankly, he was relieved.

One final glance in his mirror showed Avery still followed him. He turned in the driveway to his house, located at the end of a cul-de-sac. But he muttered a curse when he noticed his brother's truck parked along the curb. Why did his siblings always pick the worst time possible to show up uninvited? Maybe his brother had just swung by on his way home from work, and Noah could usher him on his way. Although Brody never did stuff like that very often. Usually eager to be home with his family, Brody wouldn't be hanging at Noah's place this late unless he had a good reason.

Avery pulled her car next to his in the driveway and offered him a tentative smile as she stepped onto the pavement.

"It's beautiful out here," she commented, taking in the surrounding flatlands with the town dotted in the distance. "Peaceful," she added.

"That's why I chose it. You can't hear the highway

from out here. The rest of my family prefers to live close to town, but I like my privacy." He glanced at her as she fell in step beside him, making their way up the concrete walkway. Her face was silhouetted in the moonlight, casting her skin in a milky, creamy glow. Her complexion reminded him of those little elf princess figurines his stepmother collected. They all had big, flowing, curly blond hair but their skin always looked soft, buttery, as though bathed in a glow of candlelight. Avery's face could have been cast from one of those figures. Even her pert nose looked as if it belonged on a fairy-tale character.

Man, he was in trouble if he was reveling in her skin tone and petite nose. Those particular features on a woman had never caught his eye before. His brothers were breast men, but Noah preferred a nice, round ass.

"I should warn you before we go in," he started as he stopped in front of the door. "That's my brother's truck. I'm not sure what he's doing here, but if you give me a second, I'll get rid of him."

Avery didn't respond, but she gave him a curious look, as though she'd started to have second thoughts. Maybe the presence of someone else spooked her. They had made a mutual agreement that no one would know about their arrangement. Noah wasn't worried, but she didn't know his brother and was probably apprehensive about someone seeing her here at this late hour.

The door was already unlocked. The front door opened to a great room that flowed into an eating area and kitchen, underneath a giant vaulted ceiling.

Avery hung back while he tossed his keys on the table and shrugged out of his jacket. Brody sat on the couch, arms folded behind his head, feet propped on the coffee table, watching ESPN.

Make yourself right at home, brother.

Noah cleared his throat to get Brody's attention. Hadn't his brother heard them come in?

"The front door was unlocked, so I let myself in. Hope you don't mind," Brody said, not taking his eyes off a replay of a baseball game.

Noah stepped closer to the couch and fisted his hands on his hips. This time, his brother looked at him with a questioning glance. "What?" Then Brody turned his head and noticed Avery standing in the background, hands clasped in front of her. "Ah...hi," he said, standing. "I'm Brody."

"Nice to meet you, Brody. I'm Avery," she answered politely. Noah had to give her props; she handled herself very well.

Brody's black hair stuck up in all directions from his head, making it look as though he'd stuck his head out the car window while driving. His shirt was a mess, wrinkled and with one side untucked from his pants. The only other time he'd seen his brother this undone was when his son had been born.

"Sorry to just drop in like this," Brody muttered. "Kelly and I had a fight, and I needed a place to crash. I went to Chase's, but he wasn't alone."

"Neither am I." Noah gestured to Avery.

"I see that now," Brody said. "I was going let myself into your guesthouse, but the door was locked. I can go to RJ's if you'd prefer."

Now Noah felt bad. He knew his brother was having marital problems, but he hadn't realized it had gotten to the point where they were sleeping separately. He couldn't bring himself to ask his own brother to leave so he could have forbidden sex with Avery.

"Uh, wait. Just give me a minute." When he turned and

walked back to Avery, she was already smiling and shaking her head.

"Sorry about this."

"It's okay. I'll just go." She shrugged. "I'm kind of tired anyway."

He searched her face for a moment, trying to find the look in her eye that had been there when she'd talked about her past. It wasn't there. All he saw was genuine understanding. "I can send him to the guesthouse if you'd like."

She shook her head, and her soft hair flew around her face. "That's not necessary, Noah. He's your brother and clearly needs a shoulder to lean on right now. I wouldn't feel right staying and making him leave. We can do this some other time."

You're damn right we will.

"Thanks for being so understanding." He leaned forward and brushed his lips over her cheek. Her lips had beckoned him all night, and he'd been dying to taste them, but with his brother watching, he didn't want to make her uncomfortable. So he settled for kissing her on the cheek, which was just as soft as he expected, and he even got a whiff of her hair. It smelled like coconut, reminding him of summer on the beach.

He straightened, and she gave him one more genuine smile before letting herself out the door.

There goes one hot woman.

"You want a beer?" Noah asked, walking into the kitchen.

"Sure," Brody answered and settled back down on the couch.

Noah opened his stainless steel Sub-Zero fridge, pulled out two bottles of Sam Adams, popped the tops, and handed one to Brody as he sat down.

"She's pretty hot. Where'd you find her?"

"I had to fire Belinda, so I needed some help around the office."

Brody turned around as if he'd expected Avery to still be standing there. "She works for you?"

"She works for me," Noah repeated.

Brody was silent for a second. "What are you doing with her on a Friday night?"

Noah hesitated, wondering how the conversation had gone in this direction and not sure if he wanted to tell his brother what he and Avery had discussed. "She just moved to town, and I offered to show her around. We just had some steaks." *Okay, close enough.*

"And then for dessert you decided to show her your house?" Brody asked, then laughed. "God Almighty, Noah. That's pretty thin ice you're skating on, you know."

"You don't have to tell me twice." He stacked his feet on the table next to Brody's and watched the day's recap of sporting events.

Other people's marriages weren't any of his business, and Noah tried to keep his nose out of the gossip chain. But when he'd heard his brother was having problems with his wife, Noah had been concerned. Mostly for his seven-year-old nephew. Brody had always been a private person and not one to wear his heart on his sleeve. Noah knew badgering him for details or offering brotherly advice would be like talking to thin air.

So they sat in silence, drinking their beers. And Noah waited.

"Kelly says I'm emotionally closed off. Do you think so?" Brody looked at him.

Noah shrugged. "Hell, I don't know. I think all men are emotionally closed off. At least according to women."

"Yeah, but you don't think I need to open myself up more? Kelly says I never talk to her."

"What do you mean by 'open up'?"

Brody sighed and picked at the label on his beer bottle. "That's what I asked Kelly. But she just got mad and said she shouldn't have to tell me what to say, and I needed to figure it out for myself."

Noah snorted. "Women. They expect us to be mind readers." He glanced at his brother. "What did you guys fight about, exactly?"

Brody shook his head. "Hell, I don't remember. She got upset because she dropped a pot of spaghetti sauce, and I tried to calm her down. I told her it wasn't a big deal. Then she went off, saying my response was typical, because nothing bothers me and I never tell her how I feel. I don't know how it happened, but it escalated into me sleeping in the den." He brought the bottle to his lips and took a long sip. "I'm just glad Tyler wasn't there to hear us yelling. It's bad enough he asks why I'm on the couch and his mom's in the bed by herself."

"Are things that bad?"

"I don't even know anymore. We hardly ever see each other, between work and carting Tyler around. And when we are around each other, we don't talk."

Noah kept silent, letting his brother tell him as much as he wanted to.

"I'm worried about my son and how this is going to affect him," Brody continued. "When Kelly got pregnant, it was never my intention to raise our child separately. But now..." He sighed. "I just don't know."

"You're not thinking about divorcing, are you?" Noah asked, startled. Brody and Kelly had been together for almost eight years, and Noah couldn't imagine them apart.

True, an unexpected pregnancy had brought them together, but surely their son was enough to keep them that way.

"I suggested counseling, which Kelly reluctantly agreed to. She doesn't think a counselor will be able to open me up. But if that doesn't work, then I think we'll probably divorce," he said in a soft voice. "It seems as if she's already given up."

"You don't think..." Noah hesitated, not sure if he wanted to plant this seed in Brody's head. "You don't think there's someone else, do you?"

Brody lifted the beer bottle to his lips, pausing for a moment before taking a sip. "Sex between me and Kelly has never been a problem. It's always been great."

"Yeah, but men and women are different like that. It's not always about sex with them." He hated to play devil's advocate, but he thought maybe if he helped his brother discover the root of the problem, his marriage could be saved.

Brody shook his head. "I don't think that's it. I think she resents me."

"You mean, because of Tyler?" Even though he hated to think Kelly would resent her own son.

"It's not just about Tyler. Kelly's never really liked Trouble. When we first met, she always told me she wanted to stay in Michigan so she could work on her undergraduate degree. But after she got pregnant, all that changed."

"I remember when you first brought her home to meet Dad and Carol. She seemed...less than thrilled to be here," Noah said, remembering the day his brother had introduced his new bride to their family. His new bride, everyone had found out with a jolt of surprise, who was due to give birth in three short months.

Brody sighed wearily and shifted deeper in the leather sofa. "Well, before Tyler was born, Kelly and I had a deal

that she could finish college in Michigan. After graduation, we'd move back here and I'd go to work for Dad, so
I could bring in some good money, and she could stay at
home with the baby. The only thing was—"

"You had to move back to Trouble," Noah finished
for him.

His brother nodded. "Yep. And there went her undergrad."

"You think she holds that against you?"

"It's the only thing I can think of."

The news on ESPN switched from baseball to soccer,
and Noah tuned it out, not really giving a rip about soccer.
"Does Tyler have any idea what's going on?"

Brody polished off the last of his beer and set the bottle
on the table. "He heard us arguing one time, and Kelly
calmed him down. She told him that sometimes moms
and dads fight but they still love each other. He seemed
okay after that, but . . . he's been different lately. Quiet."

"Kids are resilient, Brody. I'm sure he'll be okay."

"I'm not. I'm worried about him."

Brody's whole life was his son. Noah heard the worry
in his brother's voice, practically felt his fear. Noah's
heart went out to him. How were Brody and his wife
going to push through this without affecting an observant
seven-year-old?

"Maybe what Tyler needs is to spend some time with
you and Kelly together to see that you guys are okay.
Maybe you should take a family trip somewhere."

Brody snorted. "Yeah, I'm sure a trip to Disneyland
and shaking hands with Mickey Mouse is going to solve
all our problems."

The light from the TV flickered across the hard set of
Brody's jaw. The torment was evident, and Noah knew he
didn't deliberately mean to be cross with him.

His brother glanced at him and briefly closed his eyes. "I'm sorry. I didn't mean that the way it sounded." He leaned forward and rested his head in his hands. "I'm just trying to figure this out. I may have to stay here more than one night."

"Don't worry about it." He placed a comforting hand on his brother's shoulder and felt how tense his muscles were. "You can stay as long as you like."

Avery stretched languidly beneath his hard body, which pinned her to the mattress, and ran her legs along his. She'd never realized how completely sensual and erotic it could be to just move along a man, feeling him feel her, skimming his hands over her body. It was unlike any other sexual encounter she'd ever had.

He murmured in her ear, whispering her name. He told her how good she smelled, how he couldn't wait to be inside her. A shiver rolled through her at the feel of his warm breath, as she listened to him say how hot she made him and how he could think of no one else. She'd dreamed of this for days, wondering how it would feel to lie with him, skin to skin, with only the warmth of their body heat surrounding them.

Turns out it was even better than she expected. All her other encounters had been typical and staid. In the dark and a basic missionary position. Nothing that had ever promised to engulf her in flames. One more minute of his teasing, sensual caresses and she would burn up without ever feeling the real thing.

She should've known being with Noah would be like this. Hadn't she told herself this since first laying eyes on him? Even this morning, with the sunlight pushing through the sheer curtains of her bedroom, was just as exciting as it had been last night.

He pulled away from her and stared down into her eyes, his mesmerizing gaze holding nothing but the promise of pure ecstasy. Then he kissed her, his tongue dancing and twining around hers. And just before he slid inside her he...

Yelled in her ear?

Avery woke with a jolt, sweat gathering between her breasts. Her breathing came in short, ragged bursts, and she forced herself to calm down, along with her heart.

It was all just a dream. A dream that had her tossing and turning all night long, leaving her shaken, restless, and completely unsatisfied.

The first one had been just a teaser. She'd walked into a crowd, with no idea where she was and who all the people were. But it hadn't mattered as her eyes connected with Noah's from across the room and a current of understanding had passed between them. She could practically hear what he'd been thinking. *You're mine tonight.*

Then the next one had been explosive and animalistic, with them tearing each other's clothes off with urgency and need. He'd taken her up against the front door of his house, unable to make the long journey to his bedroom, too impatient to wait that long. And that last one... had been more about a deep connection than anything else. More about their two souls seeking each other out and grabbing on for dear life. And she'd woken up right after he yelled in her ear.

Why had he done that?

Avery sat up gingerly, as if her muscles had really gone through the sexual workout of a lifetime. She took deep, even breaths, trying to steady herself and overcome a night full of sexual fantasies.

Then she heard the same yell again and realized she

hadn't dreamed it. It had come from Rebecca, who was in the living room.

The bedside clock read ten fifteen. Had she really slept that late? Good thing it was Sunday.

She swung her legs over the edge of the bed and realized she wasn't wearing her shorts. What the hell?

I know I put them on before climbing into bed...

A flash of pink caught her eye and she noticed her shorts lying on the floor, partially under the bed. Funny, she didn't remember taking them off. Must have done it in the heat of passion...

With herself.

Lord, she was pathetic—and infuriated that she'd let her lust for her boss go so far that now she was having dreams about him.

Shaking her head, she slid her shorts back on and stepped out the door to find Rebecca standing in the middle of the living room. Her red satin robe was tied loosely and hung midthigh. And her hair was piled sloppily on top of her head, making it look as if she had little red flames shooting up from her skull. Her chest rose and fell rapidly as she focused on a piece of paper in her hands.

"Are you okay?" Avery asked, her voice still husky from sleep.

Rebecca glanced up, her eyes wide and mouth hanging open. She stared at Avery, completely paralyzed, and then a hysterical laugh bubbled out. "I got in."

"Got in?" Avery repeated as she walked into the kitchen and poured a cup of coffee from the pot Rebecca had already brewed. She was going to need a lot to wake up from her erotic dreams.

Rebecca remained silent, her eyes skimming the paper

again, and Avery leaned over the countertop, blowing into her mug.

"To Harvard," she whispered. "Harvard Medical," she said, her voice more confident and loud. "I got into Harvard Medical School!"

"Oh my God." Avery set her cup down and grabbed her roommate in a tight hug. The younger woman literally shook with excitement, and it reverberated into Avery. "Congratulations." She stepped back and peered into Rebecca's face to find tears streaming down her cheeks. Avery found herself crying along with her friend, erotic dreams forgotten.

"I thought I was just going to have to settle for the University of Michigan, not that it's a bad school, but I've dreamed of Harvard since high school." She placed a hand over her chest. "I still can't believe I got in."

Avery perched on a barstool and took a sip of her coffee. "When do you start?"

"August. Which is only in . . . four months."

"I'm really happy for you." Avery spoke from the heart and envied Rebecca's drive to have direction in her life. It was something that was always lacking in herself . . . direction. What did she want out of life? Where did she see herself in thirty years? Her parents seemed to think a marriage to Peter with a houseful of corporate-bred children was the perfect life. *No, thank you.*

She didn't know what she wanted. She felt just as lost and alone as she had the night she left home.

NINE

A S A GENERAL RULE FOR a healthy lifestyle, Avery made it a point to stay away from things like cheeseburgers and onion rings. Since she couldn't afford new clothes, she wouldn't let her waist expand past her normal size four. But her newfound hometown seemed to be blithely unaware of the ongoing cholesterol problem in the country. Her stomach wasn't used to processed foods and trans fatty acids. The cheeseburger she'd eaten last week reminded her of that fact, having left her nauseated for the remainder of the day.

Avery decided to take her lunch hour out of the office today to give herself a chance to get familiar with Trouble, something she'd made a point to do when she'd arrived in town. As her Mercedes purred down Front Street, her eyes darted back and forth and took in the people, some old, some young, walking on the sidewalks. They all had one thing in common: none were in any hurry to get to their destinations. Some were laughing, talking with friends, their gaits slow and lazy.

The all-American scene reminded her of a movie she'd once seen as a child. The name of the film eluded her, but she still remembered longing to travel to such a place, where she could skip down the sidewalk, holding hands with her mother and eating ice cream. Then she'd look out the window of their home in Beaver Creek, surrounded by the empty vastness of the Colorado Rockies, and try to imagine frolicking through the woods with a friend. It never happened.

That could be me. If I stay here, marry, and have children, that could be me walking down the street with my own child. Sharing a laugh or a banana split.

The rumble of her stomach reminded her of her quest for something that would offer her more than empty calories. Just as she was about to settle on Mel's Giant Burgers, thinking they'd have a chicken sandwich, she spotted a deli. The building looked as if it had been erected back in the early 1900s, but she didn't care. Desperation drove her past the building's initial appearance. Besides, judging something by the way it looked was something her mother would do, not her.

She parked her car in the alley next to the building and walked inside. The place was nearly empty except for two older women with beehive hairdos the color of a gloomy, rainy sky. They offered Avery a friendly smile, and she gave one in return.

After gathering the side salad and turkey half sandwich she ordered, Avery made her way to a table in the corner. Usually during lunch, she'd grab bites of a sandwich while filing paperwork. She needed a change of scenery. Something to look at other than the dull off-white walls or the glaring brightness of her computer screen. *Oh, who are you kidding, Avery? You wanted to get away from Noah.*

She'd learned quickly that Mondays were exceedingly slow, and today was no different. When Noah had come in wearing faded jeans and a white T-shirt, she'd known he had no plans of leaving the office. He'd driven her crazy with his constant pacing and chitchat. The embarrassment over making her stupid offer Friday night had motivated her to ignore him as best as she could. She'd been hasty, idiotic, and filled with regret ever since.

What kind of imbecile went around telling her boss she wanted to sleep with him? The kind of imbecile who hadn't been with a man in ages, not to mention a man like Noah. How would she face him today? He probably thought she was some kind of slut.

But it had been fun. Imagining them together, sneaking off at lunchtime or falling into each other's arms after a long day, had offered her a kind of thrill she hadn't felt in a long time. She supposed now she would only have to rely on her dreams to fulfill her fantasies. After going to his house, meeting his brother, and hearing about their family problems, she'd been blindsided by a large dose of reality.

Later on, not even Häagen-Dazs could erase the shame she felt, hence the reason for her search for something mildly nutritious.

She munched through her sandwich, picking at her salad and willing her thoughts away from the man who caused her sleepless nights. Couldn't her mind have found something else to dream about, like unicorns or skydiving?

She pushed the rest of the lettuce around her plate, not in the mood to eat anything else. One of the elderly women laughed at something her friend said and the sound cut Avery, deeply.

Looking at her surroundings, she realized for the first time in days how lonely she was. True, she'd met a lot of nice people, was even dreaming about one. But she missed the comfort and connection of her friends back home. Landon was never home and never answered his cell phone.

Teeny had been a great deal of comfort, but her childhood friend didn't really understand what Avery was going through. Their parents ran in the same crowd, but that lifestyle suited her friend. Teeny had no desire to leave her posh but empty existence for something more meaningful as Avery had, a fact that would always separate them.

She rubbed a hand over her breastbone, trying to rid herself of the ache that had taken permanent residence. For the first time in two weeks, Avery wondered if she'd made the right decision.

The lettuce on her plate grew warm. She turned her nose up and pushed the plate away. Since she still had quite a while before returning to work, she decided to read.

Just as she was about to find out if the damsel in distress was to be saved by her hero, the chimes above the door rang. The sound interrupted her concentration long enough for her to notice who'd walked in.

Heavy boots thudded across the floor, while hard thigh muscles rippled under worn jeans. She could no more control her reaction to him than she could stop the sun from rising. Her inner thigh muscles ached and her stomach twisted into knots, churning up her half-eaten lunch. It seemed as though an afternoon out for lunch couldn't offer her a break from Noah. He had his cell phone tucked between his shoulder and ear, but Avery couldn't hear the words he said, only the deep timbre of his voice.

She focused her attention on the book, forcing her eyes to skim over the words, to contemplate their meaning. His voice kept interfering with her story, muddling her brain. Suddenly he was quiet, and Avery glanced up to see him standing before her just as he hooked his cell phone on the belt of his jeans.

"Mind if I join you?"

"Ah . . . no," she said as she closed her book, her heart thudding.

"Anything good?" He gestured as she put her book back in her purse.

"I was just getting to the good part when you interrupted me."

He chuckled as he settled himself down in the chair across from her, and his knee accidentally brushed hers. Why did they always sit at tables where their legs didn't fit properly? She scooted her chair back to avoid any more contact.

"Funny running into you here," she said as he placed a bottle of unsweetened iced tea on the table and unwrapped a premade sandwich.

"I get tired of eating hamburgers and pizzas. How about you?"

"Pretty much the same." She smiled. "I get tired of sitting inside all day long."

"You're not used to that, are you?" he asked, looking at her.

She was momentarily distracted by the impact of his gray eyes, but somehow managed to push the feeling away. "What, sitting or being inside all day?"

He took a bite of his sandwich. "I'm going to say 'both.'"

If she wasn't careful, the conversation could revert back to her old life. Avery was tired of people asking about it, so she thought about her answer carefully. "I just enjoy being outside. If I sit for too long, I get restless."

"I know what you mean." He opened his sandwich, removed the sprouts and half the lettuce, then took the bottle of mustard off the table and slathered it across the top piece of bread. "What?" he asked after he realized she'd been watching with mild interest.

"Why don't you just have a sandwich made if you're going to take that one apart?"

"It's faster this way. And I don't like sprouts; it's like eating rabbit food."

"And you know what rabbit food tastes like?"

One dark brow lifted and he raised the sandwich to his mouth. "Maybe I do."

They shared a smile, and the instant connection did something to Avery's nerves. A moment ago she felt lonely and depressed. Now she felt invaded and consumed by the man sitting across from her. "You're a strange one, Mr. McDermott."

He lifted his shoulders, pulling the shirt tighter across his chest. "I try to keep things as interesting as possible."

"Really? Is that a rule you live by?"

"When I can." He flashed a quick grin before biting into his sandwich. The cell phone on his belt vibrated. Noah tilted it so he could read the caller ID. "It's my sister," he said, shaking his head. "She has a way with conversation. If I answer that, I'll never get off. She could ramble on for hours about how some guy on the street gave her a funny look."

Avery laughed, thinking Noah's family sounded loud and exciting, the type of people who would have a weekend barbecue and invite the whole neighborhood. She wondered if Noah realized how lucky he was. Generally in life, people took the things they had for granted.

"But you love talking to her anyway," she guessed.

"There's never a dull moment when she's around. If there is, then something's wrong."

"Sounds as though you have a wonderful family."

He snorted. "I have an obnoxious family. They're great, but obnoxious. Sometimes I wish my father wasn't so in my face about getting married and other stuff."

His voice trailed off when he said "other stuff," leaving Avery to realize there was much more than marriage issues between him and his father. "Other stuff?" she braved.

"Yeah, you know." He shrugged. "Just your typical family problems."

If he were to look up "family issues" in the dictionary there'd be a big color picture of her and her parents, smiling at him. Well, she definitely wouldn't smile, but her parents would, because they were always oblivious to everything around them.

She decided to let the subject drop, sensing it wasn't something he wanted to broadcast during lunch. She certainly could understand where he was coming from, in that area.

"Speaking of relationship stuff," she ventured, thinking she was either brave or incredibly stupid to be bringing this up again, "I wanted to apologize for Friday night."

Would he notice if she left it at that and ran out, leaving him sitting there all by himself? *Don't be such a coward, Avery. This is supposed to be the new you, remember?*

He looked at her as he pulled another sprout out of his sandwich. "You mean for using ketchup instead of steak sauce? I thought that was a little weird, but I haven't told anyone."

The look on Noah's face when she'd slathered ketchup on her steak hadn't been completely lost on her. He'd lifted a brow when she'd bypassed the A.1. for Hunt's and then looked at her as if she'd started shooting flames out of her nostrils. Steak sauce wasn't a staple in the Price family fridge growing up, and Avery hadn't wanted to admit that to Noah for fear of looking like a total idiot. So she'd used the old "I just prefer ketchup" line, which had earned a hearty laugh from him.

"That wasn't what I meant, but I will not apologize for my affection for ketchup. It's a perfectly normal thing to put on meat," she said, completely bluffing.

"Whatever you say." He looked at her more closely. Avery, who'd normally admit defeat, refused to back down from his gaze. Even though his stare did things to her stomach and made her feel things only her romance novels had achieved, she stared right back at him.

"You've never had real steak sauce, have you?"

"We're getting completely off subject," she said, waving a hand in the air. No way was she indulging in the reasons her parents only used things like vinaigrette and Dijon mustard.

"No, this is good stuff. Seems as though we're getting down to the real Avery Price."

Okay, so now he was deliberately goading her, perhaps even being a bit droll, but she wasn't going to buy into the boyish charm that had made dinner way more enjoyable and infectious than it should have been. Her hope had been for him to be so boring that she would have to play the movie *Flashdance* in her head just for a bit of entertainment. To her ultimate dismay and reluctant pleasure, she'd barely gotten through the opening credits when he'd reeled her in with his quick grin.

Avery remained silent while he smiled at her, wondering how they'd gotten off the beaten track to her choice of steak sauce.

"Don't worry; your secret's safe with me. I'll just have to find a way to introduce you to the many flavors of A.1."

Yeah, that would imply having to go on more dates, which she definitely wasn't doing. No matter how good he looked, or how heavenly he smelled, or even if every time he looked at her he undressed her with his eyes.

"Anyway," she started again, as he took a long sip of his iced tea, and then picked up his sandwich. "I wasn't talking about the ketchup. I meant, I'm sorry for…ah…" She shifted and cleared her throat. "The thing I said… you know, when…" A nervous laugh popped out, making her realize she looked like a royal idiot. "It was just really inappropriate…and stupid…you know…" Lord, she'd spoken in front of thousands of people at charity events, but this one man made her tongue-tied. And by the look on his face, he enjoyed her misery, the gorgeous rat bastard.

She took a deep breath. "I just meant—"

"Avery. Are you talking about rolling around in the sack until we—and I'm using your words—'get it out of our systems'?" He leaned his forearms on the table, the last few bites of his sandwich forgotten. "If I remember correctly, you were pretty enthusiastic about it."

"Yeah, well, I wasn't thinking quite clearly." Was that a reasonable excuse?

"You weren't?" He sounded surprised. "Were you sneaking sips of Jack Daniel's when I wasn't looking?"

"Jack Daniel's?"

"Whiskey?" he said, as if she was supposed to understand.

"I know what Jack Daniel's is," she sputtered quickly. She *never* drank whiskey. Well, almost never. The only time Avery had an experience with hard liquor, her mother made her live to regret it. It had been her father's beloved

Chivas Regal she'd found in his study. Being the curious and wannabe adventurous teen, she'd snuck a drink, only to be caught red-handed. Needless to say, she'd been unable to leave the penthouse for a month, in hopes to teach her that children did not drink such things, much less sneak around in places where they were forbidden.

"Sure, yeah," she said with a shrug. "Are you kidding, I drink whiskey all the time." *Great, now you sound like an alcoholic.* "I mean, not all the time, but...you know."

Now he was laughing at her. Not really laughing, but giving her one of those little smiles he had when something amused him. He smiled at her that way a lot, especially when she started rambling and making up ridiculous lies so she wouldn't look like such an...ass. But then again, her stupid little anecdotes probably made her look like even more of an idiot, because who would believe someone like her drank whiskey?

"Really, you drink whiskey all the time? Which brand do you prefer? Besides Jack, that is?" His eyes dropped down to her mouth as though he was trying to picture the liquor slipping in between her lips.

The seductive gesture almost made her forget she was trying to add on to her lie even more. Which brand? Who the hell knew? Now she wished she'd never agreed to let him sit with her. Her only intention had been to apologize for her embarrassing behavior, only to dive into even more embarrassing behavior, which she'd have to apologize again for. Vicious, vicious circles...Why didn't she keep her mouth shut?

"Uh...okay, I may have fibbed."

"Really? You sounded so convincing."

Uh-oh. "The truth is I don't drink whiskey." Confession is good for the soul. Or, in her case, good for keeping her sane.

"You don't drink whiskey?" He rubbed a hand along his jaw, which had just the slightest shadow, giving his face that roughly handsome look. Not that he wasn't already mind-numbingly gorgeous. But in Avery's opinion, he ought to go around with the half-shaven look all day. It made her want to rub her cheek against his. Then maybe she could sit him down in a chair, slather shaving cream all over his chiseled jawline, and shave the stubble off herself. Ooh, the thought gave her chills.

"You're very intriguing, Avery. I just might have to cook a steak for you myself, with the proper sauce, of course, and get you drunk on whiskey. My guess is you wouldn't be able to handle one swallow."

"Why would you say that?" she asked, leaning back in her chair and crossing her arms.

His eyes gave her a once-over, from what they could see above the table, and she had the sudden self-conscious impulse to cross her arms more tightly. Luckily, the loud floral print blouse she wore was conservative in its cut, leaving his assessment of her to the imagination.

"I'm venturing a guess here, but I'm going to say you haven't had a whole lot of hard liquor in your life." He laughed and held up a hand when she narrowed her eyes at him. "That wasn't an insult, Avery. There's nothing wrong with not being a drinker."

"It's not that I don't drink," she retorted, feeling defensive for some reason. "I just prefer a nice bottle of Costanti as opposed to something that feels like fire burning my esophagus."

His seductive gray eyes narrowed, then he shook his head. "To each his own."

He picked up his sandwich and polished off the last bite, then quickly swiped a napkin over his mouth.

"Anyway, back to what I was saying. I just don't think it would be a wise idea for us to engage in an affair," she said, with more conviction this time. "Don't you agree?"

Please, please agree so I don't feel as if I'm repeatedly putting my foot in my mouth. It's really not an attractive look.

"You're probably right." He lifted his shoulders just as his cell phone vibrated again. But he dismissed it after checking the caller ID. "Have you ever been horseback riding?"

Huh? He couldn't have surprised her more with the change of subject than if he would have dropped down on one knee and popped the question. She really hadn't expected him to dismiss her rescinded offer so easily. Perhaps he hadn't really wanted to have an affair in the first place and wanted her to call it off first. Why did that not make her feel any better?

Horseback riding was the furthest from what she'd expected him to mention. The villa her parents owned in Italy had fully run stables where she'd learned to ride as a child. She prided herself on being quite good with horses. When she was in the saddle, she felt just as comfortable as she did on foot.

"I've ridden once or twice," she lied.

Noah crumpled the sandwich wrapper and tossed it on the table. "My father and stepmother have stables on their property. I usually go every couple of weeks or so to do some riding. Maybe you'd like to come with me and show how well you can ride."

Had he meant to say those exact words in that exact order? Avery caught the meaning behind them, along with the gleam in his eye, and wondered if he took her backing out of their affair seriously. The mental picture of him

atop a horse, thigh muscles straining as he guided the animal around, was enough for her to want to decline. Then
she pictured them together, him behind her in the saddle
with strong arms wrapped tightly around her. She almost
came undone in her chair with thoughts of his thighs cradling hers. Her imagination really was overactive.

"I'm sure I can ride just as well as you can."

He lifted a brow and his mouth quirked just as he
brought the iced tea bottle to his lips. "Is that a challenge?" he asked after taking a long sip. "Because I'm
sure I can outride you."

Avery cocked an eyebrow and shook her head. "We'll
just have to see."

They stared at each other for a long moment, and she
suddenly felt the loss of their nonexistent affair. Now she
would never know what it would be like to be with him.
Not just kissing and touching, but really be with him. To
feel him on top of her body, moving inside her. To wake
up with him after a long, exhausting night. But it was best
this way. She'd been right to end it before it began. It was
not a wise decision to get involved with her boss. Even if
he probably would have been good.

"I've got to get going," he said suddenly. "I have a conference call at one fifteen."

"Yes," she said, glancing down at her watch. "It's been
almost an hour since I left."

"I'm sure it'll be okay with the boss if you're a few
minutes late," he said with a wink. Heat bloomed in her
cheeks.

He gathered their trash and tossed it in the can by the
door.

The sweltering heat outside hadn't changed any, despite
her hopes, and Avery wished she hadn't decided to wear

linen. Even though the fabric was one of her favorites, aside from silk, it was one of the worst things a person could wear when the temperature was above eighty-five. The light tan, baggy pants floated around her legs, creating a blanket of heat she didn't appreciate.

Noah slid his dark sunglasses back on his face. Avery was grateful to not be affected by his gaze for the time being. He stood so close to her she felt the heat radiating from his body, which affected her more than the stifling weather.

Just as she was about to move away from him, she sensed someone staring at her from behind. It was the same feeling she'd had before. Only this time, instead of discomfort, she felt tension. Something wasn't right. The little hairs on the back of her neck came to attention. Before she'd been unsure, perhaps even a bit paranoid, but this time was different. Somehow, she knew without a doubt someone was watching her. She also knew having this same feeling countless times since she'd been here was no coincidence. What was she supposed to do about it? Who could she tell?

She whipped her head around and saw nothing. There were no kids, no pets, no young couples laughing and holding hands as before. Funny, the only time she had this feeling was when there was nothing around to prove her point.

Only a few cars, a motorcycle, and a couple of pickups that looked decades old occupied the streets. But wait... Avery cast a sidelong glance just across the street and noticed an outdated dark sedan. She was almost sure it was exactly the same one she'd seen before. The car was empty, with a busted-out taillight. Her detective skills weren't superior, but she tried to look around for its owner without seeming obvious. There was no one.

"What's the matter?"

"What do you mean?" She tried sounding breezy and nonchalant, but the tremor in her voice surely gave her away.

Noah leaned against his SUV. "Your whole body went stiff."

"I'm just not used to this heat."

He nodded. "This is a little unusual. It's normally not so hot this time of year." He stared at her for a second, but she couldn't read his eyes behind his sunglasses. "Will you be okay to go riding this weekend?"

She smiled, appreciating his concern. "I'm sure I'll be okay." She scuffed the toe of her shoe along the pavement. "It was nice having lunch with you."

"It sure was a lot more entertaining than eating by myself. Tell Rebecca I had to make a quick stop, and I'll be back around one."

She watched his fine backside as he climbed into his truck. Did she regret calling off their affair? Most definitely not. Besides, who the hell would want to have a romp in the sack with someone like Noah anyway? Sure he was completely gorgeous, smelled divine, and had a great sense of humor, but that didn't mean he'd be good in bed.

Avery snorted and rolled her eyes. She sure as hell had come up with better lies before.

The heat inside her Mercedes enveloped her as she climbed in and started the car. Then her cell phone rang. Since she'd answer for only one of two people, she glanced at the caller ID, and saw it was indeed one of those two people.

"Where the hell have you been?" she asked after answering the call.

"That's a nice way to greet your only brother."

Avery maneuvered her car out of the parking lot and onto the street, craning her neck to see if anyone sat in the dark sedan. Still no one. "Oh, don't give me that 'I'm the only sibling you have so you have to be nice to me' bullshit. I've left you a ton of messages."

"I'm calling you back now, aren't I?"

"Landon..."

"I've been busy, Avery." Her brother sounded weary, which wasn't an uncommon thing, given the fact that he was in the process of buying a hotel so he could renovate it. But this time he sounded different, distracted.

Concern for him washed away her annoyance. "Is everything okay?"

"I've been putting in a lot of hours at work and some other things. It's nothing you need to worry about."

She slowed the car at a crosswalk to let a man and his dog cross. "What other things? Are Mom and Dad giving you a hard time about helping me leave?"

She heard him let out a heavy sigh. "No, they don't know anything about that. There are just some things I need to handle. It's not a big deal."

"If you say so," she replied, not sure if she believed him. Landon wasn't usually secretive with her, but if this was something he didn't want to talk to her about, it must be important to him. He was so supportive with her, putting their parents' trust in him on the line by helping her. The least she could do was respect his privacy. She and Landon had been each other's best friends growing up, being so isolated in their world of wealth that they'd soon become each other's confidants. Avery had always been able to tell her brother things most sisters wouldn't. They understood each other better than anyone else, and she'd never had a problem telling Landon her secrets and fears.

Something was different this time. Landon was going through something he felt he couldn't tell her. It stung, just a touch, considering everything she'd shared with him. If ever the time came that he wanted to tell her, she'd be there the way he was there for her.

"How's your new job going?"

"It's going good. I've met some really nice people… wait a minute. How'd you know I'd been hired?" This was the first time she'd spoken to Landon since starting her job. True, she'd left him several messages, but she hadn't said anything about being hired for a job. The only person who knew was Teeny. But her brother wouldn't have spoken to Teeny; they didn't even like each other.

"This woman named Rebecca called me, and I assumed you'd been hired."

"Oh," she said, still thinking it was strange he'd ask her about a job without knowing whether or not she was working.

She pulled her car into the parking lot behind the office, but didn't get out. Instead she sat there, while the Mercedes hummed beneath her. "Can I ask you something, Landon?"

There was static, muffled with background noise. Avery realized he must be in his car too. "Sure."

"Has Mom said anything to you about hiring a private investigator to find me? I mean, you don't think she'd do that, do you?"

"Mom said she talked to you, and you told her where you were."

Avery ran a finger over the top of the leather steering wheel. "We did talk."

"So… why would she hire an investigator to find you?"

"That's true," she muttered, not having thought of that.

A car honked in the background, then Landon spoke.

"Why, what's wrong? Do you think someone's following you?"

"I don't know," she admitted. "It sounds totally stupid, but I keep getting these creepy feelings, as though someone's watching me."

"It's not stupid, Boo," he said, using his childhood nickname for her. "But guys have watched you before."

Avery stared ahead at the plain stucco building and the painted sign that read EMPLOYEE PARKING ONLY. "That's not what I meant. It feels as though someone's watching my every move, but I never actually see anyone. It's really starting to freak me out."

"How long has this been going on?" He sounded alarmed. Avery definitely hadn't meant to add to her brother's stress.

"About a week."

"A week?" he asked, startled. "Do you own mace?"

"I hardly think I need mace, Landon. This is a small town. No one's going to attack me."

"Humor me. Buy a can of mace you can keep on your key chain."

"Why? It's not like I live alone." She turned off the car and stepped outside. "I have a roommate."

Her brother sighed again. "You know what I mean. Just do it for me, okay?"

He sounded irritated, a hard thing to accomplish for a man who was normally calm and easygoing. Avery wondered if his mood had more to do with his worry for her. "Okay, I promise. But do me a favor. Don't tell Mom and Dad about this. I don't need them to have another reason to tell me to come home."

"When have I ever given up one of your secrets?" His placating tone made her smile.

"I don't know what I'd do without you." Her high heels clicked loudly on the pavement beneath her, and then she paused outside the office doors. "Are you sure you're all right? You sound stressed out."

The long pause told Avery that whatever came out of Landon's mouth next was going to be a lie. "I'm fine. Call me soon."

The line went dead, leaving Avery staring down at her cell phone. She'd counted on her brother to be her voice of reason, but he'd only added to her fears by requesting she buy a can of mace. But that wasn't what concerned her. Something wasn't right with him. A problem that ran deeper than simple work-related stress, but Avery was clueless as to what it might be. He had a relatively good relationship with their parents because, to Avery's utter annoyance and bewilderment, they didn't pressure him the way they did her. And he wasn't dating anyone, so it couldn't be a girlfriend problem.

Just something else she had to add to her list of things to dwell on.

TEN

A S A RULE, NOAH HARDLY ever set foot in McDermott's before dinnertime to avoid his father. He didn't like to think of himself as being cowardly, but after years of exhausting the same argument over and over, he found it less stressful to dodge the issue altogether.

When Chase said their father was looking for him, Noah could only venture a guess as to why, although he had a pretty good hunch. He'd played the waiting game the last couple of days, thinking his dad would seek him out, but he had eventually tired of the anticipation. He'd hoped whatever had been on the old man's mind had expired. Noah knew better.

Martin McDermott never forgot anything.

Noah knew this, had repeatedly told himself this, and the notion was part of the reason he wanted to avoid the conversation. But putting it off would only give his father more time to stew. And it would give him time to build up a bigger argument that Noah would have to scratch his way out of. He had extensive experience in the area of combat with his dad, and he knew his energy would be depleted for the rest of the day.

Why Noah had chosen now to seek out the older man was a mystery to him. He supposed his father putting the time and place in his own hands would give himself more control. That was an illusion. His father had never been careless enough to let his control slip.

The steak house was only half-full, as most of the town's residents ventured out for dinner instead of lunch. Noah knew his father arrived at the restaurant around nine a.m. and stayed no later than six, leaving Chase to take care of things during the busy dinner hour.

Their father's office was upstairs, next to his brother's and the executive chef's. Noah had been up there only a few times but knew the giant two-way mirror overlooking the dining room was yet another way his father wielded control.

Noah nodded to the hostess and went through the employees-only door leading upstairs.

It wasn't any surprise his father spared no expense to give the dining room just the right look. He knew how to bring in business and how to make his customers feel as though they were getting world-class service. Martin McDermott's stubbornness went hand in hand with his knack to run a business. Noah liked to think he'd inherited the particular quality for business acumen from his father, although sometimes he thought they had only stubbornness in common.

The hallway of offices upstairs embodied everything the dining room wasn't. The rich wood paneling gave way to ho-hum white walls, and bland commercial flooring replaced the plush burgundy carpet. Noah figured he'd have decorated in the same fashion, so he didn't blame his father.

Noah's stepmother, Carol, had suggested Martin run

their business out of their home office, but Noah's father insisted he be here, in the thick of things, where he could see everything happening. Rarely was he in the dining room. He was always holed up in his office, thinking of new ways to improve and expand his business.

Even though the two of them had this business-related tension hanging over their heads, Noah had to admire the older man's drive and success. After years of struggling, his father had turned a one-room steak pit into a classy town favorite.

Noah paused outside his father's office and stared at the closed door. Trying to predict how the conversation would go was impossible. What on earth could they possibly talk about?

After briefly knocking and hearing a barked order to come in, Noah walked through the door. The sheer size of the owner's office never ceased to impress him, considering the long and narrow outside hallway. The large square room's decor matched the main dining room. Dark paneled walls blended with the burgundy carpet and a wide, coffee-colored desk sat in front of the two-way mirror, where his father read the paper.

Martin was a big man, tall with broad shoulders, a body structure he'd passed down to all three of his sons. He'd somehow managed to maintain a relatively slim waist in his old age. And his thick, once-dark hair, the same shade he shared with his youngest son, Brody, had turned stark white in the last couple of years, and the color reminded Noah of cotton balls.

Martin glanced up when Noah shut the door. "Noah. What are you doing here this time of day?" He folded the newspaper and set it on the desk.

"Chase said you were looking for me."

"Oh." Surprise flashed in his father's faded eyes. "You didn't have to come out of your way. It's something that can wait."

Of course, now that Noah had caught him off guard, his father would pretend it wasn't a big deal. But if he had sought Noah out, the encounter would've been a conversation that couldn't have waited. It was always about control with this man.

"It's not really out of my way." Noah tried to sound aloof. "I had a few minutes to spare." *Actually, I wanted to get this over with.*

"Well, now you're here. Have a seat." His father gestured to a chair.

Noah tried to gauge the older man's body language, but he was perfectly relaxed, his face impassive and calm. The air of leisure shouldn't have worried Noah, but for some reason it did.

He took the chair his father pointed to and rested his hands across his stomach. And waited. One of the things he remembered about his mother was how often she had said he and his father were alike. Every time Noah disobeyed her and deliberately did the exact opposite of what she told him to do, she'd always retort with, "You're too much like your daddy." For years he'd had no idea what his mother had meant, as he'd been far too concerned with mud, football, and chasing girls. But as the years wore on, her words had taken on more meaning in his life, especially after he opened his own business. His bitterness kept him from accepting how alike he and his father really were. And the times when his father wasn't shy about letting his resentment show, Noah tried repeating his mother's words.

The mantra had never done any good. Because Noah

had chosen not to go down the path laid before him, he knew he'd disappointed his father. Despite all that, he and his father did get along, often able to carry on a civilized conversation as long as they didn't touch on careers and family obligations. It was as if they agreed to disagree for the sake of their relationship.

Noah wondered if now would be any different.

"I'm sure you've heard of this mess going on between Kelly and Brody."

Noah highly doubted this was what his father wanted to talk about, but decided to play along anyway. "Brody mentioned it." Noah wasn't sure how much his brother had told their father and thought it best not to mention that Brody was thinking about divorce.

"I hope that boy comes to his senses. I hate to see my grandson grow up in a broken home." "Broken" wouldn't be the exact word Noah would use to describe his brother's home. Even if he and Kelly did get divorced, there wasn't any reason to believe Tyler wouldn't turn out sensible and level-headed. After all, his father had raised Noah and his brothers alone after their mother died. Never had Noah thought of his home as broken.

"Brody and Kelly are good parents. As long as they remain focused on Tyler, I'm sure he'll be okay."

"Yes, I'm sure." His father had a distant look in his eye, focusing on something over Noah's shoulder. What was going on in the old man's head anyway? "I wanted to talk to you about something other than your brother. I've decided to open a new restaurant, in Casper."

So now we get to the real reason.

"Congratulations" was all Noah could think to say. The comment had come out more condescending than he meant, because he knew what his father wanted.

"It's a decision I haven't come to lightly. I've been thinking about this long and hard. Chase doesn't need me here anymore." Martin waved a hand to the window behind him. "He's doing a good job running this place. And if Brody can keep his marital problems at home, I'll entrust the Golden Glove to him."

"So…" Noah prompted, after his father stopped talking and remained quiet.

"I feel the time is right to move on to the next project. I've been scouting potential sites and talking to investors. They've agreed to fund the building of a steak house in Casper."

Noah wasn't sure how to react. Why did his father need a special meeting with him to share this news? Unless he envisioned Noah being a part of this new business venture…But he had his own business to run.

He shifted in his seat. "I'm not sure what this has to do with me, Dad."

"I want you to run the place for me." The tone in his father's voice indicated that Noah should have known this. Words eluded him; he felt as though he'd gone back in time to the first conversation they'd had about Noah's entering the family business. The encounter hadn't gone well, both men being too stubborn to admit defeat or wrongdoing. Both walked away thinking the other would come back with some heartfelt apology about being wrong and callous. Neither had, of course, and the subject of the two of them working together had been a touchy one ever since.

Noah had come to believe that perhaps his father had finally accepted his hard work and his running his own company. He realized now that all their polite conversations about business had only been a smoke screen. The realization stung now just as much as it had all those years ago.

"I have my own business to run. You know that." The words were repetitive and redundant, but Noah didn't know any other way to explain. He sometimes felt as though he were speaking to a child, someone who was incapable of understanding, no matter how many times or ways he phrased his wishes. He knew this time wouldn't be any different.

"Maybe you could take on a partner to run things for you. I know you could do a great job, son. Of course, that would mean moving back to Casper. But it's not that far."

Though unexpected, Noah appreciated the vote of confidence. However, his father talked as if Noah had already accepted his offer. He gripped his hands tighter together to keep his frustrations at bay. "I don't want a partner. I enjoy running things on my own." He decided to try a different tack after his father remained silent. "Why don't you ask RJ? I'm sure he'd appreciate the promotion."

Martin still didn't say anything, running his hand along the edge of the mouse pad next to the computer. "RJ is a valuable asset to the Golden Glove. I need him there." Martin paused as if to choose his next words carefully. "And I don't think he's quite ready to run his own place yet."

"He's only a year younger than Brody," Noah pointed out.

Martin shook his head. "RJ doesn't have a head for business the way Brody does. RJ's more of a people person. I'm not sure he'd like being stuck in an office for a better part of the day the way Brody is. RJ's in his element when he's behind the bar. The customers love him, especially the females." When Martin smiled, he looked ten years younger and nothing like the man who carried around the pain of disappointment in his oldest son. The lines deepened in his face, but they were lines of all the life he'd lived.

"I don't know what you want me to say, Dad. My situation hasn't changed. Maybe you should hire a partner to help you run things."

His father stiffened in his chair. "This has been, and always will be, a family-run business. I don't want some stranger butting in."

Funny how he expected Noah to do the very same, but only because it suited his needs. Noah wasn't sure why he'd expected things to be different. His father still held the same illusions that had driven them apart in the first place.

"I'm sorry," Noah said, shaking his head. Man, he really needed a cigarette. "I don't want to be in the restaurant business, and I've told you that before. I have my own company to run. I build things, and I enjoy what I do. Now, if you need a contractor, I'd be more than happy to build the place for you."

"I'm already under contract with someone. We break ground in two weeks." Martin's words were cold, mechanical, and they stung Noah much more deeply than he expected. His father had all the confidence of the world in Noah to run his third restaurant, but he still couldn't take Noah, or his business, seriously.

His father had never taken the time to look at any of Noah's work or even acknowledge the awards he'd won. Noah's career was a joke to him. A kid's game, like when he used to build things out of his erector set. All he'd ever gotten was a smile and a pat on the head. That's all he'd ever get.

"Well, then this was a waste of time," Noah said curtly, trying not to let his father see the hurt in his eyes. He doubted the man cared. Noah stood and walked toward the door.

"Just think about my offer, Noah," he called after him. "And one more thing."

Noah stopped and turned around. His father was still in his seat, where he'd remained the entire time, his cold gray eyes burning back at him. "I'm throwing a party for your stepmother's birthday in a few weeks. I hope our differences won't keep you from coming."

"I would never miss Carol's birthday, Dad." With a heavy heart, Noah shut the door, not waiting to hear his father's response.

The earlier conversation had almost escaped Noah's mind by the time he returned home from work. The look on the old man's face and the smells from the kitchen were gone. But a few choice words remained with him for the rest of the day, churning a hole in his stomach.

I'm already under contract with someone.

His father's fantasy of Noah's taking over the restaurant business still eluded him. He'd never led the old man into believing he'd ever wanted any part of it. Perhaps he still held out hope his oldest son wasn't a complete loss in his eyes. His father's disappointment wasn't what bothered him anymore. He'd grown used to the familiar feeling that he'd never measure up.

He'd worked himself to the bone, poured his sweat and tears into building his business to what it was today. By making something of his life, by making his business a success, he'd hoped his father would see past what he wanted Noah to be.

All his hard work felt as if it had been for nothing, working to impress a man who would never have any intention of caring.

Never had he confided in anyone about his feelings, not when he knew what people would say. Why did he worry about living for his father? Noah hardly knew anymore, nor was he interested in figuring out why.

It was a childhood fantasy, he supposed. After his mother passed away, it seemed his father had too. He withdrew into himself for days at a time, hardly noticing his children. Noah had assumed the role of caregiver while his father worked their family farm from sunup to sundown. He'd been left to answer his younger brothers' questions about why Mommy left and why Daddy never hugged them anymore. Noah, only nine at the time, didn't know squat about taking care of kids. He'd done his best, having remembered what his mother had done in the years before she became ill.

Late at night, however, Noah had heard his father crying. After a long day out in the fields, his dad came home, barely throwing the boys a glance. Noah remained quiet through the rough years after his mother's death; he'd waited for his dad to return to his old self or maybe to thank Noah for cooking dinner and making sure his brothers got their homework done.

It seemed, all these years later, that he still tried to get his father to notice him.

Noah supposed that day would never come. After all, Martin McDermott was who he was. And as his mother had always said, he and his father were just alike.

Twilight descended on the cloudless lavender sky, smudged with hints of blue where the last lights of day disappeared behind the Wyoming hills. A few scant stars made an early appearance, trying with all their might to be seen against the purple hue. The stars made Noah think of his mother. She'd had a nightly ritual of sitting on their front porch. When Noah asked what she was doing, she'd smile and say, "Counting the stars. There isn't enough time in the night to count all of them." So she'd sit night after night, trying to count the stars, which Noah thought was a silly thing.

Now he'd give anything to see her rocking on their old, rickety swing, staring up at the sky with the barest hint of a smile. If he'd known he'd have only a few more short months with her, he'd have found something more meaningful to say.

Too late for past regrets. His mother's death had shaped the man he'd become. In one of the rare moments his father had opened up, he'd told Noah his mother was needed more in heaven than she was on earth. The statement barely managed to comfort a boy who deeply grieved the loss of a mother. But as an adult, the words had more meaning to him. Perhaps that was his mother now, painting the evening sky in all its glorious colors for him to enjoy.

Funny how the color of the sky had never caught his attention before. Was it the sudden appearance of a woman in his life who made him look at things differently?

After lunch, he went straight into his office, but not without noticing Avery. His eyes always strayed to her. He couldn't help it. She pulled him in like some sort of magnet he had no power to resist. And it wasn't just her beauty that attracted him.

Someone had wounded her deeply, forcing her to erect a wall and tell lies about herself. She was on constant guard, ready for someone to ask a personal question so she could spew out one of her rehearsed answers. Noah didn't understand how a woman could appear out of thin air, turn him on, and then turn him down. The phenomenon baffled him, but at the same time drew him in. Her mystery, her secrecy, made her all the more alluring, more beautiful.

Did women know a man loved the chase more than he did a woman who threw herself at him? Was it something they did knowingly?

He really, really needed a cigarette.

After a long workday, the sanctuary of his home loomed ahead. Two people sat on the front steps. He recognized the caramel glow of his sister-in-law's hair and a towheaded Tyler, whose nose was buried in a comic book.

Kelly looked up and smiled as Noah approached. "Sorry to drop in like this."

Her smile was tentative, laced with a trace of sadness. Noah didn't let on that he knew anything about her troubles. "It's all right. Hey, buddy." He ruffled his nephew's hair, but he only got a muffled, unintelligible response.

Kelly stood and walked a few paces away from her son. Noah suspected she wanted to say something she didn't want Tyler to hear, so he followed her. "Is everything okay?"

"Yes," she said with a bright smile he guessed was more for saving face. "Would it be all right if he stayed with you for about an hour and a half? I forgot Brody scheduled a counseling session tonight."

"He can stay here as long as he likes." He glanced at his nephew and saw the boy wasn't paying attention to their conversation. "He's a blast to have around."

"You're a lifesaver, Noah. Usually he goes to his friend's house, but..." She shrugged, breaking eye contact with him.

"I understand, Kelly. Take as long as you need."

She placed a kiss on top of Tyler's head, promised to return soon, and then left. The boy remained quiet while reading his comic book.

What went on in the mind of a seven-year-old? Did the child have any idea what his parents were going through? Brody said Tyler had been quiet and acting differently lately. Noah probably could've walked away, left Tyler sitting by himself, and the boy wouldn't have noticed.

"You want to come inside and see if we can scrounge up something to eat?"

Tyler shrugged and flipped the page of his comic. "I'm not really that hungry." He looked at Noah. "Can I make a root beer float?"

"Uh...I don't have any root beer or ice cream, but I do have Otter Pops."

The boy chewed his lip and looked at his feet. "Do you have grape? That's my favorite."

"Lucky for you I don't like grape, so I've got plenty."

Tyler looked up, and Noah gave him an encouraging smile.

The boy shuffled his feet as he followed Noah inside.

They settled at the table, Tyler with his Otter Pop, Noah with his plate of leftovers. Tyler barely took his eyes off his reading material long enough to suck the frozen grape treat. Noah didn't think Tyler seemed any different, except maybe he was a little quieter than usual, as Brody had said. He did wonder why Kelly had left her son looking so disheveled, with his unruly blond hair going in every direction. That wasn't like her.

He twirled some chow mien around his fork and paused before eating. "What're you reading?"

"Wolverine vs. Sabretooth. Wolverine is my favorite of all the X-Men."

Noah leaned his elbows on the table. "I always thought Nightcrawler was kind of cool."

Tyler set his book down and stared at him, wide-eyed. "Wolverine is way better than Nightcrawler. He has claws that come out of his hands and can heal himself. He can kill anybody. He's even better than Professor X."

"Are you kidding? Professor X was their leader. He was better than anyone."

"Not Wolverine." The boy's attention turned back to the comic. He sucked out the last of the grape Otter Pop, then laid the empty wrapper on the table. Noah scowled at the top of Tyler's head while he scooped up the last of his dinner. He wanted to keep him talking, to take his mind off the troubles of his parents, if he was even aware of them. The boy needed a distraction. He didn't want to leave Tyler sitting at the table all night, reading about the adventures of the X-Men.

He finished the last of his dinner and put the dish in the sink. "Are you a fan of Spider-Man?" he asked Tyler as he leaned against the counter.

"Spider-Man?" The light returned to his nephew's eyes. "He's my all-time favorite superhero, but he's the only one I don't have."

"I have some old Spider-Man issues if you want to see them."

"Really? My dad gave all his away, so I never got to read them." The comic book now lay closed on the table, and Tyler shifted in his seat.

As a child, Noah collected comic books but left the rare ones in the plastic to preserve them. He'd held on to them all these years with the intention of selling them or maybe saving them for his own kids one day. As of now, all they'd done was remain useless in a box on a shelf at the top of his closet. After seeing the look of anticipation on his nephew's face, he was glad he still had them.

"Come on; I'll go dig them out for you."

He led Tyler to his closet and took the big, brown box off the top shelf. When he opened it, his nephew's eyes widened again. The issue on top was still in its original plastic.

"Spider-Man and Wolverine together?" Tyler's eyes expanded, and he bounced in place. "Cool. Can I see it?"

"Help yourself. You can read it if you want."

The boy looked at Noah, his mouth hanging open. "But it's still all wrapped."

"You can take the plastic off." Tyler hesitated, so Noah took the comic out of the box and handed it to him. "Here. You'll get more use out of it than I will."

"I didn't know Wolverine and Spider-Man fought with each other."

"They also fought against each other, but I don't have any of those issues. These were hard to find." Noah opened the plastic for Tyler and handed the book back to him. Noah watched with amusement as Tyler's eyes quickly skimmed one page, then moved onto the next until he had checked out the entire book.

"Are you sure you don't mind if I read this?"

Noah dug through the box and pulled out some more books. "You can have them."

"All of them?" Tyler repeated in a soft voice. "I can't wait to show Dad."

Brody had already seen the comic books, when they were kids, but Noah didn't have the heart to tell Tyler.

"Whoa... You have Punisher? My dad told me some stories about him, but I never read any of the books."

The Punisher was one of Noah's favorites. He took a

handful of them out of the box. The pages were worn and tattered from so many readings. He had no reason to keep them. "You can have those too if you want."

"Cool. Thanks, Uncle Noah." Tyler took them and glanced at the various covers.

"No problem. Just don't tell your mom I gave you an Otter Pop before dinner."

His nephew giggled. "Okay. I don't think she'd notice anyway."

His voiced had dropped an octave, and his attention was still on the Punisher. Noah stared at the top of his head a moment and realized Tyler was more aware of the problems going on at home than his parents gave him credit for. "What makes you think that?"

He lifted his thin shoulders. "I dunno. She doesn't really cook that much anymore. She says if Dad's hungry, he can make his own food."

Noah didn't know much about what went on with them, so he wasn't going to judge whether Kelly should cook dinner.

"Does your mom cook dinner for you?"

"Usually just mac and cheese or maybe a sandwich."

Noah shifted his position on the floor to get more comfortable and moved the empty box out of the way. "Maybe you could offer to help her."

"But I don't know how to cook." Tyler looked at him with big, glistening green eyes.

"It doesn't matter if you can't cook. Maybe if you offer to help your mom prepare a meal, it might cheer her up or encourage her to cook something. It could be something as small as setting the table. Know what I mean?"

The boy picked at a corner of one of the comics. "Yeah. But my dad's not home that much cause he always works through dinner. It's always just Mom and me. She says she's tired of him never being home for dinner, so she doesn't cook for him anymore."

Why would Kelly vent her frustrations to her son? Didn't she realize saying something like that would only confuse a seven-year-old? He wondered if Brody tried to rectify the issue or explain why he worked dinner hours. Maybe his brother wasn't aware Kelly was saying such things to their son.

"Does not eating as a family bother you?"

Tyler remained silent for so long, Noah thought he was reading the comic page he'd been staring at. Then he lifted his shoulders again. "Sometimes."

"Sometimes? Have you told your dad how you feel?"

"No."

"I bet he would listen if you talked to him." The only response he got was another shrug.

Noah took the movement to mean Tyler wasn't comfortable talking about his parents, and Noah didn't want to push him for fear he'd completely shut down.

Noah let the subject drop and settled Tyler back at the table with his new collection of comics. He wasn't sure whether it was a good idea to broach this matter with his brother. The last thing he wanted to do was meddle in business that wasn't his. But Noah was concerned about his nephew. On the surface, Tyler seemed fine, but fear and confusion, two emotions a little boy shouldn't feel, lurked beneath.

He loved spending time with the boy. But Tyler should be at home, having dinner with his family, instead of sitting at an empty table while his parents went to counseling.

A loud knock on his door drew Noah out of his contemplation. He glanced up as his sister walked in.

As always, a bright smile lit up her face but an extra spark twinkled in her eye this time. A sense of happiness surrounded her that had been missing the last time they'd spoken. With Courtney, one could only guess what new drama had taken place in her life.

A long, black skirt flowed around her legs, and a silky-looking purple shirt hung so far off one shoulder that the neckline almost touched her elbow. The outfit was an odd pairing, but then again, nothing about his sister was normal.

"Noah, your grass needs watering," she announced as if she were a professional landscaper. "Hey, shorty." Tyler gave his aunt an ear-to-ear grin, the kind Noah hadn't seen from him in a while. The child loved his aunt, and the two of them had connected on a level no one else had. Noah suspected it was because they were roughly the same maturity level.

"Whatcha reading?" she asked, settling down at the table, her enormous bag landing heavily on the floor.

"Spider-Man. Uncle Noah gave me all his comic books. Wanna read one?"

"No, I only read *Harper's Bazaar* and *Vogue*."

Tyler scrunched his face in a confused look. "What kind of comics are those?"

"They're not comics, goofball, they're fashion magazines. Want to read one of mine?" She pulled two thick magazines from her bag and dropped them in front of Tyler. Both had breathtaking women on the covers, with their long hair blown back from their faces and flirty smiles.

Tyler gave both a glance then narrowed his eyes. "Those are girly magazines."

Courtney dropped them back in her purse. "What's wrong with that?"

"They're boring. They don't have cool stuff like Spider-Man does."

She stuck her tongue out at Tyler, which he mimicked. The interaction made Noah laugh. "What brings you by?" he asked, taking another chair at the table.

"I was on my way back home, but I wanted to say good-bye and tell you that James and I got back together."

"James..." he contemplated out loud. "Nope, not ringing any bells."

"Don't you remember me telling you about him a few months ago? We broke up because he, quote, needed space?" When he only stared at her, she rolled her eyes. "Noah, don't you pay attention to anything I say?"

One corner of his mouth tilted up. "Most of the time."

"Not funny."

He patted her hand. "So you and this guy got back together?"

"Yes," she continued, watching Tyler. "He realized how much he missed me. Actually he was practically begging me to take him back, which is such an ego booster. Have you ever begged a woman?" She turned the subject so suddenly that he could only blink.

"In what way?" he asked slowly.

"I don't mean like that, you sicko." She slapped his arm. "I mean, have you ever broken up with a woman and then realized you needed her back?"

Once Noah decided to end a relationship, it was usually for good. A few times he remembered getting together with an old girlfriend for one more night, but the feeling had always been mutual. The next morning he'd walk away without feeling any kind of regret that the relationship had ended. Except when Avery decided to call off their affair. That he did regret, which was strange, since they hadn't really started a relationship in the first place.

"No," he answered his sister.

"Hmm." She tapped her bare nail on the wooden table-top. "I was just wondering what could have gone through James's head. Not that it matters now, right? I mean, he was the one who wanted to get back together. I'm over-thinking this as usual. I always overthink." She tapped her fist against the side of her head.

"Your hair looks better like this, by the way." He tried taking her mind off James.

She looked at Noah. "What way? Shorter you mean?" She fingered the ends of her hair.

"No, the natural blond. It looks better than that morbid black you had."

"Black isn't morbid. Besides, the guy who did my hair said the black would make my eyes stand out. Do you think it did?"

His smile widened. "I think the combination made you look like a vampire."

Her hand fell from her hair and thumped down to the table. "That's not a very flattering thing to say, Noah. I think the color looked good. The only reason I decided to go blond again was because James said he preferred me that way."

Hell, at least James had some sense.

"Oh, some woman asked me about you the other day."

Noah's senses went on alert. It couldn't have been Avery. She didn't know what Courtney looked like. "Who?"

"She had two names. One of those cutesy, fifties-type things, like Mary Alice or Mary Sue or some shit." She slapped a hand over her mouth and glanced at Tyler but his seat was empty. The boy had moved to the couch and neither of them had noticed.

"Mary Ellen?" he asked warily. Lord, he hoped not. His old girlfriend was obnoxious and didn't know what "this relationship is over" meant.

Courtney snapped her fingers and pointed to him. "Yeah, that's it."

He sighed. "What did she say?"

"She just asked how you were and if you were seeing anyone. Then she went on and on about what a good time you'd had together, not considering that I may not want to hear about my brother's sex life. Really, Noah, where do you find these women? She didn't seem like your type."

Mary Ellen hadn't been his type. But she'd been damn good in bed and that was all he'd cared about. Noah realized now what a careless ass he'd been in his previous relationships. He only hoped his insensitive ways wouldn't come back to haunt him.

"What'd you tell her?" he asked, hoping his sister had been discreet.

"I told her you missed her terribly and are desperate for make-up sex. And that ending things with her was the biggest mistake you ever made. Then she broke down in tears and sobbed about how the relationship was meant to be and how much she missed you." Courtney picked at a fingernail. "She should be calling you anytime."

Man, he could always count on his little sister to take his mind off whatever troubled him, even if it wasn't in the most conventional way. At times she annoyed him with her rattling stories and short attention span, but she lit up his day and made him laugh.

"You didn't say that, Court."

She shrugged, making her purple blouse slide lower

down her arm. "You're right, I didn't. But you should have seen the look on your face when you said her name. Did the break up not go well?"

He leaned back in his chair and folded his hands behind his head. "Not bad. She just...couldn't accept our fling was over."

"Anyway, I told her you were single but trying to focus on your job. Is that accurate?"

Not really. He *was* trying to focus on his work but not to the point that he didn't want to be with a woman. Just not Mary Ellen. "You did well, thanks."

"I try to use my powers for good." She stood from her chair and picked up her bag. "I gotta jam. See ya, shorty," she called out to Tyler, who was still trying to figure out if Spider-Man and Wolverine were going to defeat Sabretooth.

Noah followed her to the door and opened it. "Be careful driving back."

"I always drive safe. Oh, just an FYI, I've signed up for classes in the fall."

She sashayed down the walk to her car without waiting for a response. The gesture gave her the last word, which was probably her intention. Typical Courtney fashion. He grinned at her backside and gave her a mock salute when she pulled away from the curb.

It seemed there was a light at the end of his sister's tunnel. At least, for now.

ELEVEN

LORD, HELP ME. WHAT HAVE I gotten myself into?

Noah managed to keep second thoughts of horseback riding at bay until Avery stepped out of her car and walked toward him. The sight of her knocked him to his knees as she strode across the gravel in the bright sunshine. For the sake of saving face, he remained composed.

Gone was the typical sophisticated pantsuit. In its place were jeans so straight and crisp that they could have come right out of a starching machine. Noah wondered if she actually ironed them, as that was the only way to achieve such a flawless look on blue jeans. While unnecessary to most people, it was probably one of those things Avery thought essential before getting dressed. He certainly wouldn't put the idea past her.

The dark denim looked stiff yet moved with her slim legs as though the material was actually a part of her skin. The waist rode low on her hips, low enough to give the smallest glimpse of her stomach. Her plain white T-shirt shifted, revealing pale and creamy skin, like a smile peeking at him. The sight made him want to rip her shirt off to see if the rest of her upper body was as silky.

His parents' riding stables were located a few miles away from the main ranch house, on the edge of the property line. Noah had offered to pick Avery up, but again, she insisted on meeting him there. Probably better that way. Arriving in separate cars would make the afternoon feel less formal.

"Sorry if I'm a little late," she announced when she reached him.

Noah had arrived only a few moments ago and, with his attention focused on watching her walk, didn't realize she was ten minutes late. "I haven't been waiting long." *You're worth the wait.* "Did you have a hard time finding the stables?"

Her cheeks colored, bringing out the coppery tones in her hair. "That's why I'm late. I got a little turned around on the way up here."

His parents' land was up in the hills, approximately one hundred acres spread over a lush combination of open fields and dense forest with the occasional stream cutting through the countryside. The land was a day-and-night comparison to the farm he'd grown up on, which had been only about thirty acres, just enough to produce income to raise three boys. His father had purchased the new land shortly after his second marriage.

The barn and stables had a separate access road away from the house as it was farther back on the property. The buildings were hard to find, situated at the edge of the tree line, just on the other side of a hill. Since the stables weren't visible from the road, only a person who knew they were there, or where the road was, would be able to reach them. He gave Avery the best directions he knew and worried about her finding the place. But, as always, she proved to be more resourceful than he gave her credit for.

"Do you have riding gloves?"

She averted her gaze for a moment. "No, but I'm sure I'll be okay without them."

He placed a hand on her lower back and led her to the enormous wooden structure that housed six horses. "That's okay. My stepmom has some that will probably fit you. Trust me; you won't want to ride without them."

Walter, the stable manager, took care of the horses five days a week and was on call the other two days in case of emergency. When he wasn't out riding or mucking out stalls, he could be found in the stables, grooming or feeding the horses. He was fifty-something with a quiet voice and easy disposition. Working so many long hours with the horses kept him in relatively good shape, and his hair was neither white nor blond; it was just pale, kind of like sunshine reflecting off a white wall. The only characteristic that made it easy to guess the man's age was the deep lines etched in his weathered face from so many hours in the sun.

He was good with the horses, talked to them in hushed tones and treated them as if they were his children. Noah had liked Walter from the moment he'd met him, six years ago.

"Walter, this is Avery," Noah said as he and Avery stopped just inside the barn, where Walter pulled out a box of horseshoes.

"Nice to meet you, Walter."

He returned Avery's handshake and gave a quiet nod of hello.

"Did Dad tell you we were riding today?"

Walter nodded. "Stormy Weather and Goldenrod are saddled and ready to go."

"Thanks." Noah shook the man's hand, then gathered his and Avery's riding gloves.

Noah offered to give Avery a hand, but she only shook her head no. He watched with amusement, assuming she would certainly fumble and grunt to seat herself on the saddle. But, again, he underestimated her. She swung herself up on the horse with more grace and coordination than a person who'd ridden only once or twice, as she had told him. He ought to be grateful for the opportunity to keep his hands to himself. Lord only knew what it would have done to him to put his hands on her very fine and firm derriere. The denim pulled tight across her round little tush when she placed her foot in the stirrup. The sight gave him almost as much satisfaction as actually touching her.

They settled up on the horses until they were comfortable. The quarter horses stomped their feet in a restless show of anticipation. Avery leaned forward and stroked Goldenrod's mane, then gave Noah a grand smile. "So, where to?"

"Depends on where you want to go." He tugged on the reins to turn Stormy Weather away from the stable. "There's a path that will take us through the trees. Or we can go straight ahead and down the hill. There's a stream that cuts through one of the fields." He turned his head and realized she'd trotted up beside him. "My father's land is pretty spread out, so we can ride in any direction we want."

She waved a hand in front of her. "I'll let you lead the way."

He nodded. "We can start off slow if you want. Don't

be afraid to ask for a break if you need it. Riding can be pretty hard on the knees if you're not used to it."

A slow grin spread across her flawless face. "Don't feel the need to slow down just for me. I think I can handle anything you have in mind."

Her naughty grin made him feel like he'd missed something. He didn't want to wear her out if this was something she wasn't used to. But he felt she was trying to pull the wool over his eyes.

"If you say so," he said after studying her a moment longer.

The stable disappeared behind them as they took off at a steady trot.

The peaceful, serene setting of the surrounding land drew him in. Even though he hadn't grown up here, he'd always felt more at home in the quiet wilderness than on the small farm. Not that his childhood home had been bad or harbored unpleasant memories, but he'd always felt a strange detachment. He couldn't remember a whole lot of what the house was like before his mother died, only the smells of the home-cooked meals wafting from the kitchen. In the years following her death, however, everything had changed. Not just his father, but Noah himself. He no longer thought of the modest ranch house as a home. The surroundings had faded from everyday life, and Noah had turned into a shell of a young man, only paying attention long enough to make sure his brothers were all right.

The day he graduated from high school, he left for college in Montana, to get out of the house where his mother's ghost wandered. He had no desire to return home. Thankfully he never had to; his father sold the house and bought a town house a few years later, before he met Carol.

He drove past the old house from time to time, on his

way to a job site or out of town. Some young couple had bought it and fixed it up. Noah hardly recognized the place as the same house that had grown far too empty upon the death of Julianne McDermott.

Courtney had made a comment once, not long after he'd met her, that he'd never truly dealt with the death of his mother. He wasn't sure how she could make such an assessment, since Noah hardly ever talked about his mom. But she'd said he'd never taken the time to grieve for the woman and therefore never accepted her passing.

Maybe his stepsister was right. Maybe she wasn't. Hell, he didn't know a whole lot about the grieving process. He only knew his mother was gone, his father had changed, and there was nothing Noah could do about it.

Avery reminded Noah of his mother. She was roughly the same build; a small, petite frame with creamy skin. She reminded him of his mother most when Avery wore her hair down, as she was now. The color, a rich mix of gold and cherrywood, sparkling in the sunlight, was reminiscent of his mother's.

He glanced over as Avery trotted next to him. A small gust of wind whipped strands of hair away from her face. Perhaps that was why he was so drawn to Avery. Not only was her hair similar to his mother's, but their personalities were alike as well. Both were soft-spoken and radiated a gentle air that some women lacked. Julianne McDermott had never said a bad word about anyone and never raised her voice, no matter how much her three boys tempted her. Somehow Noah could envision Avery like that with her children. Their children.

Why the hell do you think things like that, you ass?

Thoughts about his mother always made him turn sentimental, a feeling he wasn't entirely comfortable with.

"This landscape is breathtaking," Avery announced, after long moments of riding in silence. "You must have loved growing up here."

Noah debated whether to correct her and decided to go out on a limb. "I've always loved it here. But I grew up on a ranch closer to town. My dad didn't buy all this until we were grown and out of the house. The only one of my siblings who lived here was Courtney."

"Did you learn to ride here?"

"I learned when I was young. We had two horses to share between all of us, and my dad taught me when I was big enough to get on one."

"Sounds kind of like a farm."

Noah stared into the distance. "I wouldn't really call it a farm. We had a small ranch house on about thirty acres of land. My dad took care of cattle he used to sell at auction." He glanced at her. "That was how we earned our income. It wasn't much, but we did okay, I guess."

Avery looked at the scenery around her. "Looks as if he's doing okay for himself now."

"My dad didn't start to make real money until he opened his first restaurant. That was after I was out of the house."

"How many restaurants does your father own?"

Noah decided not to go into the possibility of a third restaurant. The dispute with his dad was still too fresh in his memory. "Two. The Golden Glove has a more relaxed, family-type atmosphere. We'll go sometime." He immediately regretted the words when they left his mouth. Why was he pushing a relationship with her? Getting close to Avery could only end in disaster. Yet for some reason, he still felt compelled to get to know her better.

If the statement affected her or made her uncomfortable,

she didn't show it. In fact, she looked completely at ease. She looked natural, as though she were born riding. Certainly not like a woman who'd been on a horse only a few times. Her back was ramrod straight, her chin jutted out in confidence, and her hands were relaxed on the reins. With the horse rocking beneath her, Avery's hips swayed with the motion, creating an erotic image he shoved away. But not before he got a good look at the little fantasy his brain conjured.

Inviting her to go horseback riding was a very bad idea.

"Do I hear water?" she asked out of the blue, pulling Noah's thoughts back to reality.

He looked at her and forced his eyes away from her lower extremities. "There are a number of streams around here. Do you want to go see one?"

Her face lit up as though the prospect of seeing a creek was something she'd looked forward to her entire life. "I'd love to."

"We have to go that way." He gestured toward the tree line off in the distance, and Avery took off at a gallop ahead of him.

Noah gave Stormy Weather a nudge with his boot and followed Avery. She was good, regardless of how many times she'd ridden. Either she'd lied about her skill, or riding was something that came naturally to her. He didn't have time to contemplate Avery's experience with horses and whether she was being honest with him. She and Goldenrod disappeared, the tall aspens swallowing them up.

Damn woman. Even an advanced rider could get knocked off their horse by a low branch.

The forest of aspens went on for miles, well beyond the boundaries of his father's land. Only a part of the creek that threaded its way around the skinny white trunks of the trees was accessible to them. Noah had to catch up with her so he could show her which way to go.

He slowed Stormy Weather to a walk. Avery was nowhere to be seen. He thought for a second he heard the foliage crunch under Goldenrod's hooves but then realized the sound came from him. Nothing moved. The petite leaves of the aspens hung immobile on their branches; no furry animals scurried back and forth. The silence was almost eerie, a different sort of calm than found on the prairies. The only sound was water running somewhere in the distance.

The only thing he could do was make his way to the creek and hope she somehow stumbled across it.

After a few moments of meandering through the lush and quiescent woods, he found the stream. He maneuvered Stormy Weather along the bank until he spotted her.

Noah was sure he'd be able to come up with a word later on to describe the sight of her. Right now he was too surprised, or maybe "staggered" was a better word. She looked like some sort of forest goddess, with a beam of sunshine filtering through the trees and illuminating her hair. She'd dismounted and was stroking Goldenrod's nose and cooing softly.

The two of them made quite a pair. The sleek, majestic animal and the dark-haired beauty, bent close to each other, looked like something out of a Herculean fantasy. All she needed was a toga and a harp.

The ground underneath the horse's hooves crunched when Noah approached, and Avery looked up. "I was wondering when you were going to show up. I've been waiting for ages."

He wasn't sure whether he should laugh or shake his

head. The woman just kept surprising him. "That was quite a display of riding."

Her smile faltered slightly as she averted her gaze. "This lady did most of the work." She ran the back of her hand down the horse's nose. "Didn't you, girl?"

"I wasn't sure if you'd find the creek. I was trying to catch you," he said as he dismounted Stormy Weather.

"I just followed the sound of running water. I didn't mean to leave you behind." Her gaze ran down him, in an almost intimate fashion, as he approached.

"Only because you got a head start. I could've smoked you if I wanted."

"So you were just being polite, huh?" Her teasing smile showed she wasn't the least bit offended. So she hadn't meant to leave him in the dust? Noah had the sneaking suspicion she'd planned it and only waited for the perfect opportunity. "This is a beautiful spot," she said after he stared at her for an intense moment. "You certainly can't find anything like this in Denver."

"Haven't you ever been outside of Denver?"

"Except for here, you mean?" she asked as they left the horses to munch on some slight patches of grass. "Yeah, I've been around." Her delicate shoulders lifted as she squatted down and picked up a pebble from the bank of the creek, and then she stood and turned the rock over in her hands. "Denver's not much fun," she mumbled.

Her thin fingers continued to work the rock as though she were trying to shape it a certain way. She seemed to have forgotten he stood right next to her. What went on in that head of hers? There were times when she said things, private things he guessed, as if she were thinking aloud. *Denver's not much fun?* What did that mean?

She tossed the rock, and it cut through the surface of

the water with a *kerplunk*. "Do you believe in nature or nurture?" The question came out of nowhere, and her attention remained fixed on the water.

"In what sense?"

"I mean..." She gestured in front of her, then turned to face him. "Do you think a child is a product of his or her environment?"

Tyler's face, and all the turmoil he was going through at home, immediately popped up in Noah's mind. Would a divorce affect the boy? Noah had no idea if a child was a product of his environment. It wasn't something he spent a whole lot of time dwelling on. He'd lost his mother at a young age and was raised mostly by his father. Did that mean he had issues as a result of that particular environment? Not to his knowledge.

"I think environment does play a factor in how a person turns out. But ultimately, I think a person is responsible for his own life."

"I guess that makes sense." She picked up another rock and tossed it in the water. "Why can't I skip these rocks? They keep falling."

She tossed another one, and it plunked in the water.

"You're not throwing them right. You have to angle your hand to the side." He bent and grabbed a flat rock. "Like this." The rock skipped twice before falling in the water.

Avery stood in silence then gave the action a try for herself. The rock only landed with a loud *plop* like the others. "They hate me."

Noah resisted the urge to laugh.

"Here, let me show you. First, you need to find the right kind of rock." He scuffed his boot along the bank until he found one suitable for skipping. Avery stood patiently along the edge of the water like a little child, waiting instruction from a parent. It was amazing how a woman could go from completely sexy one minute to downright cute the next. She twisted her hands in front of her and watched him approach. "You have to hold the rock like this, between your thumb and index finger."

She took the rock from him as their eyes met for a second. She looked at him as if he wanted to trick her. He felt the hesitation course through her, as though no one on earth could possibly know how to skip a rock over water. She blinked slowly, her long dark lashes sweeping down over her milk-chocolaty eyes. He'd never really taken the time to look deep in her eyes. Even though there wasn't anything spectacular about the color, there was something else that made them intriguing. He could almost see her erecting a wall just beneath the surface, so that if anyone looked in her eyes, they wouldn't be able to see her secrets. Noah wondered what they would look like if she really let herself go and loosened up. What would he see? Would they remain the same rich brown, or would they darken with passion or lighten with laughter?

"Do you want to learn how to throw it or not? Here, try." He shoved his hands in his pockets and took a step back from her.

She glanced down at her hand and positioned the rock the way he'd instructed her. After she let it go, the pebble plopped in the water without skipping. "I suck," she announced.

This time he did laugh. He'd never seen anyone take rock skipping so seriously. "You're not angling your hand in the right direction. Here." He bent and picked up another small, flat rock. "Like this." He came behind her and placed the rock in her hand, as he had showed her before. Only this time he wrapped his hand around hers, so he could show her how to throw it. "You have to move your hand in a side-to-side motion, almost as though you're swinging a tennis racket. If you throw overhand, it'll arch too high and land in the water without skipping."

Her body stiffened when he placed a hand on her waist. He didn't necessarily want the body contact. After all, being this close to her and actually touching her only made him realize how totally hot and sexy she was. Her waist was even smaller than he'd originally thought. When he wrapped his hand around it, his middle finger reached her belly button.

"Move your arm this way." He guided her arm in a back-and-forth motion.

"It feels unnatural. Are you sure this is the right way?"

He chuckled at her uncertainty. "I'm sure. Now when I bring your arm forward, I want you to let go of the rock." When she let go, it skipped once then landed in the water.

Her back was to him so he couldn't see her face, but he knew she was smiling. He felt her body relax against his. He indulged himself and let his hand linger on her hip for a moment longer before stepping back.

"Look at that. They like me after all." She peeked at him over her shoulder.

"See? It's all about how you move your wrist. Try again."

He watched with mild satisfaction, and a whole lot of lust, as she tossed another rock. This time it skipped twice, and Avery let out a gleeful laugh. "You're a pretty good teacher."

"Well, I had a good student. You learn fast. But then again, you've already proved that to me at work."

Avery lifted her shoulders, then took her shoes and

socks off and sat on the bank, dipping her toes in the crisp water. She didn't seem to care that the edges of her jeans grew damp. She'd slipped back into mysterious mode again, but Noah wasn't going to let her stay there for long.

He sat down next to her and started to ask her a question, only she beat him to it. "So what's the deal with Rebecca and your brother?"

"You mean RJ?" he asked, because he knew exactly what she spoke of.

"Yeah." She nodded. "I noticed before when he came into the office there was this thing between them."

"That 'thing' would be sexual tension. My brother is a chronic heartbreaker. I've never seen a relationship of his last longer than two weeks." He picked up a twig and tossed it in the water. "But he's different with Rebecca. She made it clear years ago that she had no interest in dating someone like RJ. So, naturally, he's gone out of his way to annoy her, thinking she'll regret her decision not to jump into bed with him." Noah laughed. "It's actually kind of funny watching the effect she has on him. Rebecca doesn't swoon when RJ enters the room, and that drives him crazy."

"How long have they known each other?"

"Let's see . . . six or seven years now. Carol moved here about a year before she married my father, bringing RJ and Courtney with her."

"What do you mean by 'someone like RJ'?"

Noah shrugged. "As I said before, his relationships don't last. He's never showed any interest in wanting to settle down. Rebecca, on the other hand, is more of a homebody. Plus, she's leaving for medical school in a few months. A relationship just wouldn't work out between the two of them." He glanced at Avery. "But that still doesn't stop RJ from torturing her. Does that answer your question?"

She laughed and rolled the bottoms of her jeans up. "Sounds like a lot of drama."

"It's harmless. I don't know why they just don't sleep together and get it over with. Know what I mean?"

He stared at her for a long while, and she finally looked at him. *So why don't we just sleep together and get it over with? Know what I mean?*

Her expression suggested she'd read his thoughts. Shit, did he say that out loud? Was he that transparent? Noah hadn't always been the type to wear his heart on his sleeve, much like most of the male gender. But something about this woman made him act strangely. When she'd called off their affair, relief had washed over him. But the feeling had also been accompanied by disappointment. He felt a sense of loss that he would never know what it would be like to be with her. He would never know how she felt naked and writhing beneath him. Or sighing out her pleasure or perhaps screaming. Would she be a screamer? Her quiet demeanor told him otherwise, but somehow he wouldn't be too surprised if she turned out to be a tiger in bed.

We can't always have what we want in life.

"So, how come you're the only one of your brothers not working for your father?" The question came out of left field, and it jerked Noah out of uncomfortable thoughts and into . . . more uncomfortable thoughts.

"I never had any desire to work in a restaurant. My passion has always been with building things." Because he'd spent so much of his youth cooking for his brothers was probably why he didn't want a profession where he would be around more food. Noah had never been one to say, "Look what I did!" He'd never thought to draw attention to the fact that he'd assumed role of caregiver after his mother died. Instead, all he wanted to do was distance himself from everything that had to do with his mother's death.

"Your family must be really proud of you. It's not easy to open your own business, much less make it a success."

He wished his dad was proud. "Yeah, they are." The truth was too pathetic.

"That must be nice." Her voice was soft, and there was something in her tone that left him bewildered. She turned her attention away from him and tossed pebbles in the water.

"I'm sure you miss your family. Are you close with your parents?"

"As close as any child is with a parent. Though they didn't really agree with my decision to leave. They supported my decision to get out on my own. I miss my brother the most."

He tried to see her face without falling over in front of her as her attention was still averted away from him. The smallest hint of a smile lit up her face when she mentioned her brother. Her expression was filled with affection and, even though she smiled, her voice almost sounded regretful.

His restraint up until this point had been remarkable given the fact he was with a woman who turned him on simply by existing. No longer able to help himself, he reached out and toyed with a piece of her hair. The strand was silky smooth and had been blowing in the breeze for the better part of their outing. He'd managed to ignore the alluring effect, but he couldn't anymore. He wrapped the strand around his finger and tested its texture against his skin. The feel was similar to silk slipping through a person's fingers, or maybe water cascading over granite. He rubbed his thumb back and forth, feeling hypnotized by something he normally wouldn't have given a second thought.

Her hair slipped from his fingers when she turned and looked at him. Something passed between them when their eyes met. Desire. Need. But also reluctance. Both of them were hesitant to cross that employee-employer boundary. But at the same time, it was as if neither one of them could rest until they tested the waters. Just one time. Just one kiss.

"You're unlike anyone I have ever known, Noah," she whispered.

His gaze dropped to her mouth. It was naked and kissable. "The feeling's mutual."

"I feel something for you, and I'm not sure what to do about it."

He shifted closer. "I have a few suggestions if you're open-minded."

"It would be a terrible idea." She moved closer, and they almost touched.

"If I remember correctly, you were the one who suggested an affair in the first place."

She shook her head. "I don't know what I was thinking. It was a stupid suggestion." Her eyes lowered to his mouth.

"Then why are you breathing so hard?" He slid his hand underneath the curtain of her hair and cupped the back of her head.

"Altitude?"

He smiled when her eyes drooped shut, then opened slowly. "We're not that high up."

Their mouths were almost touching, not quite skimming against each other, but he felt her heat and breath. Her eyes fluttered shut as though she expected him to take the step and mesh their mouths together. He continued to massage the back of her neck until she all but fell against him.

He wasn't sure what he expected. She was timid and reluctant, as if she didn't know what she was doing. Noah knew better than that. Underneath her quiet, reserved façade was a lioness waiting to scratch her way to the surface. Maybe she was waiting for him to give her the green light.

He ran his tongue over the seam of her lips, coaxing her to let him in. *It's okay*, he wanted to say. Noah was almost positive someone had done her wrong in the past. Someone she trusted had let her down.

She parted her lips slightly but didn't invite him in just yet. Her tongue snuck out and touched his and a quick, sharp jolt of fire blasted through him. It wasn't a feeling he was prepared for. Deciding not to wait for her go-ahead, his hand tightened on the back of her head, and he opened his mouth wider. Her groan traveled from deep within her chest and flowed into him.

Never before had he felt so in tune with a woman just from kissing. Noah usually entered physical intimacy with a cool detachment, knowing it was just sex, and neither he nor his partner expected more. The arrangements had worked out nicely until now. He felt far from detached from the woman who molded her lips so beautifully against his. He knew that feeling like this was only going to get him into trouble down the road, but Noah couldn't help himself.

Just as he was about to pull back, thinking if the kissing went on much longer it would turn into something else, Avery placed a hand on his thigh. Her encouraging squeeze made his leg muscles tense and certain other parts of his anatomy come to life.

Finally, she opened her mouth all the way to accommodate him, and he did not hesitate to invading her. She welcomed him with enthusiasm, even grinned against his mouth, as though this was the most fun she'd had in a long time. Noah took the gesture as a compliment and swirled his tongue around hers, loving the way it felt.

She suddenly leaned back, and Noah pulled away, knowing if one of them didn't stop it would soon progress to something she'd probably regret. He saw the question in her eyes but then it was gone, replaced by a hesitant smile. Her tongue darted out and swiped across her lower lip. Noah was tempted to mimic the gesture with his own tongue but decided not to. The action might only encourage something that was better suited for a bedroom. Or maybe a couch. Hell, anything with a flat surface.

They both stood.

"Are you sure you don't want to have that affair?" he found himself asking.

She gazed at him for a moment, then smiled. "Maybe we should, after all."

TWELVE

AVERY STARED OPENMOUTHED AND THOUGHT for sure she must be dreaming. Then she realized the appearance of Peter Hanover at her new home could only be a nightmare. Just when everything had started falling into place, the slimeball had to show his face. Surely he'd contrived the right moment to appear so it would mess up everything she'd worked for. The urge to slam the door in his face was so strong that her fingers actually twitched on the knob.

A temporary solution, she knew. Peter wasn't one to shrug his shoulders and walk away.

He emanated perfection, as usual. Polished and manicured, Peter had always reminded Avery of a Ken doll. Most women might have thought that a good thing. She never did. No one was so flawless, even if he did try to portray a certain look.

Of course, his appearance hadn't changed. He still wore the same chrome-colored gray suits accompanied with his signature power tie. His straw-colored hair, which Avery thought resembled a plastic wig, was stiff with about fifteen pounds of gel. Right now she had the urge to pound his head with a sledgehammer just to see if she could move one strand. Peter always joked that he and Brad Pitt were twins separated at birth. At first, she'd found it funny, at least enough to give him a courtesy laugh. Now she found the sound of his voice irritating, similar to a train whistle at three o'clock in the morning.

"Aren't you going to invite me in?" His voice had a practiced, smooth quality suitable for giving public speeches.

He stepped past her without waiting for an invitation, probably his way of keeping the upper hand. Avery had no choice but to shut the door behind him. She glared at him as he looked around the apartment. His face gave away nothing, but he tilted his head in a small nod, like a father pleased with his child's creation.

She knew better. Peter wasn't any different from her parents. Outside, he pretended to be supportive and even loving. Inside, he was most likely cringing, wondering why she would make such a stupid and wasteful choice with her life. How dare she choose this meager life over him?

Well, she didn't care what they thought anymore.

Peter turned in a circle, his gaze moving up and down before facing her.

"What do you want? Or maybe we should start with how did you find me?" She crossed her arms over her breasts and waited for him to talk his way out of the situation.

He lifted his shoulders under his classically beautiful suit. "I hired an investigator."

Avery told herself to show some surprise, but she couldn't manage even the smallest amount. She didn't understand why she hadn't suspected Peter all along. Now that he told her, she almost wanted to slap herself on the forehead. Hindsight really was twenty-twenty.

"You had me followed," she accused.

"What was I supposed to do? I called several times to reason with you, but you never got back to me. So I did the only other thing I could think of. This is a nice place," he said, without waiting for her reply. "Nice, but small. I think I could fit this entire apartment in my living room. So, now that we have that settled, why don't we talk about when you're coming home?"

"This is my home now." Was it just her, or did she sound like a broken record?

Peter laughed, one of those guffaws people used when they heard a really bad joke and didn't want to be rude. Avery never realized how fake everything about her supposed fiancé was, just like everything else in her former life.

"Avery," he said in a placating tone that made her want to smash a glass over his head. "I know you're upset about what happened, but don't you think this is a little extreme?"

She decided the best way of moving this along was to ignore his comment and get right to the point. "Why don't you just tell my why you're here?"

"I came to bring you back to Denver. Your parents are very worried."

Yeah, they're so worried they ran off to Europe and never call her.

She shook her head and remained in her place by the door. "I'm not going back to Denver. That's sort of what I meant by 'I live here now.'"

"You agreed to marry me, or did you forget?"

She ground her teeth together to hold her patience intact. "I never actually agreed to marry you, Peter. I said I'd think about it, and for some reason, you heard 'yes.'"

He lifted his hands in the air. "What's there to think about?"

A heavy sigh escaped her. "You and my parents bombarded me with your ridiculous idea and expected me to agree. We're talking about the rest of my life." She stared at him but he remained silent. "Why do you want to marry me anyway? We don't love each other."

"How do you know I don't love you, Avery?"

"Peter." His name came out more as a groan. "You follow me, and then show up here uninvited. Please don't add to this by insulting my intelligence. You can't possibly love me."

"Why can't I? Do you think you're unlovable?" He walked over to the mantel and gazed at some of the various photos of Rebecca's family.

She ignored the last comment. "You think you love me? What about the incident I stumbled on that afternoon in your hotel suite?"

He gave her a sidelong glance as though she had spoken in another language. "You were really upset about that? Olivia means nothing to me."

Why did men always think they could get out of being caught cheating by claiming their partner was some meaningless fling? "So you often jump into bed with women who mean nothing to you? I'm going to go out on a limb here and say this Olivia person had no idea I was in the picture."

"None of that really matters now, Avery." His gaze kept moving over the snapshots.

She walked closer to him. "It matters to me. I want to know why you asked me to marry you if you were involved with someone else."

"Olivia and I weren't involved. We had a one-time thing. I broke it off with her when I realized I wanted to be with you."

"Oh, that's why you jumped into bed with her *after* you

proposed to me. That's a surefire way to win a woman's heart."

He turned to her and opened his mouth as if he wanted to say something. Avery had a sneaking suspicion it wasn't to correct her. He was probably going to say he hadn't really been trying to win her heart. He shook his head. "Olivia doesn't matter now. You're the one I want." Placing a hand on her lower back, he guided her across the living room to the hallway. "Now, why don't you pack your things so we can go home?"

She jerked away from him. "No. I'm not going anywhere with you. It's funny how everyone is always wondering what I'm going to do with my life, and when I finally tell them, no one wants to listen."

"There's no need to get upset. If you don't want to live in Denver, we can go somewhere else. We could live here." He glanced at their surroundings.

She closed her eyes and prayed for the man to listen to her. "You're really not hearing what I'm saying. Denver isn't the problem. You are." He drew his eyebrows together, the first reaction he'd given to their conversation. "Listen to what I'm trying to tell you. I don't want to marry you. I didn't want to marry you when you first asked me, and I'll never want to marry you. Now, I'm sorry you drove all this way for nothing, but if you don't mind…" She walked to the door and opened it, gesturing for him to leave. He stood in his perfect suit with his perfect hair and his perfect smile. It was perfectly nauseating. "Look, I've worked a long day, and I just want to go to bed."

He stood his ground. "I'm not leaving here until you agree to marry me."

"Well, then you'll be here a long time, because I'm not marrying you."

"You're making a mistake, Avery." His tone dropped a notch, and he no longer sounded like a smooth public speaker. He sounded almost menacing. She knew he was probably going for seductive and comforting, but the look on his face contradicted his tone. His blue eyes darkened, a shadowy cloud crossing his classic features. She suddenly wished Rebecca were here. "I can provide you with everything you want. You'll never have to work a day in your life again."

"If I wanted that kind of life, I'd move back into my parents' house. I'm happy here." She stared at him while he gave her one last searching look. She stood her ground and lifted her chin, fully prepared to go all night if he wanted.

Without saying another word, he walked past her, and she shut the door behind him. Relief washed over her like a comforting warm blanket, and she sank to the floor.

He seemed to be exactly the same Peter she remembered, but with a hint of something else. He was far more determined this time than he'd been when she'd told him their relationship wasn't going to work. A darker side had come out in him, one he'd carefully kept hidden under his perfect façade. Something had changed in the short time she'd been away.

When she confronted him about finding him in bed with another woman, he'd apologized but hadn't put up much of a fight when she left. Now all of a sudden he was determined to take her home and marry her? The situation wasn't adding up. What had changed his mind?

She stared hard at the door, expecting him to return to drag her kicking and screaming back to Denver. He'd finally left her apartment, but Avery had a feeling it would take much more than that to get him to leave Trouble.

Much to her chagrin, an hour of yoga and a hot bath

couldn't chase away her encounter with Peter. The conversation still lingered like the remnants of a bad dream. Her muscles felt soothingly stretched out from her workout and relaxed from the steamy water. Her mind, however, proved to be a different story. She kept going over the words alongside Peter's appearance and tried to piece together what she'd missed.

She opened the freezer door and eyed Rebecca's Dove bars, thinking something sweet would do the trick. Oh, hell. Ice cream wasn't going to chase away the memory of her twisted ex-fiancé any more than her previous, wasted attempts.

What she needed was a real distraction, something to occupy her mind so she wouldn't feel tempted to think about Peter.

After all she'd done to change her life, she felt as though she'd fallen off the wagon. One conversation, one glimpse, and she'd slipped back into the same person she'd been pre-Trouble. The feeling almost made her sick to her stomach. Disgust for Peter and her parents caused a sour taste in her mouth. But the worst feeling of all was being disgusted with herself.

Sure, she'd told him to leave, had spoken her mind. A smoke screen, she knew, something she showed on the surface so he wouldn't see how weak she felt inside. Avery never considered that she had confidence problems. In fact, in most public interviews she'd given, people always told her what a strong role model she was for little girls. In reality, she felt far from the confident, independent woman people made her out to be. How could she be this make-believe person when she always shrank back to the same ungrateful, unworthy daughter her parents told her she was?

Lord, you're pathetic.

What she needed was someone to talk to. What good did she do herself to keep all this bottled up? She needed someone who understood her situation, who wouldn't judge her feelings.

She spotted her cell phone on the coffee table. She picked it up and dialed Teeny's number. And as earlier, her friend wasn't available.

Avery snorted aloud when she reached Teeny's voice mail. She relayed the events of the evening in a rushed message for her friend.

She placed the phone on the table and thought about calling her mother again. If she told her about Peter, it would only prompt the woman to nag her about moving back home.

See, he still wants to marry you. Don't let this opportunity pass you by.

Avery was sure her mother would say something along those lines, not even considering the man had violated her privacy.

Another weary sigh flowed out of her. She needed to get out of the apartment. Who knew when Rebecca would be home, and all she had were her depressing thoughts.

"Screw it." She traded her cotton pants for a pair of jeans and left her BCBG shirt on. After slipping on her one and only pair of flip-flops, she grabbed her purse and walked out the door.

Noah hadn't planned on ending up at Dave's. He hadn't been there since he first met Avery. But the deafening silence of his home had started to eat away at his nerves. At first, the solitude was the main reason he'd built such a big house far away from civilization. Now he found it repetitive, like an old TV rerun he'd seen time and time again.

In any event, he'd skipped dinner and called Chase, knowing tonight was his brother's night off. They met at the bar and decided a round of pool would be a good way of easing the day's tension. Not to mention Avery's rejection of his dinner invitation. If he couldn't eat with her, he didn't want to eat at all.

Man, he was turning into a regular loser. What happened to the carefree guy who didn't care who he went to bed with? It seemed he'd gotten lost in the shuffle of too many women with too little substance.

Perhaps some family and a bottle of beer could chase away his recent gloomy attitude.

A lively and thick crowd filled the bar, just what he'd been looking for to escape the quiet. Chase, being the good guy he was, hadn't questioned Noah's sudden need to venture to a rarely seen part of town. He took one look at Noah's somber expression and suggested pool.

Now Noah was trying to get rid of his loneliness by smacking around balls and downing a Sam Adams.

"It's your shot."

Noah had been staring off into the crowd for so long he hadn't realized his brother had been trying to get his attention.

He bent and aimed for the 3 ball, sinking it in the corner pocket.

"When the hell did you get so good at pool?" his brother asked, while he waited for Noah to take his next shot.

Another ball dropped in one of the pockets, and he grinned at Chase. "I told you not to challenge me at this game. You've never been able to beat me."

"Get over yourself. I've beaten you before."

Noah snorted and missed his next shot. "Yeah, when I let you win."

"I drove into Casper and checked out the new restaurant site," Chase said while he bent and aimed his cue. "Looks as if it's going to be nice. The location is good."

Noah hadn't thought about his father's new restaurant and wanted to beat his brother for bringing up a touchy subject. He'd come to Dave's to relax and didn't want to think about family problems and rejections.

Noah sank two balls then missed his third. "I'm sure it'll be great. Dad knows how to run a business." To his surprise, his voice came out more neutral than he felt.

Chase stood and leaned on his cue. "That he does. I suggested he give the place to RJ, but he said he had someone else in mind."

Noah hadn't discussed his conversation with his father with anyone else. The encounter wasn't something he wanted to relive, and he definitely didn't want anyone trying to analyze the relationship he had with his father. It was complicated enough without bringing an outside opinion to the mix.

"Why didn't you tell me Dad offered you the job?"

Chase, damn him, had waited for just the right moment to throw the question at him. Not expecting it, Noah let his cue slip, and he missed his shot. He straightened and glared at his brother.

Chase grinned, then laughed. If he couldn't win on sheer skill, he'd win by making sure Noah was too distracted to play well.

"What?" He lifted his hand in the air in a typical I'm-innocent gesture. Noah knew better. Nothing about his younger brother was innocent. But if the man wanted to play dirty, then Noah would take no prisoners. He would play to kill.

"Dad told me you turned it down."

Noah narrowed his gaze when Chase sank one ball

after another. "I have my own business to run. I can't take on a second."

"That's what I told him."

Chase finally missed a shot, and Noah stared at him.

"What? You thought we were all going to gang up on you for not stepping in to the family business? Don't worry; I've got your back. I told him to leave you alone."

Noah leaned his cue against the wall and took a sip of his beer. "You think he will?"

Chase shrugged and waited for Noah to take his turn. "Probably not. It was worth a try."

Both remained silent while Noah chalked his cue and sank three more balls. In the end, Noah came out the winner, just as he'd warned his brother he would. Chase only smiled and suggested another game. Considering Noah was in no mood to go home and be left alone with his thoughts, he agreed.

"Rack 'em," his brother said while he stood aside and sipped his beer and Noah set the balls up for another game. "Why didn't you tell me you talked to Dad?" Chase's attention focused on his cue while he aligned it with the cue ball.

Noah shrugged and watched his brother shoot. "It wasn't a big deal. We talked and decided I wasn't accepting his offer. End of discussion."

Chase straightened and eyed him as if he didn't believe Noah's explanation. He waited for his brother to tell him everything would be okay, as he always did, and that their father only meant well. The lecture never came. Chase drew his gaze down to where he aimed his cue and sank one of the striped balls.

"I appreciate what you're trying to do. But I don't need you to fight my battles."

Chase walked to the other side of the table and lined up his next play. "I wasn't going to. Dad mentioned it. I just wondered why you hadn't told anyone about your conversation."

A retort lay on the tip of his tongue, but he knew they could go all night. Noah didn't think the problems between him and his father were anyone's business, even if his brother was only trying to help. He lifted his shoulders in a noncommittal answer, and Chase sank another ball.

"You want to let me have a shot, or should I step back and let you play by yourself?"

A devious smirk crossed Chase's face, which was always a bad sign. The look was typical of when he was a kid and had done something he wasn't supposed to. "You shouldn't have told me you let me win. Now I'm determined to kick your ass."

Noah couldn't help but laugh. This was exactly what he needed. Chase, being the middle child, had taken on personality traits lacking in Noah and Brody. Noah and his youngest brother were most alike, neither one of them feeling the need to announce to the world what they were feeling. Chase, on the other hand, did the talking for all three of them. He never had a problem speaking his mind and not always in a quiet manner. He prided himself on being the life of the party, and he'd never been afraid of a confrontation.

In fact, that had gotten him in trouble too many times in his youth. On more than one occasion he'd spent nights in county lockup for disturbing the peace or trespassing on private property, just because he couldn't pass up a dare. For a while, Noah's amusement had turned into concern for his brother's future. Too many out-of-control parties and arrests had earned Chase a reputation as the town's hell-raiser.

Then he'd gone away to college and returned a different man. To this day, Noah had no idea what had been responsible for the turn in Chase's life. He'd left town with the plan of partying his college education away, and four years later came back with a degree and a grown-up outlook on life.

Every now and then, Noah caught a glimpse of that rebellious teenager, which no doubt lurked just beneath the surface of his adult persona. But Chase had proven himself a grown man and had earned himself a job as general manager of their father's restaurant.

Noah supposed their different personalities were the main reason they got along so well.

Chase finally missed a shot, and Noah bent to take aim. His cue hit a centimeter off and the ball bounced off the edge and rolled back to the middle of the table.

"Shit," he muttered.

"What was that about always beating me?" his brother taunted as he strolled around to the other side of the table.

"Cocky bastard."

Chase sank two more balls. "I had to learn it from someone."

Noah ignored the comment and gazed around the crowded room. All he saw were the usual suspects who'd made a career of keeping Dave's in business. Mostly truckers, a few bikers, and cattle farmers were the majority of the bar's clientele. There were a few occasions Noah knew of when the police had been dispatched because people were drinking too much. On the whole, however, Dave's had a reputation for being a decent place to unwind after work or to pick up someone.

A woman with dark, curly hair among a group of other young women caught Noah's eye. She was attractive enough, but there was an aggressive quality to her that made her girl-next-door look less appealing. It wasn't her appearance that caught his attention; instead, the way she watched him and Chase set her apart from the other women. Actually, her attention was focused more on his brother. She leaned over, whispered something to her friend, then ran her gaze down Chase's backside as he bent over and aimed his cue.

Only the mayor's niece would wrap a scrap of denim around her voluptuous hips and call herself decently dressed.

"Uh, bro?"

Chase's cue struck a striped ball and it disappeared in the corner pocket. "Yeah?"

"Didn't you say you broke things off with Jessica Reilly?"

"There wasn't really anything to break off. It was just a one-night stand."

Noah remained silent, still watching the young woman.

Chase finally looked at him before he took his next shot. "Why?"

"Because she's coming over here."

Chase sighed and relaxed his grip on the pool stick. "Does she see me?"

She strode toward their pool table with the confidence of a woman who was sure to land her prospective conquest. "She's looking right at you."

The muscles in his jaw ticked as Chase tried to focus on his next shot. He missed, as Noah guessed he would, and stood just as Jessica reached the table.

"Hey, Noah," she greeted, with a smile that could have won her a beauty pageant.

"Hi." He gave a polite tilt of his mouth in return without being too inviting. She was the kind of woman who would jump into bed with any man who had a pulse.

Jessica immediately forgot Noah as she angled her body toward Chase and placed a hand on his forearm. "Hey there, Chase."

His brother reached for his beer and took a sip. He didn't respond to her greeting; he only gave her a tight-lipped smile.

"I've been standin' over there for half an hour waitin' for you to come and buy me a drink. But you've been ignorin' me."

Everyone knew Jessica Reilly hadn't grown up in Trouble. She came from somewhere in the Deep South, like South Carolina or Georgia, and had moved here a few years ago. Her thick Southern accent still dripped from her like hot maple syrup.

Chase swallowed a sip of beer. "That's because I didn't see you."

"Maybe if you'd been lookin' for me, you would have."

"Why would I be looking for you?" He leaned his hip against the table.

Jessica glanced at Noah, and he chalked his cue, pretending not to be interested in their conversation. She focused her attention back to Chase and toyed with one of the buttons on his shirt, as though she was ready to undress him. "I thought we had somethin'."

Chase glanced at her hand, which was busy on his shirt button. Noah thought his brother would reach down to remove her busy work. He didn't. Then he realized what Chase was doing: letting Jessica think she controlled the situation by letting her touch him where she wanted.

"What we had was great sex. I told you I wasn't looking for a relationship."

"I never said I was lookin' for a relationship either." She lowered her gaze and shrugged her bony shoulders. "I thought maybe we could come to a little agreement."

Chase met Noah's gaze across the table, and they shared a grin. So she didn't want a relationship. She wanted to be sex buddies. Every man's dream, right? Apparently not for Chase. Noah raised the beer bottle to his lips and took a sip to keep from laughing.

Chase removed Jessica's hand from his shirt. "I don't think so."

She took a step back and placed a hand on her hip. "Have you turned gay since the last time I saw you?"

"Excuse me?"

"I'm offering you sex without a commitment, and you're turnin' me down?"

Chase exhaled a long breath and leaned on his cue. "Look, Jessica, we had a great time together. But it's not going to happen. I'm sure there are a dozen guys in here that would jump at your offer."

"I don't want a dozen other guys." She took a step closer to him, a territorial move, in Noah's opinion. "I want you."

Chase lifted his shoulders. "Well, you can't have me."

Wrong thing to say, bro.

The transformation was almost instant and incredibly obvious. She went from a down-home, dewy-eyed girl to a tigress sizing up her prey. Her eyes narrowed, and her painted-red lips formed into a thin line.

She took a step closer to him and lowered her voice. "No one tells me what I can and can't have." She looked him up and down. "You just turned down the wrong girl."

She turned away from them, her hips swaying under her sorry excuse for a denim skirt, as if Chase would run after her. Noah almost felt sorry for her. She had a reputation of being a spoiled know-it-all, but she was clearly starved for attention.

Whatever the case, his brother had jumped into bed with a potential problem.

Chase turned back to the pool table and his deep scowl became laughter.

"Of all the women in this town to sleep with." Noah shook his head.

"Shut up." Chase pointed his cue at Noah. "At least I'm not trying to get into the pants of one of my employees."

Well, shit. He had him on that one. Noah decided to play dumb and see how long it lasted. "I don't know what you're talking about."

"Right." Chase sank his last two balls, which left Noah the loser. "Looks as though we both tangled with the wrong women."

Noah wasn't tangled with Avery.

Just keep telling yourself that, you chump.

Even though they didn't have a physical relationship, Noah had a feeling he was more wrapped up in Avery than he wanted to admit. He hadn't quite figured out what exactly seemed to be going on between the two of them. They'd already crossed the intimate line that was generally taboo in an office. But Noah felt the invisible barrier looming closer and closer every time he was around her. Sooner or later they were going to come in contact with it. The question was, would they cross the line when the time came?

"You want to go best of three?"

Noah let Avery affect his thoughts way too much. His brother had been trying to get his attention and, once again, he'd been staring off into the crowd.

"Sure."

Chase pulled the balls out of the pockets and they rolled across the table. "Your turn."

He forced his thoughts to return to the game in front of him and off the woman who'd turned him down for dinner. Tonight was supposed to be therapeutic. All he wanted was a good, old-fashioned game of pool with his brother to take his mind off work, women, and his father. His plan had turned out to be a dismal failure. Not only had he lost the first game, but he couldn't stay focused long enough to listen to what his brother said.

After a fumbling attempt, he finally got the balls racked the proper way. He grabbed his cue and gave his brother a deceiving smile. "Prepare to meet your demise, my friend."

Chase didn't look at him, but he smiled and took a sip of his beer. "I don't think that's going to happen."

"You think you can beat me two games in a row? I've got news for you, brother; you got lucky in that last game."

An ear-to-ear grin lit up Chase's face and Noah realized he was watching someone across the room. "I think I'll be lucky this game too."

"How so?"

Chase chuckled and pointed the top of his beer bottle toward the bar's entrance. Noah followed his line of vision and admitted his brother was right. Just when he'd gotten his thoughts back on track, they veered right back to where he didn't want them, and it took only one look to get the job done.

There was no way he could win a game of pool with Avery Price standing on the other side of the room, looking out of place and lost.

Noah wasn't sure what he expected when he laid eyes on Avery standing by herself like a flower blooming among a field of weeds. Surely déjà vu or even surprise. What he felt wasn't an emotion, but it overpowered anything else she stirred inside him. Strangely enough, it was a sense of being pulled, a weird kind of magnetism that her mind had over his. He wouldn't have been able to take his eyes off her even if someone were to drop a bag of bricks on his head. His brother's voice reached out to him, but Noah didn't hear it. In fact, Chase sounded as if he were calling out to him from across the room.

Avery hadn't moved from her spot. She'd come in through the heavy metal doors and stood at the edge of the bar, her body stiff and uninviting to any guy looking to hit on a beautiful woman. Even though she was gorgeous in her casual T-shirt and jeans, her hair pulled back in a sleek ponytail, her body language said, "Don't even think about it." The classic closed-off, arms-over-the-chest look said she wasn't interested in picking up a bed partner. In fact, he'd ventured to guess she had no idea why she'd come. The move seemed out of character for her. Avery came off as a person who thought long and carefully about every decision she made. In the short time he'd known her, he'd come to the conclusion she didn't do anything on the spur of the moment.

No, she was a planner. She probably had a calendar at home where she scheduled her days' events.

For some reason, he found it endearing in Avery. He would love to watch her in action to see the gears turning in her head, and her eyes lighting up. Sort of like the woman who came to work every day.

The woman who stood by the bar looked like a completely different person. How many sides did Avery Price have?

Her eyes darted back and forth as though she couldn't decide if she wanted to sit at the bar or isolate herself at a table. Finally she made a decision and shoved her way through a crowd of people to order a drink.

"You might want to roll your tongue back in your mouth, chief."

Noah glared at his brother and forced his eyes back to the game in front of him. What Avery did with her time was of no concern to him. She made it a point to distance herself from him. Oh, sure, they talked and spent some time together. But she was keeping herself at arm's length with everyone around her. What she had with him was just a surface relationship. She wanted to get to know people and for people to know her, but not *really* know her. As everything else, she'd planned not to let anyone in too deep. If she didn't let herself get too far, then she couldn't get hurt.

In Noah's opinion, that was no way to live.

"You want to play or stare at her all night?"

"Are you in that much of a hurry to lose?" Noah walked to the other side of the table, so his back was to the room. If he didn't have to look at Avery, he could concentrate on the game.

"Something tells me you won't be winning this round."

Chase, the bastard, spoke right when Noah aimed his cue and his ball bounced inches from the pocket. He had a feeling his brother spoke the truth.

"Nothing going on, my ass. I think you've gone past the point of no return."

"I haven't gone anywhere."

"Oh, you're gone," Chase retorted as he lifted his beer bottle off the side table. "You just don't know it yet."

Even though he remained facing away from Avery, his curiosity bubbled to the surface. Surely the men hanging around had noticed her presence by now. Someone as intriguing as Avery didn't go unnoticed for very long. Would she welcome the company or beat them away with a stick? Or maybe Noah would beat them away with a stick.

"Stop trying to distract me. It's not a very noble way to win a game."

His brother laughed as he finished off his beer and lined up his next shot. "I don't care how I win as long as I win. You've beaten me for too many years. Now you're due for a loss."

"You're an ass."

"And you're a sore loser." Chase punched him in the shoulder and grinned when he sank another ball. "Why don't you put yourself out of your misery and talk to her?"

If she had wanted to spend time with him, she wouldn't have turned down his dinner invitation. Besides, the last thing she probably wanted was her boss hounding her after she'd already told him *no*.

"Or maybe you could beat up that guy who's been hitting on her since she sat down."

Noah finally took his turn, but not before checking out the scene his brother had just described. A tall, thin man with a handlebar mustache leaned toward Avery as though he was going to start whispering sweet nothings in her ear. Noah didn't know him, but he sure did recognize his body language. Mustache Man was looking to take someone home, and not for a cup of hot chocolate either. He angled his body in such a way to shield Avery from the rest of the room.

It was a typical territorial move that Noah himself had used several times in the past. Most times the move worked, making the woman feel as if no other woman existed. Seeing another man use the seductive stance on Avery made Noah want to bare his teeth and growl. Had he been raised a less civilized person, he would have stomped over there and knocked Mr. Bean Pole on his ass.

His attempt to concentrate at winning pool was almost

nonexistent now. He knew his brother had this game in the bag. His only concern was keeping some moderate composure and not coming off as an immature, lovesick fool.

Lovesick? No, he meant lust. How could he possibly love a woman he hardly knew?

His brother's presence by his side jolted his concentration away from Avery. "I'll tell you what. I'll hold him down and you can throw the punches."

"Shut up," Noah growled.

"Is it safe to say you've forfeited this game?"

He looked his brother in the eye and saw the challenge. Noah could never back away from a challenge. "Hell, no. I'm not giving this game up without a fight."

"It won't be much of a fight," Chase muttered just loud enough for Noah to hear. Noah missed another shot.

Oh, who the hell was he kidding? He could try to win the game, telling himself he didn't care what Avery did with her time. But why bother? He knew, just as his brother knew, that he was in way deeper than he wanted to admit. Now he had only one decision to make. Would he go to her or wait for her to come to him?

He stole quick glances in Avery's direction while Chase sank five more balls. The skinny guy had disappeared. Avery sat alone on her barstool, sipping something from a frosted mug. She gripped the glass with both hands, much the way a child would hold a cup, and glanced at the people around her. She tried to blend in. Man, but she had absolutely no idea how much she stuck out in Dave's. Her casual attire was a step down from how she usually dressed for work, but she was still a class above this joint.

Chase cleared his throat, and Noah bent to shoot. Surprisingly, he sank a ball but missed his next shot.

"Don't look now," Chase stated as he aimed his cue. "But Miss I-have-Noah-wrapped-around-my-finger is checking you out."

She was checking him out? Did he dare turn to let her know he saw her? Would she turn tail and run? The Avery he'd first met would walk up to him, bold as brass, and pinch his butt cheek.

He gave in to his original impulse and made no secret of seeking her out, turning and leaning back against the pool table while Chase continued to sink every ball.

The room was so crowded, the people constantly moving around, that it took him a few seconds to realize the stool she'd been perched on was empty. He told himself it was for the best that she'd left. Disappointment coursed through him as he watched someone else fill the empty seat.

"Your shot, bro."

Noah scanned the room one more time, with no luck, before he faced the table. Now that she'd left, he could get back to kicking his brother's ass.

He lined up the end of his cue with the 6 ball, taking great care with his aim, thinking there was still a chance he could win the game.

"May I join you?"

THIRTEEN

THE LIGHT, AIRY VOICE CAME out of nowhere right at the exact moment he brought his arm back to make his shot. The cue, instead of hitting the ball dead-on as it should have, barely skimmed the ball, making it roll weakly until it bumped against the edge of the table.

Chase laughed, but Noah was too stunned to pay attention to his brother's ribbing. He straightened, leaned against the table, and his eyes came in contact with the one person he shouldn't be around.

She was supposed to be gone. Who could have guessed Avery would have not only seen him, but walked over to their table? That's what he wanted, though, wasn't it? For the old Avery he first met to come back? Well, now it seemed as though he had her.

He let his eyes roam down her body. In one hand she cradled her frosted glass filled with amber liquid and the other hand was tucked into the front pocket of her faded jeans.

Noah thought she resembled a Calvin Klein ad he'd once seen. The model in the ad had on worn faded jeans and a simple T-shirt. The look was casual but sexy as hell. Some men preferred their women all dolled up with confusing lingerie. Not Noah. A woman with a simple look was more of a turn-on than one wearing garter belts and red lace.

He was really kidding himself now if he thought he was going anywhere without her tonight. She'd sealed their fate when she made the decision to join them.

He had no idea how many seconds ticked by before he realized they were staring at each other. Her gaze left his and slid to Chase, who watched the two of them as if they were about to pounce on each other.

"Noah, did you hear me?"

He let his gaze drop down to her mouth before asking, "You play pool?"

"No, I just wondered if I could watch."

"If you're going to be here, you have to play."

She lifted her hand and rubbed the lobe of her ear. "But I don't know how."

"You've never played pool?" Chase stood at the other side of the table and looked at her with his eyebrows raised.

Her gaze wavered between him and his brother. "Why, is it hard?"

Oh, he would enjoy this. Right away he thought of all the ways he could teach her to play. Bend her over the table, slide his arms around her, and show her how to hold the stick...

Chase must have sensed where his thoughts were going, because his smile widened. "Looks as if I'm going to win another game."

Avery moved away from the table, taking her drink with her, and waited while Noah set the balls up for another game. Funny how every time he turned his back, he got the feeling her eyes were glued to his butt. Served him right for every time he had checked her out.

He tried to catch her in the act, but when he turned she

averted her gaze and made chitchat with his brother. After he got their game prepared, he took aim and scattered the balls. Even though Avery's presence loomed behind him, Noah was determined not to let her affect his game this time.

He sank one solid, then missed his next shot.

Definitely distracted.

Avery sidled up next to him, clutching a cue in one hand. "So what do I do?"

"I sank one of the solids, so you're stripes. Your objective is to get all the stripes in the holes before I sink all my solids."

She spared him a look out of the corner of her eye. "If I can do that, then I beat you?"

He lifted his shoulders. "Pretty much."

"Sounds easy enough." She walked to the other side of the table, and Noah tried not to notice how nice her ass looked in those jeans. "I can shoot at any one I want?"

"Yeah, but you're going to want to take a shot at one that's pretty close to a hole."

Avery's attention was already on one of the striped balls as she licked her lips and readied herself for the shot. Her pose looked as tempting as anything out of a men's magazine. Her back curved in such a way that allowed her butt to stick out and her breasts to just barely graze the top of the table. He was too distracted by her body to notice the way she held the cue.

"She's holding the cue way too high."

Chase's voice came from somewhere close behind him. Noah's tongue was tied in too many knots for him to work out an intelligent response.

The way Avery held the cue, even the way she bent over the table, showed she'd never been anywhere near a pool table in her life. Noah would have gladly helped her out, but he had the feeling she wanted to figure it out for herself, an independent streak he admired.

Fierce resolve graced her beautiful features. Her eyes drilled into the ball in front of her, and her hand gripped the cue so tightly her knuckles turned white. She made such an adorable sight, with the amount of concentration she directed at a game she'd never played. He couldn't help her, even if she'd asked. He was having too much fun watching her.

She pulled the cue back but her angle was wrong. The ball rolled about two inches.

Her eyes lifted to his. "What did I do wrong?" she asked with a sad smile.

He couldn't suppress a grin. "You didn't hit the ball hard enough. Watch how I do it." He studied the table to determine his next best shot and walked around to stand next to her.

After lining up the cue, he glanced up to find her leaning closer than necessary. Her loose neckline made for another tempting distraction. He cleared his throat. "You want to make sure the cue is dead center on the ball. If it's off even a little, the ball won't go where it's supposed to go. Also, you don't want the cue up here, like this." He raised his cue to demonstrate her actions. "It really needs to be level with the ground." He pulled back and the ball he'd been aiming for shot across the table and disappeared in the corner pocket.

Avery's eyes were wide when he looked at her, astonishment on her face. "I don't think I could hit it that hard. My ball would go flying off the table."

"Not if you hold the cue the right way. And it's not about power as much as it is strategy." Her brow wrinkled in confusion. Noah realized if someone had never played pool, they wouldn't understand what he meant.

"Let me show you." He pointed to one of the striped balls. "You see the nine ball?"

He glanced at her, and she nodded.

"That's going to be your best shot because there's nothing obstructing its path. But because the ball isn't directly aligned with the hole, you have to angle your body a certain way."

"My body," she repeated, clearly confused. "Can't I just angle the stick?"

"No, you need to turn your whole body."

When he saw she still didn't understand, as she just stood there, he moved behind her to show her what he meant. "All right, you need to have your body pointing in the direction the ball needs to roll." He wrapped his hands around her hips and turned her so she was angled away from the table. A quick glance showed Chase shaking his head. Putting his hands on Avery was not the brightest idea. He felt her stiffen but she turned in the direction he indicated. The movement caused her hip to bump his and only his incredible restraint prevented him from pulling her fully against him. "So now, when you bend to shoot the ball, it should roll in the right direction."

"Okay." Her voice was soft, borderline husky. The whole room could have evaporated, and he wouldn't have noticed. Man, if she lost it now he would be a goner. He needed her to be strong for the both of them. Just one look and he'd be dragging her back to his house and shoving her onto the bed. Who knew how long it would be before they came up for air?

"Uh, she can't shoot with you standing behind her, bro."

The sound of Chase's voice brought him back to reality, and just in the nick of time. He cleared his throat and stepped to the side. "Sorry."

Avery threw him a grateful glance that he swore held

an undertone of desire that matched the wave of lust coursing through him. So the spark hadn't only touched him. Her delicate hand trembled as she tried to grip the cue, which had his lips curving in a satisfied smile. Nice to know he wasn't the only one affected. Maybe then her game would be as shitty as his had been.

She executed the same little bend as before, with just the slightest arch in her back. The woman had no idea how much of a turn-on she was.

This time, when she lifted her cue, Noah stepped forward to adjust it properly. He nudged the back end down just a bit, and Avery turned her head and gave him a questioning glance.

"The cue was too high," he explained.

Her gaze lingered on his a moment longer.

She took her shot, and the ball rolled in a straight line, but still without enough force, stopping a millimeter from the hole.

"That was good," he said with a nod.

"But I still didn't make it. I suck."

Chase's laughter drifted from where he leaned against the back wall, and Avery smiled.

"You don't suck. Pool takes a lot of practice. But look, you did better than your first turn. You almost made it."

She tilted her head to one side and studied where the ball had stopped. "I guess. I bet you make all your shots."

"Not tonight," his brother chimed in. Noah threw him a glare in an attempt to shut him up. Perhaps he wasn't clear enough with his message, because his brother's grin only got bigger. Maybe he ought to find Jessica Reilly to give Chase a distraction.

He tried with all his willpower to ignore his brother's knowing looks and teasing remarks and focused his attention back on Avery. After he took his next shot, he sank two more balls and purposely missed his third so she could have a turn. If she suspected he did so deliberately, she didn't show it. The only thing he saw was excitement at being able to take another turn. He supposed she expected him to sink ball after ball, and she'd never get a chance to play. He liked to think himself more of a gentleman than that.

"Brody said Tyler's been asking about your ATV lately." Chase's voice came out in a hushed tone.

He and Chase stood aside while Avery walked in circles around the table, trying to find the easiest target. Finally spotting one, she leaned so far over the table that Noah thought she would fall. Luckily, the 13 ball she hit sat close enough that it rolled in.

The look on her face when she straightened reminded Noah of a kid who'd bashed open a piñata. Her eyes sparkled with newfound delight, and her cheeks had a beautiful rosy hue to them. If he didn't know better, he'd say that was a blush creeping into her face.

Beside him Chase clapped, and Noah could only smile, like a proud father. She walked to the end of the table, her smile still lighting up her face. Then, before bending to take aim, she paused, her brow wrinkled. "Did I hear Chase say you have an ATV?"

Noah nodded. "Yeah."

"Hmm." She bent to aim. "I've always wondered if they're as fun as I've heard."

He and Chase exchanged curious glances. "You've never ridden one?" Noah asked.

The confident air once emanating around her faded away as she looked between him and his brother. She remained silent for a moment. "No," she finally said.

"Wait a minute," Noah said, holding up a hand. "Not

only have you never had whiskey or steak sauce, but you've never ridden an ATV?"

"You've never had whiskey?" Chase butted in before Avery had a chance to answer.

Avery only shifted her feet and opened her mouth to answer. Chase, being the gentleman he was, stalked over to the bar to initiate Avery to the many delights of hard liquor. Noah had never seen her drunk, nor did he know what her drinking habits were like. Something told him, however, that one sip of Jack, and he'd have to call her a taxi. Or maybe he'd take her home himself. He liked that idea much better.

When Chase returned, Noah sat back with amusement as she stared wide-eyed at the shot glass. She looked at the amber liquid as if it were some poisonous snake ready to strike. Chase moved the glass closer to her, and he and Noah shared a grin.

"Try it," his brother encouraged.

"I already have a beer." She lifted a hand to where her half-empty frosted mug sat next to Noah's bottle.

"Come on." Chase waved the shot glass in front of her nose. "You haven't really lived until you've had good whiskey."

She took the drink from Chase and turned her attention to Noah. "If I drink this, will you show me your ATV?"

"How about it, Noah? Can she see your ATV?"

Leave it to his sexaholic brother to turn an innocent question into something sexual. Fortunately Avery didn't pick up on the innuendo, because she had no idea how his brother's sick mind worked.

Noah considered her counteroffer and rubbed a hand over his chin. "If you drink that whole thing, I'll drive you over to my house tonight and show you the vehicle myself."

"Ooh, that's a deal I can't really resist."

Noah saw what she meant to do and he moved to stop her but it was too late. She lifted the glass and downed the contents in one big gulp.

Someone who'd never had whiskey before wouldn't possibly have the stomach to consume it that quickly. She coughed, and her face reddened, which wasn't a pretty sight, but Noah thought she was the cutest damn thing he'd ever seen.

He rushed to her and took the shot glass she barely managed to hold on to. "I don't think you can handle more than one of these."

"Don't take the fun away from me now. That was pretty good stuff."

She got two steps toward the bar when Noah placed a hand on her shoulder. "Not so fast. Someone like you needs to take it easy."

"Someone like me?" she asked with raised brows.

"Ah..." He looked to Chase for help, but his brother only shrugged his shoulders. "Someone who doesn't drink very often shouldn't consume too much hard liquor. It could make you really sick."

The suspicious look on her face said she didn't believe his excuse any more than he did. For purely selfish reasons, he wanted her sober. Although she would prove to be entertaining drunk, he didn't want to drag her back home, falling down. He had other plans for tonight.

She quirked one brow and hooked a thumb in the front pocket of her jeans, pulling the waist down far enough for him to get a glimpse of skin. With great restraint, he let his eyes linger for only a moment, but the brief look was enough to show him what he wanted to see. A silky little sliver of stomach Noah imagined dragging his tongue across.

"Maybe you're right."

Noah had no idea what made Avery change her mind, and he was glad he wouldn't have to change it for her.

They finished their game of pool with pleasant conversation and more sexual thoughts, at least on Noah's end. Every time Avery bent over the table or let loose an airy giggle, another piece of his defenses slipped away. The mantra he'd recited over and over about not getting involved with this particular woman was fast losing its power.

The once thick and lively crowd thinned out as most people wound down from an evening out with friends. The other pool tables were empty. A glance at his watch told Noah he'd been at Dave's longer than he'd planned.

"I need to get home. I have to be at work extra-early in the morning." Chase tossed his empty beer bottle in a nearby trash can and slapped Noah on the back. "Don't do anything I wouldn't do." His brother whispered the words so Avery wouldn't hear. Unfortunately, there wasn't a whole lot Chase wouldn't do, so his advice was pretty much useless.

Avery and Noah of them made their way through what was left of the crowd.

"Wait a minute," Avery said once they were outside and Noah unlocked his car door. "We had a deal, remember?"

Oh, he remembered all right. "What deal was that?" He leaned against his SUV.

"Don't pretend like you don't know. You were the one who goaded me."

"I wouldn't really call it goading . . ."

She crossed her arms over her chest, forcing her breasts to mush together. "Well, whatever you want to call it, it was still a deal."

He considered her for a moment, took in her body

language, and wondered if she was doing the hinting thing women were famous for. Noah had never been good with hints, but it seemed pretty clear now what she was getting at. Fate was handing him the opportunity he'd been waiting for. His self-control until this point had been damn near supernatural, considering his history with women. Before him stood a stunning, dark-haired goddess. And all he could think of was the morning after. What if she felt regret? Would their night together affect their work?

Damn, he was thinking like a woman. Maybe he should go search for his balls back at the pool table.

"Do you have something else more important to do?"

Even though she didn't come out and say the words, no man could resist; her question sounded more like a dare.

He let his gaze roam down her body for the umpteenth time and tried to convince himself to say good night and head home. However hard he searched for some plausible excuse, he came up empty-handed. Besides, as Avery reminded him, he was the one who made the deal in the first place. He couldn't have bargained a lunch or something safe and public. No, he had to offer to bring her back to his home. Just the two of them. At night, with nothing else to do.

She stood just a few, safe feet away from him, her stance casual and her head angled as she waited patiently for an answer.

"Oh my gosh." She took a few steps back. "You do have plans tonight, don't you? That's why you're not answering me."

The laugh that burst out of him wasn't meant to confirm Avery's assumption. Her lowered brows and parted lips told him his laughter was anything but comforting.

"Avery, I wouldn't have extended the invitation if I had

some place else to be." He managed to stifle his laughter by the time he spoke, but his smile still lingered.

To prove his point, he opened the car door and stood aside. She eyed him for a moment as though she were about to accept a ride from a questionable stranger.

A quick jitter of nerves passed through him at her silence. He felt exposed, as if stripped of his clothes and on display.

Noah could not remember a time when he'd felt embarrassed. Avery brought foreign feelings out in him. Her gaze had long since left his face and traveled over him as though she were trying to see through his jeans and cotton shirt. Not that he minded. He'd mentally undressed her more times than he could count. He supposed it was only fair that she return the favor.

The silence stretched on for so long that Noah considered just telling her good night. But she moved faster than he could speak. Before he opened his mouth to say anything, she walked to where he held the door open and climbed into the vehicle.

He shut the door with a mixture of surprise and anticipation coursing through him.

He'd come there looking for solitude and was walking away with something entirely different.

Teeny's feet were killing her.

She'd spent many good years molding her size sixes to slip easily into a pair of seven-hundred-dollar designer pumps and endure hours of walking around on stiltlike heels. Sashaying on heels was second nature to her. In fact, her feet were so used to the torture of four-inch spikes, she often felt unnatural in flats. The anguish she subjected her feet to was all part of maintaining a high-society image.

That was before she ended up pregnant.

The dress she had on now worked with a less murderous pair of shoes. Teeny would have done herself an even bigger injustice if she'd let her brand-new pair of Yves Saint Laurent pumps lie unnoticed in her closet. Besides, she'd bought them specifically to go with her white beaded cocktail dress. And every woman knew accessories were just as important as the dress.

When she'd first received the invitation to attend the gala dinner Darren and Priscilla Price were throwing, she'd thought about going with some other evening gown she'd worn a dozen times. Then she saw this knee-length, short-sleeved Oscar de la Renta and decided to splurge on the almost-six-thousand-dollar dress. Under normal circumstances Teeny looked for something half the price, but then she'd thought, *What the hell*. She was pregnant and wouldn't be able to wear things like this much longer. She planned on enjoying her skinny body—what was left of it—while she still could. That, and the fact she knew she couldn't squeeze her expanding waist into any of her size-two dresses.

So splurge she would. For one more evening, she'd continue to hide her condition and her affair from her parents. Although she'd heard that mothers had some weird way of sensing when another woman was pregnant. Keeping that in mind, Teeny managed to stay out of the general vicinity of her mother and father since she'd walked through the door. Thirty minutes had passed. Her mother knew she'd be there, so Teeny would have to announce her presence sooner or later.

A mustached, white-tuxedoed waiter carried a tray of champagne in crystal flutes. They called out to her. It was the second time she'd almost reached out for the bubbly liquid before she remembered not to drink alcohol. She'd had an increasingly difficult time giving up things she enjoyed, like coffee and wine. If it weren't for Landon, the man who'd put her in this position, reminding her of such things, her baby would probably grow a third eyeball.

Get real, Teeny. There's no such thing as third eyeballs.

Not only was she overly paranoid, but also she didn't know squat about kids. She'd never changed a diaper in her life, didn't know anything about calming a crying baby, and her skin crawled at the thought of breastfeeding. Teeny Newberry was what the rest of the country called a trust fund baby. Families of her stature hired nannies and in-home nurses to take care of the dirty work. She'd thought of hiring some help after the baby arrived, but when she mentioned it to Landon, he'd refused. He said he didn't want someone else raising his kid.

She grabbed a flute of sparkling cider from a passing tray and thought Landon was awfully confident for someone who knew as little about kids as she did. But then again, Landon never failed at anything. Everything he touched turned to gold.

Teeny pushed thoughts of babies and third eyes away and glanced around at the immaculately decorated room. The Prices really knew how to throw one hell of a party. Lord only knew how much money they'd spent on this thing. No doubt, whatever the number, it was probably pennies to them.

Darren Price, a publishing mogul, had his hands in almost every aspect of the business. He owned half a dozen magazines, newspapers, two radio stations, and a TV station. In fact, there wasn't a written word out there that wasn't affiliated with Price Publications. Teeny assumed it was boredom with his current profession that compelled Landon and Avery's father to run for governor.

He'd officially announced his candidacy only recently. Priscilla had put together this gala event to honor her husband's newest venture and kick off his campaign.

The decorations were grand. The best food prepared by the best chefs, a string quartet, an endless supply of alcohol, yada yada. It was no different from a million events Teeny had attended. In fact, the only thing these people did was throw parties. Have a baby? Throw a party. Get promoted? Throw a party. Spend seven hundred dollars on a pair of shoes? Hell, throw a party. Spend obscene amounts of money to decorate a big, boxy room, and dance and get smashed.

But, then again, when you had more money than the queen of England, what else was there to do but party?

Not that she was begrudging the Prices a chance to celebrate or not-so-subtly ask people for their support. What they did with their time and money wasn't any of her business. In fact, the only reason she'd accepted the invitation was so her parents wouldn't think anything was amiss. Show up, make her presence known, and slip out before she fell over from exhaustion. That was tonight's plan.

She downed the rest of the cider in one gulp and rolled the glass back and forth between her palms. The party was boring her already. The same mindless chatter, the same fake smiles.

People moved around her, clinking their glasses, air kissing, and talking about their European vacations. Teeny remained by herself, not having any desire to socialize or put on a phony smile and talk about how great things were. She'd read in some magazine that pregnancy caused mood swings and irritability, among other changes that sounded fan-freakin'-tastic.

A waiter walked by with an empty tray, giving Teeny

the opportunity to get rid of her glass. That killed about ten seconds. What the hell was she supposed to do with herself now?

A low rumble in her stomach vibrated through her entire body. Why shouldn't she be hungry? It'd been only an hour since she'd plowed through four slices of pizza. At this rate, she'd be destined to give birth to a thirty-pound baby.

A plate of chocolate-covered strawberries appeared before her like some mystical mirage. Then she realized she wasn't hallucinating. The plate was sitting on top of a hand. She turned and saw Landon, looking supersexy and debonair in his tux.

Her heart gave its usual flutter, as whenever he was near, and she had to take an extradeep breath to steady herself. His sandy-colored hair swept back from his forehead in a windblown style. A teasing grin pulled at the corners of his mouth, accompanied by a gleam in his brown eyes. Teeny was never fully prepared for the impact he always had on her.

"Are you going to eat these or stare at me?"

Teeny blinked to pull herself back to reality. "Sorry," she said on an exhaled breath. The chocolate flaked off the strawberry in big chunks as she bit down and swallowed. She downed the other two just as quickly, not taking the time to keep the chocolate intact, just to get it in her stomach. "Mmm." She swallowed the last bite. "I think I just had a tiny orgasm."

"I knew I was good, but not that good. You're welcome, by the way," he said after dodging a punch to the shoulder.

"Don't stand too close, your mother might see." Landon's parents were just about as uptight as her own. The thought of him having a torrid affair with their friend's daughter wouldn't go over well with dear old Mom and Dad.

Either Landon didn't hear or he wasn't concerned about his parents seeing them in close proximity. The truth was, she felt more worried about being so close to him than she was about Priscilla Price seeing them. Her back brushed against his chest, but she didn't move away, telling herself she wasn't that kind of coward. He didn't touch her, but he didn't have to in order to have an effect. The notion boggled her mind; the effect one man had on her. As though she were free-falling into a bottomless pit and the only thing that awaited her on the bottom was life-altering love. The kind that took a person years and years to get over if it ended.

The thought scared Teeny more than the idea of raising a baby by herself.

"They're not even paying attention. We're at a party, Teeny. You look as though you're being forced to walk over hot coals."

The tip of his finger skimmed the inside of her palm. The featherlike caress wasn't nearly as intimate as some of the things he'd done in bed, but the effect was much more devastating. She pulled her knees tight to keep them from buckling underneath her. Sheer will kept her from closing her eyes and melting into him completely.

Landon Price was a magician at seduction.

"I'm supposed to be here to support my father, and all I can think about is getting you out of this dress."

His breath fanned across the curve of her shoulder and a wave of goose bumps shimmied down to her toes.

She refocused on her surroundings and stepped away from him. "Stop. I don't want your parents to see."

"They're all the way across the room. They have no idea I'm over here."

She turned to face him. "Okay, forget your parents. I

don't want *my* parents to see. They don't know anything about us yet, and I don't want them to find out like this."

"How do you want them to find out? When you show up on their doorstep with a baby?"

She glanced around to make sure the people around them hadn't heard. "Why don't you just announce it on the loudspeaker?"

"Will you relax? No one's listening to our conversation." He took a step closer. "Those strawberries were supposed to relax you, by the way."

He was right. Again. Must be those pregnancy hormones she kept reading about. "I'm sorry. It's just... you don't know what it's like to be the only daughter of two people who are more old-fashioned than Mother Teresa. I've been trying to figure out for the last four months how the hell to tell them their daughter is pregnant and unwed."

"Well, it might be easier if you accepted my proposal."

She threw him a warning look, and he held up his hands in defeat. "All right, I'll stop."

"Thank you for the strawberries. They really hit the spot."

He pinched her chin. This time Teeny managed not to back away from him. "Do I know you, or what? You've been talking about chocolate-covered strawberries all week."

"I have?" she asked with a sheepish grin.

He shrugged. "So I went backstage and grabbed you some."

A smile slipped past her defenses, easing some of her tension. For the moment, she pushed thoughts of parents aside and focused on the man in front of her. His tux hugged him like a glove. Teeny highly resented the fact that he'd slipped into something so simple and still looked as though he'd just left a photo shoot. If they had been the only two in the room, she'd have torn his clothes off and pulled him down on the floor on top of her.

"You're totally gorgeous in that tux. How long do you think before we can leave?"

"You think I look good in this, huh?" One of Landon's thick brows lifted as he turned to the side in case she hadn't seen all of him.

Teeny rolled her eyes toward the ceiling. "Don't let it go to your head. As if you didn't know how hot you are."

"Not that I don't appreciate your enthusiasm for our extracurricular activities," he murmured in a husky voice. "But I can't leave until my father gives his speech. In the meantime"—he snagged another glass of cider for her from a passing waiter—"drink this to cool off."

"How romantic," she replied dryly, but took the glass from him anyway.

Landon's eyes roamed down her body one more time. Teeny saw him move to leave, but he stopped behind her before walking away. "If you're a good girl and wait patiently, I'll find some more strawberries and use them on you later."

Some bubbly cider got caught in her throat, forcing an unattractive cough to burst out of her. She had a witty reply all ready but when she turned, the father of her unborn child had disappeared into the crowd.

Sneaky bastard. He timed that just right to throw her off balance.

The cider churned in her stomach, doing everything except calm her down. If she drank any more, she feared she might turn into one giant air bubble.

She spotted her mother across the room, talking to

some woman. Maybe she ought to bite the bullet and tell her parents about the pregnancy now.

Hi, Mom. You're going to be a grandparent in a few months. Oh, and by the way, I have no plans to marry. See ya.

She burst out a laugh, and a man standing next to her gave her a peculiar look, as if she'd eavesdropped on his conversation. Teeny offered him a polite smile and pushed her way through the crowd.

She needed air—something to take her mind off babies and how sexy Landon looked.

She left behind the confines of the crowded room and escaped to the balcony. The sounds of laughter and music were drowned out by the floor-to-ceiling French doors. Teeny took the opportunity to exhale a giant breath and take in the fresh city air. Well, not so fresh. More like smog mixed with gasoline.

Who the hell needed fresh country air when one could breathe in car fumes?

Focus, Teeny. You're supposed to be out here to clear your head.

Her high heels clacked along the concrete as she walked over to the wrought-iron railing. The banquet room sat fifty stories up, giving the street below a miniature look. Teeny gazed down. The cars crawled along the street in the sluggish traffic as most people this time of night were eager to get home. Hell, so was she.

Right now she'd give anything for a pair of flannel pants and fuzzy slippers. Wait, did she just think flannel? She didn't even own flannel. When had she become so...domesticated? Her silk pajamas were just fine, but for some reason, flannel sounded so much more inviting.

A small cloud of breath unfurled from her mouth as she exhaled a long slow sigh. Teeny hadn't realized how cold she was until the miniature puff shape-shifted then quickly evaporated. Goose bumps rippled along her bare arms and shoulders. Rubbing her hands in a brisk motion did nothing to penetrate the chill seeping down to her bones. Shivers racked her entire body, and she turned to go inside but stopped when she heard two male voices coming from around the corner.

Normally hearing two men talking wouldn't make her stop and listen. However, when she heard Darren Price mutter his daughter's name to Hank Hanover, Peter's father, she stopped cold.

"For Avery..."

Teeny had the advantage of spotting them first and was able to press herself against the wall to remain inconspicuous. All she heard was low murmuring and had unfortunately missed what Darren said about his daughter.

Concern for her friend compelled Teeny to take the tiniest step closer. She stilled her breathing for fear she'd be heard, but her heart thumped louder in her ears.

A momentary silence lingered between the two men, and for a second, she'd thought they'd finished their conversation. Until Hank spoke.

"You have to understand, I'm only concerned about my son's future. His lack of ability to focus on one thing worried me. That's why I counted on the opportunity you'd given him."

"You know the deal we had. It ended when Avery left."

Teeny was by no means a fortune-teller but she already knew where the conversation was headed. She knew Avery's parents weren't the easiest to deal with. Never had she thought a father would sell out his own daughter.

Someone shuffled his feet, and Teeny continued to listen.

"What if Peter persuaded Avery to reconsider his proposal?" Hank asked in a quiet voice.

Darren didn't answer at first, and all she heard were the cars on the street below.

"My daughter won't listen to me or her mother. But if Peter convinced her to move back home, then we'd have something to talk about." Darren's voice rumbled out deeper and smoother than Hank's. No doubt from all those years of public speaking.

"I'm confident in my son's power of persuasion. After all, he's done it before. But Avery's proven tougher to crack than we thought."

Bastards. They were bargaining her friend for their own benefit.

"I'm a man of my word, Hank. If Peter can indeed talk Avery into marrying him, my original offer still stands. But let me make myself clear. The deal is Avery has to marry him, not just say *yes*. It's not over until they exchange their vows."

Acid churned in her stomach. If it weren't for the loyalty to her friend, she'd have abandoned this conversation so she wouldn't have to hear any more.

"Perhaps this will make it more official," Hank said in his higher-pitched, nasal voice.

Damn it. She didn't dare turn her head and risk being seen. All she heard was rustling paper. She had no idea what they were doing or looking at. A contract? Money?

"I'll take this as a down payment." Darren paused. "A very generous down payment."

Money. The two-faced, insensitive jerk-off.

It took all Teeny's womanly willpower to not turn the

corner and scratch both their eyes out. How could a parent do that to his own child?

"Do I have your word?" Hank asked in an expectant voice.

More paper rustled and Darren finally replied, "If Avery will marry Peter, then your son has a spot on my campaign team. And if I win the election, I'll bring him to the governor's mansion with me."

Red-hot fury warmed Teeny's chilled skin. The men's conversation veered away from their children and on to something else. Teeny was too sick with disgust to pay attention, and their voices became muffled.

She had to warn Avery. It was her solemn duty as her best friend to raise the red flag that Mr. Everybody-Loves-Me-I'm-Running-for-Governor was a deceitful snake. No wonder Avery had left town. The antics of Priscilla and Darren Price would test the patience of a saint.

She slipped back toward the door with a stealthlike ability that rivaled a secret agent's. There was no way she could wait to call her friend. She dug her cell phone out of her clutch and noticed she had a new voice mail.

Avery's frantic voice came through the speaker after Teeny dialed for her messages.

"I'm going out of my mind here, Teeny, where are you? I'm thinking again, and you know what a disaster that is. I could really use someone to talk to right now. Peter hired someone to follow me..."

"Shit." Somehow she managed to listen to the rest of the message while power walking through the banquet room to find Landon.

FOURTEEN

WHEN AVERY ENTERED NOAH'S HOUSE, she had a scenario all played out in her head.

In a feverish move, he'd grab her and shove her against the door, taking her in a desperate and lustful manner. The lovemaking would be quick but explosive, igniting her hormones with a brilliant spark that would burn all night long. Afterward, they'd feed each other leftover sweet-and-sour pork, both fumbling around with their chopsticks and then falling into bed. To conclude the night, he'd tuck her under his cool cotton sheets and pull his body flush against hers so their body heat could radiate together.

A foolish fantasy, she knew. But a girl could hope, right? After stepping through the front door, however, Noah flipped all the lights on, and her little dream went out the window.

She told herself not to be disappointed. Just because he didn't rip her clothes off the second they arrived didn't mean they were going to sit around and play chess.

What has gotten into you? Since when do you throw yourself at a man? Have you no dignity? You're supposed to wait for him to make the first move.

The last time Avery went to Noah's house, she hadn't really paid attention to her surroundings. She'd stood in the doorway all of five minutes before deciding she didn't want to go to bed with Noah with his brother hanging around. The short period of time only gave her enough opportunity to see that his house was big.

He moved through the kitchen like a lion prowling his den. Avery stood behind him and took the opportunity to study the way he walked. The vaulted ceiling above them must have stretched to fifteen feet, but somehow Noah's powerful frame filled the entire space. He had his back turned to her as he rummaged around in one of the cupboards, and his wide shoulders made Avery want to tear his shirt off. His hair, normally combed in a relatively neat manner, looked as if someone had ruffled the strands with their fingers. The ends brushed over his collar, curling up like fishing hooks. Avery had the urge to walk behind him and smooth his sun-kissed tresses down with her fingers. Maybe get a good whiff of his scent and let it fill her lungs. She knew from experience how intoxicating it was.

"You want something to drink?" His rumbling voice floated across the expanse of the room and curled around her like seductive little fingers.

She forced out a nervous laugh to cover up the effect he had on her. "I think if I drink any more, it'll start oozing out my pores."

"Yeah, I think I've reached my limit too," he said with a low chuckle. "It's a good thing, because I don't have much of anything here anyway."

The fridge door closed with a soft *thump*. Avery took in the natural wood architecture, fully aware of Noah watching her. Floor-to-ceiling windows on either side of the television encased their wood... perfectly framed paintings. The full m... like a beacon from heaven covering the roll... silver, creamy hue, the kind of night that allowed ... fect vision.

She felt Noah's predatory gaze drilling holes into her like two laser beams. After several anticipatory moments, she turned to face him. He leaned forward with his arms braced on the countertop, looking at her. Avery had the strangest feeling that instead of seeing her, he was picturing something else. Undressing her with his eyes maybe? Planning out the rest of the evening in his head? It was certainly possible, considering the way his wizardlike silver eyes ran over her in a perusing assessment.

Over the years, she'd grown used to the attention men often threw her way. Walking down the street, or at parties, she'd learned to ignore ogling by men of various ages. But more often than not, Avery knew it was dollar signs they saw, instead of the real her. They saw wealth, power, and a famous name instead of a real, flesh-and-blood, breathing person. In the world she grew up in, that perception was often the case. Monetary value was more important than the human being. Over time she'd come to accept it as the norm. Until her recent move to Trouble.

With the way his eyes moved over her face and down her legs, she realized he definitely wasn't seeing her earthly possessions. No, he saw *her*. She felt totally naked, as if she were standing under a giant spotlight. For the first time in her life, she didn't feel like Avery Price, daughter of a well-known billionaire. Instead she was just Avery. Your average girl next door, who grew up riding around in minivans and carpooling to T-ball.

What would it be like to live that kind of life?

"Should we head out back?"

Avery blinked herself out of her foolish thoughts and focused on Noah in the kitchen. "I'm sorry?"

He gestured with his thumb over his shoulder. "Don't you want to see my ATV?"

I would like to see other things of yours...

She gave a quick nod. "Sure."

The temperature outside had dropped significantly. Or maybe the air in Noah's living room had risen to near suffocating. There were no lights outside, just the luminescence of the moon hanging above lit the path before them.

"How much land do you have?" Her voice came out huskier in the chilly night air than she meant it to.

"Ten acres. It's not much, but it's just me living here. I don't need more than that. Just enough to take my toys out." He glanced her way with a smile that gave his features a boyish kind of charm. So the way to this man's heart was through toys, huh? Wasn't that the way with most men? Well, except for her father. The way to his heart was through money.

"How many toys do you have?"

They stopped in front of a large shed Avery hadn't noticed. The moon wasn't bright enough for her to tell what the shed looked like; only that it was the size of a small house and made of metal. "Why don't you take a look for yourself," he told her as he pulled open a heavy door to reveal an inky black interior.

Avery squinted into the darkness and tried to make out the vehicles he'd been talking about. "Is there a light in here? I can't see anything."

"It burned out, and I haven't gotten around to fixing it. I have a flashlight somewhere. My brothers get in here and move stuff around, and I can't find anything." The oppressive darkness of the shed made it impossible for her to see what Noah was doing or even where he stood. All she heard were his footsteps scuffing across the cement floor. A *thud*, like something hitting against wood, resounded out in the quiet followed by a soft, muffled curse. "I'm going to start locking this damn shed." More scuffing and rummaging, then, "Ah, found it."

She'd managed to hold in her laughter while Noah fumbled around in the dark. By the time the brilliant beam of light flicked on, she'd toned her amusement down to a grin.

The ray of light moved around the structure as Noah took a few steps farther inside. He shined the light in her direction, and she noticed his outstretched hand. She glanced at his tanned, calloused fingers before placing her smaller hand in his.

"Watch your step. There's a tire right here."

His warning came just in time for her to maneuver, with his assistance, around the abnormally large tire. Avery had never seen this sort of vehicle in person before—only on TV in advertisements with happy families tearing through dirt and rough countryside. Never in her life had she imagined her family having such...messy fun. Horseback riding and tennis. Those were the things her family did for fun. And yet, she pictured herself on top of this impressive piece of machinery. Not alone, of course. No, Noah would ride in front of her at the wheel, taking control, his powerful muscles straining under his shirt as he steered it over bumps and potholes. The thick veins in his hands pushing to the surface from the sheer force gripping the handlebars. Even better, she imagined herself behind him; straddling his backside and feeling his body vibrate against hers.

When did she develop such a naughty mind?

A tingling sensation in her hand made her realize Noah hadn't released his grip on her. No longer did he just hold it. His index finger stroked the inside of her palm, dragging the nail lightly along the surface of her skin. Avery had never been one for public displays of affection. Not that they were in public. But never had she thought a simple gesture like hand-holding could be so teasing and intimate.

His grip remained firm, yet loose enough for him to move his finger over her skin. A chilly, tingling sensation grew in the base of her arm and meandered its way across her chest and down to the balls of her feet.

Man, if his finger had this much of an effect on her, what would happen if they had full-body contact? She'd probably be reduced to a puddle.

He gave her hand one final squeeze before letting go. "So, you've never ridden one of these?" His voice penetrated the quietness of the shed.

"I've never even been around one. Do you ride it often?" She glanced at him, but his face was cast in shadow.

"Not like I used to. I also have a dirt bike, but I've been too busy these days to take them out." He paused for a moment. "It's kind of sad actually."

"What is?"

He turned to lean his hip against the seat of the ATV. "I didn't grow up with a whole lot. Raising three kids on the income from beef cattle doesn't exactly provide a lavish lifestyle. I guess you could say I bought them to make up for lost time."

Avery studied him for a moment and tried to picture what it would be like to grow up with that kind of life.

No servants, no vacation homes, no private tutors. The kind of lifestyle she'd grown to hate was the same she'd become so dependent on. But wasn't a new and different life the reason for leaving home? Had she already done that or was she merely floating through the daily grind?

She tilted her head and studied Noah more closely. Half his face was in shadow and the other half was illuminated by the flashlight. Being able to see only half his face in the distorted light gave him an almost sinister-sexy look. Like the type of man who might take a woman up against a wall in a dark, damp alley.

The old Avery would have been repulsed at the very idea. The new Avery welcomed it with open arms.

"You had a great childhood," she answered after a moment of mutual assessment.

"I can't imagine growing up any other way. We had meager surroundings, but I wouldn't go back and change anything." He lifted his broad shoulders. "Well, I'd bring my mom back."

Even though Avery had never lost anyone close to her, she felt Noah's pain. The loss of her parents was purely emotional, but she never imagined either one of them dead. And to lose a parent at a young age could only leave a child lonely and confused. Her imagination couldn't conceive the confident Noah who stood before her as a young, grieving kid.

Once again she found herself intrigued by him. By his difference, his mystery, and the pure impact of his presence. Like the first time she met him, Avery felt the pull he had over her.

His gaze dropped down to her mouth, and she took the invitation and leaned toward him. How could she have forgotten how his mouth felt against hers? It hadn't been that long since they'd kissed, but the complications of life and her idiot ex-fiancé had pushed the encounter to a distant memory. Oh, but now it came back full force. The moment his mouth descended on hers she remembered. Would she experience the full thing this time?

Her lips parted lightly under his exploring ones. His tongue was supposed to enter when she invited it to. Instead, he just ran his tongue along her lower lip like he was enjoying some delicious flavor. Avery had never thought lips tasted of anything, but apparently Noah thought hers did.

Someone moaned. She wasn't sure if it had been her or him. The sound seemed to reverberate through both of them, drawing their bodies closer. She grabbed the edge of his leather jacket, squeezing the soft material in her palm. She wanted him to take her. Just kiss her senseless and take her on the cold, hard cement floor. She was tired of waiting, tired of being the polite, high-society lady who never had indiscriminate affairs. Screw self-pride.

All she wanted was hot, down-and-dirty sex to take her mind off what a mess her life was.

To get her message across, she leaned closer to him and inserted one of her legs in between his. Noah hadn't pursued the kiss to anything more than teasing. That all changed when she lifted her knee and brought it in contact with the imposing muscle straining beneath his fly.

One minute he'd been taking his time with her, barely touching, and the next he was all over her. The flashlight clunked to the floor and rolled a few feet. An almost strobe-light effect flashed around them.

She felt so naughty and dirty, clawing a man in a darkened shed, mentally pleading for him to take her. Another moan escaped, and this time she knew it came from her.

Noah pushed himself against her so they touched from chest to feet. His body felt so hard and strong compared to her softer one that Avery pressed herself closer just to feel him.

His hands, once gripping her hips, moved up her body. One slid beneath the curtain of her hair and the other one molded around one breast. The instant his hand came in contact with the sensitive mound, a groan that sounded more like a squeak bubbled up in her throat. His hand increased the pressure, his fingers kneading her A-cup breasts.

Thick, liquid heat pooled between her legs at the way Noah touched her, the way his tongue explored her mouth. The man clearly had experience, which Avery didn't want to think about, but was grateful for. He knew his way around a woman's body. He knew all the right places to press his legs and chest against hers. The right way to grind his hips against hers so she felt only milliseconds away from coming in her jeans. The man was good. Damn good.

The darkness around them was thick and oppressive, yet she felt light on her feet, as if she could climb up his body and become one with him.

His hand loosened from around her neck, and Avery thought their tryst was over.

But we're just getting started!

He surprised her again. His mouth came away from hers long enough to grab her by the rear and place her on a solid surface behind him. *Where had this bench thing come from?*

She didn't have time to consider the layout of his shed as he inserted himself between her open legs. The assault on her mouth started again. She opened her lips eagerly and let his tongue inside to explore.

His leather jacket was way too thick a barrier between their bodies. Eager to feel him more closely, she slid her hands up to his shoulders and peeled the thick material down. She ran her hands all the way down his arms, loving the feel of his tight muscles beneath her fingers, until his jacket hit the floor.

She'd never thought a plain white T-shirt could look so sexy on a man. The soft cotton over hard muscle provided an erotic contrast that Avery had never thought to pay attention to before. As he continued to kiss her, she ran her hands over the contours of his chest, moving the shirt up inch by inch to expose the warm flesh beneath. The moment her fingers came into contact with Noah's skin, he let out a deep groan and tore his mouth away from hers.

"You're getting ahead of me here." His hands dug into her thighs. "If you don't slow down, this is going to end before we get started."

"Sorry, but I can't help myself. I've wanted to get this shirt off you all night." She pushed the T-shirt up until it bunched under his armpits. The muscles on his chest were thick and sculpted, with a light sprinkling of dark hair fanning across them. The sight reminded her of a men's calendar she'd once seen in a bookstore. "Take this all the way off," she urged, while trying to get him to lift his arms.

"As much as I'd like to rip those jeans off and take you right here," he said, molding his hands to her butt and yanking her forward, "I need more room to spread out."

Noah dragged Avery into the house so fast she didn't have time to protest or reconsider what they were about to do.

Not that she would reconsider. Or even protest for that matter. She was an equally enthusiastic participant in this scenario.

Her frenzied fantasy had come to life in spades as her ever-passionate partner kicked the back door shut behind him and stomped through the living room. She hung on with all her 120 pounds, her legs wrapped around his waist. With each step he took, she slid farther down his front, with her pelvis bumping against his.

Hmm, a preview of what's to come?

"Slow down; I'm falling." Her voice came out a touch strangled as she tightened her grip around his neck.

He shifted her position, bringing her higher without even slowing down his pace. "You're not going anywhere until I let you."

Her eyes widened at the retreating living room as he made his way down a never-ending hallway. The only time Avery ever heard Noah use a forceful tone was during phone calls at work. And those had been rare. He was one of the most easygoing and even-tempered men she'd ever met. Boy, was he anything but easygoing now. His voice had a seductive, husky quality to it she'd heard only one other time. His arms, thick and masculine, held her so tightly against his body that she had trouble taking in deep breaths. The position enabled her to feel him, up close and personal. All his hard muscle moving against her as he walked and the way his pelvis bumped against hers threatened to end her good time before it started.

He turned left into a dark room with enormous floor-to-ceiling windows overlooking the hills in the distance.

So, this is the master's domain?

Before she had time get a good look around, he deposited

her on the bed and she landed with a startled squeak. "Is this your room?"

"Yeah. I'll give you the grand tour later." He paused. "Unless you'd prefer to be shown around right now; we can postpone this."

Was he kidding? And put off ripping his shirt over his head to feel his skin against hers? Even if she were in Buckingham Palace, she wouldn't put this off one moment longer.

Standing with his hair in disarray and his white shirt barely fitting across his chest, Noah looked like some modern, dark warrior getting ready to ravish his captive. The moonlight streaming in from the windows cast his face in an eerie, mystical glow. Instead of his gray eyes darkening from the shadows, the moonlight only gave them a predator's glow. Her body quivered and hummed with anticipation.

Avery hadn't had loads of experience in the sex department, as most people assumed she did. Her sex had always been dull and unexciting. Always over much too quickly, before she had a chance to feel anything worthwhile. She had a feeling tonight would be something new for her.

"Are you okay?"

She blinked away her thoughts and looked at the man standing in front of her. He was such a sight. Definitely a prime male specimen, with his wide shoulders, narrow hips, and...bulging parts behind his zipper. *Hello, come to mama*.

"You're not having second thoughts, are you?" he asked after she failed to respond.

She shifted onto her elbows. "I'll be better once you're on top of me."

A slow, sensuous smile turned the corners of his mouth

up and caused a wave of shivers to ripple along her skin. How appreciated and wanted she felt to be stared at the way he stared at her, as though he wanted her clothes to melt away by the mere touch of his gaze.

"Stand up." His command came out so low she thought she might have imagined it.

"You want me to get up? But you're the one who put me here—"

"I changed my mind." He stepped away from the bed to make room for her in front of him.

She had no idea why he could possibly want her to stand, unless he didn't want to do this in the traditional missionary style, which was the only way Avery was used to.

Her legs shook and felt rubbery, but she managed to get to her feet. His face remained expressionless in the moonlight as she stood on feet that felt two sizes too small for her body. She somehow maintained normal breathing even though her heart was about to beat a hole through her chest and blood rushed through her ears. Heat-filled seconds ticked by in a torturous manner as she waited with more patience than she felt. Noah was either planning his next move or was having second thoughts.

He braced his feet apart and crossed his arms over his chest. "Take your shirt off."

Oh Lord, he was going to make her do this the unconventional way. Why couldn't he just tear her clothes off and place her under the covers?

She crossed her arms in front of her, grabbed the hem of her shirt, and slowly peeled it up and over her head. The cool air greeted her exposed skin like an unpleasant burst of wind on a cold day. Why she should be feeling cold in such a heated moment, Avery had no idea. After all, the way Noah watched her could ignite the entire house in flames. Maybe it was because she had never made love with a man in quite this manner before.

She let her shirt fall from her fingertips and drift to the floor by her feet. After a glance down, she noticed her shoes were still on; she toed them off and kicked them out of the way.

Even though Noah's expression remained impassive, she sensed a change in him. Just the slightest bit, but it was there. Avery seriously doubted her unimpressive chest had anything to do with the tension that tightened his jaw muscles. Yet when his eyes dropped down to her black lace–covered breasts, his brows drew together and his gaze darkened as though he'd looked upon a hunk of gold. She let her own gaze move down to her chest, just in case her pathetic assets had magically grown two cup sizes since she'd last checked.

No, still the same boring, no-need-to-look-at-me boobs. How could he be so entranced?

Only by sheer willpower did her arms remain by her side, when she so badly wanted to cover herself. She reached behind her to undo the bra clasp, sure that that's what he'd want next.

"Not yet." His husky, deep voice penetrated the silence surrounding them like a bright light forcing its way through a heavy fog. Avery hardly recognized the gruff tone that escaped his mouth. "Your pants, sweetheart." His words choked off at the end, and he cleared his throat.

"I beg your pardon?"

The muscles in his jaw ticked for the gazillionth time in the last ten minutes. It was actually quite pleasing to know she had this effect on him.

"Take your pants off. Slowly."

Her panties were damp from her impromptu striptease. But it wasn't as if she could help it. Not with the way Noah ordered her to undress and the way his eyes ate up every last inch of bare skin. Just wait until it was her turn.

Her hands moved to the snap of her pants as if controlled by a puppet master. After much struggling, she finally got the bastard unsnapped and the zipper lowered. Had her pants been that hard to fasten when she put them on?

She slipped her thumbs inside the waistband to push them down. Then she paused.

What underwear had she put on? She thought back to that morning and tried to remember which pair she had pulled out of the dresser. Definitely not the leopard print. Normally she wore a matching set, but her black panties to match the bra had gone missing. She was pretty sure she had on the lemon-yellow thong with tiny rhinestone flowers on the front. Satisfied she was presentable in a semisexy fashion, Avery pushed her jeans over her hips, slowly, as instructed. She had to wiggle just the slightest bit to get the skintight denim down to her thighs. Her hips shimmied back and forth in a teasing manner as she struggled to get the material down until it slid to her feet.

Her gaze remained fixed to the floor as she stepped out of her pants and shoved them aside to rest next to her shirt. Call it cowardice, but she felt Noah's burning gaze on her naked flesh and couldn't bring herself to look at him. Clothed was one thing. Naked was an entirely different matter. Well, almost naked, anyway.

She slowly straightened, running her fingers over her stomach in a pathetic attempt to cover herself.

Noah stared at her. "Don't do that."

Her gaze snapped to his face. He'd moved sometime in the last few seconds and now he stood in shadow. The moonlight streaming through the windows gleamed off the sun-bleached tips of his hair, making it look as though he had little flecks of gold on his head. The rest of his face remained relatively hidden in darkness.

Her fingers continued to move over her stomach.

"Don't cover yourself. I want to see you."

"But I can't see you," she complained, trying to make out his features.

"There'll be plenty of time for that. I've waited too long for this for you to cover yourself up. Drop your hands."

It wasn't as if her fingers were covering that much, anyway. What's a little more flesh when they were about to do the deed? Teeny always hated it when Avery referred to sex as "the deed."

And why the hell was she being so shy? She'd never in her life had a confidence problem, and she worked damn hard to keep her body looking trim and fit. She ought to be proud to show it to a man who was more than eager to see her naked. For some reason, being under Noah's scrutiny was similar being under the scrutiny of someone who held her entire future in his hands. As though her whole grand, escape-for-independence plan had prepared her for this one moment.

Her arms hung at her sides as though fifty-pound weights pulled them down by the fingertips. Noah stood stock-still next to the footboard, his body rigid and practically humming with tension. Heat radiated off him in giant, palatable waves and surrounded her in a thick cloud of sexual awareness. By some otherworldly miracle, she remained firmly on her feet, when all she wanted to do was sag into him.

Noah took a step, close enough for him to stand within a fingertip's reach. Avery sucked in an anticipatory breath, waiting for his next request with her heart pounding a loud drumbeat in her ears. Her chest heaved up and down with each shallow breath she took, waiting... waiting...

Then, after eons of silence and heavy breathing, he lifted his arm and traced his index finger over the flesh of her breast, just above the edge of her bra. Back and forth his finger went, over her sensitive, tingling flesh in a featherlike caress. He moved from one breast to the next, giving each one equal attention.

Avery's already heavy eyelids drifted shut. Her head dropped back, almost lopping off onto the floor. Her whole body quivered, itching to be touched more than just a skimming of fingers over her breasts. For some reason, Noah was fascinated with them, rubbing little circles over the swell above her bra. Then his hands floated over her skin to her shoulders, where he pushed her bra straps ever so slowly down until they hung on her arms. Would he ever get her completely naked or just play with her?

Her arms were trapped at her sides, leaving her at his mercy to do as he pleased. Of course he didn't need straps to achieve that. He'd had this power over her for quite some time.

"This is so sexy." His gaze was transfixed on her chest, his hands molding over the bra cups.

He thought her boobs were sexy? When she looked in the mirror, she saw two mediocre, barely there lumps. Nothing like Teeny, whose ample C cups could stop any man in his tracks.

"You think I'm sexy? I always thought I was too small."

"Are you kidding? This is one of the most beautiful sights I've ever seen."

The man had a way with words, making her feel like she was the only woman on the planet. Or was it possible his suave lines were just a ruse to get her into bed? Had he said the same things to other women? More ample women?

Who are you kidding? He doesn't have to say anything to get you into bed, you little slut.

A moment later her bra was undone and fell to the floor. Her breasts, now free of their restraints, were open and free and begging to be touched again. Noah molded both his palms around each breast, kneading and squeezing, and a quick spurt of breath escaped her. Never had any man paid such close, careful attention to her breasts, or any body part, for that matter. Not unless her bank account counted as a body part.

A thousand sensations coursed through her, making her body come alive after so many years of feeling nothing more than a material possession to wealthy men. How could this be happening now? What was it about Noah that made her feel so unlike herself? Or maybe this was the real her, breaking through a plastic shell that had merely existed in a world revolving around Swiss bank accounts and six-hundred-thousand-dollar yachts.

And it had only taken a two-hour drive and one gorgeous man to bring it out. Avery loved Noah for that.

Uh-oh.

Boy was she in trouble now.

Noah's magical fingers moved from her breasts, leaving them abandoned and wanting more, and skimmed down to the edge of her panties. No ripping or yanking of the delicate material happened yet. Just a light teasing along the edge to let her know his intention.

Keep on going…

"Could we speed this along?" she managed to get out.

"Why are you in such a hurry?" Both of Noah's hands were at her hips, toying with the thin elastic covering her skin. Any minute he would push them down and move to the next phase of their night. "Why don't you just relax and enjoy yourself?"

Easy for him to say; he still had his clothes on.

His thumbs finally slipped beneath the edge of the silky fabric. Avery held her breath for no other reason than to keep from passing out and waited with greater restraint than seemed possible. Noah, bless him, had buckets more willpower than she originally gave him credit for.

After her panties landed on the floor, she was truly and completely naked. No covering herself, no hiding behind designer clothes. There she was, flaws and all, open to his scrutiny and assessment. It should have been horrible. Being vulnerable under Noah's gaze should have made her want to crawl under the covers until he closed his eyes.

Instead she felt nothing she'd ever felt before. Beautiful. Not just on the outside but on the inside, as clichéd and corny as that sounded.

Enough of this slo-mo seduction. Time to get down to business.

Avery grabbed fistfuls of Noah's shirt and lifted it over his head in one fluid motion. This time he didn't stop her. His chest, beautifully magnificent and sculpted, practically cried out to be felt. After waiting all night, she traced her fingers over the contours and hard planes of muscle. It was so unlike anything she'd touched before. Hard, yet smooth and soft at the same time. Warm, with light dustings of hair that felt like silk beneath her fingertips. How could something look so masculine and still be heaven to feel?

She couldn't tear her eyes away from where her hands journeyed over his skin. Noah remained still, allowing her to do as she pleased. Everywhere her hands touched, his muscles twitched and tensed.

Her eyes moved to his shoulders, then his arms. There, circling his right bicep, was a tattoo of a thick green python or some other mean-looking snake. The reptile, long and scaly, wrapped around Noah's muscle with its mouth open in a fierce hiss. The snake's forked tongue lashed out between elongated, pointy teeth. On any other man the tattoo would have looked hideous and sinister. On Noah, it was incredibly sexy.

She traced her finger along the serpent, starting at the tail and ending at the curly tongue.

"My brothers and I all got tattoos when we turned eighteen. Sort of a rite of passage."

"I like it," she found herself saying.

"You do? Most women get turned off by it."

How could this man not turn on any woman?

She bit her lip and circled the whole tattoo with her hand. "I think it's sexy."

His gray eyes bore into hers as her hands slowly meandered their way down his flat belly. She trailed her fingers along the taut lines and grooves of his muscles until she reached the edge of his jeans. She teased the way he had, dipping the tip of her index finger beneath the rough material. The skin she found was just as warm and smooth as the rest of him.

His stomach pulled tight as he drew in a harsh breath. Her fingers circled around the button of his fly, suddenly wanting to yank his pants down and see every magnificent inch of him. Avery didn't wait for his invitation. Impatience and going too long without intimacy were driving forces a girl couldn't ignore. Especially when there was a tall, masculine, and entirely-too-good-looking man standing in front of her. Slowly, she lowered the zipper, the metal scraping together to create a grating noise in the quiet night.

She gave him a teasing smile, which he answered with a lift of his brow, and slipped the button through the opening. "Something funny?"

"What? Oh," she said, realizing not only had she smiled, but giggled—like some love-struck teenager. "Nothing's funny."

When had she become so skittish? She could handle men. After all, it wasn't like she was a virgin.

Noah's jeans slid over his hips, not without some difficulty on her part, and eventually made it to the floor. Along the way her fingers brushed the hair-roughened skin of his hard thighs. She loved how they tensed beneath her touch.

When she finally had him naked, Avery realized the sight was well worth the wait. If she thought seeing him clothed turned her on, it was nothing compared to the knee-weakening effect of his nakedness. Ancient Greek sculptures could have been carved from his example.

All lean muscle and hard contours, his wide chest tapered down to narrow hips and thick, powerful thighs. Even his calves turned her on, hard-looking and sprinkled with hair like the rest of him. Forget making love. She wanted to spend all night running her hands over him and exploring all the little grooves and bulging parts. Speaking of bulging parts...

Avery searched her brain for the correct adjective to describe the most impressive sight. Even "impressive" was

a gross understatement. Nestled between his thighs—
no, "nestled" wasn't the right word—the muscle stuck
straight out at a ninety-degree angle, like a lightning rod.
Long and thick, it gave her the sudden urge to lick her
lips. Noah stood still, as he had for most of their time in
the bedroom, while Avery wrapped a hand around him.
Again, he sucked in a breath, this one louder and deeper
than the previous ones. She squeezed, then ran her hand
up his length to the very tip. The tension in his thighs
grew until they looked hard as steel.

"Is this for me?" she asked in the naughtiest voice she
could manage. Just for effect, she squeezed him again.

He groaned and braced a hand on her shoulder. "It's all
for you, if you want it."

If she wanted it? Who would be crazy enough not to
want this?

Instead of telling him, she decided to show him. In
heels she was still about three inches shorter than him.
On flat feet, he practically towered above her. She had to
stand on her toes to reach his mouth. When she did, the
contact was explosive. He responded instantly, shaping
his big hands around her waist and pulling her closer. His
warm skin pressed against hers. She wanted to feel him
all over, climb inside, and become one with him. Their
tongues slid along each other, performing an erotic dance
of heat and desire. She abandoned her efforts between his
legs and sank her hands into his hair. For so long she'd
ached to feel his hair, ached to run her fingers through the
strands, brush them away from his forehead.

She fisted her hands, grabbed chunks of his hair, and
pulled gently. She smiled against his mouth as he gripped
her hips harder and ground them against his. His startling erection turned her smile into a surprised gasp. He

was oh-so-hard and...big. The feel of him caused all the blood to drain from her head and gather between her legs, making her acutely aware of her female parts. He rubbed himself back and forth along her sensitive flesh, all the while kissing the hell out of her. The interaction was so erotic and intimate that Avery felt like her head was going to pop off her shoulders.

Noah moved with her until the softness of the bed-spread brushed against the backs of her knees. The man proved to be incredibly gifted, shifting her around while maintaining contact with her mouth and other iron-hard parts of his.

She pulled her lips away from his. "Not to sound impatient or anything, but can we move this along?"

FIFTEEN

THE CORNERS OF NOAH'S MOUTH tugged in a come-let-me-seduce-you smile. Every way this man moved turned her on. "Am I doing a bad job so far?"

She narrowed her brows. "What?"

"The only reason I can think of that you'd be in this much of a hurry is if you're not satisfied. Are you not satisfied?" he asked in a low voice with just the tiniest hint of a smile.

Was she satisfied? They hadn't even gotten to the good stuff yet, and this already beat any other experience she'd ever had. In fact, the other times weren't even in the same universe.

She grabbed his hand from her waist and put it between her legs, where she was moist and swollen. "Does that feel satisfied to you?"

He rubbed his finger back and forth, sending her hormones into a frenzy. "Well, I won't be satisfied until we're both limp and you're begging me to stop."

Oh, my.

"Well, in that case..."

She took the liberty of placing herself on the bed and

crawled backward until her head lay on the pillows. His scent wafted up from the sheets beneath her, wrapping her in a cocoon of masculinity. This time she gave in to her foolish impulses and turned her head to his pillow. She drew in a deep breath, pulling the delicious aroma that made up Noah McDermott. Manly soap and shampoo gave her a perfect visual of him lying in this big bed, the dark sheets tangled around his legs and barely concealing his nakedness. The image had her smiling to herself again and biting her lip.

"Did you just smell my pillow?"

Busted. Quick, deny it so he doesn't think you're a nutcase.

"Yeah." The word came out before she could stop it. "You always smell so good. I couldn't help myself."

"I smell good?" Instead of crawling on the bed with her, he crossed his arms over his naked chest. "What do I smell like?"

Okay, now he was mocking her. "Just soap and"—she waved a hand in the air—"you know."

One corner of his mouth kicked up. "Soap and you know."

Not only was he mocking her, but also she was naked and totally alone on his bed while he stood and stared at her. She just *had* to go and smell his pillow.

"You know, whatever it is you spray on yourself. That's what smells so good."

He placed one knee on the bed, followed by the other. He crawled toward her, his biceps muscles straining and bunching as he walked on his hands and knees. His gaze never left hers, and she lay there waiting for him to reach her. When he settled his body along hers, their skin touching in all the right places, he lowered his head and whispered in her ear.

"I don't spray. I just"—he inhaled a deep breath next to her ear—"shower and go."

If it had been possible for her to die on the spot, she would have. His weight felt so good, heavy and solid. She squirmed beneath him as he pressed featherlight kisses down her neck and along the curve of her shoulder. Her breasts smashed against his chest, and his hands—the masterful instruments they were—roamed down her torso and gripped her thighs. He brought her legs up until her knees bent and wrapped around his lean hips.

Her breath came in short, rapid bursts. She squeezed her eyes shut tightly, ran her foot along the back of his leg, and lifted her hips so they ground against his. Even though he wasn't inside her, she still needed the contact of all his hardness.

His kisses made their way to her shoulder and then her breast. She lifted her hips again to get her message across, but he didn't cooperate. "Noah," she said in a part sigh, part whine.

He grabbed her hands and pinned them above her head. Now she was at his complete mercy.

His gray eyes stared down into hers. "Do you trust me?"

Oddly enough, she did. She trusted him more than she'd ever trusted anyone in her life. What did that say about her? What did that say about the people she surrounded herself with?

She looked in his enigmatic gray eyes. "I trust you."

He smiled another heart-melting smile. "Then be patient. We have all night."

Easy for him to say; he was the one in control.

He bent his head and continued his assault on her breasts, moving from one to another. Minutes, hours, days, eons—she had no idea how long—went by while he kissed his way down her body and back up again. Her head thrashed back and forth on the pillow, as she tried to keep the rest of her body as still as possible. He wreaked havoc on her with his little kisses, swirls of tongue, nipping of teeth.

Before she could stop herself, she blurted out, "Noah, I have to tell you something." Was she really going to do this now? They were a breath away from making love, and there she lay, ready to spill her guts.

He lifted his head once again. "I know you're not going to tell me you're a lesbian. No one can fake reactions like this."

She laughed despite her sudden apprehension. "I think you already know how attracted I am to you."

"So what is it?"

"I…" His erection brushed up against her thigh, distracting her from her train of thought. "I just needed to tell you…" Her voice trailed off again when she looked Noah in the eye. Never had she known anyone like him. He trusted so easily and accepted her in his life, no questions asked. It made her feel like she was treading on foreign territory, and she had to keep glancing over her shoulder to see if someone was playing a practical joke on her.

She cleared her throat and put up her bravado. *It's like ripping off a Band-Aid. Just tell him who you really are and get it over with.* "I've never done anything like this before. I don't go around throwing myself at men I hardly know."

You're the worst sort of coward, Avery.

"I guess that makes me special," he said with a grin.

"You are." Too special for her.

Noah didn't respond, but something flashed in his gray

eyes, darkening them for a second. He kissed his way back up her body and then, just as she braced herself for his entry, he leaned over and opened the nightstand drawer.

She lifted her head off the pillow. "What're you doing?"

A little silver package appeared between his index and middle finger. "Condom."

"I'm glad one of us is thinking clearly."

"I must be doing a pretty good job if you're not thinking clearly." He tore the package open with his teeth, a very skilled move, in her opinion.

"Do you mind if I do it?" she asked when he lowered his hand to don the protection.

He passed over the rolled-up condom. "Be my guest."

The material felt smooth and slick between her fingers. Avery had never actually touched a condom before; she usually let the man do the work. She pushed Noah onto his back and snuggled up next to his side. His erection stuck straight up toward the ceiling, begging to be touched. She stared at it, in all its rigid perfection, and wondered how a single male organ could have such a dizzying effect on her.

"Are you going to suit me up or stare at me all night?"

"Sorry," she muttered and placed the condom on the tip and rolled the thin rubber down his length. Avery couldn't imagine how wearing rubber could be comfortable. The lacy-thin material suctioned to him like shrink-wrap, barely reaching the bottom, where a thick patch of dark hair surrounded his shaft. She took the liberty of running her fingers back up to the top and reveled in the way his thigh muscles tightened.

She licked her lips in anticipation of him being inside her.

"Is there a reason you're stalling?" A bemused smile pulled at the corners of his mouth, softening his masculine features.

His hands were on her shoulders then, flipping her over onto her back. He nudged her thighs apart with his knee, settling himself for entry.

Here it comes. Just hold your breath, and it won't hurt.

Avery had come to the conclusion the reason sex was more painful than pleasurable was because there was something wrong with her. That maybe she just wasn't good at it. Maybe she was one of those women who would never experience really phenomenal sex.

She still held out a small glimmer of hope that sometime before she died her mind-blowing orgasm would come. Something told her Noah was her chance to experience what so many other women talked about.

"Are you okay?" Noah gazed down at her, his face poised above her like the dark god of sex that he was.

"I'm just a little nervous."

He stroked his thumb down the side of her cheek. "Don't worry; I'll take care of you."

That's what she was afraid of.

One minute he spoke softly to her, and the next he pushed his way inside. Slowly he invaded her, his thickness opening her up, splitting her softness as though he were made to fit there. She waited for the burning, uncomfortable sensation that always stole sexual pleasure from her. To her surprise, the feeling never came. In its place was the most exquisite, dizzying feeling, warming her skin from the top of her head to the bottom of her curled toes.

A moment later, Noah completely filled her. Their bodies meshed, their sweaty skin gliding slickly together while he ground his hips against hers in a slow, gyrating motion that stole her breath.

Noah stilled his movements and pushed himself up on stiff arms. "You're so tight," he said through clenched teeth.

She wrapped her legs tighter around his lean hips. "It's been a while since I've done this." Heat crept to her cheeks that had nothing to do with the pleasure of the man inside her.

"So you're not a virgin?"

His pupils were dilated to almost black but there was a hint of surprise in his voice. Why would he think she'd still be a virgin? Most men assumed she'd screwed any man she came in contact with. Apparently this was how the outside world viewed rich heiresses.

She ran her hands up his biceps, then down his back to grip his buttocks. "You can rest easy, I'm not a virgin."

Noah didn't respond to her comment. Something flashed in his eyes, too quick and dark for Avery to tell what it was or if she should be worried.

He stared at her a moment longer, then lowered himself and moved his hips against hers. She closed her eyes and hung on for the greatest, wildest ride of her life.

When it ended and he lay on top of her, breathing heavily and spent, she knew. She knew if she hadn't been in love with him before, she definitely was now.

A much-welcomed silence filled the house.

No more heavy breathing. No more moans and grunts. No more beautiful feminine voice screaming his name.

For a woman who had limited experience in the sex department, Avery Price knew how to rock a man's world in bed. The first time had been for the record books. Her throaty, begging words and roaming hands had sent him over the edge in about two-point-five seconds.

Over the years, sex had taken on a mechanical, unexciting feel. He'd become more discriminate with his choice of partners than he had been in his twenties. Even though he'd had some incredible sex with some unbelievable women, he'd lost his passion for screwing as if there were no tomorrow. Avery rekindled his enthusiasm.

Not the screwing-any-woman part, but the passion and desire for making love. She'd brought all his long-dead sensations bursting through to the surface. Now he feared they'd never decrease, at least for her.

After the first earth-shattering orgasms, he'd lain back on the passion-heated sheets to catch his breath and let her take the lead. She'd been more than eager, her nimble little fingers tiptoeing across his chest before she straddled his hips.

Noah wasn't sure if the whole thing about multiple orgasms with women was true. But Avery had experienced her fair share of them tonight. At least he thought she had. Noah liked to think he was pretty good at telling if a woman faked it. He'd be willing to bet the farm hers had been real. Not only real, but pretty damn powerful.

He lay on his back staring at the dark ceiling with Avery curled by his side. Her breathing was deep and even, letting him know she was sound asleep.

Satisfying orgasms and a beautiful woman in his arms was as close to heaven as he got. All he needed now was a cigarette.

Her light, warm breath tickled his chest just before she stirred.

"Tell me about your mom." Her words were thick and mumbled from sleep.

His euphoric state disintegrated with her statement. Noah didn't discuss his mother very often. Not only did he not remember much about her, but the memory of his dead mother and the vulnerable children she'd left behind was something he'd pushed away years ago. The faraway look in his father's eyes and Brody's questions about where Mommy went were things he hadn't thought about in a long time.

He forced the tension out of his shoulders. "I don't remember that much about her, to be honest. I was only nine when she died."

"You have to remember something about her. What did she look like?"

Avery's head rested in the crook of his shoulder. Her lithe, soft body lay along his, tempting him to distract her from her line of questioning. He cleared his throat. "She was about five seven with long, curly brown hair." He chuckled. "She had these massive waves that flew around her face as if she'd just stuck her finger in a socket. She wore her hair down all the time. Never pulled it up, never attempted to straighten it. Dad used to always ask her why she didn't just cut it off or go to the salon. But she would smile and say she believed in presenting herself exactly the way God made her."

"Sounds like a noble attribute."

He smiled in the dark. "Mom was pretty religious. She used to make us go to Sunday school when we didn't want to. Especially Chase. He'd put up a fight more than anybody."

Noah remembered his brother, the little towheaded devil. He'd run down the hallway and refuse to put on his church clothes. Their mother, with all the patience of a saint, would tell her son that if he didn't go, God would see to it he couldn't go riding that day. Chase always obeyed in the end, not wanting to disappoint their mother.

Avery leaned on one elbow and looked down at him. "But you never put up a fight, did you? I bet you were a pretty obedient child."

He snorted. "Don't be too sure about that. I had my moments, until my mother threatened to send me to bed without any supper."

"Were you one of those families who all sat around the table and ate together?"

He shifted his gaze from the shadowy ceiling to her face. The full moon cast her classically beautiful features in a cool, milky glow. She resembled a goddess with her pale skin and chocolaty-caramel hair falling over her shoulders and curtaining her face.

"We either ate at the table together, or we didn't eat at all."

Her eyebrows knitted together with confusion. "Your mom cooked for you every night?"

She asked the question as though the idea of a mother cooking for her family was a strange concept. Had Avery never had a home-cooked meal?

"Every night, except when she volunteered at church." He paused to run his finger down her arm. "Didn't your mom cook when you were a kid?"

She lifted her delicate shoulders and the sheet slipped to her waist. "When she was around. Usually it was just me and my brother."

"Were you and your brother left alone a lot?" Noah couldn't imagine parents not around to share a meal with their children. Yet Avery made the statement with the casualness of someone who'd never expected anything more from parents. He thought for a moment that he detected a hint of resentment, but she spoke in such soft tones it was hard to tell for sure.

"We were never completely alone. But my parents were . . . busy people."

He opened his mouth to ask her to elaborate, but she continued. "You know, just doing stuff around the community." She drew circles on his chest with a finger. "Normal parent stuff, I guess. Landon and I understood."

Landon must be her brother. She indicated she'd had a normal childhood, but he suspected that was a well-crafted lie, since she rarely spoke of her family.

"What was your favorite meal your mom used to cook?" she asked before he had a chance to ask her more.

He wrapped a silky strand of her hair around his finger. So soft, like velvet. "No question, chicken and dumplings. I remember walking home from school and being able to smell her cooking from a block away. My mom was one of those women who spent the entire day in the kitchen. And dinner always came with dessert. Peach cobbler was her signature dish."

If Noah closed his eyes and concentrated hard enough, he'd be able to recall the smell of his house right before dinner. As soon as he opened the door after school, the scents of homemade bread or some kind of pie drew him right to the kitchen. He could see his mother's back, her long, unruly hair puffed around her shoulders, as she stood at the stove humming a hymn. Of course, at the time he'd taken the scene for granted and had always run straight to whatever she cooked and tried to sneak a bite. She let him, knowing he'd never leave her alone until he had his taste.

A longing ache settled around his heart as he remembered things about his mother he hadn't allowed himself to think about in a long time. This was why he tried to forget her. It was easier than to deal with the pain her death had left in his life. Would he ever find anything to fill the gap? He'd never thought so. Until he met Avery. She ignited emotions in him he hadn't felt since he was a child. Happiness, contentment, and the desire for a family.

What did all that mean? That he was in love with Avery? He wasn't sure. But what he felt for Avery was pretty close to resembling love.

"You miss her a lot, don't you?"

Her petite hand rested on his chest. His finger slid across the top of her hand, loving the way her body shivered at his touch. He gazed into her luminescent brown eyes. "Have you ever lost anyone close to you?"

Her gaze flickered away from his for a brief moment before settling on a spot below his chin. "Not really, no."

Not really? What kind of answer was that? He didn't want to probe into something so personal, but she was hiding something. Sooner or later he intended to find out what.

"My stepmother is having a birthday party next week. I want you to be my date." The words were out of his mouth before he could stop them. Yet he wanted to show his family this incredible, sensitive woman who made him feel alive again.

She remained quiet for a few seconds, then offered him a tight smile that didn't quite reach her eyes. "I would love to."

Was she reluctant to meet his family because of their working relationship? Or was she afraid to get any closer to him emotionally? Hell, they'd already had sex; he didn't see a problem with her accompanying him to his stepmother's BBQ. And if she felt uncomfortable about it, wouldn't she have said no?

"How long has your father been remarried?" She laid her head back on his shoulder.

He folded one arm behind his head and wrapped the other one around her, resting his hand on her hip. "Let's see," he said. "About six years. He was alone for a long time. He didn't even start dating again until I was a teenager."

"He took your mother's death pretty hard?" Avery's satin-smooth leg brushed along his, sending blood straight to his groin. He took a deep breath, enjoying the contact.

"Yeah. He's never really been the same since." Emotion thickened his voice as he recalled how withdrawn his father had become after his mother passed away. He pulled in another deep breath.

"I bet it made the two of you closer."

"Just the opposite, actually."

She stirred, drawing her arm across his chest and rubbing her knee over his penis. "The two of you don't have a good relationship?"

"We're not exactly close." Not wanting to elaborate any further on the complexities of their father-son relationship, Noah left his answer at that and hoped Avery would accept it.

She didn't.

"How so?" Her bodily pursuit of him stopped as she lifted on one elbow again and gazed at him. He stared at her for so long that she lowered her eyes and toyed with the edge of the sheet. "It's okay. You don't have to talk about it if you don't want to."

He ventured into uncomfortable territory. "He resents me because I don't work for him."

"His restaurants?"

"Yeah."

"He asked you to come and work for him, and you wanted to do your own thing. And now you think he's bitter and holding a grudge against you."

"That's pretty much it." How had she guessed it so easily? Was he that easy to read? Maybe the situation wasn't as complex as he thought.

"Maybe it's not about you."

Her response was unexpected. Most everyone in the family took his side and said his father needed to accept that his oldest son was his own person and needed to get over it and move on. Noah couldn't agree more.

"What do you mean?"

"Well, maybe instead of being angry and resentful, his feelings are hurt."

He mulled over her words and tried to imagine his father being hurt by Noah's career decision. For some reason, he couldn't imagine his father, the big, tough rancher, with hurt feelings. Maybe it was the older man's attitude and curt words whenever they spoke. Maybe it was the way his father refused to acknowledge all the progress Noah had made in his career.

"I don't think so," he finally said.

"Have you ever really talked to him about it?"

"It's not a happy conversation between us," he said, in a drier tone than he intended.

"Well," she paused. "Then how do you know?"

"I just do." Maybe he was being a little immature. But Avery didn't know the first thing about what had gone on between him and his father. He wasn't going to tell her because it was totally pointless. His father wasn't going to change his attitude toward Noah, and Noah wasn't going to change his mind about working in one of the restaurants. They had agreed to disagree years ago and had been living with the bittersweet decision ever since.

"Noah." Avery placed her fingers on his chin, turning his head so he had to look at her. "I don't think you're giving your father enough credit."

Their conversation was treading into dangerous territory. He never should have answered her questions or made her believe he was comfortable talking about his father. He didn't even like to talk about the topic with his brothers; they were more relentless than Avery.

The warmth he felt a moment ago faded away to a stiff, lukewarm feeling, slowly traveling across his body. He knew he'd regret it later, but he untangled his body from hers and got out of bed. Her questioning gaze drilled into his backside like a heat-seeking missile. Well aware he'd left her confused and frustrated, he remained silent while he searched for his jeans.

She didn't say anything, but watched his movements as if trying to send some unspoken message.

"Maybe I should just go," she said in a quiet voice that reached out to him from across the room. And, damn it, she didn't sound confused or frustrated. Just hurt. Now he felt like an ass for shutting her out.

"No, it's okay," he said, pulling on his jeans. "I'm just going to step outside for a cigarette." He went to the nightstand, pulled a cigarette out of the package, and picked up his lighter. "I won't be long. Stay and go to sleep if you want."

He tossed out the invitation as though it he didn't give a rip one way or another. The truth was, he did. He couldn't remember the last time a woman stayed the entire night in his bed. His sexual encounters were usually bang and run. With Avery it was different. He wanted her in his bed the whole night. He wanted to roll over and feel her body next to his, smell her hair next to his pillow. He wanted to wake up in the morning and cook her breakfast, even though he couldn't cook for shit. Maybe just pour her a bowl of cereal or something.

She didn't respond to his invitation to stay the night. Did that mean she planned to leave?

She remained propped on one elbow, staring at him as he flicked his lighter on and off. "You really should quit smoking, you know."

He smiled. "You told me that already."

"Well, it's true." Her voice became firm, not that of the soft woman who'd just spoke to him of family problems.

"I'm working on it. I haven't had one since last night."

She raised her brows. "And?"

"And," he said patiently, "I usually smoke five or six in one day."

A coy little smile crept along her scrumptious mouth, making him want to lean down and take a bite out of its fullness. "That's progress, I guess."

One corner of his mouth kicked up. "You think?"

"I believe in you."

Something inside him tightened and twisted. He had no idea what it was, considering he'd never felt such a profound effect from four little words before. They shouldn't have made him feel like his guts were being ripped out. But they did, especially since no one had spoken them to him before. There'd be no walking away from this relationship, or whatever they had, unscathed. Avery did things to him and affected him in a way no woman ever had. Hell, because of her, he wanted to quit smoking. No woman he'd ever known had been worth giving up his addiction.

Avery made him want to be a better person.

He leaned down to take her mouth with his when something vibrated from across the room.

"I think that's my phone." Avery sat up higher. "It's in the back pocket of my jeans."

It continued to vibrate until Noah was able to retrieve it from her pants. He tossed it over to her after seeing it wasn't a call but just a new message.

Avery scooped it in her hands and touched the screen. After several moments he realized her message must have been a text. Her brows pulled together while she scanned the small screen.

"Anything important?" he couldn't help asking after she'd been silent.

A few beats without an answer went by before she offered him a tight-lipped smile. "It's nothing that can't wait."

Bullshit. Noah was getting pretty damn tired of her secretive ways. Anytime he tried to get closer to her, she pushed him away. What was she so afraid of anyway? What horrible secret did she have? He wanted to think their relationship had progressed enough that she'd be open with him. Especially since he'd told her things, personal things, he didn't normally share with people.

Her body had become tense, like she was suddenly self-conscious about being naked. She pulled the sheet tighter around her and refused to meet his gaze. Something was definitely up, and it involved whatever message she'd just received.

SIXTEEN

A VERY," NOAH STARTED, DETERMINED TO make her include him in her troubles, when a knock sounded from his front door. A heavy sigh escaped him. The bedside clock read eleven fifteen. "Only someone in my family would knock this late."

Avery remained silent in his bed as he grabbed a hooded sweatshirt out of his dresser and walked to the front door. He yanked the heavy wood open, ready to tell whoever it was on the other side to piss off, when he locked gazes with his brother.

Disheveled and burned-out looking, Brody leaned against the door frame with a black duffel bag at his feet. Apparently the marital counseling wasn't going well.

He stepped out onto the porch and shut the door behind him. "Tell me what happened while I smoke."

"I thought you quit." Brody followed Noah to the two wooden rockers. His brother's voice sounded worn out and scratchy, like he'd spent the better part of the night yelling. Brody was one of the calmest people Noah knew. The man hardly ever raised his voice and never got riled about anything, unlike their brother, Chase.

"I'm working on it. I can't just quit cold turkey." He settled into a chair and it creaked under his weight. He inserted the cigarette between his lips, lit the end, and exhaled a puff of smoke. "So, what happened? Kelly kicked you out?"

Brody stretched his long legs out in front of him. "Not exactly. I chose to leave, but the feeling was pretty much mutual."

"What started it?"

"I had to work late and missed our counseling session. I guess that was the last straw. She said I was more committed to work than I was to our marriage." He paused and tipped the chair back. "When I got home two hours after our appointment, she started yelling the second I walked in the door. Then I yelled back, saying I work hard so she can stay home with Tyler. Then she said, 'Maybe I never wanted to stay home; maybe I wanted to work.'" Brody shook his head and sighed. "It just escalated into this huge thing, so I packed a bag and quietly left."

Noah took a puff of his cigarette. "*You* yelled?"

"Believe it or not."

"What about Tyler?"

His brother was silent for a few seconds before answering. "Tyler's at a friend's house tonight and luckily didn't have to hear yet another fight. He's been asking questions, which I try to answer, but he knows what's going on."

Noah's heart went out to his seven-year-old nephew. No child should have to hear a fight between his parents. Although he had to admit his brother's marriage had lasted a lot longer than the rest of the family anticipated. Considering how the two of them got together, it wouldn't have been any surprise if Brody and Kelly had divorced after the birth of their son. They'd always had a pretty amicable marriage, but Noah never sensed a deep and abiding love between the two of them. They got along okay, and both were great parents. He supposed they had done the right thing by marrying, only now maybe it was time the two of them went their separate ways.

He took another drag from his cigarette and expelled a puff of smoke.

"I hope you don't mind me dropping in like this," Brody said after a quiet moment.

"Nah. The guesthouse is yours if you want it." He looked at his brother. "What're you going to do now?"

Brody lifted his shoulders and let them fall in a tired gesture. "Give Kelly a couple of days to cool off. She's pretty pissed."

"Are you going to continue with your counseling?"

"I don't know," his brother said in a quiet voice. "I'll leave that decision up to my wife."

Noah drew in one last puff of smoke, then crushed the cigarette out in the ashtray on the table between the rocking chairs. "Was the counseling even doing you guys any good?"

He could see only his brother's dark profile, so getting a good read of his expression was impossible. His tense shoulders and white-knuckled hands gripping the arms of the chair told Noah that Brody's answer wasn't going to be good.

"It's hard to say. The therapist said we needed to work out our issues at home before things could change. If you asked Kelly, she would probably say no."

"What would you say?"

Brody tipped the rocking chair back. "I don't think it's helping."

The full moon high overhead shone down like a beacon

from heaven and bathed his quiet neighborhood in a soothing, milky glow. While the big cities got bigger and busier, out here, where cowboys and ranches hadn't yet gone extinct, it seemed as though time stood still. He only hoped their little golden valley stayed untouched by the rest of the world while he was still alive.

"Do you love her?" Brody may have thought it a silly question, but for some reason, Noah felt the need to ask.

"I've grown to love her over the years, sure."

"No." Noah stared hard at Brody until he turned his head. "Are you *in* love with her?"

Brody stared at him a moment longer before returning his attention to the street in front of them. He remained silent, tipping back and forth in his rocking chair. But Noah knew what the answer would be before his brother opened his mouth. If he had to think that long and hard about being in love with his own wife then he obviously wasn't.

"She gave me my son, and I'll always be grateful to her for that," his brother replied after a long, tense moment. "She's a good mom and a good wife. But I've never felt a burning desire to be with her forever. If that means I'm not in love with her, then I guess I'm not. What's most important to me is Tyler's happiness." Brody scuffed his shoe along the wooden planks. "I don't think he's happy right now."

"Maybe he just needs to know you're still around. You know what it's like to lose a parent. He's probably really scared."

"He's always been more open with Kelly than with me. Every time I try to talk to him, he clams up and shrugs his shoulders."

A cool burst of wind whipped across the porch, making Noah wish he'd taken the time to put on socks. He rubbed his feet back and forth on the wood in a pathetic attempt to warm them.

"He talked to me when he was here."

Brody threw him a sharp look. "When?"

He probably shouldn't have said anything. Brody felt bad enough as it was. Noah tried to downplay the incident as not being a big deal. "When Kelly dropped him off when you guys had a session. He didn't say that much."

"I'm sure it was more than he's ever told me." Brody's gaze dropped to his lap, and his voice took on a hushed, sad quality. Not having children of his own, Noah couldn't imagine what his brother was going through. He'd never had any intention of repeating his and Tyler's conversation to Brody. But now he felt like he needed to reassure his brother.

He clamped a comforting hand on Brody's shoulder. The muscles were hard and tense. "All he said was that he misses you, and he doesn't like seeing his mom sad all the time."

Okay, so maybe he paraphrased just a bit. No need to tell him all the details. Brody just needed to be reassured that his son still looked up to him and needed him. "Just because he's shutting you out doesn't mean he doesn't love you."

"I know." His brother expelled a heavy breath. "I just feel as if I'm losing him. Like every day that goes by without me and Kelly working this out, he gets farther and farther away."

A dog barked in the distance, the only sound coming from their lonely little town. "I think you're giving him too much credit, Brody. He's only seven. He's probably just confused and scared." He glanced at the other man's profile. "Maybe if you just reiterate that you're not going anywhere, it'll help him relax."

Brody shook his head. "That's the thing. I can't promise him that. If Kelly and I do get divorced, it'll probably be me leaving. He's fragile enough without me breaking a promise."

Hell, he had a point there. Maybe Noah shouldn't be giving out advice, especially since he didn't know much about kids and knew even less about being married. Brody was going through something Noah knew nothing about. All he wanted to do was lend a solid shoulder for his younger brother to lean on. Now, if Brody wanted advice on how to piss off their father, Noah was a first-class champ in that department.

"Hell, don't listen to me. I'm talking out of my ass."

Brody laughed, a sound Noah hadn't heard from his brother in a long time. Maybe he should have just made jokes instead of trying to spill out useless advice.

"You've been more help than you realize," Brody said with a smile lacing his voice.

Noah tipped his rocker back. "I'm always here for you, bro."

Even though his advice had been for the birds, Noah couldn't help but think he'd helped his youngest brother in some way. Even if it was only to offer a listening ear. He had a feeling things with Kelly would get more complicated before they calmed down. He only hoped his nephew would come out of it as unscathed as possible.

"So, are you screwing your secretary yet?"

The question came completely out of left field and was so far off the subject that Noah had to plant his feet on the porch to keep from falling out of the chair. "Huh?"

"Don't play that fake shock with me. What's her name, Amanda, Ashley?"

Pleading the Fifth or perhaps continuing his fake

ignorance sounded like a good way to veer into another subject. "Avery," Noah answered, against his better judgment.

"Avery." His brother said her name with a slow smile, as if it were the most beautiful thing he'd ever heard.

"Don't even think about it," he warned. Where had this sudden fierce possessiveness come from?

Brody held up two hands in surrender. "Hey, I may be having problems at home, but I am still married. Besides, sounds to me as if you've already staked your claim."

Noah didn't respond, not sure how to without sealing his fate. He *had* already staked his claim on Avery, and beware to any man who crossed his path.

"Hell, she's here, isn't she?"

Brody apparently had taken Noah's silence as admittance of guilt. What was he supposed to say now?

"So, is she already naked and disheveled, or did I interrupt something?"

Noah smiled at what Brody could have interrupted and thanked the Lord he hadn't.

His brother laughed again, and this time Noah didn't bother hiding his satisfaction.

"Be careful that doesn't blow up in your face."

Wise words for a man who should heed them. Problem was he'd already gone past the point of no return.

Incredible sex had a way of making a woman forget who and where she was. For Avery, the feeling lasted all of twenty minutes.

Of course, she couldn't blame her cell phone for sucking the euphoria right out of her. The blissful feeling left when Noah pulled away emotionally after discussing his father.

Just call her the Queen of Delusion. After so many years, she'd gotten good at wearing different masks, depending on her circumstances. Wanting to fit in with a certain type of person, she'd always tried to appear acceptable. Until now.

Noah may not be as deep into the troubles with his father as she was with her parents, but he was well on his way. She and Noah were in equal denial. The only difference between the two of them was that she'd realized her problem soon enough and done something about it.

Granted, she didn't know much about the situation between the two men, only what Noah had told her. However, it seemed to her Noah buried the problem with his father as a way of coping with the guilt. He may not have admitted to feeling that way, but Avery knew. He'd almost have to be inhuman to not feel some sort of remorse for their lack of relationship. Noah didn't strike her as the type of man who went around shouting out his feelings to the world.

Yeah, like you've so boldly put your parents in their place?

Entirely different matter. Her situation was much more complex. If Noah knew, he would no doubt understand her lack of forthrightness.

If Noah knew.

He'll never know unless you tell him, you wuss.

Hey, she'd almost told him. Didn't that count for something? Courtesy for his feelings had propelled her to stay silent, not to mention they'd been in the middle of a romantic moment. Not the best time to announce something so...deceitful.

Was she deceptive?

Man, she had issues. Here, she thought she'd left all her issues behind with her suffocating parents only to be even more messed up than before.

Again she wondered if she'd made the right decision by coming here.

Romantic feelings had a way of mucking up a person's clear thinking.

Now here she was, naked in his bed, having a bipolar moment and admitting to her true self. Not the most opportune time to do so. Tomorrow. Tomorrow would be better. A good night's sleep would lend a clear mind.

She nestled herself back under the covers and read Teeny's message again.

> call me asap. it involves peter. T

The only time her friend sent a text message was when she was too busy to talk.

Teeny must have something important to tell her to send a text so late at night. The only thing that came to mind was to warn her about Peter's appearance. As noble as her friend's efforts were, it was a few hours too late. Hadn't she listened to Avery's message?

The only thing visible outside the bedroom door was the dark hallway Noah had disappeared into. She'd heard him open the front door, talk to whoever stood on the other side, then step outside.

She ran her thumb over the keypad of the cell phone and stared at Teeny's text message. Should she call her friend back? Did she really want to have such a discussion while she lay in Noah's bed when he could return at any moment? Not one of her smarter ideas. That would not be the way she'd want him to find out the truth about her.

She pursed her lips and took a deep breath. When she did, all she smelled was Noah.

Instead of placing a call, she responded to Teeny's text with one of her own.

call u in the morning. A

Considering the matter taken care of for the time being, Avery placed the phone on the bedside table.

The cotton sheets were warm and soft around her. After settling back on the pillow, she moved her naked limbs along Noah's bed. His scent wafted around her like a delicious after-sex cloud of sensuality. She loved the way he smelled, the way he looked, the way he looked at her. She loved everything about him. Hell, she loved *him*.

Avery had never been in love before. There had been a few select times when she'd had the illusion of love only to discover her significant other had been using her to get to her father. Within a few years, she'd come to the conclusion there was nothing more to her than wealth and power. That prospect would have been more than satisfying for some women. People who struggled thought money and power were everything, the gateway to happiness. And maybe that kind of life really was meant for certain people, people who had the tough skin to deal with the pitfalls that came with extreme wealth.

Instinctively, she'd known from a certain age she was not one of those people. "Fake it till you make it" had been her motto for years, and it had worked pretty well. After a while, the faking-it had gotten to be so cumbersome that she knew she'd never make it, at least to the point where she'd be truly happy with herself. She'd been dancing with the decision of what to do with herself when she met Peter.

Peter had presented himself as different from all those other power-hungry, self-absorbed nitwits who were supposedly worthy of an actual relationship. He'd presented himself in a seminormal manner, driving himself everywhere rather than relying on a driver. Jeans, instead of expensive Italian suits, had been his choice of threads, making her believe he wasn't an image-conscious freak. His easygoing manner and golden looks made her salivate quicker than a starving man standing in front of a buffet table. He hadn't tried to get into her pants or mentioned her father. For a few blissful months, she'd thought she'd finally struck gold. Peter and she could eventually marry and have a life independent of their parents.

Then her rose-colored glasses fell off, revealing Peter's true nature. After she turned down his first marriage proposal, they'd decided to stay together and marry sometime in the unforeseen future, which she thought was a real possibility, and Peter had agreed.

He'd taken a business trip to New York, and Avery had made an impulse decision to surprise him. Impulses were something she'd rarely indulged in until recently.

Using her charm on the desk clerk at the Waldorf Astoria, she gave her father's name and got a key to Peter's penthouse suite. It had surprised her, the fact that he'd chosen to stay in such a ritzy place when he'd made it clear he wasn't a part of that crowd. His hotel of choice should have been a sign. In that case her naïveté had gotten the better of her.

She'd let herself into his room and adjusted the negligee she was wearing underneath her red trench coat. Shortly after shutting the door, she heard the noises that couldn't possibly have been mistaken for anything else. The sounds grew louder as she followed them, not really sure why, knowing what she'd find. Sure enough, in the master suite, evidence of her fiancé's betrayal had smacked her in the face. Sunlight pouring in from the enormous windows gleamed off Peter's sweaty backside as he pounded into the woman beneath him. He later identified her as his assistant and insisted she meant nothing.

Bile rose in Avery's throat as she thought about it, even now. Not because she'd been in love with Peter and heartbroken by his actions, but because he'd appeared to be one thing and spoken a certain way, she automatically believed he could be the one for her. How could she have been so blind and stupid? He'd ended up being no better than any other man she'd been with. Worse, in fact.

She loved Noah, but what good would it do her? He had no idea who she really was. Her parents would never approve. And now she had Peter breathing down her neck.

Darkness descended as she closed her eyes. Noah remained outside, leaving her alone to brood with her depressing thoughts.

SEVENTEEN

AVERY LET HERSELF INTO HER apartment at ten forty-five the next morning only to be greeted by Noah's golden younger brother.

She shut the door slowly, not sure what to make of the tall, broad-shouldered man leaning against the kitchen counter and drinking from a coffee cup. His faded jeans looked worn and his brown T-shirt, which read "I Love Backseats," looked as if it had seen better days. He stared at her over the rim of the cup, then offered her a smile as though he owned the place.

The vertical blinds hung closed in front of the sliding glass door, making the apartment feel like a gloomy cave. Rebecca was nowhere in sight. What was this man doing here on a Saturday morning, sipping coffee as though he lived here?

"Would you like some coffee?" he asked in a deep but quiet voice.

"Uh...no, thank you."

Her confusion must have shown on her face. Noah's brother...what the heck was his name again? BJ?

Noah's brother with the blond hair stepped forward,

a smile lighting up his boyish good looks, and refilled his coffee cup. "Rebecca's still asleep. It might be a while before she gets up." He smiled again before taking another sip from his mug. "She had kind of a wild night."

Her gaze narrowed at the devious look that crept across his face. The image of him flashing the same grin to a teacher after misbehaving came to mind. Or tempting the innocent girl next door into doing something her parents wouldn't approve. Had Rebecca become that girl?

"Avery," he said, pointing a finger at her as if he'd just remembered her name. Too bad she couldn't say the same thing about him.

"You don't remember me, do you?" The laughter in his voice indicated that he wasn't offended she hadn't thought him important enough to remember his name. "RJ."

He extended a large, tanned palm. Avery took it for a moment; his warm, calloused hand grasped hers firmly. His blue eyes danced with amusement or mischief—she wasn't sure which—as he let go of her hand and leaned against the counter.

"So you and Rebecca are friends?" After quiet moments of him sipping coffee, Avery felt the need to make conversation, however futile the question.

His smile grew wider, this time showing a row of straight, white teeth. "Friends?" he responded with a chuckle. "Not exactly."

So what was a non-friend of her roommate doing here on a Saturday morning?

"Are you a friend of my brother's?" He threw the question back at her in a casual manner as he set his mug down in the sink.

The risk of anything she said to RJ getting back to his older brother was too great for her to tell him anything.

"We work together." She left the statement at that and hoped he would too.

RJ slowly nodded as if placating a child.

Confusion filled her, as if she wasn't already confused enough by his presence alone. Did he know something she didn't? Had Noah said something about her to his family?

"Pardon me for asking but . . . why are you here?"

Something chirped in the quiet of the apartment, and Noah's younger brother dug a cell phone out of his back pocket. He glanced down at the screen and clicked a few buttons while saying, "Your roommate had a little bit of trouble getting into bed last night." He replaced the phone in his pocket. "So I helped her." He lifted his blue eyes back to hers.

One corner of his mouth curled upward, indicating he relayed some hidden message in his words. Avery was too tired and hungry to try to figure it out. All she knew was this guy would be nothing but trouble for any woman he got involved with. He had "heartbreaker" written all over him.

"You've got a trail of broken women, don't you?" Avery leaned against the counter and tried to ignore her growling stomach. The breakfast invitation Noah had offered her that morning now sounded pretty tempting.

RJ placed a hand over his chest. "Me? I've got nothing but love for women."

"That's my point."

He stared at her for a moment as if her words hadn't registered. His caramel-colored, thick brows pulled together in a scowl. "I'm sorry, your point is what?"

Men could be so obtuse. "I don't know you very well," she admitted. "But I like Rebecca. I care about her. I don't want to see her get hurt."

"And you assume I'm the one who'll hurt her?" He crossed his arms over his wide chest. "What if she hurts me?"

"How could she? She's leaving."

Tension-thick moments ticked by like a countdown to someone's execution. RJ's scowl deepened but his stance remained the same. His blue eyes darkened and his forearms grew hard and coiled looking. Avery shifted her feet, suddenly uncomfortable under his scrutiny. Perhaps she'd told him something she wasn't supposed to.

"What do you mean, she's leaving?" he asked in a gruff voice.

"She got accepted to Harvard. She's moving out in a few weeks."

A faint shuffling sounded from the living room, cutting off anything RJ might have said. Avery turned to find Rebecca, moving into the living room at a snail's pace, in red flannel pants and a white T-shirt with a picture of Tigger on the chest. Her dull-looking hair, brick red instead of its usual vibrant fire engine, was a knotted rat's nest flying in every direction. Dark smudges of mascara lined her eyes, as if she'd been punched in her sleep.

A unladylike groan reverberated from her, and she slowly moved herself onto one of the barstools. "Hangover" was the only word that came to Avery's mind.

RJ remained silent while Avery threw looks between him and Rebecca. Finally she turned to her roommate, who'd dropped her head in her hands.

"What exactly happened last night?"

"Not really sure." Her muffled response was barely intelligible.

Avery turned back to RJ and lifted her brows in question. His attention remained focused on the hungover woman. "Maybe I should explain. Apparently our little party animal here is bad at telling people things."

"Why are you here?" Rebecca lifted her head and focused her bleary green eyes on the man in front of her. "Did we have sex?"

Avery cleared her throat and wished she could disappear. She felt like she was in the middle of a lover's spat. Or maybe it was more like a not-quite-friends-but-not-quite-lovers spat. The complexities of their relationship eluded Avery. There were definite currents flowing between the two of them.

RJ threw his head back and laughed, slapping his hand on his thick thigh. "Yeah. I have the scars on my back to show for it too."

Rebecca narrowed her gaze at him. "I don't doubt it. How do you know they're mine?"

His laughter died down to a smile as he rubbed a hand over his chest. "Ouch. You know, instead of insulting me, you could say something like, 'Thank you, RJ, for driving me home last night, carrying me up two flights of stairs, then putting me to bed when I was too drunk.'"

"I'm sure I could have done it myself."

He turned and retrieved a mug from one of the cabinets and filled it with coffee. "Trust me; you couldn't have." He placed the cup on the counter in front of Rebecca's pathetic form, then walked toward the front door. "Nice talking to you, Avery."

The door shut quietly behind him, leaving the two women in his brooding aftermath. Avery turned to face Rebecca. Both her hands held the mug, turning it slowly in circles, as she gazed down into the black liquid as though the drink held a rerun of the previous night.

"I was kind of a bitch, wasn't I?" she asked in a soft voice after several moments.

Avery leaned her hands on the counter and smiled, even though Rebecca hadn't looked at her. "A little. It sure was entertaining, though."

"Gee, thanks. I don't mean to be like that around him. Something about that man brings out the worst in me," she said and finally took a sip. "Mmm, you make good coffee."

"I didn't make it."

"You didn't?" Rebecca set her mug down and finally gave Avery a good once-over, letting her gaze drop down her wrinkled jeans and back up. "Were you out all night?"

Lie. Just tell another lie, so you don't have to explain. You've gotten good at it.

But she was lonely and had spent so much time keeping things to herself. The need to spill her guts bubbled so close to the surface, she feared she might let everything erupt like a volcano. She trusted Rebecca. The younger woman had become a friend in the few short weeks they'd lived together.

"Yes," she finally answered.

"All night?" Rebecca asked again. "With who?"

Oh, what the hell?

"Noah."

Rebecca chose that exact moment to take another sip of coffee, only to spit it right back out, spewing hot, black liquid across the white tiled countertop. Avery laughed despite the mess, mostly at the expression on her roommate's face. Coffee dripped from Rebecca's chin, which she wiped off with the back of her hand. Avery grabbed the roll of paper towels, and the two of them sopped up the mess.

"I'm sorry; I must be more hungover than I thought. I could swear you said 'Noah.'"

Another laugh bubbled out of Avery at Rebecca's reaction. "I did."

Rebecca's smile faded, and her hands stilled on the counter. "Noah McDermott," she said as if they knew more than one Noah. Then she gestured between the two of them. "*Our* boss?"

Avery nodded and Rebecca sat straighter on her stool, brushing her flyaway hair back. "I had no idea you guys were together."

This was where it got tricky. The terms of their relationship were not clear. Last night she'd drifted off to sleep while he'd still been outside, only to be woken up by his lips on her inner thigh. He'd made love to her one last time with a devastating slowness only found in erotic novels. Slow, burning heat crept into her cheeks as she thought of all the places his mouth and hands had explored. It had been only about an hour ago that she'd awakened, draped across his body, the sheet barely covering them. He'd tried to persuade her to stay for breakfast, which she politely declined, not wanting to make the situation any more intimate than it already had been.

What could be more intimate than making love, Avery?

"If that blush is anything to go by, I'd say it was a pretty hot night."

It was about damn time she learned how to put on a good poker face. She wanted to confide in Rebecca, but she didn't really want the other woman to know specifics. There wasn't anyone she was comfortable with knowing specifics. The deeper she dug herself, the faster she'd have to talk herself out of it. On the other hand, Rebecca was probably the one person she could tell. Avery doubted her roommate would go and blab such a huge thing to their boss, especially now that Rebecca knew they'd spent the night together.

"Can you keep a secret?"

Rebecca pulled her neatly trimmed, dark brows together. "Sure."

"It's a really big secret."

Avery opened her mouth to spill her guts as her cell phone vibrated from her back pocket. Just when she worked up the nerve, probably the one and only time, she got a text message.

"Hold that thought."

Rebecca picked up her coffee again and watched as Avery pulled her phone out.

Where r u??

Teeny.

Geez. She'd never called her friend back as she'd said she would. She needed to take care of this. "Can we talk later?"

Rebecca lifted her shoulders. "Whenever. I don't have any exciting plans today."

Avery walked into her room, closed the door behind her, and dialed Teeny's number. Her friend picked up on the second ring.

"Where the hell have you been?"

The loud urgency in Teeny's voice forced Avery to wince and hold the phone away from her ear. Had her friend been sitting up all night waiting for her?

"I'm here now," she responded.

"Where were you last night?" Her friend was damn persistent.

Avery didn't really want to go into another explanation of her night out with Noah. A sigh flowed out of her as she sank onto the edge of the bed. "I was just out…with friends."

"Oh." The hurt in Teeny's voice reverberated through the phone. Okay, so it hadn't been a lie; she'd been out with friends. But she'd called to discuss Peter, not her affair with Noah.

The thought sent little spirals of guilt swirling through her. After all, Teeny had done a lot to help her. The least Avery could do was be up-front with her.

She inhaled a deep breath. "I was out with a man."

Silence rang from the other end. "The same man you told me about before?"

"The same one," she confirmed.

"It's about damn time." Teeny hooted with laughter. Avery stared down at the brown carpet and waited for her friend to quiet. "You were overdue for a dirty one-night stand."

"Yeah, well…what can I say?"

"Well, I say congratulations. I'm proud of you."

Avery's lips curled into a satisfied smile. Last night had been pretty damn amazing. "My life's goal is to serve you, T."

"As much as I would love to hear all the details, that's not why I called."

Avery heard rustling in the background, like Teeny had just gotten out of bed. Very peculiar, since she'd never been one to lie the day away.

"I already know Peter's here. He paid me a visit yesterday."

Another beat of silence sounded. "That's not why I called either." More rustling, then what sounded like a male voice. "Will you hush?" Teeny whispered.

Avery pulled her brows together and listened as hard as she could. All she heard was whispering. "Who's there with you?"

"Will you just listen for a minute?" her friend said with a hurried urgency. "Anyway, I was at your father's fundraiser last night, like I told you I would be. Remember?"

Teeny wasn't making sense. Avery had no idea what her father's party had to do with Peter. She decided to play along until the other woman made her point. "Yeah, I remember."

"So, this thing was really boring and losing my interest real fast. And the only reason I wanted to go anyway was so my parents wouldn't make me feel guilty and—hey!"

Shuffling took the place of her friend's voice for a brief moment. Avery waited with practiced patience, knowing Teeny would eventually come to the climax of her story. She always had her own roundabout ways of making a point.

"What're you doing?" Teeny's voice came across the line as muffled, almost whispered. Avery wasn't sure if the question was directed at her or not.

"Teeny?"

"You're taking too damn long."

The voice registered instantly, but she thought for sure she was mistaken. No way could that actually be her brother.

"Avery." Sure enough her brother's voice came on the line, as though he'd been listening the whole time. What the hell was going on at her friend's house?

"Landon?" she asked with hesitation, after letting the sound of his voice sink in.

"Surprised to hear my voice?"

Resounding shock was more like it. She shook her

head, knowing her brother couldn't see but was unable to form actual words.

"Uh…" was all she managed.

"Okay, here's what was taking Teeny so long to get out—"

"Wait a minute." She stood and paced to the door and back. "Why are you at Teeny's house on a Saturday morning?" Her free hand gestured wildly in the air. "Why are you even over there at all? You guys hate each other."

Landon fell silent. "There's a thin line between love and hate, Avery."

She gripped her cell phone tighter. "Excuse me?" she whispered.

Off in the distance, a flock of birds flew past her window. A long, drawn-out groan sounded from the other end of the line. "This is not how I wanted to do this," her brother said in a low, hesitant voice. "I guess I have to now."

Avery's eyes widened as she stared out the window without really seeing the scenery beyond. Had her bedroom door really been a door to *The Twilight Zone*?

"Teeny and I have sort of been"—he paused—"seeing each other," he finished after mumbling a few incoherent words to Teeny.

"Describe 'seeing.'" Not that she wanted to know details.

Landon cleared his throat. "'Seeing' as in we spend most our time in bed and occasionally go out to dinner."

Yep, that's pretty much what she thought. Although hearing him confirm it did nothing to squash the total and complete disbelief clouding her thoughts. Apparently, she *had* entered *The Twilight Zone*. The Landon and Teeny she knew wouldn't have touched each other with a ten-foot pole, even if they were the last people on earth.

Her mouth snapped shut after several gaping moments as she sank on the bed.

"Did I render you speechless?" No doubt Landon meant the touch of amusement to soothe her. The laughter lacing his words, under other circumstances, would have had her laughing right along with him. This time, his easy, brotherly banter didn't have the calming effect it was supposed to.

"Avery?" he said, after she sat silent for several moments, his voice a touch more hesitant.

"So you guys are together," she stated, trying not to act bewildered.

"I'm sorry we didn't tell you sooner. We just...we weren't ready for people to know."

"Teeny always tells me everything." Did her best friend feel resentful because Avery left?

"Don't start doing that," Landon said in a firm tone as if he'd read her mind. "The fact that we kept this a secret for so long has nothing to do with you. No one else knows."

She heard the shower being turned on from the other side of her bedroom wall. Rebecca must be trying to wash off her hangover.

"What do you mean, 'for so long'? How long have you two been together?"

"Uh." He chuckled. "About five months."

"Five *months*?" Her mouth fell open again. Landon and Teeny had been the only two people she cared about spending any time with. How had she not known? Her friend and brother were obviously excellent liars. Plus she was also puzzled by the fact that her playboy brother had never had a relationship lasting longer than a few weeks. How had he and Teeny managed to stay together for this long? A relationship based on sex wasn't usually designed for the long haul. *Unless*...A startling thought occurred to her.

"Teeny's pregnant, isn't she?" Avery stared at her reflection in the ancient seventies mirror above the dresser and waited for her brother to charm his way out of this one.

Was that a hickey? She rose from the bed and angled her head to get a better view of the red blotchy spot just below her right ear. Good Lord, she had a hickey! Never in her life had a man given her a hickey. Noah had sucked on so many spots last night that the memory of how this one came about eluded her. The heat in her cheek warmed her palm as she touched her face. Noah's brother and Rebecca had probably seen this. What a hussy she'd turned out to be since she'd arrived in this town.

She gave Noah's love bite one last glance before walking to the window. A few wispy, featherlike clouds floated across the crystalline sky, as if they were headed for someplace in particular. Avery's eyes followed their movement as she waited for Landon to spit out his answer.

"Landon?"

Scuffling and whispers that sounded like a lover's spat came across the line. "Okay, Avery, listen." Teeny came back on the line, her voice all businesslike. "I—no, you suck at this," her friend said in a firm tone to Landon, who muttered an unintelligible reply. "This is a woman thing. Let me handle this. As I was saying. The reason I didn't tell anyone right away was because Landon and I needed to figure some things out. Well, mostly I didn't want it to get back to my parents without me telling them first, and I figured the best way to avoid that would be to keep it a secret. It's been getting harder to do these days because my jeans don't fit anymore and your boneheaded brother wants to tell everyone he meets."

"Keep *what* a secret? You really are pregnant?" *Stupid question, dummy. You're the one who asked in the first place.*

"I'm four months," Teeny said in a matter-of-fact tone, as though they were discussing the weather. Her friend, who stayed out all night at parties and took three-week vacations, was having a baby? Was this person on the phone the same Teeny who helped her escape?

In all her adult life, Teeny had never expressed any desire for a family. In fact, she'd been perfectly content to live off her trust fund and let others cater to her. The lavish lifestyle suited Teeny. She was born into it as naturally as a kitten to a cat. Not that she begrudged Teeny the kind of life Avery had walked away from. Her friend was happy. With a baby? Avery wasn't so sure.

Landon, on the other hand, was more domesticated than Teeny. Oh, sure, he'd spent his fair share of time in Europe, but mostly for business. Her brother had voiced on a few occasions that he wanted a family someday. At thirty-three, she assumed family would come further down the road, after he married. Not by knocking up her best friend after one short month. Was the baby the reason they'd lasted this long, or were there deeper feelings going on?

"I know what you're thinking," Teeny interrupted. "Yes, this baby was an accident, but we're happy. We haven't told anyone else, and considering your parents hate me—"

"My parents don't hate you." They'd had this exchange countless times.

"Well, they aren't fond of me."

Avery sat on the bed and picked at the multicolored pastel quilt. "They aren't fond of anyone. It's nothing personal."

Her friend sighed. "Anyway, I just don't want anyone else to know until Landon and I get our story straight."

"Which is?"

"I don't know," Teeny said in a quiet voice. "I don't want to talk to you about babies. I wanted to talk to you about Peter. When you saw him, what exactly did he say?"

Her annoying conversation with her ex-fiancé wasn't something she wanted to rehash. She decided to humor her friend anyway. "That he's sorry for the whole Olivia thing and I'm the one he still wants, yada yada yada. Pretty much the same BS as before. Why?"

"He didn't happen to mention his dad or your dad in any way?"

"No," she answered slowly, unsure of this line of questioning.

"Okay," her friend started, before exhaling a deep breath. "When I was at the party last night, as I was telling you before your brother rudely interrupted me, I overheard your father and Peter's father talking about you."

That was nothing earth-shattering. Her father was no doubt using the opportunity to tell yet another person how ungrateful and careless she was. What her father said about her didn't matter anymore.

"And?" Avery prompted.

"They were saying things, Avery. Things like Peter needs to be steered in the right direction, and if he marries you, your dad will put him on his campaign team. Now, I never actually saw them, but I'm pretty sure your dad gave Mr. Hanover some money and said he trusted

Peter to get you to come to your senses. I didn't hear the entire conversation but..."

The rest of Teeny's words fell on deaf ears. Her friend continued to ramble on, and only a few select words caught Avery's attention. Her father's false support and backstabbing shouldn't mean anything. The man whose blood ran in her veins had sunk to such a low level that she felt as though her heart had been slit with a rusty knife. Of course, she should have been used to things like this over the years, the constant pushing and nagging to follow the golden path they had so carefully laid before her.

She wasn't completely destitute. There were worse things in the world besides her pathetic life, like starving people in Africa and orphaned children in Mongolia. Didn't she deserve to have two loving parents who cheered her on through the bad and good? Someone she could call after a promotion at work or a marriage proposal?

Her knuckles had turned white, gripping the bedspread. It wasn't until she heard Teeny say her name that she realized how stiff she'd been holding herself on the bed. She rolled her head from side to side and forced her body to relax.

"Avery?" Teeny said her name again, this time with a touch of impatience.

"Put Landon on the phone." However hard she tried, her voice still came out in a strained whisper.

"What's up?" Her brother came across relaxed as always, which she tried not to resent.

"Did you know about this?"

"Don't you trust me, sis?"

Trust. There was a word that had frequented her brain in the past few weeks. Who did she trust? That list of people had dwindled down to practically no one, leaving her to feel alone and abandoned more than ever. Luckily for her, her brother had repeatedly proved his worthiness to her. Well, except for the whole thing with Teeny and her pregnancy, which Avery decided she would forgive. But only because it was her brother and best friend.

"You're one of the few people I can trust, Landon."

"So, do you really believe I had any idea what Dad was doing?"

A deep breath filled her lungs as she paced to the window, trying to work out some of the tension coursing through her muscles. "No. But don't you think the fact that Peter shows up here at the same time as Dad making his deal is too big of a coincidence?"

Her brother whispered something to Teeny, then said, "Hard to say. Just because our dad and his dad are in cahoots doesn't mean he knows anything. He could be as innocent as you."

Avery watched the sun disappear behind a long wisp of clouds. A loud snort popped out of her at Landon's words. "Nothing about Peter is innocent. I don't trust him."

"You shouldn't trust him—he's an ass. But just because he cheated on you doesn't mean he's accepting money to push you into marrying him."

Her shoulders once again stiffened, and she pulled them back. "Whose side are you on?"

He chuckled. "Don't get so pissy. Of course I'm on your side. I'm just saying you should get all your facts before you run off and accuse him of bribery."

"You're right as always. What would I do without you?"

"Lord only knows. Here's Teeny."

"Hey, girlfriend. Are you going to be okay?"

Her friend's concern always had a way of warming her

heart and reminded her someone still cared. Would she be okay? Not any time soon. She had a battle ahead of her that included people other than her parents.

"Eventually," she said with a sad half smile.

Teeny fell silent for several moments. Avery listened to the quiet hum of the other line while watching the outside scenery. "What're you going to do?" Teeny finally asked.

"I have no idea. I need to think for a while." She ran a hand through her uncombed hair and thought about confronting Noah and telling him the truth about her. Honestly, she'd rather deal with Peter.

"Well, I'll leave you to think, then. I haven't eaten in over half an hour, and it's time for me to go stuff my face again. I swear, at this rate the kid is going to weigh thirty pounds when it's born. Ciao."

"Wait a minute," Avery said in a rush before Teeny hung up. She paused a moment to gather her thoughts, which were a jumbled mess. In all her stress over her situation, she'd completely overlooked her friend's happy news. After all Teeny had done for her, she deserved better than that. "Congrats on the baby. You and Landon will make great parents."

Teeny chuckled. "Thanks. I don't have a clue what I'm going to do, though."

"Yeah, but you have Landon. He won't leave you to deal with this by yourself."

For a moment, Teeny didn't speak. "That's what I'm afraid of," she replied in a low voice. "I'll let you go. Call me if you need anything."

Avery smiled without saying good-bye. Trust Teeny to lift her spirits when they hit rock bottom.

EIGHTEEN

LANDON WATCHED THE SUNLIGHT SIFT through the sheer curtains and play across his lover's beautiful face, illuminating her expressive eyes. Eyes as green as a precious emerald, he always thought, though they weren't completely green. Flecks of light brown dotted the irises, something only a person who stood close enough could notice. He'd always noticed that particular trait about her, even before they became involved. Teeny Newberry had never been far from his thoughts. Even as a child, when she never left the side of his baby sister, she'd wreaked havoc with his sanity.

Then she'd blossomed into a young woman. Her simple denim shorts and T-shirts turned into miniskirts and halter tops, showcasing her ample breasts for any young man to appreciate. He ought to know. He'd spent many a night trying to get the sight of her out of his head as he tossed and turned in his bed. As a teen, or even in his twenties, he thought his lust for her had been a phase, a simple crush most boys his age went through. Then he'd gone away to college and returned after a few years, thinking surely whatever thing he had for Teeny would have dissipated with time. Much to his chagrin he returned to find his lust for her was still very much inside him, like a creature living in the deep recesses of his mind.

After a while, he convinced himself all he had was an itch, a desire for a woman he knew would be totally wrong for him. The only way to rid himself of such ever-consuming feelings would be to sleep with her and get her out of his system. Right? Man, he never could have been more wrong. Taking Teeny to bed hadn't in any way dissolved the craving he carried around for her. Instead it had opened a Pandora's box of passion and hot, steamy nights filled with incredible orgasms. Who knew Miss Fifth Avenue was so wanton and so much more willing to give than take? Plain and simple, his little Gertrude was a naughty animal in bed.

And he was in love with her. Yes, he would be the first to admit he did love her, pure, no-turning-back love. He hadn't planned it. Hadn't even expected it. But his feelings were there just the same, causing him to walk around in a lovesick-fool haze twenty-four hours a day. He ought to be happy and planning the rest of his life. Only the woman in question didn't return his sentiments. Oh, he knew she had some feelings toward him. But he suspected it had more to do with the sexual release he gave her than wanting to spend the rest of her life with him. Yes, they would be connected, at least for the next eighteen years, by the child she carried. Call him selfish, but he wanted more than that. He wanted more than joint custody and an occasional meeting to discuss the goings-on in their child's life.

Apparently she was satisfied with remaining sex buddies. Not that he was complaining. However, she'd shot down hints at marriage enough times for him to know exactly where she stood on the subject. She blamed her reluctance on her parents. Granted, he understood her fears, but she was a grown woman. Her parents shouldn't have so much influence for her to be scared to be seen in public with him. Then she tried to drag his parents into the equation. Yes, he did plan on telling them sometime, but he didn't give a shit what they thought. He wanted them to know their grandchild and have a relationship with him or her. No way would he let their feelings stand in the way of marrying the woman he loved. He made too much money on his own for them to dangle the financial card in front of his face as a means of keeping him where they wanted. And they knew it. He supposed that's why they didn't get all over his case the way they did Avery's. They viewed his sister as too much of a liability to let her flit around on her own.

Teeny tossed her phone on the rumpled bed and paced across her enormous master suite. The nightshirt she wore brushed the tops of her knees, covering her naked body beneath. He crossed his arms over his bare chest and leaned against her dresser, watching her feet move back and forth across the champagne-colored carpet.

Teeny was by no means a modest woman. She never had any problem parading her nudity around for him to enjoy. Only recently had she covered herself more. He knew it had everything to do with the baby growing inside her and causing her stomach to swell slightly. He'd tried on several occasions to convince her that she still looked beautiful and the tiny bump wasn't noticeable. But she'd only stood in front of her mirror and complained she looked like she'd eaten too much. Flattery didn't go very far with this image-conscious beauty.

"I'm worried about Avery," she said, shaking her head and walking across the room.

"Why? She's a big girl; she can handle herself."

She stopped midstride and pinned him with an exasperated look. "When has Avery ever handled *anything* herself?"

She had a point there. "She is now. Just give her some time and she'll figure it out."

"I guess you're right." Teeny resumed her pacing. Her body nearly brushed his. He resisted the urge to reach out, grab her, and pull her back to bed. "I still think you need to talk to your father."

"What good will that do?"

"Your father respects you. He listens to you in a way he doesn't with Avery. Maybe if you convince him what a scumbag Peter is, he'll back off."

Landon wasn't so sure about that. Darren Price saw only what he wanted to see. The man didn't allow himself to be concerned with morality when it came to things like affairs and bribery. As long as the people around him made him look good and his career was on the right track, he was one happy man. Landon tried not to let himself think about how self-absorbed and mechanical his parents were. He just lived his life, making his millions developing real estate and sleeping with an incredibly sexy woman.

He shook his head. "I'm still not convinced Peter had anything to do with the bribery."

"Oh, please," Teeny said with a roll of her eyes. She flipped her long blond hair over her shoulder and placed a hand on her hip. "Avery walked in on him screwing his secretary."

"Just because he slept with his assistant doesn't mean he's being paid to marry my sister."

Teeny only continued to stare at him with one raised

brow. "Then why would he drive all the way up to Wyoming when she made it clear she didn't want to marry him?"

He lifted his shoulder in a nonchalant shrug. "Maybe he really does love her."

This time she snorted and resumed her pacing.

His eyes followed her, taking in her shapely legs and the soft, creamy skin on her neck. "I'm just saying, don't start hurling accusations if you can't prove anything. Innocent until proven guilty, right?"

She inhaled a deep breath, pushing her full breasts against the white nightshirt. "You're too trusting, Landon."

You're not trusting enough.

The words almost left his mouth. Then he remembered that Gertrude Newberry always had to have the last word. Just one of many things he loved about her.

"Okay." She placed her palms together and held them in a prayerlike position in front of her face. "Just promise me you'll try to talk your dad."

He pulled in a deep breath, taking in a mixture of her vanilla scent and the lingering scent of sex on the bed-sheets. "If it'll make you happy. I don't think it'll do any good."

Teeny seemed to ponder his words. Her pliant, pink, kissable lips pursed into a little Cupid's heart as her enig-matic green eyes gazed into his. He stared right back, visions of sex and babies muddling his thoughts about their conversation. He loved his sister and resented what his parents did to her. To be perfectly honest, though, Avery's life and her decision not to marry Peter was the last thing he cared about right now. He wanted to give his child a good life, a life with two parents who loved each other and were committed to each other. Teeny's evasive answers and mysterious thoughts were chipping away at his patience. Yes, they'd been together for only five months, but that was longer than any woman he'd dated before. So he'd been sort of a playboy in the past. Why not? He'd be a fool not to take sex when a woman offered it freely. There was nothing wrong with a no-strings-attached one-night stand. As long as the woman agreed, why push for more? With Teeny he couldn't get enough. She was like a drug. Every time they were together, her throaty moans and back scratching seeped into his soul like an addictive substance. He always woke up the next morning wanting more.

"Marry me," he blurted out, more to see her reaction than to hear an actual answer.

"Landon," she said on a groan and glided out the double bedroom doors.

He knew she'd headed for the kitchen, and he sauntered after her. The stainless steel door to her fridge stood open as she bent over, her perfectly round ass sticking out beyond the edge of the door. She reappeared holding a to-go carton, then pulled a fork out of a drawer.

"I don't even know why I'm eating this. I hate chow mein," she grumbled as she twirled some thick brown noodles around her fork.

He leaned against the kitchen doorway, stuck his hands in his back pockets, and watched her. How could he have ever thought just one night would satisfy him?

"You have that look on your face again," she said after swallowing more noodles.

One corner of his mouth tilted up. "What look?"

"Like you know some inside joke, and you don't want to share it with me."

"Maybe I do want to share it with you."

She paused with the fork halfway to her mouth. "If it's about marriage, I don't want to hear it."

"You know," he said, pushing away from the wall to stand in front of her. He took the carton of leftovers from her and placed it on the black granite counter. "I do think about other things besides marriage and sex."

He watched her eyes darken as he slid his hands beneath her shirt to find her bare bottom. He squeezed once, loving how firm and round her cheeks felt.

"Yeah, I can tell." Her voice had gone from sarcastic to husky in a matter of seconds. She wanted to push away. He knew she resented herself for letting him disarm her so easily. All he had to do was give her a look, a touch, to let her know where his thoughts were headed.

His hands skimmed along her satiny skin to her belly, circling his fingers over the slight swell where their child grew. Her head tilted to one side, allowing him access to her softest part. Never in his life had he imagined anyone tasting so good. Like biting into a hot apple pie with melted vanilla ice cream. Her groans fueled him to nibble harder, dropping little bites accompanied by a swirl of tongue. He grinned against her velvety skin when her fingers gripped his shoulders like she was in danger of sliding to the floor.

"Landon, I..." Her pleading turned into a gasp when his hand meandered up her stomach to her breast. When his thumb brushed across her pebbled nipple, her breath came out in short, swift bursts, tickling his ear. Then she shoved his shoulders, forcing him to remove his mouth from her neck and hand from her breast. "I have things to do today. If you keep this up, we'll just end up having sex again."

He brushed his thumb along her plump bottom lip. "You say that like it's a bad thing."

"We can't spend all day in bed."

"Why not?"

She maneuvered around him, leaving him hard and unsatisfied. He stared at the leftover noodles before turning and following her back to the bedroom. When he walked in, the shower was running, and she'd tossed her shirt on the floor. She stood gloriously and beautifully naked, as though she was waiting for him to join her. Hadn't she just said a minute ago they needed to stop?

"We can kill two birds with one stone if you hop in with me."

Damn, he loved the way her naughty mind worked. With her lips curving into a come-hither smile, he shucked his pants and joined her under the hot, steamy spray.

Forty-five minutes later, clean and sexually satisfied, Landon steered his Maserati into the underground parking garage of his father's office building. After a quick phone call, he'd learned his father had gone into the office. It wasn't an uncommon thing to find one or both his parents working on a Saturday. He knew he didn't need clearance to get in to see his own father, but he called anyway just to make sure the older man was free.

The elevator took him to the fortieth floor and the lush, contemporary offices of Price Publications. The Denver office, the company's headquarters, was just one of about a dozen located around the world.

Landon made his way down the long, quiet hallway toward Susan's, his father's secretary, empty workstation. He made a left past the large, dark wooden desk and walked to the double doors of the president and CEO's office.

The man of the hour Darren Price leaned against his ultracontemporary glass desk, his gaze fixed on something Landon couldn't see. No doubt, it had to be the two dozen or so TVs taking up most of the side walls. Just as he thought, all the television monitors were turned down to a respectable level. The monitors were on at all times, covering everything from CNN to ESPN. Landon had never understood how a person could pay attention to so many talking things at once.

Even on a weekend, Darren Price was dressed to kill in a stark black suit with his signature red tie. No one was in here, for chrissakes, and the man couldn't even loosen his tie.

Landon shook his head and opened one glass door. The floor-to-ceiling picture windows lent an awe-inspiring view of the Rocky Mountains that looked like an oil painting. Only the tallest peaks boasted light dustings of snow surrounded by the bare, gravely lower peaks.

"Aren't you supposed to be meeting with developers today?"

His father didn't even turn his head at Landon's entry, much less move from his spot in front of his desk. It was hard to tell which television held the older man's attention.

Hello to you too, Pops.

"Not until later. I came to talk to you about Avery." He knew small talk would be wasted on a man who knew nothing but business. At the mention of his daughter, Darren Price turned and locked gazes with Landon. However, his father remained in position, his arms firmly crossed over his chest.

"Don't tell me she finally came to her senses." His father's mouth barely moved when he said the words. Landon always had the hardest time gauging the man's mood, even when he spoke. The man was like the proverbial FBI interrogator, or something.

Landon decided not to respond, knowing it would do no good to give his opinion, and waited with his hands in his pockets.

His father, still stony-faced and unmoving, gazed at Landon for several moments before retrieving a remote from his desk and quieting the wall of televisions.

"I have a feeling you don't want to give me your opinion on her recent antics."

Did he know his father or what?

Landon took a seat in one of the cushy red chairs when his dad walked around the desk and sat.

Age had been particularly kind to Darren Price. Where most men his age had earned deep grooves from years of laughter and sun exposure, his father had only thin, barely visible lines, leaving the majority of his face smooth as a thirty-year-old's. Landon had no idea how his father had ceased to age, but it was probably due to all those years of never showing any emotion. The only attribute that gave away his age was the streaks of white cutting into his natural rich mahogany hair. Caramel-colored eyes, which Landon had inherited, stared back at him, cool and unblinking. Sometimes he wondered if he and his father were even cut from the same cloth.

Landon rested his foot across one knee and gave his father a levelheaded stare. "I need to ask you something, and I would appreciate it if you gave me an honest answer."

His father's thick, dark brows rose like he was surprised to hear his son making demands of him. "You can ask me anything you like, son."

We'll just see about that.

"Have you had any dealings with Hank Hanover recently?" He deliberately made the question vague, just to see the other man's reaction at the mention of Hanover's name.

As usual, his smoothly practiced, political stare gave away nothing. "As you know, I deal with any number of men on a daily basis. Hank Hanover is one of them."

"I don't mean for business. This is personal."

The older man's brow twitched, pulling together just a fraction before smoothing back out. The small, almost unnoticeable expression was the first reaction his father had shown since Landon had entered his office. Not even so much as a smile for his only son.

"Perhaps you could expand, Landon. I'm not sure what you mean."

Like hell you don't. "Do you mind if I speak frankly with you?"

His father lifted a hand off the desk and gestured toward him. "Please do."

Landon linked his hands across his stomach and thought of the gentlest way of wording his accusation. And, after all, no matter how he looked at it, he was here to make a basic accusation. His father wasn't the kind of man to respond well to threats or anything else of that kind. Not that Landon would ever dream of threatening his father. He just wanted an honest answer. To know why the man sitting across from him would stoop to such low levels of controlling his own flesh and blood. Why couldn't he just be content to let his children live their own lives and be proud of what they did no matter what? When he'd found out about Teeny's pregnancy, he'd vowed he would never be the kind of father Darren had been to him.

"I'm concerned about Avery," he started, thinking he could soften his father up with those words. Not likely to happen. "I don't think she should marry Peter."

"Well," his father said with a sadistic sort of smile. "I think your sister made her choice when she abandoned her family."

Landon decided to let the "abandon" comment slip. They could be here all day debating *that* one. "Are you going to tell me you didn't give Hank Hanover, and possibly Peter, money to ensure a marriage between him and Avery?"

Once again his father's brow narrowed. Only this time it was more than a twitch. His brows pulled together in a scowl, darkening his eyes and creating deep lines in his forehead. Landon stared right back at him, making sure not to look away or blink. He was here for Avery. And he wasn't leaving until he got at least some answers from the older man.

"Are you accusing me of something, son?"

Landon shook his head and forced the expression on his face to remain neutral. "No. I was just asking you a question."

His father was silent again; his narrowed eyes remained relentlessly on Landon. Then he stood, pushed back his chair, and walked to the windows overlooking the Rocky Mountains. Landon stayed seated, watching the way his father held his shoulders back, his spine rigid. When was the last time this man put on a pair of sweats and let himself be loose?

"Your sister doesn't know what she's doing. Over the last few years, she's failed to prove to your mother and me that she's capable of making a rational decision. She's done nothing but disappoint us. She needs help being steered in the right direction."

It wasn't quite the confession he'd come looking for, but he supposed it was about as close as he'd get. As always, his father spoke like a true politician: evasive, smooth, and rehearsed.

Landon willed a response out of his mouth, anything to let his father know how he really felt about the disgusting situation. Nothing came. Not even a snort. Instead, he remained in his chair and glared at the man he called father, a man with whom he had never felt any real connection. And why should he? It's not like Darren Price was any contestant for father of the year. Oh, sure, he and Avery had never wanted for anything. They'd lived their lives in the lap of luxury. What was luxury and wealth compared to the love and compassion of a parent? No wonder Avery left without so much as a backward glance. A person could take only so much, and apparently his sister had reached her limit.

"Maybe if you gave Avery a chance and let her prove herself, you might find she's more than capable of standing on her own." Landon forced the words to come out even, without emotion.

His father turned; his hands remained clasped behind his back. With the other man looking down on him, Landon suddenly felt like a little kid again, when he used to get scolded for disobeying their ridiculous rules. He forced himself to stay seated.

"Why do you care? You have your life in order. Let your mother and me worry about Avery."

That's what he didn't want.

"Why wouldn't I care what happens to Avery? She's my sister. You know," Landon said as he stood, bringing him eye level with the other man. "She's really happy. She's doing well for herself. If you gave half a shit about her, you'd pick up the phone and call her."

With that, he turned and walked toward the door, not

giving a rip about his father's reaction. When he got to the double doors, he paused and turned.

"By the way, Teeny and I have been having an affair for the last five months. And you're going to be a grandparent."

Landon walked out with a satisfied tilt of his mouth.

Chew on that for a while, you prick.

"Come to your senses yet, sweetheart?"

Damn you, Peter.

Avery used one hand to put the finishing touches on her makeup while trying not to cringe at the world's most annoying voice.

She should have known, when her phone said "restricted caller," not to answer.

Thinking about Noah and seeing him this afternoon had distracted her. And about the sex they had last week and last night. It had been one of Rebecca's late nights, thankfully. After a knock on the door, she'd opened it and hadn't been able to resist his disarming smile and gorgeous eyes. So she let him take her, again. Then again after that. Early this morning he'd left, but not before brushing a kiss across her cheek and whispering in her ear that he'd be back later to pick her up. The softly spoken words had left a silly, ear-to-ear grin on her face for half the day.

Yep, she was definitely in love. And there was no way she would come out of this with her heart intact. Not after she told him the truth about her. Okay, so last night would have been the perfect time to spill her guts and give him every detail of her life. She just hadn't wanted to spoil the after-sex glow. Maybe she'd tell him today.

"Avery, have you listened to a word I've said?"

She stroked more mascara along her lashes and forced

a smile. "Peter, you already know how I feel. I don't know why you waste your time. Go home." She said those last two words with emphasis just in case he hadn't heard her the first hundred times. The man gave new meaning to the word "tenacious."

"You know I'm not leaving without you. Why can't you just meet me somewhere? All I'm asking is for you to listen to me."

She pulled in a deep breath and let it out slowly before digging through her cosmetics. "I've listened to you already," she said, after finding her eyebrow brush.

"Damn it, Avery." Frustration more than anger laced his voice. Frankly she didn't really give a shit. All she wanted was for him to leave her alone. However, she knew just merely speaking to him wouldn't do the trick. What she needed was something drastic, something to make him believe she really didn't want anything to do with him. The man was like a damn leech. He'd latched on to her, and now he refused to let go.

"What could possibly be in this dust bucket that's better than what I can offer you?"

"You know, not everything is about you, Peter." The words came out harsher than she intended, as she tossed her brush back in her makeup kit. "I'm here because I like it. Not because it's better than you. Now leave me alone."

"There's a man, isn't there? You've met someone."

Yeah, and he's ten times better in bed than you ever were.

She didn't say the words out loud. For some reason, letting him know he was right didn't sound like such a smart idea. Who knew what he'd do with the information?

Apparently she'd stayed quiet too long. Peter must have taken her silence as acquiescence.

"What can some low-life, dirty cowboy give you that I can't?" His words were laced with disgust.

Oh, that did it. No way was he going to start taking jabs at Noah and get away with it. Not only was he wrong about Noah being a dirty lowlife, but once again, Peter thought it was all about him. That Avery just needed coaxing into coming back to her old life.

"You know what?" she bit out as she stood. "I don't care how long you stay in Trouble, but you can take the money my father gave you and shove it up your ass."

Her poor phone took the brunt of her frustration when she threw it on the bed and it bounced off, landing on the Berber carpet with a *thump*.

Did the refined Avery Price just utter those naughty words? She'd never spoken to someone like that before. Her emotions were something she always made sure to keep in check. Her mother always told her tears or angry outbursts never did anybody any good. It certainly never earned her any sympathy from them. Why was Peter the one person who brought out that unattractive side of her? The man really knew how to push her buttons.

She inhaled another deep breath and closed her eyes, trying to slow down her erratic heartbeat. Maybe she shouldn't have spoken to him like that. He'd probably only use it as fuel to further whatever sick and twisted thing he had in mind next.

So, now what? She could either sit and stew by herself or she could finish getting ready for a party. Ultimately her future plans won out. She changed out of her work clothes and pulled on a pair of faded jeans and a white tank top.

The red numbers on the bedside clock glowed 3:45. Noah said he'd pick her up at four then drive them over to his parents' house. Avery had tried not to think about this afternoon and give herself a chance to second-guess her decision to attend. It was nothing serious. Just an outing with other people. She was allowed to do that, right? Just an afternoon with Noah, being near him, smelling him, falling deeper in love with him. Yeah, nothing serious. Then there was the little fact of meeting his family, possibly judging her. The knowledge was enough to send any sane person into a panic attack.

Suddenly fidgety, she retrieved her cell phone and the gift she'd purchased for Noah's stepmother and walked into the living room.

She'd been at her job for more than a month now. And for the last thirty-some-odd days, the routine of getting up and going to a place where she did actual work fueled her motivation for independence. It gave her purpose, a reason to get up in the morning and look at her life through different lenses. The friends she'd made here, the money she'd saved so far, made her feel...important. Although she still held on to things from her former life, like her car and the designer clothes, she had made steps to better herself. They were baby steps, but that was better than going backward. Her parents would say she'd gone downhill. She didn't care. The longer she went without contact with them, the easier it became to push them out of her thoughts completely.

The only time her ray of sunshine faltered was when she thought of Peter and the potential problems he brought with him. After all, how many ways were there to say, "I don't want anything to do with you"? Yesterday she'd driven past the town's one and only motel, trying to spot his car. No luck. That didn't mean he wasn't lurking in some alley with the rest of the bottom-feeders, waiting to make his next move. What had she ever seen in him? Good looks, money, and all that were great, but in the end, none of that meant anything if the person was psychologically unbalanced.

Maybe hanging up on him was a clear sign that she didn't want to talk to him. No, that wouldn't be strong enough of a signal. Instead of giving up, she could picture him sitting somewhere and outlining a way to get to her with his stupid PI. Or maybe he was counting all the cash her father had given him on her behalf. She didn't need her father's sick and twisted game of matchmaker. She was perfectly capable of finding her own man, thank you very much.

In fact, she'd already found one. Just thinking of Noah, his powerful presence and steely gray eyes, caused a weird tingling sensation in the pit of her stomach. As though no matter how deep of a breath she pulled in she could never quite get enough.

The time would come, sooner or later, when she'd have to tell Noah the truth about her. Their relationship had blossomed and turned a corner sometime when she hadn't been looking. She deemed it only fair to the man who held her heart to be truthful with him. He deserved to know what he was dealing with and who he'd gotten involved with. The thought of having that particular discussion with Noah made her almost as uneasy as thinking about Peter. This charade had gone on for too long. The time to out Avery Price had come. Only she was too much of a coward to do it. What would he say? Would he hate her for lying to him this whole time? Was not telling the entire truth considered to be a real lie?

Of course it is.

She needed to know how he felt about the *real* Avery and not this other person she'd created out of thin air.

Her phone chimed for the second time in half an hour. Somehow she knew before even looking it would be a message from her nemesis. She dug the phone out of her purse. Sure enough . . .

You can't ignore me forever, Avery.

A snort burst out of her lips. "Wanna bet?"

Then, just before slipping her phone back in its place, she did something she almost never did. She turned her phone off.

"That ought to silence you for a while." She placed the phone back in her purse.

Unfortunately she knew, just as she knew her own name, that turning off her phone wouldn't make Peter disappear. It was sort of like finding mold in your bathroom and painting over it. She would have to deal with him sooner or later.

A soft knock came from the door as soon as she sat down on the couch. Jumping up again, she grabbed her belongings and opened the door to see Noah in all his gorgeous glory standing on the other side. Her mouth immediately broke into a smile upon seeing him.

He looked relaxed in a pair of worn blue jeans and a light gray polo. His eyes roamed down her body as if he were trying to picture her as naked as she'd been when he left her that morning. "You look hot."

"Thank you," she replied, stepping out and closing the door behind her. Her eyes dropped down to where the soft denim hugged his rear like a second skin. "You look pretty good too," she managed to get out after lifting her gaze to his. "Mmm, and you smell good."

Did she really just say that? Could she sound any more desperate?

Just as she was about to lead him down the hallway, he leaned forward until his face was buried in her hair, with his mouth and nose brushing up against the sensitive skin on her neck. He inhaled deeply. "You smell delicious. I could eat you up right here." Then his teeth took a little nip of her ear, and she gasped.

He straightened and started down the hallway, leaving her gaping and wishing they could miss this party to do other things.

"You coming?"

He stopped a few feet ahead, one hand extended toward her. By God, she could suppress her sexual urges for one afternoon. She walked to him, linked her fingers with his, and headed for the elevator.

NINETEEN

So much for keeping his distance. He was in too deep to consider staying away. Hell, he couldn't even take a shit without thinking about Avery, as romantic as that sounded. Noah had never prided himself on being a hopeless romantic anyway. But then, bam! In the last week his romantic side had decided to show all its brilliant colors, which had really started to affect his masculinity, if you asked him. He was so hung up on the woman sitting in the car next to him that he hadn't made it home from work yesterday without needing to see her. His plan on a short visit, maybe dinner, had turned into full-blown lovemaking. Twice. And then he'd gone and stayed the night, barely missing Rebecca as he slipped out the door. Not a wise move. How was he supposed to keep Avery at arm's length if they were already spending the night together?

Not that he regretted last night. No way. In fact, he'd do it again every night if he could. When Avery opened the door, she'd practically dragged him by the collar to her bedroom, and they hadn't come up for air for another hour. Only the rumbling of their stomachs had reminded them that a world did exist outside the bedroom of Avery Price.

There was nothing in this world quite like great sex accompanied by cold pizza. Yep, he was one happy SOB.

He stole a glance at her before returning his attention back to the road. Her hair tumbled around her face and brushed along her collarbones, like rich, silky caramel with touches of honey. Every turn or tilt of her head caught the sunlight and illuminated the strands of her hair. They glinted and shone like precious jewels.

To hell with his stepmom's party. What he wanted to do was turn the car around and go have a little party of his own with Avery.

What he needed was something to take the edge off. He eyed his pack of cigarettes in the cup holder. Just one. One tiny, little smoke to ease his nerves. Then he could relax for the rest of the day. Hell, with Avery around, the cigarette would only buy him about thirty minutes.

He lifted his hand from the steering wheel and was about the grab them when Avery beat him to it. She took them from the cup holder, rolled down the window, and tossed them outside.

"Hey!" What the hell was she doing?

"I said you needed to quit those." The confident tone of her voice told him she'd planned on doing that the entire time.

"I am. I was only going to have one."

"Just one?" She crossed her arms over her perky breasts and shot him a challenging look.

He looked at her for as long as driving would allow before turning back to the road. This woman just wouldn't quit.

"Noah," she said in a firm tone. "I better not see you smoke any more of those."

He snorted. "I can't. You threw them out the window.

It was almost a full pack, by the way." He shot her another glance to see a satisfied smile pull the corners of her full lips. "How long have you been planning that?"

She lifted her shoulders. "Long enough." She continued to stare him down until he finally conceded defeat.

"Fine." He dug out a stick of gum from the middle console. After popping it in his mouth he said, "Happy?"

She smiled. "Very."

Chee-rist. Sleep with a woman a few times and she thinks she has the right to toss out your cigarettes or change your lifestyle. He knew she meant well, but did she have to waste an entire pack? Man, oh man.

"So, tell me the names of the rest of your family so I know what I'm dealing with."

"My father's name is Martin and my stepmom is Carol. Her kids are RJ, who you've met, and Courtney, who's still in college."

"The one you were telling me about?"

"Huh?" He took his eyes off the road for a split second to glance at her.

"Remember at lunch? You said she rambles on and on."

She remembered that? He cleared his throat. "Yeah, that's her. If she corners you, be prepared to camp out the rest of the night. And don't feel bad if you can't keep track of what she tells you. She could put a teenage girl to shame."

"Okay," she said on an airy laugh. "Who else is there?"

"Let's see. You've already met Chase and Brody. Brody's wife, Kelly, will be there. My seven-year-old nephew, Tyler, is their son. He's a little shy around people he doesn't know." He drummed his fingers on the steering wheel and stopped at a red light. "Carol's younger sister, Charlotte, will be there. You'll know her because she'll be the only person carrying around her Chihuahua like it's a baby. Her kids live far away, so they may or may not be there." He lifted his shoulders and pressed on the gas when the light turned green. "Everyone else is just friends. I don't know half of them. Oh, and Rebecca will be there."

"I didn't know she knew your stepmom."

"She and Courtney are good friends. And Rebecca used to walk Carol's dog before he got hit by a car."

"Aw, how sad."

He turned onto the long, dirt road leading to his father's ranch. "He was old, anyway."

Tall, leafy trees lined the road, along with a wooden fence marking the McDermott's property. *My own little slice of heaven*, his father always said. With the serenity and privacy the land offered, Noah supposed he was right. Although he and his brothers never enjoyed such luxury as children, he didn't begrudge his father his success. Even if they didn't see eye to eye. Martin McDermott worked his tail off fourteen-plus hours a day bringing his dream to fruition. Noah understood the concept, even respected it. Years of dedication and business savvy provided his father and stepmother with the kind of life they enjoyed. Noah liked to think his own independence was what drove him to succeed in his own business. He knew better. He and his father were more alike than he wanted to admit on better days. It included his drive to push himself to his limit, among other things. Like being bull-headed. Yes, he admitted it. He was bull-headed, and he knew so because his sister never failed to remind him every chance she got.

"Is the house you grew up in close by?" Avery asked, clearing his thoughts.

"No, it's on the other side of town." They came to the end of the long road and Noah made a right turn onto the dirt road leading to the main house. "I suspect my father wanted to be as far from there as possible."

"Too many memories?"

The softness in her tone indicated she understood. Noah hardly ever talked about his childhood or his mother. But Avery was the one person who pulled the memories out of him as though she had some magnetic field. He constantly found himself opening up to her. It scared him. No woman ever had that effect on him. He knew the cause. It stared him in the face like the bright sun making its descent across the Wyoming sky.

Love.

He snorted.

Who knew? Who knew that he, Noah McDermott, confirmed bachelor of Trouble, would fall for a mysterious, beautiful woman? He knew she kept her past a secret, but it didn't matter to him anymore; she had him. Like she'd reached straight into his chest and stolen his heart. Vulnerability, a feeling he wasn't all too familiar with, had blindsided him. She held his fate in her petite hands. What would she do with it?

"Do you ever go there?"

What had they been talking about? "I beg your pardon?"

"Your old house. When was the last time you were there?"

"I drive by it all the time. But I haven't been inside since I left for college."

Avery was silent for a few seconds. "Maybe it would help?"

She was doing it again. Pulling out all the uncomfortable

feelings he knew were better left alone. How did she do that?

"Help with what?"

She cleared her throat. "It just seems to me your mother's death left you...I don't know, incomplete. I just think going back there would help you resolve whatever issues you have."

What was she? A psychic? All she had to do was look at him and see his old insecurities buried deep inside him, as if she had X-ray vision. No one in his family possessed that power. Not even him. Granted, he *chose* not to look at those insecurities anymore. In any event, Avery said those words like they were staring her in the face.

"Maybe" was all he was willing to admit at the moment.

He could feel her brown-eyed gaze on him from where she sat. "You're a very mysterious man, Noah."

"Me?" he asked with a laugh.

"Yeah. Every time I bring up your mother, you clam up. Why is that?" Her thin, slightly arched eyebrows pulled together in scrutiny.

"I told you; I don't remember much about her."

The road curved farther up the hill, and Noah maneuvered his SUV around the turn. One of his father's mares grazed along the fence line, not sparing them a glance as they drove past.

"I don't believe that for a minute. It's okay if you don't like talking about her. I understand. I just think your feelings go deeper than you're letting on."

He shifted in his seat, unsure of what to say next. Did he remain quiet and let her continue with her observations or spill his guts like his initial reaction told him to? So far she'd figured it out on her own. No woman he'd ever been with had bothered to look any deeper than what he did for her in bed. And that had always suited him just fine. With Avery, he treaded in unfamiliar territory. One wrong turn and he'd sink to the bottom.

Noah glanced at her to reply, but she focused her attention out the window. They came to the end of the drive, and the front yard of the house came into view.

"Oh, wow," she exclaimed in whispered wonder.

The sprawling, lush green lawn surrounded the rambling house, reminiscent of a fifties-style ranch. The L-shaped home, done in a mixture of brick and wood shingles, sat behind a white fence with a cobblestone path meandering through grass and multicolored flowers. His father had designed the home himself, wanting something airy and spacious but also something that dominated the space it sat on. Noah had never really taken the time to look closely at the home or the way the yard, with all its bright flowers and lush bushes, always looked impeccable.

Yet Avery looked at it as though she'd never seen a real house in her entire life. Her eyes darted from one thing to the next. He supposed, as he drove to the other side of the circular drive and parked behind Chase's truck, that looking at it for the first time it would be easy to be taken in by the home's beauty. And it wasn't just the house itself. The whole package of the surrounding, wooded hills and quiet countryside could easily draw anyone looking to escape from a hectic life. Perhaps that was what his father wanted, a peaceful retreat after raising three hardheaded boys and his success as a restaurateur.

"This place is breathtaking," Avery stated as Noah put his car in park and opened the door.

When he rounded the front of the car and opened her door, he realized she'd waited for him.

"You must love spending time here."

He shut the door and inhaled the coconut scent of her hair as she stood next to him. "Yeah, it's nice," he said with a shrug of his shoulders. Truth be told, he didn't really spend that much time at the ranch. Oh, he paid his dues and spent quality time with family—dinner once a month. But most often he was at the stables, far from the house. Maybe he ought to come around more often to appreciate the home his father had built. It was something he never really thought about before. Perhaps he should. He was really starting to do a lot of things he didn't normally. All because of the woman next to him.

"I could spend a lot of time up here."

He fell into step beside her, the two of them meandering in and out the dozen or so cars already parked in front of the house. "Maybe we will." The words were out of his mouth before he had time to think.

"I'd like that." She surprised him by stopping and placing a hand on his cheek. Her brown eyes gazed into his. He could see his reflection in their swirling brown depths, like hot chocolate on a cold day. She leaned into him, her soft mouth a breath away from his.

"About damn time you got here."

Their moment was abruptly broken by his sister's statement. He glanced over Avery's head at Courtney's fire-engine-red hair. The sunlight shone down and made her head look as if it were engulfed in flames. Looking at anyone else with such a mane would have made his eyes bug out of his head. With Courtney, he only smiled. Her unpredictability was one of the things he could count on.

"Your dad's barking orders at anyone who has a set of ears," she said.

He turned Avery into his shoulder and put an arm around her. "So you thought you'd escape for a minute?"

"My mom's stressing me out. First she doesn't like my outfit, then she says my hair looks like a Crayola melted all over my head." She came to a stop in front of them and pulled a cigarette and lighter out of her back pocket. "You like my clothes, right?" she asked as she placed the cigarette between her hot-pink lips.

Her denim shorts cut up to her ass and black T-shirt with a skull on it weren't anything he'd let his daughter wear. "Sure," he said anyway to avoid a big debate.

She punched his arm after lighting her cigarette. "Liar." Her gaze shifted to Avery. Courtney's laserlike blue eyes roamed down Avery's pristine frame like she didn't approve of her ironed shirt or the normal pants covering Avery's entire legs. His sister took a puff of her cigarette and turned her head to the side as she expelled a puff of smoke. "You're Avery Price."

Avery's tall, thin frame grew stiffer than a starched shirt. Noah was pretty confused himself. He'd never introduced the two women, so how could Courtney know her? Was his sister trying to add "psychic" to her already long list of attributes?

He withdrew his arm from around Avery's shoulders so he could see her face. Her eyes, normally cool and calm, were wide with surprise and unblinking. Tension flowed off her in giant palpable waves. Her white-knuckled grip on her purse made him think of someone who was ready to ward off any attacker who might try to steal it from her.

"How do you—" he started to ask his sister, who stared at Avery, when the woman in question interrupted him.

"I'm sure Rebecca mentioned me," Avery said with a

wave of her hand and a tight-lipped smile. "Aren't you two friends?"

Courtney's thin, dark eyebrows pulled together across her pale skin, causing lines of confusing to mar her forehead. She flicked her cigarette and some flakes of ash landed by his feet. "Well, yeah, but that's not—"

"Courtney Noelle Devlin, I know you don't think you're escaping me." His father chose that moment to barge out the front door, his tall, wide frame filling the entryway. "This is your mother's party, and I will not have her doing any work. Now get back in here. I can smell the potatoes burning."

He went back in the house before Noah's sister had a chance to respond. Courtney, a smart-ass remark never far from her lips, only rolled her eyes and tossed her cigarette into a nearby rosebush. After the rebel of the family disappeared through the stained-glass front doors, Noah turned to his date and tried to gauge her expression.

Gone were the tension and the wide eyes. She looked much like the woman who showed up to work every day. Cool, confident, and elegant. He had the very distinct feeling that he'd just missed something important.

He slid his hands in his pants pockets and narrowed his eyes at her.

She only gave him a bright smile. "She's…interesting," Avery finally said.

"I warned you." His eyes searched her face. "How does she know you?"

She lifted her small shoulders. "I'm sure Rebecca mentioned she had a new roommate."

A very possible explanation. But that didn't explain how Courtney knew Avery by sight. Would Rebecca describe what her new roommate looked like? He didn't think so.

Avery took a deep breath, pushing her pert little breasts against the thin cotton of her shirt. "Whatever they're cooking smells wonderful. Should we go?"

She was doing it again, pushing aside whatever questions he might have for her. Noah prided himself on being a patient man and decided that the driveway of his father's house wasn't the place for a grand inquisition. He relented, took her hand, and led her through the front door.

Noah hadn't seen this many people in his father's house since RJ's college graduation. People milled about the backyard, standing poolside or wandering through his stepmother's prizewinning rose garden. He didn't know half of them, but apparently they knew him. He got the occasional "How are you?" or "You're looking good." His only response was a polite nod of his head, since his attention was elsewhere.

After an hour of making small talk with strangers and charming his brothers, Avery had retreated to a lounge chair, where she was deep in conversation with Rebecca. No matter where she moved, or whom she spoke to, he knew her exact location. All he had to do was turn his head and she'd be there. Her head would be thrown back in laughter or her brow furrowed in concentration as she listened to a story. She fit in here. As much as the notion made him nervous, she seemed relaxed with his family. She'd glided into the house, kissed his father's cheek, and hugged his stepmother as though they were long lost acquaintances. He'd never seen someone work a room like Avery Price. She laughed at the appropriate times, nodded and smiled in all the right places. Hell, she practically glowed.

"Hide me."

Courtney appeared out of nowhere, wedging herself

between Chase and RJ. A longneck beer was cradled between her palms and her red hair curtained her face as she lowered her head. She angled her body toward RJ, and the three men stood there, speechless.

"What're you doing?" RJ finally asked.

"I think Mom might have seen my nose ring, but I was able to slip out before she could say anything. I don't want her to see me."

Nose ring? When had she done that? Noah took a closer look and that's when he noticed a small silver stud dressing up her right nostril. Nose jewelry wasn't something that particularly attracted him to the opposite sex. However, he was surprised his sister hadn't pulled something like this earlier. After all, the two tattoos on her ankles were a few years old.

"Why the hell did you pierce your nose?" Chase asked. "Only bulls have nose rings."

Her sharp elbow jutted out and caught Chase in the ribs. "They do not." She straightened from her hunched-over stance and peered around the yard. "Do you see her? Where'd she go?" Then she slowly blinked and her shoulders slumped once more. "Great, she's talking to Mrs. Pratt, the most judgmental twit in the entire county."

Noah glanced over his shoulder and found Carol talking animatedly to the elderly Elvira Pratt. The old woman reminded him of Auntie Em from *The Wizard of Oz*, only frailer and with one foot already in the grave. Courtney was right. Mrs. Pratt did have a way of preaching to those whom she deemed had questionable lifestyles. Noah always thought it was because of boredom in her old age. She didn't have any children whose lives she could meddle in, so she meddled in the lives of those around her. That wasn't to say she wasn't a nice old lady, in an abrasive sort of way. She was just a little too self-righteous for his taste.

"I don't think your mom's looking for you, Court," he said, turning his attention back to his worried sister. "Either that or she didn't even see the ring."

"So what have you been talking about over here?" she asked as if she hadn't heard his statement. It wasn't something he took personally. Courtney had very selective hearing. "How many women have the two of you banged this week?" She looked from RJ to Chase.

"Geez," RJ muttered before taking a sip from his own beer. Chase only chuckled.

"Or maybe none, since you're so infatuated with Curly Sue," Courtney nudged RJ in the ribs, using her nickname for Rebecca, who sported curls tighter than Shirley Temple's.

RJ, who'd been watching Rebecca with more interest than someone who had no romantic feelings, shot his sister a scorching look. "I'm not infatuated with her."

Courtney tilted her delicate chin up. "You are."

"Not."

"Are."

"Not."

"You two are like a couple of five-year-olds," Noah said, breaking into their argument.

Courtney turned her gaze to his. "Would you please tell him I'm right, and he needs to put himself out of his misery?"

"Why don't you just tell him that?"

"Because he doesn't want his baby sister giving him sex advice. Do you?" She aimed her lethal gaze back to her brother, who did his best to ignore her.

Chase took a sip of his beer and lowered the bottle. "Why don't you just take her to bed and be done with it?"

RJ slid his hands in his back pockets. "Because I don't sleep with every female I come in contact with, unlike you." He pinned Chase with a glare that said to let the subject drop.

Courtney, however, had other plans. "Yes, you do," she said a little too loudly. A few people standing around them turned their heads in their direction. Noah glanced at Avery and Rebecca, who were still talking. Neither one of them seemed to have heard.

A gust of wind picked up, rustling the leaves in the trees and stirring Avery's hair. She swiped it out of her face just as she let out a soft giggle. He'd been there only an hour and already he wondered how long he'd have to wait before he could drag her away without his father noticing.

"Will you shut up?" RJ's demand brought Noah back to their conversation. Instead of being intimidated, like most people, Courtney only smiled and took a sip of her beer. The little five-foot-six pistol wasn't afraid of any of her older brothers.

"Rebecca's different," his brother continued, looking back at the woman in question.

"Yeah, she doesn't swoon at your feet," Chase threw in.

RJ grumbled. "I'm going to get something to drink." He stalked away, leaving the three of them to watch his retreating back.

"Why's he so pissy today?" Courtney asked, lifting her bottle in the direction their brother had just gone.

Noah didn't know how to answer that, and apparently neither did Chase, as he remained quiet too. Who knew what went on inside RJ's head? He and Rebecca had a strange relationship. Half the time RJ ignored her, and the other half he spent driving her crazy.

"You know," Courtney started slowly, "Rebecca tells me things."

Noah narrowed his eyes at her as he considered her cryptic words.

"Like what?" Chase asked when their sister didn't elaborate.

She lifted her bony shoulders. "Like maybe she's not all that different."

Why did women always have to speak in code? Why couldn't they just say what they meant? "What the hell does that mean?" Noah asked.

She downed the last of her beer. "Nothing." A sly smile lifted the corners of her pink lips. "See you chumps later."

She sauntered off.

"I can't follow her," Chase said, shaking his head.

"I stopped trying a long time ago. Now I just smile and nod."

The two of them were silent. Someone in the background roared in laughter. His father darted from one guest to the next, making sure everyone was happy. The only people missing were Brody and his family. Trouble in paradise again? The party had started over an hour ago and so far his brother was a no show. Perhaps Noah should call? No, his brother was a grown man and could handle anything thrown his way. Against his better judgment, Noah stole another glance at Avery over his shoulder. For a brief second, he watched her without her knowledge, completely riveted by the picture she made. Glittery rays of sun pierced through the thick foliage of the trees and gave her brown hair an almost golden glow. The subtle highlights were magnified in the buttery light of the sun, and whenever she turned her head he found a new color. Sometimes it was caramel, other times chocolate. How many shades did she have?

She nodded at something Rebecca said and her gaze caught his. Her smile froze, then grew a fraction wider. The swirling depths of her light-brown eyes sparkled as if remembering the night before. Hell, he'd been remembering last night all damn day. It was entirely possible he'd never get it out of his head. She'd cast a spell over him, the little witch. For a moment they were the only two there, their eyes communicating as intimately as last night.

"If you stare any harder, you'll scorch the clothes off her back."

Chase's words made Noah tear his attention away from Avery. "I can't help it."

"How deep are you?"

He pulled in a deep breath. "Pretty deep. I think this one's for good."

Chase's brow raised on his forehead. "Really?" His brother gave Avery a once-over, a smile of appreciation crossing his mouth. It would have sent Noah's back straight, but he understood what Chase saw. "She's pretty hot. But there's something about her..."

His words trailed off as if he'd lost his train of thought or couldn't find the right words. "What do you mean?" Noah asked.

"I don't know. I just feel like I know her from somewhere. When we played pool last week, I kept thinking I'd seen her before, but I can't place my finger on it." He lifted his shoulders and returned his gaze to Noah's. "I don't know. Could just be one of those things, you know?"

No, he didn't know. First Courtney, now Chase? What was it about her that made everyone think they knew her? Noah didn't see what they saw. No, he saw something entirely different. A sexual goddess who had the power to turn him into a muttering mess.

The back doors flew open; his nephew came barreling through the crowd and didn't stop until he landed in the pool. Water splashed over the sides, hitting a few people who mingled too closely to the edge. Tyler popped up a few seconds later, an ear-to-ear grin on his face.

Brody came ambling through after his son with Kelly on his heels. The two of them split ways, Kelly heading over to his stepmother and Brody in the direction of Noah and Chase. Brody had a particularly smug and satisfied look about him, from the tilt of his mouth to the relaxed gait in which he moved. Noah knew that look. It was universal with all men.

"Looks like things are better on the home front," Chase muttered just before their brother reached them.

"So," Noah started when Brody stood before them. "Things are good?"

Brody lifted one shoulder. "They were this afternoon."

Noah and Chase exchanged a glance, trying to figure out what was going on. Finally Chase furrowed his brow and said, "I thought you two were having problems?"

"Doesn't mean the passion isn't there. This was the first conversation we've had in a while that didn't end in an argument."

Noah and Chase exchanged another glance. "So you've made progress?" Noah asked. "No more counseling?"

Brody's face went from satisfied to wary, his brow creasing and his gray eyes darkening. "Just because we had sex doesn't mean the problems aren't still there. We have another session tomorrow. Who knows?" His brother's gaze sought out his wife, and his dark brows pulled down over his eyes as if trying to figure something out.

Noah turned, and once again found Avery watching him. She said something to Rebecca, then stood from the lounge chair and walked to the rose garden. He felt her beckoning him as if her body sent out some telepathic message to his. His eyes automatically dropped down to her sensational ass and the way the tight denim molded around her curves like shrink-wrap. She had no idea how mesmerizing she was. All a woman like her had to do was crook her finger and she'd have any man eating out of the palm of her hand.

He turned back to Brody, slapped him on the shoulder, and said, "Good luck."

She had wandered down one of the six rows of the rose-bush display. The way Carol set up her flowers reminded him of a nursery. There were cement paths in between each row of flowers like she expected people to come with their shopping carts.

He stopped next to Avery.

"Yellow roses are my favorite. They're so bright and cheery." She tilted her face to his. "Don't you think?"

All he could think about was how beautiful she was. Damn, he wanted to tell her how he felt. And he wanted her to tell him.

"Sure" was all he could manage. Truthfully he'd never really thought about flowers or which ones looked bright and cheery. He took the Swiss army knife he always carried out of his back pocket and cut one off. He didn't want her to prick her delicate skin so he cut the thorns as well, and handed her the fully bloomed rose. Her eyes never leaving his, she accepted the flower and brought it to her nose. Her eyelids drifted shut as she inhaled the fragrance.

"Thank you," she almost whispered, and he gave in to his impulse and trailed a finger down her cheek. Her skin was warm and soft like a baby's. How did she do that? Never had he thought it was possible for a person to have skin that felt like pure heaven.

Her eyes bore into his as her fingers twirled the rose around and around. He stepped closer to her, wanting to press his lips to hers, when she took a step back.

She was withdrawing again. He could practically see the wall erecting around her like a protective shield. Frankly, he was damn tired of this.

"Avery," he said and took a step toward her.

"Noah, wait." She took another step back, and her eyes darted around them, almost as if making sure no one was listening. "There's something we need to talk about. I wanted to do this in private but...I can't wait anymore." Her chest expanded as she pulled in a deep breath. "I'm not who you think I am."

Her words could've had so many meanings that he wasn't sure what to think or how to react. Immediately his body tensed. Whatever she had to say couldn't be good. Gone was the peaceful, relaxed Avery who'd charmed his brothers. In her place was someone who looked petrified, as if she were about to give a speech in front of ten thousand people. Her back had gone ramrod straight and her fingers gripped the flower so tight he was glad he'd cut off the thorns.

"I haven't been completely honest with you about... things." The leaves on the rose were being mutilated by her fingers as they twisted around. She wouldn't look at him. He willed her to, but her attention was on the sunny rose as though whatever she wanted to confess was for the flower and not him. "I—"

She lifted her head and stopped when her gaze focused on something over his shoulder. He'd never seen anyone's face freeze up so fast the way hers had. Her breathing turned rapid, her eyes widened. A fine sheen of sweat beaded up on her forehead. Her throat worked in rapid succession and just as he started to ask her what was wrong, a man wearing faded jeans and a black leather jacket shouldered past him. The newcomer, whom Noah had never seen before but instantly disliked, put an arm around Avery's stiff shoulders.

Something exploded inside him. Whether it was a need to protect Avery from this clown or pure untapped jealousy, he wasn't sure. But fierce fingers of fury uncurled deep in his belly and shot throughout his body, setting his teeth on edge and making his back rigid. The muscles in his jaw worked tighter than ever, practically grinding his back teeth into dust. The look of complete discomfort on Avery's angelic face should have made him feel better. On the contrary, it made the fiery pit in his stomach grow even bigger. The look only told him she knew this person. Whatever she'd been about to tell him had something to do with this other man.

"I've been looking all over for you, sweet cheeks," the pompous ass said with a sadistic sort of smile, his mouth lingering a little too close to Avery's temple.

She leaned slightly away from him but didn't pull away completely.

"Who the hell are you?" Noah managed to ask after he eased the tension from his jaw.

"I'm sorry; I've been so rude. I just waltzed in here and didn't even introduce myself." He stuck out a palm, and that's when Noah noticed the expensive-looking gold watch peeking out from the edge of his jacket. "I'm Peter."

Peter left his introduction at that and waited for Noah to take his hand. Noah stared down at the man's unblemished, soft-looking palm but didn't take it. He raised his eyes to Avery's for the first time, but her gaze averted to something in the distance. Probably the nearest exit.

When Noah didn't shake hands, Peter said, "I'm Avery's fiancé."

Whatever had been inside him allowing him to keep his cool for the last several moments evaporated. Madness, like he'd never known before, replaced the fresh jealousy flowing through him. He reacted quicker than his mind could think, grabbing Peter the Jackass by his jacket. The other man was a good three or four inches shorter than Noah, so when he jerked Peter up, the bastard rested on his toes. Noah's eyes narrowed as Peter's grew wider with surprise and fear. Noah yanked him closer, and the movement wrenched Peter away from Avery and she let out a gasp. But Noah's attention was focused on the man in his hold. They were almost nose to nose. The urge to knock the man to his ass and bust a few teeth out of his too-pretty face almost made Noah raise his fist. Then Tyler let out a shout of laughter, and reality sank back in. He didn't want to cause a scene at Carol's party. So he pushed Peter away, and the man stumbled back a few feet, dragging Avery with him.

Noah turned and stalked away, hearing Avery call out his name. He didn't pay attention and told himself the desperation in which she said his name didn't mean anything. All he could think of was getting away from her.

TWENTY

COMPLETE BALD-FACED HUMILIATION. THAT WAS the only way to describe how Avery felt. Oh, and resentment. The way her body hummed and fingers tightened around her purse in a death grip could be caused only by the bone-deep loathing for the man sitting next to her.

Would she ever in her life be able to do anything without someone stepping in and screwing it up? It was as though every time she took a step forward someone said *Not so fast, Avery. We have other plans for you.* And it usually involved her parents or people associated with them. He just couldn't let it go. It was as though the man didn't understand English or he had cotton balls in his ears. But that wasn't even the worst part. No, he had really hit where it hurt. Driving an arrow right through her heart by completely destroying her new life. Showing up at the worst possible moment and pretending they were still engaged or even had a relationship. It wouldn't have been so bad if they had been in private. Then she could have told him off and torn his eyes out to her heart's content. But with Noah and all his family around? This time he had really crossed the line.

Why couldn't he just disappear?

After dragging him away from the party as fast as her size-eight feet would carry her, she ordered him to drive the two of them to town. Not that she had any idea where they were going. The only thing in her mind was the driving force to get him away from Noah.

Never in her life would she forget the look on his face when Peter uttered the word "fiancé." She'd watched, with horror, how his face changed from easygoing to downright frigid. It was the look of someone she wouldn't want to have an encounter with in a dark alley. His face had turned to granite, his gray eyes had narrowed into icy slits, and his brows had pulled into dark, fierce slashes over unwelcoming eyes. His mouth, usually so soft, had formed into a harsh line. At that point, Avery hadn't been sure whether or not to hide behind Peter or pull Noah aside and try as best she could to explain things to him. It was when Noah had grabbed Peter that she realized talking to him would have been like talking to air. He would have been too emotional and confused to listen to anything she would have to say. In a split second, she'd decided her best course of action was to take Peter away from there and deal with him first. Give Noah time to cool off and handle him after she had things figured out.

This was assuming, of course he would even speak to her. Peter wasn't really her fiancé. But had she told Noah that first? No. She had to keep it all to herself, and now all Noah knew was what Peter had said. Stupid. This was entirely her fault. Things had been going so well, and Noah, the one man she'd fallen in love with, wouldn't speak to her.

A small part of her wanted to place all the blame on Peter. But she couldn't. Only a weak, self-absorbed person would do that. In order for her to right things, she needed to start with number one. Who was she? What had she hoped to accomplish by coming to Trouble in the first place? It was at this moment, as she sat in Peter's expensive car, that she realized she'd messed up from the beginning. Instead of being up-front with the people in her life, she'd hidden behind her hurt and taken off without having any real plan. What an idiot she'd been.

Peter drove down the hill, toward the town of Trouble, neither one of them saying a word. Avery didn't feel compelled to speak to him except to give directions. Wound up tighter than a coil, she sat next to the man who was the bane of her existence. On the other side of the car, Peter looked like a man who didn't have a care in the world. Was he really that clueless?

A hysterical scream bubbled up to her throat, and she only managed to tap it down seconds before it burst out.

"Take a right at the light," she instructed in a tight voice.

He made the turn with one arm draped casually out the open window. "Where are we going?"

Good question. The only place that sprang to mind was the coffee shop next to the one and only dry cleaner. And one thing she did know about Peter, the man inhaled coffee as though it was the elixir of life.

She loosened her grip on her handbag. "There's a coffee shop at the end of Main Street. You'll see it at the corner."

Out of the corner of her eye, she saw Peter glance at her. His eyes were hidden behind a pair of Roberto Cavalli sunglasses but Avery knew what he thought. He took their departure as her wanting to reconcile. Why would she want to reunite in such a public place? Peter was pretty much one-dimensional. He only saw what was right in front of him and wouldn't, or couldn't, look beyond that. The time had come for her to set him straight once and for all.

The rest of the ride to the café stretched into an eternity, which she spent ramrod straight in the soft leather seat. The blessed sanctuary of a public place finally greeted them as Peter slid his car along the curb. Avery jumped out as quickly as possible, not wanting to give Peter the chance to pretend to be gallant by opening the door for her.

Once inside, they sat opposite each other and ordered their drinks. They waited, and Avery took the opportunity to study the man across from her. Peter was very handsome in a pretty sort of way. At one point she had been attracted to his well-polished looks, without ever a hair out of place or callouses on his hands. But now, she couldn't find a thing that appealed to her. When they walked in, she noticed several women glance his way. He'd returned their looks with an interested gleam in his blue eyes. The look had caused a shudder to ripple through her. If she'd married him, she'd have to deal with that sort of thing for the rest of her life.

She'd rather stick bamboo shoots under her nails.

The gray-haired waitress set their coffees in front of them. Avery picked up her cappuccino and took a sip.

"Tell me what you planned on accomplishing by following me today," she said after setting her mug back on the scarred tabletop.

Wispy strips of steam curled up from Peter's mug, which he hadn't touched yet. His eyes darted around the café, touching every woman within eyeshot. Considering his next possible affair maybe? She wouldn't put it past him.

"Peter."

His eyes snapped back to hers.

"I want an answer."

He wrapped a hand around the mug but didn't drink. "I said you couldn't hide."

What the hell was that supposed to mean? That he was merely trying to prove a point?

"That doesn't answer my question." Aggravated to the breaking point, she inhaled a deep, calming breath and twirled her mug around on the table.

"What would you like to know, Avery? I thought I made myself clear."

"And I thought I made *my*self clear. On several occasions, in fact." He'd averted his gaze again. Her frustration gave way to maddening, hair-pulling resentment, bringing a warm flush to her entire face. Only the presence of other humans kept her from reaching across the cheap Formica table and choking out his last smug breath.

Instead, she took another sip of the still-hot coffee. "What do I need to do to convince you that I don't want to marry you? How about every last dime from my trust fund? That would keep you more than comfortable for the rest of your life." *Maybe buy a house on the other side of the planet.*

For the first time since seeing him that afternoon, he laughed. Oh, sure, he'd been flashing those smiles that made her want to rip every last hair from her head. But his laugh sent her to a whole new level of head banging. It was one of those I-know-better-than-you-little-girl laughs.

His laughter subsided to a wolfish grin. "I have plenty of my own money. I don't need any of yours."

For a moment she only stared at him, narrowing her eyes and trying to read his features. It didn't look like he was hiding anything. In fact, he looked quite normal, sipping his coffee and lounging back in the seat. What possible hidden meaning could his words have? She tried her hardest to wrap her mind around them.

Avery leaned forward in her seat. "If you don't need any money, then why has my father been giving you some?"

"Your father's never given me money," he said, as if they were commenting on the weather. Oh, the nerve of the man.

"Okay, so then your father is giving you money. Either way someone is paying you to marry me, and I just wanted you to know"—she jabbed a finger at him—"that I'm aware of it. And," she continued when his eyes narrowed at her, "I'm not going to put up with it. So you can just take all your money and your new career with my father and stick it where the sun don't shine." She ended her tirade by scooting out of the booth. There, let him sit on that for a while and see if he still wanted to come around. Hopefully this time she got her message across.

Before she had a chance to make it away from their booth, Peter's hand wrapped around her arm and stopped her in her tracks.

"Hold on a minute. Sit down."

"We're done talking. If you don't leave me alone, I'll get a restraining order."

The fingers around her arm tightened. Avery looked down at where he had a hold of her. The veins in his hand rose to the surface as his fingers dug into her flesh. A prickly sensation stirred from her arm where he cut off the circulation down to the tips of her fingers. Avery tossed a nervous glance over her shoulder. Their gray-haired waitress narrowed her eyes at them from behind the counter as if she suspected an outburst just around the corner. Avery tapped down her annoyance and pinned Peter with a levelheaded stare.

"Peter." She tried to reason with him but he interrupted her.

"Sit. Down." The words were ground out through gritted teeth. Well, she could either wretch herself away from him, and he would only follow her, or she could obey. Ultimately, she decided the latter was the most effective course of action and retook her seat.

Peter pinched the bridge of his nose and pushed his coffee mug away. "What would make you think someone was paying me to marry you?" he said after a long stretch of silence.

She debated telling him but decided against it. "It doesn't matter," she said with a shake of her head. "The important thing is that I know. And once I talk to my father, the money train is going to stop."

He remained stony faced, and his eyes bore into hers as if he were waiting for more of an explanation than that. As far as she was concerned, she didn't owe him any more than that. What he'd done was bad enough. He could consider himself lucky she was willing to spare him this much time to talk.

"Excuse me," he said as he scooted out of the booth and walked out of the café.

Once outside, he pulled out his cell phone, punched in a phone number, and raised the phone to his ear. Now would be the perfect chance to make her getaway. She could sneak out the back door and walk to her apartment. But the way Peter held his body stiffly and the thunderous look on his face told Avery she should probably stick around.

The more minutes that ticked past, the more uncomfortable she grew. The remnants of half a dozen napkins lay in a shredded heap in front of her. Her coffee mug, which she'd turned in about a hundred circles, now sat in the middle of the table. Her leg developed that nervous bounce it always got when she couldn't sit still. Out of the corner of her eye, she saw Peter, still on the phone, pacing back and forth on the concrete. Who would he call in the middle of their conversation?

Something told her she'd misjudged Peter. Hadn't Landon warned her to get all her facts together before she accused him? Yes, Peter was a jerk for cheating on her and couldn't be more wrong for her. But bribery? She'd been so quick to put him in his place that she hadn't given him the chance to give her an explanation.

The bell above the entrance dinged, and Avery glanced up as Peter came back in. A dark scowl pulled his thick brows low over his eyes. His mouth, set in a hard line, was bracketed by lines of irritation. She waited for him to give an explanation after he reclaimed his seat.

"Apparently my father doesn't trust me to make my own decisions."

The words came out with a slightly lighter edge than she'd anticipated.

"I owe you an apology, Avery."

He couldn't have stunned her more if he had announced he was gay.

She cleared her throat. "I don't understand what you're getting at, Peter."

"You were right." He ran a hand through his wind-blown hair, a look she hadn't ever seen on him. "Both of our fathers have been conspiring to get us together. If we were to marry, your father would have offered me a job on his staff. And my father would have received a hefty amount of cash."

Confusion still clouded her thoughts. "So . . . you didn't know about any of this?"

He picked up his mug and took a sip of what had to be stone-cold coffee. "No."

His answer was short and clipped, telling her the situation pushed him as close to the edge as it did her.

She cleared her throat and chose her words carefully. "You really do want to marry me?"

He looked at her with raised brows. "How many other ways do I need to say it?"

She closed her eyes. For the first time Avery realized he was just as much a victim as she'd been. For two puppet masters pulling the right strings to control their children, they'd been nothing more than guinea pigs.

Time to try a new approach. "Peter, look at me." When he did, she reached across the table and grabbed his hands. "You don't want to marry me."

"I don't?"

"No. You think you love me, but you don't. You can't make me happy and I know I could never make you happy. This is my home now," she said, glancing around at the small and meager café. "I like it here. I don't have any plans to return to Denver, no matter what my parents say. So do yourself a favor. Go home and find a woman who can give you what you want." He opened his mouth to argue. "Please," she said, squeezing his hand for effect.

He removed his hands from under hers and leaned back in the booth. Defeat slumped his shoulders and darkened his eyes.

After a moment of silence, Avery gathered her purse and slid out of the booth. "I hope I've made myself clear this time." He watched her but didn't say anything. "Good-bye, Peter."

The next day, Noah forced thoughts of Avery and the events at Carol's party to the bottom of his list of priorities. That wasn't to say the hurt didn't still course through his veins like ice. Or that he couldn't still see the look of dismay on her face when the other man had touched her. No, after only twenty-four hours, the knife in his heart was still very much present. And not only there, but every time he thought of her, the knife twisted, embedding itself deeper.

He should have known a woman like her was too good to be true. Ever since he'd met her, he'd tried his hardest to find a flaw, some sort of quirk or idiosyncrasy. All to no avail. No wonder falling for her seemed too easy.

Until the fiancé.

Even now, standing at the site of his father's new restaurant in Casper, the word "fiancé" set his teeth on edge.

For all he cared, she could go back to her fiancé. Hell, he never wanted to see her again. That way there wouldn't be any reminder of what they almost had and how he'd lost it.

There was just one problem. She worked for him. Normally problem solving came quite easily to him, especially in his line of work. But he didn't have a clue how to solve this puzzle. He supposed he could just leave his office door shut and wear earplugs so he didn't have to listen to her melodious voice.

Suck it up. So you had a fling and it ended badly.

It wasn't like he was the first man in history to have this happen. And that didn't mean he couldn't be a professional when in the office and work beside her. Sure, he could do it.

He slid his sunglasses on and walked closer to the

construction site. When he'd decided to take the day off today, it hadn't been with any real plan in mind. His only goal had been to decide what to do about Avery. By about ten o'clock, he'd come to the conclusion he'd not do anything. Then he'd gotten in his car and driven. He'd made it to his father's new restaurant, or just the foundation of it, without even realizing he was headed in that direction.

As he got closer to the foundation, he started to notice flaws in the construction. Minor flaws that the untrained eye wouldn't notice, but he did. Things like cracks, the foundation sloping off to one side, and unevenness in thickness. Noah narrowed his eyes when he realized the site stood empty. Only the foundation and a couple of trailers occupied the lot. Where the hell was everyone? In the middle of the day, this place ought to be bustling with workers. The only person present, besides himself, was RJ. Standing alone on the other side of the foundation, his brother stared at the site through dark sunglasses. Why Noah hadn't recognized his brother's fully restored '66 Shelby Mustang was beyond him. Just went to show him how thoughts of Avery still clouded his brain.

RJ hadn't spotted him yet, so Noah walked around to the other side.

"What're you doing here?" Noah asked him when he came to a stop.

RJ's head came up in surprise, his brow crinkling above his sunglasses. "I could ask you the same thing. Since when do you have an interest in this?"

Not wanting to get into the real reason, Noah shook his head. "I just wanted to get out for a little while and thought I'd come check this place out." He glanced around at the empty lot and the busy commercial corner it sat on. "Looks like a good location."

"It's a damn good location. I'm the one who found it."

"No shit? And Dad approved?" His father was one of those control freaks who didn't like other people, even his own children, messing with business decisions. Martin ran a well-oiled machine and had enough manpower and money to step back and enjoy his retirement. Which would make Martin and his children a lot happier. But, as he continued to age, his dad worked as many if not more hours as he had when he first opened McDermott's.

"After he saw the research I did, he was pretty happy. I came here on my days off, counted traffic, checked out the competition within a ten-mile radius, talked to the locals. I even typed it up in a report and presented it to him without him even knowing what I was up to." RJ shook his head and a breeze ruffled his blond locks across his forehead. "I have to say I think I did a pretty damn good job."

Noah slapped him on the back. "I'm proud of you." He glanced back at the foundation. "Wish I could say the same thing for Dad's choice of contractor."

"I was just noticing that. Is it just me, or is the foundation tilted to one side?"

Noah slowly nodded as his eyes scanned the construction site. "Not only that, but there are already cracks and one side is thicker than the other. Why is no one here working?"

His brother lifted his shoulders then let them fall. "Hell if I know. Maybe they're taking a lunch break."

No, an entire crew wouldn't leave the site to take lunch. Something wasn't right. He needed to talk to his father. If the man would even listen to him.

"Hey, uh..." RJ cleared his throat. "How're you holding up?"

"What do you mean?" Noah played dumb without

making eye contact, even though he knew exactly what his brother meant. *Plead ignorance and you don't have to answer questions.* That was his motto.

"I saw what happened at Mom's party. You stormed out of there like your ass was on fire, and Avery's eyes looked like they were about to bug out of her head. Is everything okay?"

"Sure." Why bring it up all over again anyway? It's not like venting to his brother would change anything. Besides, men didn't vent. That was for women.

Out of the corner of his eye, Noah saw RJ nod as if placating a child. "I was just going to get some lunch. You hungry? It's my treat."

"I could eat."

Fifteen minutes later, they were sitting in a booth at a local restaurant and contemplating the best way to plug their arteries. Should he go with a hamburger or chicken fried steak? Having decided on the steak, Noah handed his plastic menu to the server, who looked about fifteen.

RJ leaned back in his seat and watched the dark-haired jailbait sashay away.

Personally, Noah preferred his women with a little more life experience and less . . . oh . . . rail thin. She looked like one of those models out of a magazine whose ribs you could count and with cheekbones that could poke someone's eyes out. RJ had a track record of going for women who could disappear behind a telephone pole.

"How's the GTO coming?" Noah draped his arm along the back of the booth. Everyone had different passions in life. For some it was fishing, others . . . well, in Chase's case it would be women. RJ's passion was old cars, although his brother continually referred to it as his hobby. Noah knew better. RJ spent the better part of his time off at auctions, snagging beat-up rust buckets, and then pouring hours of sweat and money into beautifying and selling them. However, he had kept a few for himself. One was his Mustang, the other a sweet little '55 Corvette Roadster painted a color called Gypsy Red. How RJ had landed his hands on such a gem, Noah had no idea. Pure luck would be the only explanation he could come up with, considering that particular model and year were rare, to say the least.

RJ's newest project to date was a '64 Pontiac GTO that he'd completely gutted. "Don't think you're getting off the hook," RJ chided him after peeling his eyes off the child waitress. "What's the deal with you and Avery?"

Play dumb. "What do you mean?"

"Well, you had a thing, and now you're... what?"

"Now we're nothing, since she's"—he twisted his head to the side to work a kink out of his neck—"engaged."

RJ held up a finger. "Pardon me if I'm wrong. Isn't that the kind of information you should have found out before you jump into bed with her?"

Noah gave him a tight-lipped smile and forced himself not to walk out on his brother. "You think?"

"Sorry." His younger brother held up his hands in defense. "We can talk about something else." RJ leaned back and drummed his fingers on the Formica table. "So, why don't you just go after her?"

"RJ," Noah said with a groan. "Do me a favor and drop it, okay?"

"I mean, obviously you have feelings for her," his boneheaded brother went on without hearing him. "You clearly have chemistry. What's stopping you?"

"Oh, I don't know. An engagement ring maybe?"

RJ gave him a pointed look. "I don't remember seeing a ring on her finger. Do you?"

Gee, his brother had a point there. Avery never wore any kind of diamond ring on her left hand. But still... "What about the guy she was with?"

RJ threw him a look like Noah had just spoken Greek. "Him? You're going to let that guy stand in your way? He looked like a schmuck to me. He had gel in his hair, for chrissakes. Hell, he probably gets manicures. My advice? Beat down her door and drag her back."

Sure, just like that. She'd no doubt leap into his arms and shower him with kisses. *And they lived happily ever after.* Yeah right. Things like that didn't happen in the real world, especially to guys like him.

RJ, who'd never had a relationship that lasted longer than the time it took him to run out the front door, was advising him to go after Avery?

Then he continued. "How do you know this guy is really her fiancé? Maybe he's just an ex-boyfriend who's pissed off because she left him. Have you even talked to her about it?"

Noah glanced around the half-empty diner. Where the hell was their food? He needed a distraction. The waitress would come back and give RJ something to focus his attention on other than him. Much to his chagrin, it wasn't the subject of conversation that really got his back up. His carefree little brother was right. At least Noah was man enough to admit that much, even if it did piss him off. He hadn't given Avery an opportunity to explain herself, which wasn't like him. Noah had always considered himself a fair and reasonable man. So why wasn't he willing to display his most cherished trait with the one woman who meant more to him than any other woman?

Because you're pigheaded and stubborn, just like your daddy.

The voice in his head sounded suspiciously like his mother's. She didn't come to him that often, but when she did, she was usually right.

RJ lifted his shoulders in a negligent shrug. "What do I know? I'm sure your way is better. Let her walk away and marry Mr. *GQ*."

Their food was delivered, giving Noah something to do other than respond to his persistent brother. They ate in silence for a while, until RJ reached for a newspaper that lay on an empty table next to them.

"Holy shit," his brother said in hushed tones after a minute of reading.

Noah glanced up from his steak to see RJ holding an article in front of his face. There, next to the article, was a black-and-white picture of four people.

"Recognize anyone?" RJ asked after Noah only stared.

Noah took the paper and read the caption under the photo.

Pictured above, Darren Price with wife Priscilla, son Landon, and daughter Avery at a fund-raiser last fall.

Noah looked at RJ with a furrowed brow. "Darren Price? As in—"

"Billionaire publishing mogul Darren Price? Yeah, that's him."

Noah glanced down at the picture one more time. The other people in the picture didn't matter. Avery's stunning face jumped out at him from beneath the black-and-white ink. Dressed in a light, knee-length dress, she outshined the three people surrounding her. So she was the heiress to a giant media corporation. No wonder she never seemed to fit in in Trouble. No wonder she never wanted to discuss her family. Did she think he'd go after her money? Why hadn't she just been honest with him in the beginning? Maybe he'd been the problem. Perhaps she didn't think he cared enough to know more about her. That couldn't have been farther from the truth. He wanted to know everything about her from the day he met her.

So why did he feel like the heel in this situation?

"Bet you didn't know *that* about her, did you?" RJ asked as he took a whopping bite of meat.

No. Hell, no, he didn't.

TWENTY-ONE

IT HAD TAKEN AN AMAZINGLY short amount of time to drive back to Denver. She'd been hoping, as she packed that morning, for there to be a reasonable amount of traffic on Highway 25 so she'd have time to ruminate over her thoughts. The highway was as empty as a desert road. What was it called when that happened? Murphy's Law? Or was it plain old shit luck? Either way, she'd reached her parents' penthouse sooner than she'd expected. In order to give herself some get-it-together time, she'd remained in the underground parking garage, gripping the leather steering wheel until her fingers made indentations. What had she hoped to accomplish by sitting here? For the dull gray wall in front of her to provide all the answers and tell her what to say? Perhaps there'd be pearls of wisdom on the wall of the elevator on the way up to the top floor. Who was she kidding? Could she be more unprepared?

You can't think your way through this one, Avery. You have to experience it.

Besides, she was a grown woman. What were they going to do to her? Ground her? Lock her in her room? She had a job. She could stand on her own two feet. She didn't need them anymore. As long as she chanted that to herself again and again, she'd be fine.

They're just people. You don't need them.

Closing her eyes and pulling the new car smell into her lungs, she stepped out of the vehicle and headed toward the elevator. By the time she reached the penthouse, she had her emotions firmly in check. Calm. Cool. In. Con. Trol.

The elevator's doors swooshed open, revealing the elegant hallway and the golden double doors standing majestically at the end. The doors always reminded Avery of walking into Willy Wonka's Chocolate Factory. They possessed a nearly whimsical feel with their ornate carvings and reflective surface, so anyone drawing close could get a full view of themselves. Another piece of her father's vanity?

She used her key to let herself in, then paused for a second. Stoic muteness. That was the only way to distinguish the interior of the impeccable Price home. No clutter. No family pictures. Absolutely nothing out of place. Avery had never paid attention to such particulars in the past. Nevertheless, after spending a month in Rebecca's apartment with its shabby-chic decor, Avery now realized her former home was uninviting.

A quiver undulated through her. How could she ever consider spending time here? Thankfully she didn't have to anymore.

Indulgent, female giggles drifted into the foyer from the rear of the penthouse. There were too many rooms to tell precisely where the noise originated. Could be the family room, the media room, the kitchen, or the dining room.

Her heels produced delicate clacking noises on the polished marble floor as she walked as softly as she could across the foyer. The family room straight ahead of her was empty. No females giggled in the media room either. She walked back across the family room toward the kitchen. The laughter became brassier as Avery drew near, and more hysterical. The gruff, breathy tone couldn't be mistaken for anything else. No way could that be her parents. Landon always liked to joke that he and Avery were really delivered by a stork. How could her parents have conceived two children when they never touched each another, outside of the casual arm-around-the-shoulder in public? No. Unquestionably not her parents. If it were, Avery would surge right out of here and enroll herself with the nearest shrink.

The quality of the laugh was too young to be Gina. Besides, her former nanny wouldn't be so audacious as to bring a lover into her employers' home.

As she approached the archway leading to the kitchen, the laughter hushed to make way for male whispers. Landon.

The scene before her would have made her gasp if it had been anyone other than two people she loved more than anything. Across the area of the stainless steel monstrosity her parents called a kitchen, were Teeny and her brother locked in an intimate embrace, both of them scantily clothed. Teeny sat perched on the counter, her bare legs locked around Landon's hips as he nuzzled her neck. He pulled the man's shirt Teeny wore away from her shoulder and kissed along her collarbone. Teeny panted and tilted her head back while stabbing her fingers into Landon's naked shoulders. From the way they were clothed, along with her brother's tousled hair, they looked like they'd just tumbled out of bed.

Avery was just about to leave the room when Teeny

opened her eyes and spotted Avery. She pulled away from Landon and unwrapped her legs from around his hips.

"Avery," her friend said in a surprised voice. "What're you doing here?"

"I was just thinking the same thing about you guys. Aren't you, uh"—she turned her head to glance about the empty space—"worried about being caught?"

"Mom and Dad aren't here." Landon stepped away from Teeny, and she adjusted the shirt over her thighs.

Avery set her purse on the counter and crossed her arms under her breasts. "So what are *you* doing here?"

"Your moronic brother here"—Teeny jumped in before Landon could respond—"blurted out our situation to your father, and now we have to try and smooth things over."

Avery transferred her attention to her brother, who'd picked up an apple from the fruit bowl and was busily munching. "He pissed me off," he explained with a negligent shrug.

"So while you were waiting, you decided to"—Avery waved a hand in the air—"make the best of your old room?"

Landon took a noisy bite of his apple. "Don't worry; I made the bed."

Teeny rolled her eyes and slid off the counter. She made her way across the kitchen and hooked her arm through Avery's.

"Not that I'm not happy to see you, because I am. But why exactly are you here?"

She and her friend walked out of the kitchen and over to the picture windows that offered a view of the west and the Rockies in the distance. "I just felt it was time to have a real heart-to-heart. I need to put all this to bed and move on. Who knows if they'll agree with me or even if they'll listen?" She leaned her head on Teeny's shoulder. "I'll always be looking behind me if I don't get a chance to have my say."

Her friend sighed and lowered her head to Avery's. "Good luck, sister."

"Hey, you're having their grandkid. You're going to need more luck than me."

"Thanks," Teeny muttered.

"On the other hand," Avery said, lifting her head, "you have Landon on your side."

Furrows appeared on Teeny's brow.

"They adore Landon."

Her friend's features loosened into a droll expression. "Your parents adore you, Avery."

She dropped her gaze and noticed a red mark on Teeny's neck. "Not the way they do my brother. They don't seem to care what he does."

"I can't believe I'm about to defend them but"— Teeny ushered them to the curvy staircase that led to the bedrooms—"you're their baby and the only girl. It's only natural for them to be more protective of you."

"There's protective and then there's suffocating."

"I think it's harder for some parents to draw that line," Teeny explained as they reached the top of the stairs and started down the long, morose hallway.

"How do you make them?"

They stopped at Landon's old room, where Teeny opened the door and led Avery inside. "I don't think you can." She walked over to her clothes, which lay in a pile at the foot of the bed.

Just as Landon said, his queen-size bed had been made to perfection, not a single rumple spoiling the dark-brown comforter.

Avery sat on a lounge chair by the balcony as Teeny peeled off the light-blue men's shirt to reveal bare skin and a pregnant belly. Her friend had never been abashed about walking around in her birthday suit. As kids, Avery had wished she had half her friend's courage.

"I do believe you have a little belly on you, Miss Newberry," Avery pointed out, and smiled when Teeny narrowed her eyes.

Teeny slid on a pair of cotton shorts and a loose-fitting T-shirt. After slipping on her sandals, she addressed Avery. "Don't make light of this. I can hardly fit into anything I own."

Avery's smile faded as she watched her friend pull her ash-blond hair back into a ponytail. "Have you talked to your parents yet?"

A few seconds of silence filled her brother's old room. Teeny disappeared into the bathroom, and when she spoke, her voice echoed among all the marble. "I've decided to invite them to the kid's first birthday and let them figure it out for themselves." She came back into the room, looking polished and beautiful as always. "Do I look pregnant in this?"

Avery eyed the baggy shirt, with a college emblem on the front, which completely concealed her little bulge. "No. But I think you need to follow your own advice, T."

Teeny sat down on the edge of the bed. "I think you're right." She buried her face in her hands and made a whimpering sound. "How did I get myself into this?"

Seems they were two of a kind: both unsure how to get themselves out of their current situations. When would they ever start using their heads? Sensing her childhood friend needed comfort, Avery rose from the chair and sank down on the bed next to Teeny.

"That's easy."

Teeny lifted her head and pinned Avery with a pathetic look.

"You fell for my brother."

The mother-to-be lifted her eyes to the ceiling. "I did not fall for your brother."

"You did," Avery insisted.

Teeny stood and paced to the French doors. "Just because we're involved doesn't mean I'm in love with him." Teeny puffed her cheeks out as she pulled in a breath of air then slowly let it out. "I mean, I don't go around falling in love with my best friend's brother."

"Yes, you do."

"He may be funny and charming and amazing in bed," Teeny added as if she hadn't heard Avery. "And he's completely sexy and occupies my thoughts all the time and—what?"

A smile crept along Avery's mouth as she listened to Teeny list her brother's attributes. Her friend was in really deep. Avery could that tell by the way Teeny's breathing had picked up in only the last few seconds; even the way she talked about him was a dead giveaway.

"All you're doing is proving my point. The sooner you're honest with yourself, the better off you'll be."

"How do you figure that?"

"Because once you stop lying to yourself, the two of you can start being honest with each other and move forward."

Teeny turned away to stare out the doors to the multitude of buildings beyond. Instead of lecturing or giving advice, Avery waited, knowing Teeny would figure it out for herself. Finally she slowly lowered to the lounge chair Avery had vacated.

"What do I do?"

Her voice came out small and meek, like a child asking a parent for help. Teeny was one of the most headstrong people Avery knew. She'd never needed anyone's help or advice.

"Marry him, let him pamper you, and have a houseful of babies."

Teeny leaned her hand back against the chair and stared at the ceiling. "The pampering sounds nice," she said, almost grudgingly. Teeny drew her knee up and picked at a scab on her ankle. "I guess this is what I get for wearing heels too small for me. So what're you going to say to your parents?"

Avery watched, grossed out, while Teeny picked the scab until it was almost completely off. "I don't know." Her shoulders sagged. "I guess I'll figure it out when I see them."

Teeny finally looked up. "I can tell you've given this a lot of thought." Sarcasm laced her friend's voice, which should have offended Avery. However, she didn't take offense, because Teeny was totally right. Even though she knew what she had to say—to a certain extent—she had yet to make up the exact words.

"I hate to break up your makeover session." Landon's voice came from behind them, in the doorway. Avery turned on the bed to glance at him. "But Mom and Dad are here."

"Avery's gone."

Noah considered his employee as she stood in her doorway. Her hair, a rumpled, frizzy mess of fiery-red, rotini-like curls that looked like she'd either just fallen out of bed or let a man run his hands through them, momentarily distracted him from the words that had just left her mouth.

"What kind of gone are you talking about?"

Please don't let it be the permanent kind. Please don't let it be too late to fix this.

He forced his hands to remain relaxed in the pockets of his worn jeans and waited impatiently for Rebecca to explain. A television blared in the background, something about the most fuel-efficient car in America getting even more fuel efficient. Noah couldn't have cared less. If someone announced he'd won the lottery, he'd be disinterested.

Rebecca leaned against the jamb and adjusted the reading glasses that were nestled among the bird's nest on top of her head. "She packed a bag last night and said she needed to go home for a little while."

"Go home for a little while" could have any number of meanings. Vacationing with family, getting away from the city, or the dreaded making up with the supposed fiancé, which Noah refused to explore further.

"Did she say anything else?" *Like "That guy isn't my fiancé and I'm in love with Noah"?*

Rebecca shook her head and thinned her lips into a slight frown. "No, she was pretty tight-lipped about it."

His disbelief and frustration must have been evident by his lowered brow. A look of worry crossed Rebecca's face.

"If this is about her missing work," Rebecca tried to reassure him as she straightened away from the door, "don't worry. I'm going to cover for her."

Work-schmurk. That was the last thing on his mind. This morning he'd finally put aside his anger, though it went against his better judgment, and Avery wasn't even around to talk to. Now he faced a whole new dilemma, which, by the way, he was really starting to grow tired of: did he follow her to Denver and invade her quaint, oh, excuse him, *posh* family home? The answer to that question would probably take him another three days to figure out.

"Noah, are you all right?"

Only when Rebecca said his name did he realize he'd been staring at her like an idiot.

"Uh... yeah. Sorry. I'll see you later." He left his puzzled secretary standing in the doorway and decided to go home. Why, he wasn't sure. He really did have work, but none of it seemed important. However, as much as he'd love to, there was no getting out of his meeting with one of his subcontractors. Considering the appointment important enough, he'd decided at least to shave the two—or was it three—days of stubble off his face. And maybe take a shower. And he should probably change out of his paint-stained jeans. Then he ought to at least appear human enough to converse with someone on a professional level.

At least at home he'd have some peace and solitude to wallow in self-pity for about an hour.

However, when he pulled into his driveway twelve minutes later, he saw Brody's car. How many times this month did that make? Three? Four? Hell, at this rate, he'd have himself a new roommate by the end of the year.

Telling himself not to put his inner grouch on his face and to listen with at least half an ear, Noah walked into his house. And into an empty living room. Empty kitchen... and... sure enough, empty bathroom. On his way back to the front door, movement from the backyard caught his attention. His younger brother, looking like he'd been run over by an eighteen-wheeler, paced back and forth on the other side of the sliding glass door, cell phone tucked between his shoulder and ear.

Noah, deciding it was impolite to burst out there and demand an explanation for Brody's presence, kicked off his shoes and opened the fridge to quiet his growling stomach.

If nothing else, food would help. Food always helped. Yep, a nice, big, cholesterol-laden omelet ought to clear his troubles right away.

After making his, he decided to make one for Brody, and that's when his brother entered the house. Noah glanced over his shoulder and took Brody's uncombed hair, unshaven face, and grease-stained shirt to mean that all was not well on the home front. He'd seen his brother look better than he did now. But, given the circumstances, Noah understood. Hell, Brody looked on the outside the way Noah felt on the inside. Like shit.

Brody tossed his cell phone on the counter with a weary sigh.

Noah transferred the second omelet to a plate and placed it under his pathetic-looking brother's nose. Brody only looked at it like it was infected with some sort of disease.

"Sorry to drop in on you again." Brody's gravelly voice meant either he was coming down with laryngitis or he'd been up all night without a wink of sleep. Noah guessed the latter.

"That's all right." As much as he loved his brother, Noah wasn't particularly in the mood for dealing with more problems. On the other hand, the dejected, unkempt aura Brody had going on only made Noah feel like an ass for being so worried about himself. After all, the mess

Brody had been trying to deal with, of keeping his family together for the sake of his son, would be taxing on anyone.

Brody stared at the omelet as if he expected the food to feed itself to him. After a moment, he picked up a nearby fork and cut a bite. Noah took that as a sign that his brother was, in fact, still breathing and picked up his own meal.

"Want to tell me about it?" Noah asked after the two of them had eaten in silence.

Brody sucked in a deep breath, his eyes still downcast. "Kelly left me. She says she wants a divorce." His monotone words made Noah worry that his brother had withdrawn so far into himself that no one would be able to help him.

Unable to offer any real words of comfort, because Noah seriously doubted that at this point in time Brody would find anything anyone had to say of comfort, he only placed a hand on his brother's slumped shoulder.

"She packed Tyler up and said she was going to stay with her parents in Michigan."

Since the day he was born, Tyler had always been Brody's entire existence. Everything Brody did, every decision he made, had been with his son's best interests at heart. His brother was one of the most loving, involved parents Noah had ever seen. And now Kelly had taken his son away. Noah couldn't begin to imagine being apart from his child for any length of time, however temporary. But if he had to venture a guess, he'd have to say it was one of the worst feelings for a parent. It was a wonder Brody hadn't thrown himself under a semitrailer. On second thought, maybe he had, considering the way he looked this morning.

Noah wasn't about to ask for the specifics of what

Brody and Kelly had discussed, *if* they had had a discussion at all. The only thing Noah could offer was silent consolation. Brody, being the closed book he was, would no doubt not want anything more than a solid presence beside him.

Since walking in the door, Brody had yet to lift his gaze off the floor or his food. He ate in silence, keeping his head down as if repeating a silent prayer. Hell, maybe he was. Maybe Brody felt that was the only way to make sense of this pile of shit his life had become.

"I promise I won't stay long. I just…" His little brother gripped the edge of the counter so tightly Noah was afraid the skin over his knuckles would tear, much like the Incredible Hulk's shirt. "I can't be at home right now."

"Brody," Noah stated in a firm voice, wanting his brother to look him in the eye and know Noah meant what he said. When Brody lifted his head, the tears that swam beneath the gray depths of his eyes were enough to make Noah forget all about what had happened to him the last week. "Stay as long as you want. You're my brother, and this is your home too."

Noah added a squeeze to Brody's shoulder for extra reassurance. His brother's only response was a slight but weak nod of his head as he returned his attention to the counter.

"Don't worry about Tyler," Noah urged, abandoning his original rule to stay silent. "He knows you love him."

However much conviction Noah put behind his words, they didn't seem to do a lick of good with Brody. He left his omelet half-eaten and trudged to the back door. "I have to get ready for work."

By "get ready for work" he surely meant "call my wife and try to fix this." Right?

"You can't possibly be effective in this condition. You look like you're on drugs."

"Maybe I ought to be." Noah only stared after his younger brother when he paused with his hand on the door. "Look, I know you mean well, and I appreciate that. But I need to be doing something where I'm not thinking about this."

Noah gazed at Brody's retreating, sullen back as he made his way to the guesthouse.

Wasn't life just peachy-feakin'-keen?

Later that afternoon, after a mind-numbingly boring meeting with his subcontractors about punch lists, Noah decided not to return to his office. The only thing to do there was mull over the spectacular turn of events that had taken place in his life over the past few days. Not that taking a trip to his father's restaurant would push the...how should he put it...inconvenient thoughts out of his mind in any way, shape, or form. Nevertheless, he wanted to get something that had been nagging him off his chest.

Parked in front of McDermott's were a surprising amount of cars, which made Noah wonder what kind of person ate dinner at four thirty in the afternoon. Couldn't be the geriatric crowd. His father always thought Early Bird Specials were only for places like Denny's. And McDermott's, as his father also said, was no Denny's. He guessed people in this town were just so darn eager to get a steak they couldn't wait until the regular dinner hour. Whatever.

His father was rarely found in the dining room. Martin McDermott spent most of his work time in his office doing...whatever the hell he did up there. So one could only imagine Noah's utter astonishment when his old man was nowhere to be found in or around the general vicinity of the dining room or the kitchen. His brother, however, was there... shocker. Noah always wondered how Chase found time to be human with all the hours he put in to managing Trouble's best steak house.

Noah stood on the sidelines while Chase spoke to a dark-haired teenager who held a bin of dirty dishes.

Chase stepped closer to Noah after the busboy walked away. "What brings you here?"

"I need to talk to Dad about something. Do you know how busy he is?"

Chase's answer was a shrug of his shoulders. "He's been in his office all day. If you want to catch him, you'd better hurry. You know how he likes to leave before the dinner rush."

Noah eyed the dining room, which was about one-third full. "Speaking of rush, isn't it rather busy for this time of day?"

Clothed in black slacks with crisp creases down the center of the legs, Chase placed his hands on his hips. "Actually, this is normal," his brother replied as his gaze roamed around the room, his eyes touching briefly on a blond-haired waitress.

Normal? Just went to show how much Noah knew about his father's business. The blond waitress who'd captured Chase's attention laughed at something one of the male customers said, like the huskier her laugh, the higher her tip would be. Noah spared her a moment of interest before moving his attention elsewhere. And yet, his attention moved back to her. There was something vaguely familiar about her. The slight build, like that of a ballet dancer, the short, choppy blond hair, and the way she carried herself like someone used to handling things herself all rang familiar with him. But he couldn't quite put his finger on why.

"Where do I know her from?" Noah asked when she all but floated across the dining room to the kitchen.

"That would be Lacy Taylor," Chase said with the slightest touch of resentment in his voice.

Lacy Taylor...Lacy Taylor. Nope, not ringing any bells.

Wait a minute. Noah watched Lacy Taylor when she returned from the kitchen and walked to the ordering station, where she smiled and placed an affectionate hand on the server already punching in his order. Then it dawned on him.

"*That's* little Twiggy Taylor?" Noah asked Chase, using the name given to her in high school because of the way her less-than-womanly body sort of resembled a golf club.

Even though her body was still slender, like she needed to eat a few more cheeseburgers, there was nothing... golf-clubbish—yes, that was the technical term—about her body now. Although she was a few years younger than he, having graduated with Brody, Noah remembered her. And the reputation that had followed her wherever she went. Something to do with her low-life felon of a father.

"Yeah," Chase finally said in a deeper voice than usual. "But don't call her that. She hates it." His brother shook his head as his gaze followed Twiggy—oh wait, *Lacy*—to one of the other tables.

Noah was no expert on the way his brother's mind worked, but he thought Chase was paying too much attention for someone who had never given Twiggy—shit, *Lacy*—the time of day as a kid.

"I thought she was in New Mexico or one of those desert states."

Chase returned his attention to Noah. "Arizona. Apparently Ray's got lung cancer, and Lacy came home to take care of him."

Ray was Tw—Lacy's—grandfather, who had raised Lacy since she was about fifteen and her father had been taken to jail, again, but on a more permanent basis.

"And guess who she came crawling to for a job?" his brother added, with a somewhat smug smile turning up the corners of his mouth.

"You don't sound overly enthusiastic about it."

Judging from the way Lacy turned her friendly eyes to Chase and they became, well, not friendly upon seeing him, Noah had to guess she wasn't kicking her feet up in a fit of glee either. But why would she be here if she and his brother weren't exactly best friends?

Chase turned his smile, which didn't quite reach his eyes, to Noah. "Let's just say Lacy brings out my uglier side."

Noah, not fully understanding what was going on between Chase and little Twiggy, just patted Chase on the back and headed upstairs to the offices.

His plan was to have a productive and informative meeting with his father where they could talk without disagreeing. Yeah, if that actually panned out he'd make an appointment to have his chest waxed.

He rapped lightly on the door before opening it and stepping inside. A day planner held his father's attention. It was only after Noah shut the door that the other man looked up.

"Noah. What're you doing here?"

Well, it wasn't quite the warm and fuzzy welcome he'd been hoping for. He supposed it was better than *What the hell do you want?*

"Do you have a minute to talk?" Noah paused in the middle of the office before sliding his hands into his pockets and approaching the desk.

"Sure. I was just going over some figures." He flipped the planner closed and leaned back in his black leather chair.

"What about?" Noah figured since he was here, and was a silent partner in the business, he might as well show some interest.

His father ran his hand along the leather book like it was a cherished baby. "The new restaurant."

Noah settled himself in one of the chairs. "Ah," he replied, unsure of what else to say. "Actually that's what I want to talk to you about."

"Oh? What about it?"

"Well." Noah fidgeted and crossed his ankle over his knee. "I was there the other day. Looks like a good site."

His father offered a condescending tilt of his lips. "Thank you, son. I'm glad you approve."

"What I mean is, I checked out the construction. I think there are some things you should take a closer look at."

Martin was silent for a moment, resting his hands across his elderly round belly. "Such as?" he asked.

"For one thing, the foundation is cracked. Which worries me because it means they didn't do a proper job leveling the land first."

His father's thick, white brows shot up his forehead. "Worries you?"

"Yeah, and it ought to worry you too." For some reason, Noah had the vague impression his father still didn't take him seriously, like he didn't know squat about construction.

"Not that it concerns you, but the company I hired came highly recommended."

Not that it concerned him? Hell, he was only a silent partner. Besides, call him sentimental, but it was still a family business. He didn't want to see his father get screwed by some two-bit operation that couldn't even level off a piece of land. Noah could have done a better job in his sleep.

The other man remained silent and waiting behind his desk.

"Recommended by whom?" Noah finally asked.

Martin rubbed a weathered, sun-spotted hand along his chin. "A friend. A friend I trust."

But you don't trust me?

"Obviously this friend doesn't know anything about construction. I think you need to take a trip out there and closely inspect the place."

His father sighed and pressed his lips together. "I'll think about it."

Well, slap a pair of tights on him and call him Nancy. His father was going to *think* about it? That was the equivalent of, well, something big. Right now he was too downright giddy to think clearly.

"Was there something else you wanted to talk about?" The question his dad asked was a clear sign their conversation had come to an end.

Noah decided it was best not to push his luck; he might as well leave the conversation on a somewhat high note. He forced a smile and stood. "I'll let you get back to your work."

As he left his father behind the oversize wooden desk, Noah told himself, even if it was a stretch, that today's visit hadn't been a total loss.

TWENTY-TWO

ER FATHER HAD DEVELOPED AN annoying tick in his jaw sometime during the past month. Avery supposed it was stress, or maybe fatigue, to which she had—and she was being modest here—probably, in some small way, contributed. Not that she wanted to give herself too much credit. She was just one tiny woman.

Her mother, a blond version of Susan Lucci, except more robotic, had offered her everything under the sun to drink. Would she like coffee? No, thank you. How about tea? No, thank you. Gina could bring in some Pellegrino, or water, or wine, or perhaps she'd prefer some champagne, even though it was barely five o'clock. No, no, no, and no. After Avery had plastered a muscle-straining smile to her face and said she was fine, her mother conceded defeat and settled herself in her antique George IV gilt-wood-edged, black-upholstered confidante. Personally, Avery had never liked the chair. Her parents had bought it from an antiques dealer in England who swore it was an original piece that King George himself had used during the early 1800s. She always thought the four individual seats quartered together into one chair looked like it belonged on a children's playground.

"I'm so glad you've decided to come home," her mother said in a breathy, airy voice like some women get after a really good orgasm.

Come home? Good heavens. Gardening tools were more cooperative than this.

"I don't think she's here to stay, my love. Are you, Avery?"

Her father, who at this point was more patronizing than helpful, had opted to stand instead of sit in any of the horrifically uncomfortable antique chairs littered throughout his downstairs study. Darren Price could often be found entertaining a wide variety of people in here with every type of cigar known to man, endless amounts of cognac or bourbon, and mindless chatter. Her mother rarely entered the room, even though she'd decorated it much to resemble a sixteenth-century English drawing room.

No, instead of sitting, the patriarch of the Price household chose to stand in front of the bar, which housed his vast collection of expensive liquor. She supposed standing made him feel superior since it enabled him to look down at her. The belittling feeling was something Avery had grown quite used to over the years. So much in fact that she hardly ever expected her father to sit down when he spoke to his children.

"You're right." *For once.* "I'm not here to stay." Avery crossed her legs then uncrossed them in an attempt to get comfortable. "But there are some things I need to say."

"And what, pray tell, would they be?"

She decided to ignore her father's sardonic tone and the way he stood over her like a sentinel, again, and chose her words carefully. After all, her parents, although highly intelligent people, didn't often seem to understand the words that left Avery's mouth.

A glance at her mother showed the woman's smile had faltered slightly. But no matter how big the smile, it still wasn't enough to put even a hairline wrinkle on her surgically altered face. In fact, Avery always thought that if her mother had any more work done on her face, she'd soon be able to blink her lips. The picture, even though it was somewhat humorous, didn't sound the least bit flattering to someone who was trying to appear younger than her fifty-nine years.

"First, I want to say that my leaving has nothing to do with you being my parents." Lie, lie, lie. If they refused to believe the truth, then use an alternate version. Hey, desperate times call for desperate measures. "I just feel like it's time for me to be independent."

"Honey, you can do that with Peter. You don't even have to continue living here. You can go someplace else with him."

Truthfully, Avery was quite surprised by her mother's reaction. Gone was the demanding tone and condescending reasoning. Had some Botox leaked into her system and drugged her somehow? Who was this person sitting in front of her?

"Before I continue, let me say it's over between me and Peter. We've talked, and I've convinced him I don't want to marry him. I'm happier without him." She looked from one parent to the next. They both stared back at her much the way a dog stares at you when it's trying to understand human lingo. Not that she was comparing her parents to dogs. Really, she wasn't.

"Avery," her father began, then turned to his bar and poured two fingers of bourbon. "Drink?"

She inhaled a deep breath and prayed for the strength not to strangle him. "For the last time, no. But thank you."

"Suit yourself." He paused to take a sip of the drink he'd poured for her, then cradled it in one hand. "Your mother and I never intended to push someone on you with whom you weren't happy. We only thought Peter was a good match."

She balled her hands into fists. "You mean he was a good match for *you*."

Her father lifted his shoulders, covered in an expensive Italian slate-gray silk shirt. "However you want to look at it. But if you say it's truly over, then your mother and I are willing to move past the whole thing." He took another slow sip of his drink, prolonging what was probably going to be another lecture. "That's not to say we aren't disappointed the two of you couldn't see eye to eye. I have no doubt in my mind most of that is due to your sudden independent streak. Which you inherited from me."

What was supposed to be, she was sure, a compliment sounded more like an insult. After hearing things like that most of her life, Avery knew not to read between the lines.

And even though she still had mixed feelings about the whole Peter fiasco, a small but significant sense of closure settled over her. That was one out of a handful of problems on which she could close the book. She thought.

"I appreciate your understanding." Finally. Planets were created in less time than this. "Not that I'm not grateful for all you've done for me. I understand your intentions were in the right place," she said after they both stared at her as if expecting her to be more thankful. How many alternate truths had she said so far? Maybe she didn't need to keep count.

"Does this mean you're coming home?"

Geez, her mother was obsessed with her coming home. Did the woman sit in her room at night and make wishes on shooting stars? Surely she didn't expect her grown daughter to live at home forever.

The woman had yet to move from her spot on the oddly designed chair. In fact, Avery was sure her mother hadn't so much as blinked or even taken a breath.

"Mom," Avery started as if talking to a child. "I'm twenty-eight years old. Don't you think it's time I got out on my own? And stopped being a dependent to you?"

Her mother tilted her elegant blond head to one side sort of like a dog—she really wasn't comparing them to dogs—would do when it heard a strange sound. Eyelids slowly blinked over deep, royal-blue eyes.

"Of course." Her voice deepened, closely resembling the commander-like tone Avery had grown used to. "We just thought it would be with a husband and not to some"—the other woman waved an unnaturally smooth hand in the air—"no-name cattle town in the middle of Wyoming. You can have your independence here in Denver."

"I don't want to be in the city anymore. I like being in a small town."

Finally, her mother's smooth face cracked with shallow wrinkles pulling her too-thin, dyed-blond eyebrows together. "But—"

"Give it a rest, Priscilla," her father interrupted as he downed the last of his bourbon and set the crystal down with more force than was necessary. Honestly, didn't the man know how easily things like that cracked? "She's not coming home."

Both Avery and her mother tossed the head of the household looks of confusion.

"You don't want to be with Peter? Fine, your mother and I have accepted that. But you want to be on your own? Then you have to be on your own."

Avery cautiously decided to remain silent, knowing her father's words had more meaning, and he wasn't finished laying out his plan for her. In order to retain control, the other man no doubt had a plan of contingency in the back of his mind all ready to bring out if need be. She had a feeling she was about to hear whatever he'd concocted.

"I want to be on my own." A childish urge to stand up so she'd feel equal to him almost had her leaving the antique chair, which had caused part of her butt to go numb. She remained seated in a grown-up show of control, which her father pointed out she'd inherited from him. She'd only done it to prove to herself that the way her father loomed over her like those giant glowing sentient gate-things from *The NeverEnding Story* didn't bother her in the least.

"Let me make myself a little clearer."

Please do. I'm quivering with anticipation.

"You want independence and freedom? Then you have to take all that comes with it. That nice little savings you've been living off of—you know, the one that bought you the car you love so much—is no longer yours."

Avery could only stare. She wasn't sure any words that would leave her mouth at this point in time would be a sufficient response. Mostly because she still didn't understand what the hell her father was getting at. Actually she did have a small, tiny clue. But the conclusion her mind currently formed was not one that left her with a comfortable feeling.

"Perhaps you should explain a little bit better, Darren. I don't think our daughter fully grasps what you mean."

Apparently her mother's enigmatic eyes had the capability of seeing into her mind.

"Being independent means you have to earn for yourself.

If you do have a way of supporting yourself, as you have said several times, then you should have no need for the money you've been living off of. Correct? If that's the case," her father went on without even giving her a chance to answer—yet another way of maintaining control, "then your mother and I are going to find other uses for it. Donating it to charity perhaps. You are, after all, a big supporter of charity."

Oh, the bastard was using her charity work against her.

His intention to give her money—she supposed it really was her parents' money—away to people who really needed it was for all intents and purposes noble. But she still couldn't help but feel that her father was being anything but noble. He had chosen the word "charity" to strike a chord near and dear to her heart. And not in a good way. No, his intention was to twist an ice pick in her heart until all the blood dripped free and she was left with nothing but emptiness. To make a long analogy short, what he wanted from her was *You're right, Daddy. Please don't give my money away. I'll move back home and do whatever you want.*

No way would she give them the satisfaction.

She inhaled a deep breath and pulled her lips into a satisfied smile. "It's your money, of course. You can do whatever you want with it. I'm perfectly capable of surviving on my own." She looked from her mother to her father, neither of whom showed any kind of reaction other than an occasional I'm-trying-to-comprehend-what-you're-saying blink. "As for giving it to charity, I think that's a wonderful idea. You might want to look into Autism Speaks." She widened her smile for sheer effect. "It's my favorite."

There. Take that.

Maybe she had, for the first time, ended a conversation with the upper hand.

"I was thinking the St. Jude Children's Research Hospital, but your mother and I have decided to leave the decision up to you. The money is in your name."

At this point the decision on what to do with the money was moot. They could go back and forth all night. They had made up their mind and that, as they say, was that. Not that she wanted to be selfish and hoard all the money for herself; she hadn't been lying when she'd said she was capable of supporting herself. What killed her was leaving there, knowing her father thought he'd won yet another battle. And it shouldn't even be about winning and losing. For some reason, though, it always felt that way with them, no matter how hard she tried to tell herself otherwise. Let the money go to people who would put it to good use. If she kept it, she'd only end up having more things she didn't need.

"Give it to St. Jude's, then. It doesn't matter." Time to give up the battle and let her father do with it what he wanted. St. Jude's needed it more than she did. The point was, they were willing to give her what she needed more than millions of dollars: independence.

Her father puffed out his chest, then let out a long exhale of air. A sign of weariness maybe? "If that's your wish. If you're willing to give that money away, you can leave and do whatever you want with your life. We won't interfere with it anymore."

Ever again? The vague answer left her uncertain. Her intention wasn't to cut her parents out of her life. They may be controlling, old-fashioned hypocrites, but she wanted to maintain some kind of relationship with them. Even if it meant seeing them only on holidays, so she could hold on to her sanity.

She stood, only because the tingling sensation in her butt had turned into numbness.

"Look," she started, trying to salvage what was left of their relationship. For as hard as she thought, she had no idea how they'd gotten this way. "I didn't come here to fight with you. All I want is to live my life the way I want to live it and have you . . ." She started to say "support" but that seemed a tad too eager. "Accept that."

Her father remained unmoving from his post, his eyes unblinking, as if her words were still turning over in his head.

"We have accepted it, Avery," he finally said in a tone unlike she was used to hearing. It was almost filled with . . . regret. More than likely her ears were playing tricks on her.

Neither one of them made a move. Avery assumed the conversation was over. She'd gotten what she'd wanted hadn't she? Come there, staked her claim, and gotten them to agree to leave her alone? So why didn't she feel like the better half here? Maybe because most parents hugged their kids, and it didn't look like either of them were going to do that. Neither even twitched. Hell, at this point she'd settle for a handshake.

She looked at her mother. Her beautiful, angelic-looking mother. Avery so badly wanted to lean down to press a kiss to her smooth, flawless cheek. But she didn't, knowing the sentiment would likely not be returned. Avery wasn't into giving one-way affection. Instead the woman had averted her gaze to her coral-colored linen pants, picking a piece of imaginary lint off her thigh. Then she brushed her soft, manicured hands down her legs as if satisfied they were clean, even though the pants were as unblemished as the rest of her.

Her mother was avoiding her. Fine. Two could play at that game.

Giving her father a hug would do as much good as an umbrella during a hurricane.

Then he spoke. "You don't have to leave right away. Even though you're on your own, this is still your home. You can stay longer if you like."

Avery supposed that was as much of a peace offering as she would get. She decided to take it at face value and not wish for the moon.

She smoothed her suddenly sweaty hands down her Bermuda shorts and plastered a smile on her face. "I know you won't kick me out. But I've already missed two days of work, and I need to get back."

"Understandable," her father replied with a curt nod of his head, like he was speaking to one of his subordinates.

So...no need to stay and chat about the weather. With business finished, they probably expected her to leave so they could get back to schmoozing more people out of their money for the governor's campaign. Avery really did hate politics.

"Thanks for listening" was all she could think to say, which, to her surprise, really wasn't a lie. They had listened and given her what she wanted. For that, she could leave here completely satisfied.

So, why did she still feel like there were things left unsaid?

Yes, the tiny little detail of her father exchanging money to barter her happiness had crossed her mind. On several occasions. Okay, more than a few occasions; like every day since she'd found out. In fact, on the drive there, she'd planned on confronting her father and demanding an explanation. After she sat down and put her game face on, every argument on the subject of her engagement had failed to come to fruition. It had been at that point in time, gazing at the people who'd given her life, that the reality of the matter had smacked her in the face.

It would have been pointless. Oh, she knew her father wouldn't deny it. He wasn't that kind of man. In fact, he probably would have admitted it with a big, wolfish smile on his aging face. Which was one of the reasons she'd opted not to bring it up. She was sure somewhere out there were those women who would have urged her to have some self-respect and put her father in his place. The truth was, she just didn't care enough anymore. The whole thing had exhausted her, and frankly, she was sick and damn tired of letting this run her thoughts. What was done was done. Arguing about it wouldn't change anything. Things were over with Peter. She'd gotten her parents off her back. And even though she was leaving there not as completely elated as she'd originally planned, Avery supposed that she had taken a few steps forward.

After gathering her overnight things, saying good-bye, and wishing Teeny good luck, Avery headed for the palacelike front doors.

Landon stood with his back to her, his head bent down over something. When she stopped by him, she saw the thing in his hand was an engagement ring with a center diamond big enough to sink the Titanic.

"You must have spent a small fortune on that thing," she said before giving the ring a good look and noticing the way the different angles caught the lights overhead. Teeny would have a heart attack when she saw it.

"You think she'll like it?" Her brother's normally confident air had been replaced by uncertainty, something she didn't see in him very often. She supposed having a baby on the way and a potential proposal could do that to a person.

She set her bag down. "Depends on how many carats it is." When she saw her brother's expression didn't lighten any, she placed a hand on his shoulder. "That was a joke, Landon. I'm sure she'll love it. Think she'll say yes this time?"

He snapped the box shut and slid it in his pocket. His lowered brows turned his hesitant expression into an annoyed one. "I see you two have been talking."

"Girls tell each other everything. You ought to know that by now."

"How'd it go in there?" He changed the subject with a jerk of his head in the general direction of their father's office.

She lifted one shoulder in an oh-well shrug. "As well as can be expected, I guess. I got what I wanted, though."

"You know, I wasn't going to tell you this," he started with a nervous chuckle, "but I talked to Dad about the deal he had with Hank."

"What'd you tell him?"

Landon lifted his shoulders. "I told him to leave you alone and let you live your life."

I could have handled this myself would have been the first words out of her mouth with anyone else. With Landon all she felt was a crushing sense of appreciation and love. Her brother had his own set of problems with Teeny and the baby. He didn't have to come riding in on his white horse with a sense of brotherly duty. As always, he'd been looking out for her when nobody else had.

She stepped forward and grabbed him in a fierce hug, locking her arms around his neck and squeezing her eyes shut. Tears formed, seeping past her closed eyelids and saturating her mascara-coated eyelashes. One lone tear slid down her cheek and soaked into Landon's shirt.

"Aw, don't tell me you're crying," he said as he stepped away from her.

"Sorry." She ran the tip of her pinky finger along her lower lashes to dispel any remaining moisture. Wouldn't do to have black mascara streaks down her cheek.

"So, what are you going to do now?"

"Go home."

Wasn't it some king from biblical times who said "This too shall pass"?

Noah had never been very Johnny-on-the-spot with his ancient history, but whoever coined the phrase knew what they were talking about.

Life eventually got back to normal, by the time the weekend came, a couple of days after Avery's departure. Had it been only a couple of days? Felt more like a year.

In fact, life had become so normal it was almost eerie, like Avery had never even existed.

Of course, no matter how long she stayed away, he would always know in his heart that she'd been as real as anything else. Otherwise how could he explain the achy emptiness with which he missed her?

Saturdays sometimes gave him a chance to work in his office with a few hours of uninterrupted time. Today he didn't have the drive to leave his house. Instead he decided to use the sunny but windy weather to tear down the rotted railing on his front porch.

Some people might say he was drowning his sorrows in good, sweaty, backbreaking work. So what? Noah figured it was better than drowning his sorrows in alcohol, which he'd already done last night, with a just as-pathetic Brody by his side.

The two of them had their own little pity party in his living room, talking about how women were good for nothing else than ripping men's hearts out. On the flip side, upon waking up in a hungover haze this morning, he knew that wasn't true. If it were anyone's fault it was his own for letting her get so close. He'd jumped into a relationship with a woman he didn't know anything about. Hell, he knew more about his mailman than he did Avery Price. And he'd never exchanged more than a cursory hello with the guy.

By the time noon hit, he'd showered and had sufficient coffee to feel human enough to step out in actual sunlight. Brody's car was gone, Noah had no idea where he was. He only hoped his brother hadn't decided to trek it all the way to Michigan in a pathetic attempt to win back a woman who clearly didn't want to be won over.

He had no idea what the future held for his separated brother. Divorce? Shuffling Tyler back and forth between two different houses? As long as the boy was taken care of and loved, Noah supposed that was okay.

The sun beat down ruthlessly on his bare back, cooking him like a Thanksgiving turkey and causing the sun damage Carol had always warned him about. Little rivulets of sweat danced and skittered down his spine, each racing the other to the edge of his jeans. He dropped his sledgehammer on the grass next to a pile of time-worn, weather-beaten wood and grabbed his water bottle. The cool water lent instant, if only temporary, relief to his heated, dehydrated body.

He swiped a hand across his brow and was about to resume his destruction when his father's white Cadillac pulled into his driveway. Great. Just what he needed.

Despite his father's meandering walk up the path, Noah grabbed the sledgehammer and knocked down more railing. All the while pretending he wasn't secretly anticipating what the other man had to say. Noah hardly ever received impromptu visits from his old man.

A shadow descended over the partially ripped-up railing, but Noah didn't immediately turn. He brought the sledgehammer down hard, splintering the wood with a loud crack. After wiping sweat from his brow and taking another chug of water, Noah turned and faced his father.

"Pretty hot out today," his father mumbled as he eyed the pile of wood.

Not a very intellectual way to start a conversation. His father was known for getting right to the point, which Noah had come to expect. When he started a conversation with a pointless remark about the weather, Noah knew there had to be something weighing on his mind.

"Yeah" was all he said in response.

"This looks like a pretty big job." The older man nudged some wood with his brown tasseled shoes. "You sure you should be doing this on your own?"

Noah shrugged and picked up his water bottle again. "It's not that big a job. I can have this done in a few weekends. I do know a little bit about construction," he added just in case his father had forgotten.

"Yes, actually"—his father cleared his throat and folded his arms across his chest—"that's sort of what I wanted to talk to you about."

Noah took a long sip of water, deliberately staying quiet. Besides, a prolonged conversation with his dad would be an easy distraction from other things occupying his mind. He waited while the older man looked everywhere but at Noah. Of course, it was hard to tell exactly what held his father's attention considering the sunglasses he wore showed Noah nothing but his own reflection.

"I took the day off yesterday and had a rather interesting trip to Casper."

"Oh?" Noah decided playing dumb was his preference at this point in time. Better to let his father grovel a little. A bit childish, he knew. But what the hell? This phenomenon didn't happen very often.

"And I—uh," he cleared his throat again. "Actually when I got there..." He bent over and picked at a weed that had poked its head past the ground cover lining the porch. "Well, shit, this isn't coming out right."

At first, Noah thought his father was speaking of the weed. "Just say whatever it is you came to say."

"You were right." The words that left the other man's mouth were so low, Noah thought they were a figment of his imagination. Then he realized his father's sincerity came from the heart when he removed his sunglasses and his gray eyes bore into Noah's.

"Those aren't easy words for me to say," he continued. "But when I'm wrong, I say I'm wrong. I fired my contractor and construction's been put on hold for now."

"And?"

His dad didn't respond. He eyed the surrounding destruction that used to be Noah's front porch as if trying to envision the finished product. Noah waited patiently for an answer.

"And," the other man said slowly, while tilting his head briefly to the brilliant sun overhead, "I'm in a bit of a jam. Frankly, I could really use your help."

If Noah didn't know any better, he'd say he and his old man had almost done a complete one-eighty. All he'd ever hoped for was to have a conversation that didn't veer into business or life choices. Maybe Carol slipped something into his father's breakfast. Or maybe Noah was still hungover. Either way he wasn't quite ready to believe the two of them were having an amiable discussion.

Noah cleared his throat and chose his words carefully. "I don't want to be snide and say I told you so. After all, this is your business and money on the line."

A deep guffaw burst out of his father's mouth, seeming to come from deep down in his chest. When was the last time he'd heard laughter escape the other man's lips? "You have every right to say 'I told you so.' Hell, I'd probably say it." Then his face sobered, and his lips pressed into a thin line, causing the brackets around his mouth to deepen. "The point I'm trying to make is…you're the only one I trust to do the job right. It's yours if you want it."

If he lived to be a thousand years old, Noah would never fully understand the way his father's mind worked. But what he did understand was the length his father went to admit he was wrong. His mother had always said Martin McDermott had more pride than every man in the county put together. Not that Noah was an innocent party in their weird relationship; he certainly hadn't helped things with his own stubbornness. All he'd ever wanted from the man was some kind of recognition. Recognition of his talents that didn't include what everybody else in family did. He supposed this was his father's roundabout way of showing that. And after all this time, Noah realized that was more than enough for him.

"I haven't been very fair to you over the years," his father continued while Noah gazed at him. "I took your branching out personally, like you didn't want anything to do with me. It was hard enough losing your mother, and the restaurants were my way of keeping the rest of the family together."

Noah pushed the heels of his gloved hands into his eyes, telling himself the bright sun was what made his eyes water. "You don't need a business to do that, Dad," he said, after lowering his hands and noticing the way his father had bunched his fists in his pants pockets.

"I know that. It took me a long time to figure it out, though." His voice had become gruff, like he'd swallowed a fistful of sand. "But I don't want you to feel guilty because you made a life for yourself outside of what I created. You're good at what you do, and I'm proud of you. I—"

"Dad, stop." Noah had the sudden urge to wrap his old man in a bear hug and say something like *You had me at hello* like a freakin' woman. Instead he just cleared his throat so he could maintain some semblance of his masculinity. "I've been stubborn too. This"—he gestured between the two of them—"was a joint effort. I owe you an apology too."

The corner of his father's mouth twitched, then his thin lips pursed together like he was trying to hold back whatever else he wanted to say. Noah figured anything else was moot. It didn't matter who was at fault or who was more stubborn. Hell, neither one of them were great communicators. They'd be better off speaking to each other in sign language.

"Well, uh…" The other man cleared his throat—there sure was a lot of throat clearing going on—and slid his sunglasses back on. Noah took that as a sign their current conversation was over. "You know," his dad said with a jerk of his thumb over his shoulder, "I can run home, change my clothes, and give you a hand with this. I might be old, but I can swing a sledgehammer with the best of them."

Noah's lips cracked into a smile at the image of his old man, his bare chest covered in thick white hair, doing manual labor with someone half his age. "Nah, I got this. Go home and enjoy the rest of your day off. Take Carol out to dinner."

"That sounds like a better idea," he responded with a bob of his head and a smile.

"Dad?" Noah called out after his father had made it halfway to his car. The other man turned. "Thanks." It certainly wasn't poetry, but Noah figured it was enough for the both of them. Besides, his father's smile was all he needed to know they were headed in the right direction.

With a grin splitting his face, Noah returned to his work. He got only about three good swings in before his mood shifted once again into the depressing category. Funny how piles of broken and splintered wood could start to resemble a woman's face. A certain woman's face. Or how the smell of fresh-cut grass from his neighbor's yard suddenly turned into the scent of a certain some-one's coconut shampoo after she had stepped out of the shower. *She* being the woman who had taken residence in his thoughts and refused to leave until he acknowl-edged just how much he missed her. What a ruse. Even as his brain admitted he missed her more than any woman before, with the exception of his mother, she still hung around. His own mind had turned against him, flash-ing her face every time he blinked. Or reminding him of things like how her tanned, toned legs looked in a skirt, or the way her eyes narrowed at him when she suspected he held his thoughts back from her. If he had known their time together would be so short, he would have spilled his guts like he'd never spilled them before. Even now, saying something like *I love you* didn't seem as detrimental as her leaving.

As the day wore on and his old railing disappeared, he knew the decision not to go after her had been wrong. So she may or may not have a fiancé? So she had more money than Donald Trump? What a fool he'd been to let such trivial things stand in the way of the one woman with whom he could picture himself walking down the aisle. Before Avery, the only way he'd wanted to walk down the aisle was as a groomsman.

Just as he brought his sledgehammer down with another crack, he heard the low purr of an engine as a car pulled into his driveway.

TWENTY-THREE

A VERY HAD DECIDED TO THROW her plan of action out the window. Considering she'd put the plan together in haste as she pulled out of the parking garage in Denver that afternoon, she figured it wasn't all that much of a loss. Besides, she'd never been any good at sticking with plans anyway. The only thing that made any sense in her life was Noah. And he was the one thing that threw her life into total chaos to begin with. Funny how things worked out.

Her original agenda included getting in touch with Noah and letting him now she could no long work for him. The message she'd left on his work phone before leaving for Denver hardly seemed sufficient. And it only explained about needing a few days off. To be honest, getting his voice mail had been a relief. At the time, she hadn't had the strength to have a conversation with him, or even hear his voice. Just listening to the deep bass on his voice mail had been torture enough. After squeezing thoughts of her job in with all the hundreds of thoughts revolving around Noah, she decided to inquire about employment at a local youth center. She'd yet to actually visit the place, but she knew deep down she'd be happier there than stuck in an office all day.

That conversation, Avery had decided after driving into Trouble's town limits, could be held just as easily Monday morning as it could on a Saturday night. The conversation she had in mind with a certain man with wizardlike gray eyes and sun-kissed hair would have much more impact on her future. Avery knew she wouldn't have a problem finding a job. But there was only one man she had her sights on. Only one man who had captured her heart in a way she hadn't imagined. And if she didn't take her earliest chance to fix the mess she'd made, her fears of losing him for good would certainly become reality. If they hadn't already.

Too much time had passed since the Peter incident in which she'd been most unceremoniously outed before Noah's entire family. Not the way she had planned on telling him the truth. Of course, it wasn't Peter's fault. She was certainly adult enough to admit if she'd been truthful from the beginning she'd be snuggling in Noah's arms right now. Perhaps sharing a meal after intense but tender lovemaking. Maybe making wedding plans? Not that she wanted to get ahead of herself. For all she knew, Noah wouldn't even give her the time of day.

She let out a long, tired sigh as she pulled off the main highway and onto the road leading into Noah's neighborhood. She realized, with much chagrin, she was taking a gamble that he'd be home on a Saturday night. Perhaps he'd be out, trying to find someone new to warm his bed. After all, wasn't that what men did? Moved on to their next conquest without really thinking about their previous one?

Stop it. Noah isn't Peter.

There was a chance that he was at home feeling just as alone and miserable as she. Hopefully, anyway.

Her heart squeezed in her chest, followed by several palpitations, when she pulled into Noah's driveway and saw him hard at work. What used to be his front porch railing now lay in messy heaps all over his grass. A wheelbarrow, half-full of wood scraps, was being loaded by the man she had come to see. The desecration of the front porch wasn't what captured her attention and caused a thin sheen of perspiration to develop between in her breasts, however. The last time her heart beat this hard, she'd had to run a mile for PE in the ninth grade.

Mustering up what courage she had left in her five-foot-ten frame, Avery cut the engine and swung the car door open. Either Noah hadn't heard her approach or had decided he wasn't ready to acknowledge her presence just yet. Oh, but she was ready to see him all right. Especially since the early-evening sun, casting long shadows over the lawn, still managed to make his bare back glow as if he had stepped out of a Greek cartoon. His hair, an uncombed mess, curled up at the ends around his neck, letting Avery know that his coif hadn't seen a pair of scissors in quite some time.

She stood on jellylike legs and held on to the roof of the car as he bent down and grabbed more wood with his glove-covered hand. When he straightened, every muscle in his back constricted and bunched. And if he stayed still long enough she'd be able to count every muscle and sinew that lined his back. When he turned in just the right direction she was able to see the faint, shiny glow of sweat making his muscles seem more like satin over bone. She never really realized how much sweat could be a turn-on until now.

Ignoring her erratic heart and forcing even breaths, Avery pushed away from the car and made her way across the lawn. As if powered by some extrasensory perception, Noah turned just before she reached him. The full impact of his mesmerizing stare, as she came to a stop before him, brought back memories of the first morning she laid eyes on him. She'd known then her heart didn't stand a chance and nothing had changed.

"You sure have made a mess here." *Good opener, idiot.*

"Yeah, well," he said, taking a swig from his gallon-size water bottle, "I figure this is a good way to release all my energy. It was either this or go get myself laid."

Ouch. Okay, so he was still a little upset and not afraid to lay it on thick. Perfectly understandable. Even though she knew she deserved them, his words still stung.

Noah placed the water jug on the grass and when he straightened she was hit again by his scrutinizing eyes. Now they held nothing of their former likeness. Almost as if the life force that gave them their mysterious seductiveness had died out. Had she caused him that much pain?

Unable to stand still under his penetrating stare, Avery circled the crumbled wood on the lawn and ran her gaze along the torn-up porch. "I've spent the last two hours in the car wondering what I would say to possibly explain my..." What word could she find to properly describe how she'd treated him? "Inexcusable behavior. Normally, I'm really good at giving speeches. It's one of the things my parents groomed me for," she added, tossing a cautious glance his way. He remained in his spot, only turning far enough to track her movements.

"The only thing I can do now is tell you the truth—finally," she said with a tight smile, "and hope you'll find it in your heart to"—she waved a hand in the air, almost afraid to say the word—"forgive me."

She slowly lifted her eyes to his, trying to gauge his reaction, hoping for anything beyond the statuelike quality his body had taken on.

The lingering scent of fresh-cut grass and sweet mountain air filled her lungs when she pulled in a deep, steadying breath.

"My father is the head of Price Publications, which I'm sure you've heard of. He and my mother...well, we've never really seen eye to eye, even though I've always led them to believe we did. They've wanted certain things for me, and until recently, I thought those things were going to make me happy." Avery knew Noah probably didn't care about any of this. Her background with her parents wasn't important to making amends with Noah, even though she'd kept it from him. But she felt he needed to know everything about her before they could make things right. "Anyhow, Peter was a mistake that never should have happened. If you were to ask me to give you an honest answer about our engagement I would have to say I simply don't know. He did ask me to marry him, and I honestly thought I wanted to. That is, until I realized what he was really like. Then I told him I wanted nothing to do with him."

She circled the wood again, this time coming to a stop in front of Noah. Her fingers itched to trace the hard lines of his shoulders, to feel the steel beneath the warmth of his skin. Would he brush her hand away or welcome it like he had before? Avery decided it was safest to leave her hands at her sides.

"After I broke things off with Peter," she continued, running her sweaty palms along her shorts, "he couldn't accept that I didn't want to be with him. Both he and my parents kept saying it would be best for me if we married. I was so furious with all three of them that I packed my bags, got in my car, and didn't stop until I pulled into Dick's Motel parking lot. Then I met you, and I knew I'd made the right decision."

Over the course of her brief please-forgive-me speech his face had changed subtly but in a way that let her know maybe, just maybe, her words were having an impact. His eyebrows, instead of two harsh lines pulled together over his eyes, were a tad more relaxed with only a hint of a frustrated furrow in between. His lips, which she had wanted to press against hers upon first seeing him, had lost the tightness that caused lines to bracket them. Or maybe she saw only what she wanted to see. Maybe it was her own wishful thinking that had Noah looking like he wanted to pull her into his bare, sweaty arms.

A nervous chortle popped out of her. "You know, your silence isn't making this easy."

Of course that was probably his intention. What reason would he have to make it easy? How easy had she made things on Peter after she learned of his infidelity?

"What did you expect? I'd welcome you with open arms and drag you to bed?" His voice didn't have the hard, steely edge she'd expected, but it also didn't have the husky welcome she'd grown to love. Perhaps this was for show just to teach her a lesson and all wasn't lost?

"Maybe not to that extreme," she joked with a half smile, trying to lighten his mood. "Look," she said on a sigh. "I know it was wrong of me to be dishonest with you. But I was trying to close a chapter of my life that made me really unhappy. I just wasn't ready to drag somebody new into it."

"You think that's a good enough reason not to be truthful with me? I would have understood if you'd just included me from the beginning." He hooked his thumbs in the pocket of his jeans, pulling the waistband down to expose the white elastic band of his briefs.

Avery spared the exposed area a quick glance, knowing how perfectly sculpted his hips and thighs were beneath his jeans, before swallowing and looking away.

"I know it's a pathetic reason, but that's all I've got. As for your understanding, I couldn't have known for sure without getting to know you better first. And the more time went on, the harder it got for me to spill my guts without it looking like I'd been hiding it from you."

"That's exactly what you were doing, though. You didn't come to Trouble to start a new life. You came here to hide."

Even though she'd known that, to hear the words come from his lips that he'd figured her out had her lowering her gaze in shame. "I realize that now. My head was still too wrapped up in other things for me to be honest with myself, much less you." In fact, the full impact of the truth hadn't hit her until the words had just left her mouth.

He lifted one thick shoulder, and she didn't fail to notice how his gaze ran down her body. "So now what? Did you come here to explain things so you could go back to your other life with a free conscience?"

"I have no other life now." She glanced around her, at the neighborhood and the surrounding hills. "This is it. My parents have cut me off, not that I cared about the money anyway. But I'm on my own." She ventured a step toward him to see what he would do. He did nothing, nor did he reach out to touch her even though they were close enough. "I came here to see if maybe you'd be interested in starting over. You don't have to make a decision right now. At least think about it."

When he didn't move, with his eyes still burning into hers, she decided she'd said all there was to say. She'd put the ball in his court. The only thing she could do was give him space and pray he remembered how good they were together before she messed things up.

She pulled in a deep breath, catching some of his delicious male scent with a hard day's sweat. The aroma brought back memories of long nights entangled in each other's arms and not thinking about tomorrow. With a heavy heart, she pivoted on her sandal-covered heel and took slow steps back to her car. She kept the vehicle in sight, barely resisting the urge to turn around to get one last glimpse of him. What reason would she have to see him again, since he clearly didn't want to give them another chance? She had no one to blame but herself. Finally something real had entered her life, and she'd screwed it up with her own stupid mistakes. On the other hand, how could she have thought she'd be ready for a relationship with substance when she couldn't even deal with other issues in her life?

The Mercedes finally came within touching distance. She groped for the handle, grasping it with a firm hand and jerking the door open. Tears built up, forming little pools beneath her eyelids and turning the charcoal-gray interior of the car into a watery blur. She drew in a shaky breath while gripping the top of the car door until her knuckles hurt. When the tears became too much, she blinked, and they ran over, dropping to the paved driveway beneath her. Even though she'd prepared herself for this, the reality of it proved more difficult to swallow than she'd thought. She'd told herself, as she left the penthouse,

You're taking a gamble. He probably won't take you back.
That was just so she wouldn't get her hopes up only to be let down when he actually did turn her away. No amount of inner pep talks could have prepared her for the heartbreaking defeat that washed over her from head to toe.

She took a more steadying breath and had just placed a foot inside the car when a firm hand wrapped around her elbow. With the last tear dropping off the edge of her jaw, she turned and saw Noah's rugged face, his eyebrows lowered against the setting sun.

"That's it? You're just going to get in your car and drive away?" His voice, always calm, had turned husky, as if he'd swallowed a piece of sandpaper. His hand, warm and calloused, burned into her elbow.

Stunned by his sudden change in demeanor, Avery only blinked at him and blotted her damps cheeks with her free hand. "But you—"

He turned her fully, forcing her foot out of the car, and now had both hands on her arms. He gave her a gentle shake. "You think I'm going to let the woman I love walk away from me?"

The tips of her breasts brushed against his bare chest through her thin button-down linen shirt. If she leaned forward just a little more she could press them fully against him like she had when they'd been naked together. The last thread of her will was just about to give out when the words he spoke hit her full force.

"You...you love me?" she managed to get out on a strained whisper.

His hot gaze lowered to her lips, which she chewed out of nervous habit.

"I was a fool to almost let my pride keep you from hearing how I really feel." He said the words as his hand left her arm and brushed along her cheek. His thumb roamed across her bottom lip, wiping away traces of moisture left by her teeth. Her tongue darted out and touched the tip of his thumb, coming away with a salty, masculine taste. His brow lowered even more as his burning gray eyes zeroed in on where the digit disappeared into her mouth.

"I guess this means you're not mad at me?" She'd meant that as a statement, but it came out more as a question, still not confident he meant to keep her around.

"Oh, I'm mad at you all right."

Disappointment had her shoulders sagging, and she took a small step away from him, bumping into the car behind her.

"Mad enough to take you inside and give you a good spanking." The corners of his lips turned up in a wicked grin.

Warmth filled her chest, and liquid pooled in between her legs as Avery lifted her arms and entwined them around his thick neck. He hefted her up easily, and she wrapped her legs around his waist, trying not to wince at how his belt buckle dug into her pubic bone.

"Let me show you just how mad I am." He carried her into the house, kicking the door closed behind him.

An hour and a half and two rather spectacular orgasms later, Avery and Noah lay on his bed with some Chinese takeout containers littered between them. Noah had fumbled around with the chopsticks for about thirty seconds before tossing them aside and using a fork to dig the pineapple out of the sweet-and-sour pork. The corners of Avery's mouth had tilted in a smile at the sight of her lover's masculine hands trying to grasp the thin wooden sticks.

Those hands are mine.

All of him was now hers.

"So," Noah started as he tossed aside another container and reached for the fried rice. "When you say your parents cut you off, you mean..."

"They literally cut me off. I have no money." She lifted her shoulders beneath Noah's worn white T-shirt. "Sure I'll get my inheritance one day, but the money I've been living off of is no longer mine." She popped one last wonton in her mouth and shifted her eyes to his. "Does that bother you?"

"Hell, no. I have enough money for the both of us." He shifted from his seated position and leaned on one elbow. Steely muscles rippled beneath bronzed skin when he moved, tempting her to abandon their conversation and press herself against him. Just a short while ago, she'd been running her tongue along the hard, defined ridges of his stomach. She'd taken her time, savoring every moment of feeling him against her, just in case he still wanted to change his mind.

"Is that what's bothering you? You think I only want you for your money?"

She licked her dry lips and abandoned the rest of the wontons. "Every man in my life has been after my father's money. After a while, I just started to assume that's all I was good for."

Noah's gaze roamed over her figure, starting at her breasts beneath his shirt and moving down her bare legs. "That's not all you're good for," he said when his smoldering eyes lifted to hers.

Heat filled her cheeks at his suggestive words, which brought back memories of what they'd been engaged in earlier. She forced the intimate memories aside. "I'm serious. That's mostly the reason I didn't tell you about all that in the first place." Her voice lowered an octave. "I got tired of always being seen as someone with connections instead of an actual person. But," she went on when he opened his mouth to interrupt her, "you've proved me wrong."

"I don't think you should be giving me all the credit," he said, his tone more serious.

Avery nodded slowly and dug her chopsticks into the cold sesame beef. "Yes I should. In fact, you're the only person in my life who can take the credit. By the way," she added, wanting to drop the current subject, "I quit my job."

Noah's thick brows shot up his forehead, leftovers beside him forgotten. "You're quitting? Was I that bad to work for?"

"Just the opposite, actually." She abandoned her food, pushed him to his back, and straddled his hips. "You were great to work for. And not that your scrumptious backside wasn't nice to look at every day, but I think I'd be happier doing something else."

His large palms gripped her hips and ground them against the growing bulge beneath his jeans. "Something else?" he asked absently as his gaze drifted over her bare legs.

Avery smiled, liking how she put him under a spell so quickly.

Avery was sure he hadn't been paying attention to half of what she'd said. His eyes started to glaze over as his hands ran up and down her thighs. He only nodded and occasionally gave her an "mmm-hmm" until she finally gave up and leaned down to kiss him. After his tongue found its way in her mouth and had her seeing spots behind her closed eyelids, she pulled away slightly. "I'm sure I'll have to repeat that later. In the meantime there's one more thing I wanted to tell you."

"What's that?" he asked while he lifted his shirt over her head.

She skimmed her sensitized nipples across his hairy, hard chest. "I love you."

"I know." His magical hands roamed their way down to her hips, where he gave a gentle squeeze.

Just one short month ago, Avery Price had been a lost, hurt soul with a bruised ego the size of Alaska. Who would have thought that her spur-of-the moment, whirlwind plan of escape would have handed her what she never realized she'd always needed?

BONUS MATERIAL

The following scene is the reader's first glimpse at Landon and Teeny as a couple, though Avery doesn't know they're a couple. These two were a fun extra I added in and they kind of took on a life of their own.

Unfortunately, this scene was one of the casualties of editing and it had to get cut. But I love this scene so much that I decided to share it with you. Here is Teeny dealing with that pesky morning sickness.

Happy Reading,
Erin Kern

DELETED SCENE

TEENY NEWBERRY HAD EARNED HER nickname on the first day of kindergarten. She knew the second she stepped foot in the classroom and saw she was a head shorter than everyone else, the nickname that followed would be inevitable. A dark-haired boy ran up to her and said, "Wow, you sure are teeny!" Not that she minded. It was a whole lot better than the alternative, the horrible old woman's name that was imprinted on her birth certificate. Teeny had always hated her real name and had secretly jumped for joy when her classmates had decided to give her a much more attractive alternative.

Her father told her she ought to be proud to be named after her great-grandmother Gertrude. After all, she was one of the women who pioneered a town in Idaho or some important shit like that. Teeny didn't know exactly and never really cared. All she ever wondered was why she couldn't have been named after her other great-grandmother, who had the wonderful fortune of being named something pretty like Julia. Or even her Grandma Betty. Anything was better than Gertrude.

In any event, the girl formerly known as Gertrude

Newberry was now Teeny Newberry. The nickname had always driven her mother crazy. She used to tell Teeny her nickname reminded her of a cartoon, like one of those little mice who talked when they should have been squeaking. One time her mother had tried to implement Gertie as a compromise. Teeny didn't know why the woman thought a shortened version of the worst name ever invented was any better. To make a long story short, it had taken about a year of back-and-forth bickering in order to get her new name to take hold.

The two of them had lived with a mutual understanding ever since. It hadn't been hard. Teeny had a relatively easy relationship with her parents. Like every other teenager, there had been times when she'd rebelled in high school after her mom and dad tried to enforce too many rules on her. They backed off eventually, realizing their only child needed to experience life and make mistakes for herself. For that much Teeny would be forever grateful. However, the one thing she faulted them for was their intensely old-fashioned beliefs. They were two of the most conservative people she'd ever known. In fact, they were conservative to the point where they were almost archaic.

Growing up, she'd never really paid attention to such things or listened when they chastised the lack of solid family values in most American homes. These things never really concerned her. As long as she appeared to be the daughter they raised her to be, it wouldn't affect her right? She'd lived with that belief her entire twenty-eight years. She went about her day-to-day life, got up, went to work, and never really harbored thoughts of whether she'd turned out the way her parents wanted her to.

After all, she was her own person, free to live her own

life. She made everyday decisions, not really being concerned about what her parents thought.

Until three months ago. It was a moment, right here in this very bathroom, that something had happened. Something that made her think, *Shit, what're my parents going to say?*

It wasn't something she'd thought many times over the years. The feeling was so foreign to her that a desperate laugh had popped out followed by a rainfall of tears.

At this moment Teeny didn't have any tears left to cry. In fact, there wasn't a whole lot left inside her. She'd thrown everything up.

Her sensible diet had escaped her recently. She'd inhaled everything in sight since last night and now it all stared back up at her in a gooey, disgusting manner. She took a deep breath to steady herself, now pretty sure everything, including her small intestine, was in the toilet bowl.

Feeling mildly better, for the time being, Teeny flushed and leaned over the sink to rinse her mouth. She was pretty positive whoever invented the term "morning sickness" hadn't actually been pregnant. In fact, it had probably been a man. Only a man could coin a completely off phrase about a woman's body. Morning sickness happened only at night, after she'd eaten herself out of house and home for the better part of the day.

Teeny wished she could call her mother and ask if it was normal to be sick this late in her first trimester. She'd never known anyone who'd been pregnant before, except her mother. However, the woman was unaware of her daughter's unexpected pregnancy so Teeny suspected a call this late at night with such questions wasn't a brilliant idea.

The jerk who'd knocked her up her was sleeping like a damn baby. He hadn't even woken when she ran out of bed, stark naked, to hurl the contents of her dinner. She glared at him as she walked back into her bedroom. Entirely his fault she could no longer fit into her designer jeans.

Grow up, Teeny. No one put a gun to your head and forced you to have unprotected sex. Condoms aren't that hard to come by.

She curled back underneath the down comforter and pulled the heavy blanketing around her shoulders. Running around naked could really make a person cold.

"You okay?" The muffled voice came from next to her.

She stared at the ceiling and slowly blinked. "Fabulous. I'm just wondering how the noodles came up whole when I know I chewed them."

His deep chuckle vibrated across the mattress and did absolutely nothing to soothe her mood. Maybe it was her hormones, but she didn't see how throwing up noodles was amusing. Typical man.

All his fault.

The mattress dipped and gently shook when Landon rolled over to face her. Teeny kept her attention focused on the darkened ceiling. She knew if she looked at him and saw his handsome face and messy hair she'd want him again. Sex was the last thing she needed right now.

"Let's go to Vegas."

She looked at him out of the corner of her eye. "Gambling really isn't my thing."

He rolled his eyes and brushed a strand of hair off her forehead. "I mean to get married."

"Be serious, Landon."

"I am serious." The small tilt of his lips told her otherwise. It was hard to take him sincerely when they were lying naked.

"I want a real wedding. Not one where the man walking me down the aisle is wearing polyester and a bad wig." He opened his mouth to say something and Teeny rolled to her side to face him. "A woman dreams about her wedding day her entire life. We want the perfect dress, the beautiful flowers, and a big diamond ring. Get it?"

His gaze dropped down the edge of the sheet. "So let's do it in a couple of months."

She gave him a droll look. "I really don't want to squeeze my fat belly into a ten-thousand-dollar wedding dress. I want to do it right."

He snorted. "We already went past doing it right, Gertrude."

"Call me that name one more time and this'll be only kid you ever have," she said, smiling sweetly.

He ran the tip of his finger over her shoulder. "Ooh, you sure are grouchy when you're pregnant."

She batted his hand away. "Stop distracting me. I don't have the energy for more sex."

"You were the one who practically shoved me through the door," he said with a half smile that had been torturing her for years. Landon Price was very good at turning on the charm when he wanted to. It was one of the reasons she'd grown up with a love-hate relationship with him.

"Hormones," she replied with a shrug.

His grin grew to the size of Rhode Island, one of the features that Teeny had never been able to resist from him, no matter how hard she tried.

The Newberrys had raised their daughter to be independent, outspoken, and strong-willed. She'd held up to those standards as best she could in every aspect of her life. Except where Landon Price was concerned. She knew the moment she met him, he would be the ultimate undoing of every good intention her parents tried to instill in her.

He'd always been rude, obnoxious, and too damn sexy for Teeny to notice anything else. She hated to love him and loved to hate him. The feeling had been one of those strange phenomenons she'd never experienced with anyone else. The realization had made her want to run in the opposite direction whenever he was around, yet at the same time she'd never been able to think about anyone else.

For years, they'd sparred, teased, insulted, and danced around their desire for each other. Teeny thought the game would never end, or at the very least she'd spontaneously combust, then one night it did end. No, "end" wasn't the right word. "Intensify" was more like it. No, there was no end to what they had now.

Her fate had been sealed four months ago when she'd run into him at a fund-raiser. The encounter hadn't been planned, even though she knew perfectly well he'd be there. He had some ditzy brunette pawing him like he was a newborn puppy. Teeny tried to ignore him and his dark-haired Barbie doll but every time she looked across the room their eyes would connect. One time he had the gall to wink and all the other times there was an intensity about him like he was trying to tell her where they were going to end up before the night would end.

She hated when he was right, especially when he was cocky enough to know it.

The sex had been phenomenal. They'd barely been able to keep their hands off each other long enough to rip their clothes off.

"Teeny…"

She looked at him when she realized he'd been talking to her. "What?"

"I said we can get married however you want if it means that much to you."

She shook her head and ran a finger down his biceps. "It's not just that. I don't want to get married just because you feel obligated to me. I want to marry for love." She looked him in his brown eyes. "Do you love me?"

"Maybe I do," he said in a soft voice.

"Maybe isn't an answer, Landon. Either you do or you don't." When he only stared at her she continued. "Like I said, I don't want to rush into a marriage just because you're obligated to me."

He pulled back from her slightly. "You think I feel obligated?"

"Well, I am pregnant." She pulled back too and gazed at him for one intense moment. "You're telling me you don't feel obligated? This is your baby too."

A weary sigh escaped him. "Teeny, it's more than just obligation. I feel something for you." Her skin quivered when he cupped a hand around her waist then rubbed it across her belly. "I care about you."

She dropped her head down to the pillow and watched as he skimmed his hand across her stomach, like he was trying to feel the baby growing inside. It was still fairly early in her pregnancy, almost four months, and Teeny had never really felt anything until now; except for her bouts of nausea. But seeing his hand, the tanned skin a stark contrast to her pale skin, made the life they'd created together seem more real.

When she first told him she about the pregnancy, Teeny had still been getting over the initial shock herself. But

Landon had taken the news better than she expected him to. He'd been stunned at first. Then he'd pulled her against him and shoved her onto the kitchen table, where they'd made love.

She looked at him and wondered how she was supposed to have been able to resist him in the first place. His sandy-colored hair lay in disarray like he'd been tossing his head over the pillow. His eyes, a deep chocolate brown, were focused on her stomach, where his hand rubbed in circles. Teeny had always been fascinated with his hands. Landon had grown up with privilege, surrounded by some of the wealthiest people in the country; people like her family. Most men like him were always polished and had perfect appearances. They got manicures and their hands were soft and smooth from never doing a hard day's work in their lives.

Landon's, on the other hand, were big and strong looking. His fingers were thick, like those of a man who used them in everyday life. She'd grown to love the feel of them on her; cupping her cheek, playing with her hair, or caressing her skin.

His height was the most impressive part.

That's not the most impressive part of him, Teeny. You've seen him naked, remember?

He stood at six foot two, almost a foot taller than her pathetic five foot three. When she stood next to him she felt small and very . . . feminine, like he was her big, strong protector and could fight off any guy who pursued her. His shoulders, which Teeny had to stand on her toes to reach with her elbows, were wide and powerful. She loved to run her fingers in the grooves of his well-defined muscles, kept in shape from early-morning trips to the local gym.

Everything about him turned her on, always had. From

his deep voice to the way his eyes burned into hers to the way his long legs looked in a pair of athletic shorts.

"We don't have to talk about this right now." He lifted the covers and slid under. Teeny moved to pull him up when he stopped halfway down and placed a soft kiss on her stomach. His thumb stroked back and forth over her belly button and her eyes drooped, and not from fatigue.

She sifted her fingers through his hair when he looked up at her. "You're trying to distract me."

He grinned. "Is it working?"

She lifted her shoulders and combed his hair back from his forehead. "Maybe."

He lifted a brow like he knew he had her right where he wanted her. Shit, he'd always had her where he wanted her, whether she wanted to admit it or not.

He dropped a few more light kisses on her stomach before crawling slowly up her body. "Just promise me if we have a girl, not to name her after your great-grandmother."

She smiled against his mouth and let him take her.

Growing up in Trouble, Wyoming, Lacy Taylor learned to be ready for anything. She can handle a jailbird dad who won't stay lost and a sister she didn't know she had, but sexy Chase McDermott might be her ultimate undoing...

Please turn this page

for a preview of

HERE COMES TROUBLE

ONE

THE SECOND LACY TAYLOR OPENED her front door, she knew the two men standing outside weren't members of the Publisher's Clearing House Prize Patrol. She'd watched enough *FBI Files* to know a federal agent when she saw one. Remarkably bland, dark suits, crisp white shirts, and cheap ties could only be an ensemble put together by an officer of the government.

Lacy stood with her hand on the frame, not bothering to invite them in for drinks. They probably wouldn't accept, anyway.

"Miss Lacy Taylor?

He'd called her "miss." How polite.

The taller man who'd addressed her, roughly the size of Santa Claus with thick sandy hair, looked at her with amber-colored eyes and a bored expression.

The other man, whose skin was as dark as the coffee beans she'd ground up that morning, also looked at her with a bland expression. Was that something they were taught in FBI school, or wherever these two exciting gentlemen were from?

"Yeah, I'm Lacy," she answered, after holding them in

suspense long enough. They were the type of men who didn't appreciate being held in suspense.

The larger man, who'd been so patiently awaiting her answer, pulled a black wallet-looking thing from inside his suit coat. "I'm Detective Whistler and this," he said with a jerk of his head at the shorter, wiry man, "is my partner, Detective Parks."

Detective Whistler held his impressive-looking identification in front of her face. To appease him she leaned forward and read the ID. Yep, according to the minuscule piece of paper, he was indeed Detective Paul Whistler, from the St. Helena Police Department. But then again, what did she know about government IDs? She could be staring at a forgery and not even know.

Detective Parks also held out his ID, like the good little partner he was: DETECTIVE JON PARKS, ST. HELENA POLICE DEPARTMENT.

"You two are an awfully long way from St. Helena." Okay, so it wasn't the most cheerful way to greet two men who'd traveled so far to see little ol' her. Call her suspicious, but no good could come of two police officers coming to visit.

"Do you mind if we come in, Miss Taylor? We have a few questions to ask you."

So Detective Parks really *did* have a voice. The deep timbre, like Darth Vader's, didn't match his thin, lanky frame at all. Maybe that's why he waited so long to speak: shock factor.

"Questions about what?" she asked, instead of inviting them in. Sweat, which had nothing to do with the lack of air-conditioning in her ancient house, beaded on her upper lip and trickled down her back. A warm breeze ruffled the thick, overgrown trees in the front yard but it only made her swelter even more.

She waited for them to hit her with the words she knew were coming.

"We're looking for Dennis Taylor. Your father."

I just knew it!

Lacy never referred to Dennis Taylor as her *father*. That was a term a man had to earn. Someone who showed more devotion to his cheap whiskey and the hard cement floor of a jail cell was a man who definitely hadn't earned that name. The mention of him still played hell with her emotions, and the emptiness his absence had created inside her had yet to be filled. For years, Lacy had searched for a way to fill it, but she'd lost hope. But she didn't tell them that. They didn't need to know the sordid details of her depressing childhood.

"He's wanted for questioning in a series of robberies. We have reason to believe he may be in this area," Detective Parks continued in his deep Darth Vader voice.

Robberies? It seemed good old Dennis had not progressed past petty thefts.

Lacy shifted from one bare foot to the other, the wooden floor slick beneath her sweaty feet. "What makes you think he'd be here?"

Detective Whistler withdrew a handkerchief from his pocket and blotted his forehead. "For one thing, an eyewitness spotted him about a mile from here."

"And the other thing?"

"*You're* here, Miss Taylor," Detective Parks said.

Lacy shifted her attention to him. "I'm not on speaking terms with Dennis. I haven't seen him in almost five years." Lacy had filed that day away in the part of her brain labeled "Never Think About Again." Showing up at your daughter's place of employment with broken hand-cuffs attached to one wrist and demanding money was not a good way to get back in her good graces. She remembered reading somewhere that he'd been arrested—yet again—shortly after she'd sent him away empty-handed. That was the last time she'd heard anything about him. Five years later, she assumed he would still be rotting in jail with the rest of society's losers.

"Really?" Detective Whistler and his partner exchanged curious glances. She couldn't fault them for being skeptical. She resisted the urge to stomp her feet like a child and demand they believe her.

"Did you know this is listed as his home address?" asked Detective Whistler.

Lacy resisted the urge to sigh. "I'm sure it is," she said with great patience. "But, like I said, it's been a long time since I've seen him." Her hair brushed along her back when she shook her head. "That's all I can tell you." When the men exchanged yet another doubtful glance, she reiterated, "Look, I would love nothing more than for Dennis to slip into a dark hole somewhere and never emerge again. I don't know where he is."

The muscles in Detective Park's jaw clenched as he pulled a business card out of a shiny silver card holder. "Here's my card. It has both our cell numbers on it. If you hear anything or if he contacts you in any way, call either of us immediately. Doesn't matter what time."

Oh, she would definitely do that. For nothing more than to see the look on Dennis's face at being ratted out by his own daughter. Again.

Lacy took the plain white card with their information printed on it in basic black letters.

"Thank you" was all she could think to say.

Detective Whistler gave a nod. "Have a nice day." And the two of them walked down the cracked sidewalk to their unsurprisingly boring black sedan, got in, then drove away.

Lacy stared down the street long after the detectives had disappeared. So Dennis had returned to his old haunts, had he? She hoped to hell he didn't think he'd find help here. *Except maybe help back to jail.*

She shut the door on the heat outside and walked through her even hotter house. Middle of summer was such an inconvenient time for a broken air conditioner, especially since she couldn't afford to fix the stupid thing.

Boris, her late grandpa Ray's beloved English mastiff, lay snoring on the threadbare area rug in the living room. The dummy hadn't even flinched when the doorbell rang.

"Some watchdog you are."

His response was nothing more than another loud snore and a twitch of his leg. Boris was a very twitchy sleeper.

Ray had purchased the mastiff as a pup about eight years ago and affectionately named him after the famous old-time actor Boris Karloff. Boris wasn't too bright and refused to sleep on the bed Lacy had purchased for him.

She took the hair tie out of the pocket of her jean shorts and pulled her hair into a ponytail. Hell, she couldn't even afford a haircut. Waitressing didn't exactly qualify her for a life in the lap of luxury.

That was another thing she'd inherited from Ray: a mountain of debt.

Something licked Chase's face. Something with a very small, warm, and prickly tongue. It moved from his chin up to his nose. Unless a stray animal had somehow meandered into his house during the night, Chase would say he was in someone else's room.

He opened one bleary eye and was greeted by blinding sunlight.

Son of a bitch.

The bright, cheery light pierced his skull like a thousand nails hammering into his brain. The pressure made every part of his head throb. He recognized the symptoms for what they were: signs of a hangover.

Now, if he could figure out where the hell he was, all would be right with the world.

The thing licking his face moved to his ear. Chase struggled to lift his arm, which had turned leaden along with his pounding head, and swatted the creature away. His hand came in contact with coarse fur and a deep growling meow sounded in his ear. His brain just about pounded through his skull. He groaned and rolled over onto his stomach.

Maybe Garfield had a shotgun and could put him out of his misery. The arms of sleep wrapped around him once again, but retreated when a soft, warm, bare leg rubbed along his.

Dark, curly hair came into fuzzy view when Chase managed to open both his eyes. He thought he recognized her, but...no. Who did he know with dark, curly hair? Hell, he knew a dozen women who fit that description.

Great.

"Hello, lover." The husky, sleep-riddled voice was like ants crawling down his legs.

"Why are you shouting?" he mumbled into the pillow. "No shouting. Must be quiet."

The nameless woman next to him cackled like a witch and her leg slid farther over his. "I think someone had too much to drink last night."

Chase's only response was a grunt. Maybe if he ignored her, she'd shut up and go away so he could go to sleep.

The persistent woman didn't get his hint. "Come on, Chase. You promised me one more time," she whined. Chase hated it when women whined.

One more time his ass. He had no clear memory of last night, of even the first time, never mind one more time. He couldn't even keep his eyes open long enough to get a clear picture of her face. Maybe if she closed her curtains at night like a normal person, he could wake up without staring straight into the sun until his eyes boiled in his skull.

Slowly, images from the last twelve hours or so formed in his mind. He remembered closing up the restaurant after work, and walking to his truck. It had been late, around midnight, the parking lot mostly empty. Chase squeezed his eyes shut more tightly as the mystery woman next to him scraped her fingernails over his ass. What the hell was her name? She had been standing leaning against his truck when he walked out of the restaurant. She'd held a six-pack of beer in one hand and a bottle of Jack in the other. That would explain the hangover.

"Chasey..." She placed a kiss on his shoulder blade.

Ah, hell. Only one woman had the balls to call him "Chasey."

Sonja Hartley, a woman with more beauty than brains. Her hair had been straight the last time he'd seen her; that's why he hadn't recognized her. They'd gone on a few dates about a year ago, but their relationship had never progressed past casual dinner and inventive sex. He remembered driving her to her house. Using his elementary detective skills, he deduced they'd gotten shit-faced and then tumbled into bed. Great. It was like being back in college.

He groaned again and rolled over, if only to stop her from groping his ass. No way was he going another round with this woman. Had he been sober, he probably never would have gone the first round.

"You promised me, Chase." Her tone had gone from sweet and pleading to more demanding.

He tried one more time to open his eyes. The light was still blinding, but this time he managed to hold them open and blink the room into focus.

Holy hell! It was like Walt Disney had thrown up in here. What was the name of the princess who had her own castle at Disneyland? Cinderella? Chase imagined her room looking something like this. The bed was one of those four-poster canopy things with a sheer, gauzy curtain draped across the top. The rest of the room had white furniture and pink, girly shit strewn about every available surface. If he had to wake up in this room every day, he'd throw himself in front of a truck.

"Chase, I'm serious. I have to be at work in an hour, and I know how you like to take your time."

Work. Shit.

"What the hell time is it?" He rasped, his throat sore and dry, as if he'd spent the night swallowing pinecones.

Sonja leaned across him to check her watch, which she'd discarded on the nightstand. Her breasts scraped against his chest. He had to get away from this woman. His mind was pretty logical about these things, but his manly parts weren't. They tended to respond whenever they saw a remotely attractive woman.

"It's eight o'clock," she responded.

Fabulous. He should have been at work an hour ago. He hoped his father had had a late morning too and wouldn't notice his tardiness. *Not likely.*

He kicked off the hideous, flowery, girly comforter and stood on weak legs. Not a great morning to skip his customary jog. He could really use the opportunity to regain his strength. Hell, he didn't even have time for a shower.

"Where're you going? I have a whole hour."

"I don't." He heard her moving underneath the sheets and avoided looking at her. "Where the hell are my clothes?" He'd spotted his jeans on the other side of the room, but the rest were nowhere to be seen.

"I think your shirt and shoes are still in the living room."

He swiped his jeans off the floor and was about to pull them on when he remembered he was still buck naked. "Where's my underwear?"

"I don't know." Fake innocence laced the morning huskiness of her voice. She'd pulled herself upright and held the lavender sheet around her breasts. She watched him with deep blue eyes while nibbling on a baby-pink nail.

The last time they'd been together she'd somehow gotten hold of his watch. Reluctantly he'd driven back here to retrieve it, at which time she'd tried to get him into bed. Heck, maybe she did have brains after all.

"What'd you do with them?" He was starting to feel foolish, standing bare-ass naked in the middle of her room.

She pulled her knees up to her chest. "I swear I didn't do anything with them. Maybe they got kicked under the bed. You were kind of in a hurry," she said, with a wicked and knowing smile.

He regarded her with suspicion; she only returned his stare with the same naughty tilt of her unpainted lips. His underwear wasn't under the bed. It could be anywhere, considering he couldn't remember taking it off.

"Screw it," he said, pulling the jeans on. "I'm going commando."

Naked, Sonja walked on her knees to the edge of the bed and ran her index finger over his chest. "Why are you in such a hurry? I'm offering you more sex." Her finger continued its journey down his stomach and into his pants, along with the rest of her hand.

Damn, persistent woman. He managed to tear her hand away right before it wrapped around his not-so-sensible parts. "Will you stop molesting me? I'm late for work."

She sat on her heels and crossed her arms under her breasts, completely unconcerned by her nudity. "I see you still live by the same bang-and-run motto."

"You got that right." He tossed the words over his shoulder as he walked out of her room. Sure enough, his shirt lay by the front door, along with his socks and shoes. He gathered them up, and walked outside to his truck.

The early-morning air was already warm, promising another unbearably hot day. Chase left his shirt off and tossed it on the passenger seat as he climbed into the vehicle. His phone, which had been left in the cup holder all night, beeped annoyingly at him from the second he sat down. The leather seat burned his backside, and one spot in particular on his left shoulder blade. He ignored the pain and picked up his phone.

One voice message. Probably his father ripping him a new one for being late.

"Where the hell are you? There's food missing from the refrigerator. Drag yourself out of whoever's bed you're in and get your ass here."

Yep, his father definitely didn't sound happy. Maybe he'd just say his alarm clock broke.

What a morning to have a hangover.

• • •

Twenty minutes later, with combed hair and fresh clothes, Chase walked into McDermott's to face a less-than-pleased Martin. At eight thirty in the morning, the restaurant was empty except for his father and Henry, the head chef, who were gathered in the kitchen, and the sous chefs, who, like every morning, were at work pressing fresh pasta and cutting vegetables for the day's meals.

"What happened?" Chase walked across the large room and came to a stop in front of the two men.

His father turned to acknowledge him. "You're an hour and a half late."

"Sorry. I overslept." That was as close to the truth as he'd get. "Your message said there's food missing from the fridge."

"Five pounds of halibut are missing." A muscle in his father's jaw tensed.

"How do you know?"

"I did a supply check last night when I left. I counted fifteen pounds of halibut. When I got here this morning, there were only ten pounds," Henry said. Unlike most chefs, Henry's demeanor was calm. He was one of those men with very unremarkable looks, except for the russet-colored Fu Manchu and the sideburns that grew all the way down to his jawbone. Other than that, his five-foot-nine-inch height made it hard to for him intimidate anyone. But the man could cook anything.

"What were we doing with fifteen pounds of leftover halibut?" Chase wanted to know. They rarely had leftover food. Extra food equaled money lost, unless it was something they could puree or add as a side dish. Neither could be done with halibut.

"That's not the point," his father interjected. "We have

over a hundred dollars' worth of seafood missing and no explanation. Where do you think it went, Mr. GM?" Martin directed his question to Chase.

"What're you asking me for? We shouldn't have had any leftover seafood anyway."

Henry threw a cautious glance at Martin. His throat worked before he answered. "We had a slow night."

Chase slid his hands in his pockets and jingled the change. "Have you asked Meryl and Phil?" Meryl and Phil, the sous chefs, were the backbone of Henry's operation and nothing went on in the kitchen they didn't know about.

"Meryl wasn't here last night. And Phil doesn't know what happened to it." Henry's thick fingers pulled at one of the buttons on his pristine white jacket.

"Seems to me we have a dishonest employee on our hands."

"Wait a minute, Dad." Chase knew exactly where his father's thoughts were heading. "That fish would have been thrown away anyway. And you don't know that someone stole it. There could be a dozen explanations for this."

"Such as?"

Well, shit. He didn't have any ideas off the top of his head. His brain was still beer-foggy.

"I didn't think so. I have some paperwork to go over in my office. But I want you," Martin said with a glance at Chase, "to start going over the security tapes. Have something ready to show me by the end of the day. In the meantime, I don't care for tonight's specials. You and Henry need to come up with some new ones." With that, he disappeared through the heavy metal door that led to the offices upstairs.

That was his father for you, ever the consummate order-giver. Why was the man even here? He should be at the new restaurant that opened a few months ago. Hadn't Chase proven he could handle things here without the need for a babysitter? His father was such a control freak. Chase tried not to resent the particular trait that ran strong in his own blood. In fact, it was what made his father so successful. He just knew now Martin would use this whole someone-is-stealing-from-me thing to breathe even further down Chase's neck. Like he was some teenager in training who didn't know shit about restaurants.

As Henry walked away, Chase stood in the empty kitchen and couldn't ignore the burning on his back. Had Sonja held a lighter to his skin last night while he slept? The same small spot had burned all the way to work. It almost felt like someone had seared off his flesh. He rolled his shoulder, as if that would ease the burning. It didn't help.

A heavy sigh flowed out of his sleep-deprived body. Might as well start watching those tapes. As if he didn't have anything better to do.

"Rough morning?"

The light bedroom voice floated over his skin and washed away any fatigue he'd been feeling. His senses went on instant alert. Funny how Lacy Taylor, a woman he hadn't given a passing thought to in his youth, managed to do that to him.

He turned and let his gaze meander down her body. A thin cotton shirt, draped loosely over small but perky breasts, fell almost to the hem of some frayed denim shorts. The cutoffs did a piss-poor job of covering creamy, slender thighs, thighs that were built to be wrapped around a man's hips. Chase's type was usually a busty brunette. He didn't make a habit of going after skinny blondes who cut their jeans into shorts and were always ready to verbally spar with him. Lacy had a way of making his body rebel against his own mind.

"You're brooding," she added when he didn't respond to her.

"I don't brood."

She flipped a strand of long blond hair over her shoulder. "All men brood. It's an occupational hazard. Plus I could hear your teeth grinding together when I walked in."

One corner of his mouth kicked up. "You think you're cute, don't you?"

"Noticed that, did you?"

He crossed his arms over his chest and ignored her comment. "You're here a little early."

Her teasing smile fell a fraction. "I need next week's schedule."

"You know Anita doesn't post it until Wednesdays."

"I was hoping she'd be here working on it."

"Sorry to disappoint."

Her teeth sank into her full lower lip as she gazed around the empty restaurant. The mischief lighting up her green irises faded. Chase wanted to coax that light into her eyes. Getting her all riled up had become a favorite pastime of his. Lacy wasn't one to take flak from anyone, least of all him. She met him head-on every single time.

"She'll be here later, if you want to come back," he suggested when Lacy continued to gnaw on her lower lip.

She glanced at him but didn't say anything.

"Or she might already have it started in her office. I could take you back there." *Okay, now you just sound creepy.*

Her emerald eyes narrowed at him as though she'd just

read his thoughts. "I'll just get it tomorrow night when I come to work."

"Is something wrong?" he found himself asking.

Her steady gaze dropped down to his midsection for the dozenth time in the past few minutes. He forced himself not to react.

"Nothing's wrong," she replied.

"You really can't lie worth a damn, can you?" he countered as he took a step toward her.

She didn't bother backing up. "I can lie a lot better than you think."

He lifted his brows, and took another step until he was a whisper away from her. Lacy stood her ground and for once didn't have some smart-ass comment. Chase prided himself on being excellent at reading people. Lacy always pretended indifference around him, but her eyes gave her away. All he had to do was look into their depths to see through her.

"Really?" He bent over and whispered in her ear, "Because your attention is focused on things it probably shouldn't be."

Her jaw just about hit the floor as he brushed past her. Point one for Chase.

THE DISH

Where Authors Give You the Inside Scoop

From the desk of Debra Webb

Dear Reader,

I can't believe we've already dug into case five of the Faces of Evil—REVENGE.

Things are heating up here in the South just as they are in REVENGE. The South is known for its story-telling. I can remember sitting on the front porch in an old rocking chair and listening to my grandmother tell stories. She was an amazing storyteller. Most of her tales were ones that had been handed down by friends and family for generations. Many were true, though they had changed through the years as each person who told them added his or her own twist. Others were, I genuinely hope, absolute fiction. It would be scary if some of those old tales were true.

Certain elements were a constant in my grandmother's tales. Secrets and loyalty. You know the adage, "blood is thicker than water." Keeping family secrets can some-times turn deadly and in her stories it often did. Then there were those dark secrets kept between friends. Those rarely ended well for anyone.

Jess Harris and Dan Burnett know a little something about secrets and I dare say in the next two cases, REVENGE and the one to follow, *Ruthless*, they will understand that not only is blood thicker than water but the blood is where the darkness lurks. In the coming cases Jess will need Dan more than ever. You're also going to meet a new and very interesting character, Buddy Corlew, who's a part of Jess's past.

Enjoy the summer! Long days of gardening or romping on the beach. But spend your nights with Jess and Dan as they explore yet another case in the Faces of Evil. I promise you'll be glad you did.

I hope you'll stop by www.thefacesofevil.com and visit with me. There's a weekly briefing each Friday where I talk about what's going on in my world and with the characters as I write the next story. You can sign up as a person of interest and you might just end up a suspect! We love giving away prizes, too, so do stop by.

Enjoy the story and be sure to look for *Ruthless* next month!

Cheers!

Debra Webb

From the desk of Katie Lane

Dear Reader,

One of the highlights of my childhood was the New Mexico State Fair. Every year, my daddy would give me a whole ten dollars to spend there. Since I learned early on what would happen if you gorged on turkey legs and candy apples before you hopped on the Tilt-a-Whirl, I always went to the midway first. After a couple hours of tummy-tingling thrills, my friends and I would grab some food and head over to the coliseum to watch the cowboys practice for that night's rodeo.

Sitting in the box seats high above the arena, I would imagine that I was a princess and the cowboys were princes performing great feats of agility and strength in order to win my hand in marriage. Of course, I was never interested in the most talented cowboys. My favorites were the ones who got bucked off the broncos or bulls before the buzzer and still jumped to their feet with a smile on their face and a hat-wave to the crowd.

It was in this arena of horse manure and testosterone that a seed was planted. A good forty years later, I'm happy to announce that my rodeo Prince Charming has come to fruition in my newest contemporary romance, FLIRTING WITH TEXAS.

Beauregard Cates is a cowboy with the type of smile and good looks that make most gals hear wedding bells. But after suffering through a life-threatening illness, he has no desire to be tied down and spends most of his time traveling around the world...until he ends up on a runaway Central Park carriage ride with a sassy blonde from Texas.

Jenna Jay Scroggs is a waitress who will go to any length to right the injustices of the world. Yet no matter how busy her life is in New York City, Jenna can't ignore the sweet-talkin', silver-haired cowboy who reminds her of everything she left behind. And when her hometown of Bramble gets involved, Beau and Jenna will soon be forced on a tummy-tingling ride of their own that will lead them right back to Texas and a once-upon-a-time kind of love.

I hope y'all will join me for the ride. (With or without a big ol' turkey leg.)

Much Love,

Katie Jane

♥ ♥ ♥ ♥ ♥ ♥ ♥ ♥ ♥ ♥ ♥ ♥ ♥

From the desk of Erin Kern

Dear Reader,

A few months ago, my editor put me on assignment to interview Avery Price. Little did I know that Avery would end up being the heroine of my latest book, LOOKING FOR TROUBLE. I got such a kick out of following her journey that led her to Trouble, Wyoming, and into the arms of Noah McDermott, that I jumped at the opportunity to revisit with her. What better way to spend my afternoon than having a heart-to-heart with the woman who started it all?

We settle on the patio of her home in the breathtaking Wyoming foothills. After getting seated, Avery pours me a glass of homemade lemonade.

ME: Thank you so much for taking the time to meet with me. I know how much you value your privacy.

AVERY: (*Takes a sip of lemonade, then sets her drink*

down.) Privacy is overrated. And I should be thanking you for making the drive out here.

ME: It's nice to get out of the city every once in a while. Plus it's beautiful out here. I can see why you chose this place.

AVERY: I'd say it chose me. (*Her lips tilt up in a wry little smile.*) I actually didn't plan on staying here at first. But anonymity is something anyone can find here.

ME: Is that why you left Denver?

AVERY: (*Pauses a moment.*) If I wore a pair of heels that were too high, it got commented on in the society pages. No one cares about that kind of thing here. It's refreshing to be able to be my own person.

ME: That's definitely a tempting way of life. Your family must miss you terribly, though. Are you planning on being an active part in your father's campaign?

AVERY: I'll always support my father no matter what he does, which he's almost always successful at. No matter what happens with the race, he'll always have the support of his children. But I've had my fill of the public eye. That life suits my parents and brother just fine. I think I'll leave the campaigning to them.

ME: That's right. Your brother, Landon Price, is one of the biggest real estate developers in Denver. Are you two close?

AVERY: We grew up pretty sheltered so the two of us were really all the other had. I'd say we're closer than your average brother and sister.

ME: Do you think your brother will be moving up here with you any time soon?

AVERY: *(She chuckles before answering.)* Even though we're very close, my brother and I are very different people. He lives and breathes city life. Plus my parents aren't nearly as concerned with his activities as they are mine.

ME: Meaning?

AVERY: *(Pauses before answering.)* Maybe because he has a different set of genitals? *(Laughs.)* Who knows? For some reason they focus all their energy on me.

ME: Is that the reason you're not active in your father's business? Is this a rebellion?

AVERY: I wouldn't really say it's a rebellion. I made a decision that I thought best suited me. The corporate life isn't for me, anyway. I doubt I'd have anything valuable to offer. My father has enough VPs and advisers.

ME: *(I smile as I take my first sip of lemonade.)* I've got to say, you are a lot more down to earth than I expected. And there are a lot of girls in this country who wished they were in your shoes.

AVERY: *(She lifts a thin shoulder beneath her linen top.)* Everybody always thinks the grass is greener on the other side. Growing up in the public eye isn't for everyone. I've developed thick skin over the years. But I wouldn't change my life for anything.

ME: Well, I certainly appreciate you granting me this interview. Good luck with your father's campaign.

AVERY: Thank you. I'm going to grab a copy of the magazine when the article is printed.

Erin Kern

♥ ♥ ♥ ♥ ♥ ♥ ♥ ♥ ♥ ♥ ♥ ♥ ♥ ♥ ♥ ♥

From the desk of Jami Alden

Dear Reader,

As I look back on the books I've written over the course of my career, I'm struck by two things:

1) I have a very twisted, sinister imagination, if my villains are anything to go by!
2) I love reunion romances.

Now in real life, if you ran into someone who was still hung up on her high school boyfriend and who held on to that person (consciously or not) as the one true love of her life, you might think she had a screw loose. Unless you've ended up with your high school or college sweetheart, most of us grow up and look back at those we dated in our youth—hopefully with fondness but sometimes with less affection. But rarely do we find ourselves pining for that boy we went to senior prom with.

So I wondered, why do I love this premise so much in romance? Well, I think I may have figured it out. In real life, for most of us, those early relationships run their natural course and fizzle out with little more than a whimper and a gasp.

But in romance novels, those relationships that start out with unbridled intensity end with drama and more drama and leave a wagonload of unfinished business for our hero and heroine. It's that lingering intensity, combined with the weight of unfinished business, that draw our hero and heroine together after so many years. So when they finally find themselves back in the same room together, the attraction is as undeniable as gravity.

When I was coming up with the story for GUILTY AS SIN, I found myself fascinated by the history between my hero, Tommy Ibarra, and my heroine, Kate Beckett. Caught up in the giddy turmoil of first love, they were torn apart amid the most excruciating and tragic circumstances I, as a parent, could ever imagine.

And yet, that intensity and unfinished business lingered. So when they're brought back together, there's no force on Earth that can keep them apart. Still, to say their road to true love is a rocky one is a huge understatement. But I hope in the end that you feel as I do. That after everything Tommy and Kate went through, they've more than earned their happily ever after.

Happy Reading!

Jami Alden